"Kathy Herman has the power to dig deeply into the hearts of readers everywhere with lovable characters, great tension, and a totally satisfying conclusion. *All Things Hidden* is her best story yet."

—HANNAH ALEXANDER
AUTHOR OF *FAIR WARNING*

In *All Things Hidden,* Kathy Herman once again displays her gift for weaving spiritual truths into a page-turning story. A powerful portrayal of the consequences of sin—and God's limitless grace."

—CAROL COX
AUTHOR OF *SAGEBRUSH BRIDES*

"Packed with emotion, *All Things Hidden* is not your average suspense novel. I could not put it down. Satisfying and thought-provoking."

—LYN COTE
AUTHOR OF THE *WOMEN OF IVY MANOR* SERIES

"Kathy Herman writes stories abundant in the emotions we all share, enhanced with hope and happy endings. *All Things Hidden* takes this even further by adding the theme of redemption. This is a glorious tale of God transforming our deepest hurts and our biggest mistakes into witnesses for His glory. I couldn't put it down."

—JANELLE BURNHAM SCHNEIDER
COAUTHOR OF THE *BRIDE FOR A BIT* ANTHOLOGY

"Kathy Herman's *All Things Hidden* is another powerful family tale of intrigue and restored relationships that tugs at the heart's strings."

—ERIC WIGGIN
AUTHOR OF *THE HILLS OF GOD, BLOOD MOON RISING* AND *THE GIFT OF GRANDPARENTING*

"Kathy Herman's signature fast-paced, breath-catching style takes the reader deeper into the core of suspense than ever before. *All Things Hidden* proves that no greater intrigue hits home harder than the mystery of family."

—DEIDRE POOL

AUTHOR OF *LOVING JESUS ANYWAY*

A SEAPORT SUSPENSE
BOOK THREE

ALL THINGS HIDDEN

KATHY HERMAN

Multnomah® Publishers *Sisters, Oregon*

ALL THINGS HIDDEN
published by Multnomah Publishers, Inc.
© 2006 by Kathy Herman

International Standard Book Number: 1-59052-489-6
Cover image by Stephen Gardner, PixelWorksStudio.net
Interior typeset by Katherine Lloyd, The DESK

All scripture quotations, unless otherwise indicated, are taken from
The Holy Bible, New International Version.
©1973, 1984 by International Bible Society.
Used by permission of Zondervan Publishing House

Multnomah is a trademark of Multnomah Publishers, Inc.,
and is registered in the U.S. Patent and Trademark Office.
The colophon is a trademark of Multnomah Publishers, Inc.
Printed in the United States of America

For information:
MULTNOMAH PUBLISHERS, INC.
601 N. LARCH STREET • SISTERS, OREGON 97759

Library of Congress Cataloging-in-Publication Data
Herman, Kathy.
All things hidden : a Seaport suspense novel / Kathy Herman.
    p. cm.
ISBN 1-59052-489-6
I. Title.
PS3608.E762A79 2006
813'.6--dc22
                                                        2005025581

06 07 08 09 10 11 12—10 9 8 7 6 5 4 3 2 1

To Him who is both the Giver and the Gift

Acknowledgments

This book required considerable research and professional counsel regarding Alzheimer's disease, social services, and crime investigation, and I'm grateful for those who shared so generously from their storehouse of knowledge. I did my best to integrate those facts as I understood them. If accuracy was compromised in any way, it was unintentional and strictly of my own doing.

I owe a special word of thanks to Jane Boreman, Health Services Director of Pinehurst Alzheimer Special Care Center, Tyler, Texas, for answering my many questions about this disease and its effect on patients; to my friend, Anna Allison, whose willingness to share candidly about her experience caring for a mother with Alzheimer's and a father with dementia has added to the realism of the story; and to Anita Maish, a beloved member of our family, whose decade of living with Alzheimer's touched each of us in a different way and taught us to appreciate what a wonderful gift good memories are.

I extend a warm thank you to my buddy, Will Ray, private investigator, state of Oregon, for taking his valuable time to give me input on the chapters involving DNA evidence, interrogations, and law-enforcement procedures. Will, your willingness to respond quickly to my many questions has made my job much easier.

I'm so grateful to my friend, Carolyn Walker, who is actively involved with Texas Foster Family Association, for enlightening me about procedural aspects of child protective services and explaining what takes place behind the scenes and in the hearts of those involved when a child is put in foster care.

I wish to extend a loving thank you to my little sister and zealous prayer warrior, Pat Phillips, and my newly formed online prayer team for your amazing support. How God is using you! Thanks also to Susie Killough, Judi Wieghat, Mark and Donna Skorheim, my friends at LifeWay Christian Store in Tyler, Texas, and everyone in my Bible study class and Sunday school class for your many prayers for my writing ministry. I have felt your prayers.

To those who read my books and those who sell them, thanks for encouraging me with e-mails and cards and personal testimonies about how God has used my words. He uses you to bless me more often than you know.

To my novelist friends in ChiLibris, thanks for sharing so generously from your vast storehouse of knowledge. It's a privilege to be counted among you.

To my editor, Rod Morris, can you believe this is number *nine*? I remember wondering during the intense rewriting of *Tested by Fire* if I had made a mistake to think I had what it takes to write professionally. Thanks for requiring me to stretch with each book and for encouraging me every time I did. Your insights and suggestions have been invaluable, and your honest way of conveying them constructive and gentle. How grateful I am for your mentoring.

To the staff at Multnomah, whose commitment to honor God through the power of story is so very evident, thanks for the privilege of working with such dedicated professionals. Without your hard work, my books would never reach the shelves.

And to my husband, Paul, who attentively listens to all my chatter about the characters in my books and about twists and turns each plot may take, your partnership in what I do has made all the difference. If you were the only audience I ever had, it would still have been a ball. But thanks to your support, input, creative marketing ideas, and prayers, tens of thousands of my books are keeping people up at night. Isn't it fun?

And to my Father in heaven, who listens not only to my words, but also to my thoughts and motives, thank You for gifting me to write stories that touch and challenge, and for refining my character during the process. I'm realizing more and more that it is precisely because of my weaknesses that the strength of Your truth stands out on the pages. I am merely the vessel.

Prologue

*"Do not be deceived: God cannot be mocked.
A man reaps what he sows."*
GALATIANS 6:7

Owen Jones felt a blast of humid air as he pushed open the glass door of the Spartan Hotel and staggered down the front steps, his hand clutching the shiny brass railing. How late was it? He pushed the button on his watch and the face lit up green, but he couldn't make out the numbers.

"Do you need a cab, sir?" the doorman asked.

Owen grabbed the man's arm, feeling as though the sidewalk were moving under his feet. "Yeah, thanks."

The doorman motioned with his hand, and a red and white cab pulled up under the awning, the passenger-side window down.

The cab driver peered up at him. "Oh, it's you again. You wanna go back to the Kennett Hotel?"

Owen suddenly recalled leaving tonight's fundraiser for Senator Poston with a blond bombshell clutching his arm.

"Buddy, you gonna get in?"

"Uh, yeah. Sorry." Owen slid into the backseat of the cab.

"So, am I takin' you back to the Kennett?"

Owen reached into his pocket and pulled out a valet parking ticket. "Yeah, I need to get my car." It was all coming back to him: the schmoozing, the martinis, the gorgeous blonde in the slinky red dress, the cab ride to her hotel.

The driver pulled to the end of the circle drive and turned onto Honeycutt Boulevard and then right on Sixth.

Owen started to loosen his tie and realized it wasn't there. He smiled. A nice souvenir for the lady. What was her name? Candy? Connie? *Corinne*. That was it. Corinne.

He pushed the button on his watch again and squinted until he could read the numbers. "Is it really 2:00 a.m.?"

"Three minutes after," the driver said.

Owen leaned his head against the back of the seat and let his mind replay the highlights of his one-night stand. He figured the lady had ten years on him, but what a knockout!

"I've got to stop doing this on weeknights," he mumbled.

"How's that?"

Owen looked up into the dark eyes reflected in the rearview mirror. "Oh, nothing. My appetite for good-looking blondes is competing with my work schedule. I'm going to be dragging all day. Oh well. Gotta grab a little gusto, right?"

"Why do I need gusto?" the driver said. "I've got a steady job, a roof over my head, a wife who loves me—and three beautiful daughters."

"I want to get married someday, but I want to have fun first."

"Marriage isn't a death sentence. There's a lot to be said for settling down. So whaddya do?"

"I'm a CPA. I specialize in management accounting."

The driver chuckled. "Yeah, same here. I make sure whatever I take in lines up with what the meter says. So what's your hang-up with gettin' married?"

"I'm not hung-up about it. Just not in a hurry." Owen rubbed the stubble on his chin. "Actually, I'm seeing a gal I could get serious about if I'd let myself. Her name's Hailey. I would've taken her to the fundraiser tonight, but she's away at an HR seminar." *Why am I telling this guy all this stuff?*

"Is she blonde?"

"Yeah, but that's not the only thing that attracts me to her. I like hanging out with her. She's smart. Really sweet. When I decide to get married, it'll be to someone like her. But I'm not ready to stop playing the field—not by a long shot."

"So many women, so little time?"

Owen smiled. "Something like that." He spotted the neon sign on the Kennett Hotel up ahead.

The cab driver pulled up to the front entrance and nodded toward the meter. "The fare is four seventy-five."

Owen peeled off six dollars and reached over the driver's shoulder and handed him the money, aware of a silver cross dangling from the rearview mirror.

"Don't worry," Owen said. "I'm not driving till I've had a few cups of strong coffee."

"Good." The driver turned around and looked at Owen. "You seem like a nice kid—remind me of my nephew Eduardo. Why don't you do yourself a favor and stop tryin' to sleep with every blonde in Raleigh? Find one who'll make you happy and marry her."

"I *am* happy." Owen slid out of the cab and leaned in the passenger window. "Every guy should sow a few wild oats before he gets tied down. I mean, it's not like I'm hurting anyone."

"Don't be so sure, amigo."

Owen snickered. "I think you're jealous."

The driver's face was expressionless. "I did my share of bar hoppin' and sleepin' around. I didn't realize there were consequences till I became a Christian."

"That's because you never had guilt till then. Guilt's a by-product of religion."

"Or a by-product of *sin*."

Owen swatted the air. "Sin is nothing more than religious lingo. No one has the right to decide for me what's right and what's wrong, so don't waste your time trying to convince me I need to be saved. It's not gonna happen."

There was a long pause.

"What's your name, kid?"

"Owen Jones."

"Mine's Juan Rodriguez. I'm going to be praying for Jesus to change your heart and bring the right woman into your life."

Owen felt a smile stretch his cheeks. "Hey, knock yourself out."

The guy kept staring at Owen as if he knew something he wasn't saying. "You be careful, hear?"

"Yeah, I will."

Owen backed away and watched the taillights of the cab until they blended into a sea of gleaming red. He put his hands deep in his pockets and shuffled toward the hotel coffee shop, feeling surprisingly sober and thinking Juan the cab driver was about as gullible as they come.

I

D on't eat the candle, son!" Owen Jones was laughing so hard he was sure he had blurred the three pictures he had just taken. "Let Mommy light it so you can blow it out. Honey, hurry! This is going downhill fast."

Hailey Jones wiped the tears off her face and tried to look serious as she bent down and put a yellow candle in the middle of the red fire-truck cake. "Remember what Mommy told you: The candle is hot. Don't touch it."

Hailey struck a match and lit the candle and began to sing slowly until everyone in the room joined in:

> Happy birthday to you,
> Happy birthday to you,
> Happy birthday, dear Daniel,
> Happy birthday to you.

"Okay," Owen said, "blow!"

Daniel's mouth formed an O, and he produced noise and drool, but no wind.

"Let Grandma help." Ellen Jones stood behind the boy's highchair, then bent down and put her cheek next to his. "Ready? One...two...three...blow!" She let out a quick puff of air and the candle went out. "You did it! Good job, Daniel!"

Everyone cheered and clapped.

The birthday boy squealed with delight and grabbed a fistful of icing. He squeezed it through his fingers, then brought it to his mouth.

"Are you going to let Grandpa eat part of that fire truck?" Guy Jones said.

Daniel offered a handful of red goo to Guy, who pretended to take a bite. "Mmm…that's good. I want more. *More*! Give me more!"

Daniel giggled and grabbed another handful of icing and held it up.

"Better let me cut the cake before he grosses us all out," Hailey said.

Owen heard the phone ringing and went out to the kitchen. "Hello."

"May I speak with Ellen Jones, please?"

"Sure. May I tell her who's calling?"

"My name won't mean anything to her. I'm her father's neighbor."

"Did something happen?"

"It isn't an emergency, but I need to make her aware of something. If this isn't a good time, maybe she could call me back."

"No, it's fine. Hold for just a minute."

Owen went into the dining room and motioned to Ellen. "Mom, the phone's for you. It's Granddad's neighbor. She says it's not an emergency."

"How would she know to call me here?"

Guy smiled sheepishly. "I forwarded our calls here. If the tailor calls, I thought we could pick up my suit on the way home."

Hailey turned to Owen. "Darling, would you get the ice cream? Oh, and the plates, napkins, and forks? They're on the countertop."

Owen followed his mother into the kitchen and took the ice cream out of the freezer and listened to her end of the phone conversation.

"Have you ever noticed this behavior before now?" Ellen said. "I didn't know that…Did you ask him about it afterwards…? I'm sorry. My father can be really blunt…Yes, I can see that…I guess I need to drive down there…No, not at all. I appreciate your letting me know." Ellen hung up the phone and seemed to be staring at nothing.

"Is everything all right with Granddad?" Owen said.

"Sounds as though his mind is slipping."

"Mom, he's what, almost ninety?"

"Eighty-seven, actually, and this isn't normal forgetfulness. Sybil, his neighbor across the street, found him sitting in her porch swing yesterday afternoon. She went outside and asked if there was something she could do for him. He said no, but for her to go ahead and make herself at home. She didn't know what to say and went back inside. When she looked out again, he was standing in his own yard, watering the flower beds."

Owen smiled. "He was probably kidding around. You know how he is."

"Sybil's convinced Dad didn't have a clue he wasn't sitting on his own porch. She asked him this morning if he liked the new cushions on her swing, and he got huffy. Asked her how he should know since she never invites him over. Apparently, he's over there all the time. She thought he looked scared."

"I can't imagine Granddad being scared of anything."

"Me either, Owen. This is disconcerting. Unless the neighbor is overreacting, it sounds as though he shouldn't be living alone." Ellen breathed in and exhaled. "I've been dreading something like this since Mother died."

"What're you going to do? He'll never agree to move."

Guy breezed through the doorway. "Hey, what's holding up the ice cream? What did the neighbor want?"

Ellen told Guy everything Sybil Armstrong had said. "I don't know what we should do. Dad and I wouldn't last a week under the same roof, but he's certainly not ready for nursing care."

"Honey, both our fathers would be better off in Seaport where we can watch out for them. Maybe it's time to look into assisted living."

Ellen raised her eyebrows. "Yes, we could hog-tie my dad and haul him here kicking and screaming. I can hardly wait."

"Too bad they couldn't move in together," Owen said.

There was a long moment of silence.

"Why couldn't they?"

"Mom, I was kidding."

"They've always seemed to get along. It's certainly worth considering. Dad's in reasonably good physical shape even if his mind's slipping. And Roland's mind is sharp, even if his arthritis slows him down. They might be good for each other."

"You're serious," Guy said.

"It would solve our immediate problem of getting them to move out of their houses and transition from being independent. This could be a huge first step in preparing them for assisted living, don't you think?"

"Well, I...I suppose they could move in together," Guy said. "But would they? Better yet, *should* they? I mean, is it feasible to think—"

Hailey poked her head in the kitchen. "Where's the ice cream? The birthday boy's getting antsy."

"Sorry, I got sidetracked." Owen picked up the stack of plates and utensils and the ice cream and looked over at his parents. "I really was kidding. But if you decide to go through with it, you know Hailey and I will help you any way we can. It'd be great having them closer, and I'd love for Daniel to have a chance to know them."

"Well," Ellen said, "Daniel may be just the hook we need to get your grandfathers to consider this."

Ellen sat on the veranda of her home, listening to the crickets and aware of her heart pounding much too fast.

Guy came outside and pulled the other wicker rocker next to hers and sat. "I heard your wheels turning all the way in the living room. You want to talk about it?"

"I don't even want to think about it, much less say it out loud."

"Honey, you knew your father couldn't be independent indefinitely."

"He's managed this long, I actually thought he might." She glanced up at one bright star visible between the tree branches. "I dread the thought of him living nearby, and I feel guilty for feeling that way."

"Well, there's a lot of bad history between you two. Maybe that'll change now."

"I can't erase a lifetime of hurt just because Dad is suddenly needy."

"No, but maybe he's mellowed. You've hardly seen him in—"

"Don't remind me how long it's been. I feel bad enough his *neighbor* had to call and inform me his mind is slipping."

Guy took her hand in his. "Well, let's take one step at a time. At least we know my dad is open to sharing an apartment with yours. All we have to do now is convince Lawrence it's a good idea."

"Surely you don't think he's going to give up his house and move here without a fight?"

"Probably not. But he can't stay in Ocala."

2

Four weeks later, Ellen Jones stood next to her white Thunderbird in front of her father's house in Ocala, Florida, her eyes fixed on the Sold sign in the front yard, and the sound of her mother's laughter echoing in her mind.

She took one last whiff of orange blossoms, wishing she could bottle the sights and sounds and scents that evoked the good memories of this place. It had been a long time since she enjoyed coming here, but the thought of leaving it forever was bittersweet.

"I hope you're happy now that you've ruined my life," Lawrence Madison said.

No, Dad, you had an eighty-seven-year head start. Ellen looked in the open car window at her father sitting in the passenger seat. "We've been over this a dozen times. Your moving in with Roland is the best possible scenario."

"Sure, best for *you.*"

Ellen bit her lip. *"Do the right thing, Ellen,"* her mother had always said. *"Everything else will take care of itself."*

"All I have left is in that dinky U-Haul trailer," Lawrence said. "Why didn't you just sell the shirt off my back?"

"Dad, I asked you what you wanted to keep. If it got sold in the estate sale, it's because you gave the green light. You could at least be grateful that those nice young men on the corner loaded up your things for us."

Lawrence sat with his arms folded and stared out the windshield.

Ellen heard a voice calling. She turned around and saw Sybil Armstrong crossing the street.

"I brought you something to take with you." Sybil handed her a Baggie chock-full of cookies. "Oatmeal raisin. Lawrence's favorite. I even added a little flax meal. All that fiber will be good for him."

"Thank you. That was thoughtful of Sybil, wasn't it, Dad?" Ellen glanced over at her father, surprised to see his eyes welled with tears.

Sybil poked her head in the driver's side window. "Now, don't worry about your flowers. I'll keep them watered till the new owners move in next month. Ellen has my e-mail address. I want to hear all about your new place."

Ellen glanced at her watch. "We really should get on the road. My family's expecting us before noon."

Sybil turned and lowered her voice to just above a whisper. "I don't know what I'll do without Lawrence to take care of."

"I can't thank you enough for all you've done. I had no idea Dad wasn't paying his bills or driving his car. He sounded okay the times I talked to him on the phone." *For all of five minutes.*

"Well, it had been quite some time since you'd actually seen him. He just can't do for himself the way he used to."

"I would've stepped in sooner had I realized," Ellen said.

"I'm sure you would have, but Lawrence is a proud man. I knew he wanted to be on his own as long as possible, so I did what I could to help him manage. But lately he seems so confused. I don't think it's good for him to live by himself anymore."

"You did the right thing by calling me."

Sybil's blue-gray eyes filled with tears. "It's so hard to say good-bye to my old friend."

"I'll e-mail you and let you know how he's doing."

Sybil nodded and dabbed her eyes with the hem of her apron, then walked across the street toward her house.

Ellen opened the driver's side door and slid in behind the wheel. She glanced over at the blue gingham curtains in the kitchen window and fluttered her eyelashes to clear the moisture. *Goodbye, Mom.*

"You going to get this sardine can on the highway?"

Ellen waited several seconds more, then turned the key and pulled away from the curb, painfully aware of the ending of an era—and the dawning of a potential nightmare.

Ellen reached for her sunglasses over the visor and put them on, then opened her eyes wide and blinked several times, feeling the effects of a restless night. She picked up the Styrofoam cup in the holder and drank the last of the lukewarm coffee.

"Dad, would you like a cookie?" She picked up the Baggie on the console.

Lawrence stared out the side window and didn't answer.

Suit yourself. Why did her father have to be so obstinate? She took a bite of cookie, her crunching exaggerated in the steely silence. Ellen savored the taste, her mind wandering back to her mother's kitchen, to an incident that happened when she was a junior in high school…

"I'm so proud of you," her mother had said. "I think running for class president is an excellent idea."

"I'll have to really campaign hard," Ellen said. "Mary Pat's a cheerleader, and Kent's like the brainiest kid on the planet."

Mother put a plate of oatmeal raisin cookies and a glass of milk in front of Ellen. "Well, you're very smart—and persuasive. Plus, you can get along with anybody. Don't defeat yourself before you even get started."

Her father walked into the kitchen. "Get started with what?"

"Ellen's decided to run for class president. Isn't that something?"

"Big waste of time, if you ask me," her father said. "Why don't you sink your energy into something more useful—like joining the homemaking club or becoming a candy striper?"

Ellen glanced over at her mother and then locked gazes with her father. "What's wrong with running for class president?"

"It's pointless, Ellen, that's all."

"But Dad—"

"Honestly, Lawrence," her mother said, "why must you be so negative? It'll be a good experience for her whether or not she wins. Learning to compete will help her in college."

"College is a waste of time and money for women. Their place is in the home, taking care of their children."

"What if I don't ever get married and have kids?" Ellen said.

His face softened. "You will." He stroked her cheek. "Just look at that face."

"So if I were ugly, going to college might be worth it, but since I'm not, I should plan on being a housewife? Come on, Dad. That's not fair."

"Listen to me, young lady. What's not fair is women trying to change their natural bent toward being wives and mothers. It's upsetting the entire social order."

"I never said I don't want to get married and have kids. But can't I be a journalist, too?"

"Women flooding the workplace is creating problems you have no idea about."

"But all I've ever wanted to do is write."

Her father's eyes were suddenly like stone, his voice stern. "And I'm telling you to develop practical skills that will benefit your husband and family and not your own selfish ambitions!"

Ellen dropped out of the race for class president, but her father's disapproval of her going to college made her only more determined. She secured the loans she needed and struggled through all four years without his financial support or approval. But nothing between them had ever been the same…

Ellen spotted the Seaport exit up ahead and put on her blinker, her father's silence registering the defiance she feared would only escalate.

Lord, he brings out the absolute worst in me! Unless You intervene, we're just going to go on making each other miserable.

Owen Jones looked out the picture window of the furnished

apartment at the Colony Reef Retirement Center that would soon be home to both of his grandfathers. He didn't see any sign of his mother's Thunderbird. He went over and sat on the couch next to his paternal grandfather, who was watching Daniel push a toy lawn mower across the living room carpet.

"We're so glad you've moved closer, Papa. It means a lot to us that Daniel will get to know you."

"That little boy is probably the only reason I didn't put up a stink," Roland Jones said, glancing over at Hailey. "I could've stayed right where I was. I'm not incapable, you know."

Owen glanced at the black-and-blue splotches on the back of Papa's hands—and his gnarled fingers. "Of course you're not. We're counting on you to help us with Granddad. Mom says he gets confused sometimes."

"Last time I saw Lawrence was when you graduated from college. He looked really great. Moved a whole lot better than I did. Then again, most people do." Roland reached over and tickled Daniel's tummy. "That's why I get along with this little fella. We both waddle when we walk." He leaned his head back and grunted. "It's a real pain getting old. Seems like just yesterday I was your age and Guy was Daniel's. Better make the most of it, Owen. It goes by too fast."

Guy Jones came out of the kitchen and sat in one of the two chairs opposite the couch. "The groceries are put away. I still think it would be better if you and Lawrence would eat your meals at the clubhouse."

"I'm not giving up my cooking," Roland said. "That's one thing I enjoy and can still do."

"All right, Dad. At least the option's there if it gets too bothersome—or if Lawrence won't eat your cooking."

Roland laughed. "Then let the old rooster go to the club by himself."

Owen heard a car door slam and got up and looked out the window. "They're here!"

He shot out the door and jogged to the car. "Granddad!" He threw his arms around his grandfather as unabashedly as he'd done when he was a kid. "It's so great you're here."

"Tell that to your mother," Lawrence said, his arms at his side.

Owen turned around and saw that the others had followed him out of the apartment. "Granddad, I want you to meet my family—my wife, Hailey, and this is your great-grandson, Daniel."

Lawrence reached out and wrapped his fingers around the baby's arm. "Solid as a rock. What's his name?"

"Daniel."

"Hello, old friend." Roland patted Lawrence on the back. "Guess we're going to be roommates. Think you're up to it?"

"Didn't know I had a choice."

Owen looked at his mother and saw the tension in her face. "Granddad, why don't you let Papa show you around the apartment while we unload the U-Haul?"

"Not much in it. Ellen sold off nearly everything I own."

"Well, just show us where you want it and we'll help you put it away."

"I'm not helpless."

"Neither of us is helpless," Roland said. "That's why we get to enjoy this place. Come on, let me show you around. It's the next best thing to what we had."

Lawrence turned and shot Ellen a crusty look. "Guess it's better than a nursing home."

Ellen sat out on the veranda of her home, absorbing the night sounds and enjoying a balmy south breeze off the gulf.

"Mind if I join you?" Guy said.

"No, come sit with me. It's so peaceful out here. I've missed being home."

Guy sat in the wicker rocker across from Ellen. "I'm sorry

all the driving back and forth to get your dad's affairs in order was the pits. But things might get more hectic before they calm down. This is a huge adjustment for him."

Ellen rolled her eyes. "Well, he's not the only one having to adjust—not that he even noticed, the selfish old goat."

"He'll probably come around once he's done trying to punish you."

"I wouldn't count on it," Ellen said. "He's the most headstrong man I've ever known and has never forgiven me for anything."

Guy rocked slowly and seemed to be thinking. "I'm proud of you for not reacting to his digs at you. Though he won't admit it, he has to understand we're doing the right thing by bringing him here."

"It's hard to know *what* he understands. I was shocked that Sybil had been paying his bills, chauffeuring him everywhere, even bringing him meals. I honestly can't tell how capable he is or isn't. Then again, he's clearheaded enough to torment me the way he always has."

"It's all I can do not to jump to your defense, honey. But I keep thinking if you and I both stay cool and don't react, he'll realize it's getting him nowhere. And since it's obvious he wants attention, maybe he'll change his method."

"We can only hope. Thank heavens Roland seems to have a calming effect on him."

"Yes, but Dad's not going to let Lawrence get away with anything."

Ellen sighed. "What if this was a mistake? What if it's too much to expect them to watch out for each other?"

"We left it in God's hands. If it doesn't seem to work, then we'll explore other options. Getting them here and moved in was the most difficult part."

"For you, maybe," Ellen said. "If Dad doesn't change his attitude, you may have to put *me* in a home."

3

On Sunday evening, Ellen Jones was seated next to Guy at the kitchen table in their fathers' new apartment, enjoying the cold chicken pasta salad her father-in-law had made.

"This is good, Roland," Ellen said. "What gives it the zing?"

The corners of Roland Jones's mouth turned up. "I can't let that out. Claudia would turn over in her grave."

"Are you liking the new apartment?" Guy asked. "You haven't said much about it."

"It'll take some getting used to, but I think it's going to work out fine."

"What seems to be the biggest challenge?"

"His roommate," Lawrence Madison said.

"*Actually,*" Roland said, "I'm finding it hard to remember where things go after putting them in the same place for forty years. I can tell I'm going to like the dishwasher, though. It holds more than my old one. Trash compactor's a nice addition."

Ellen watched Lawrence push the chunks of salad around his bowl with his spoon till she wanted to shake him. He had hardly taken a bite.

"So did you take some time to explore the facilities?" Guy said. "I saw a lot of folks at the pool when we drove up."

Roland added a shake of salt to his bowl. "Oh, there'll be plenty of time for that later. Right now, I'm just trying to get used to the feel of the place."

Ellen heard the sadness in his voice and thought how sweet he was to stay positive about a difficult adjustment. She glanced over at Lawrence. "Dad, you've hardly touched your dinner. You're going to give Roland a complex."

"I don't need you monitoring what I eat. Stop treating me like a child."

Then stop acting like one! Ellen felt Guy kick her under the table, and she tried to will away the frown on her face.

"Actually, Lawrence ate earlier so he'd have room for dessert." Roland winked. "I made lemon meringue pie."

Lawrence got up, picked up his bowl, and put it in the refrigerator.

Ellen looked at Guy and rolled her eyes, convinced her dad had staged the whole picking-at-his-food act just to torment her.

Owen Jones shut the door to the nursery and walked softly into the living room where Hailey lay on the couch reading a travel magazine.

"Daniel's out like a light," Owen said. "I think Granddad and Papa wore him out this afternoon."

"He certainly loved the attention. I just hope having Granddad here doesn't prove too stressful for Ellen."

"Mom'll be fine. They just need to call a truce."

"Easier said than done. It's obvious he's needling her every chance he gets."

Owen flopped in a chair. "It's been going on my whole life. I just blow it off. Drives Mom nuts."

"What does your dad say about it?"

"Dad learned a long time ago to stay out of it. Mom doesn't want him running interference. I've only seen him tell Granddad off one time."

Hailey closed the magazine and sat up on the couch. "When?"

"Oh, back when Mom was a reporter. She'd gotten some kind of award for a feature story she wrote, and Granddad was ragging on her. Really hurt her feelings."

"Why would he do that?"

Owen raised his eyebrows. "He's never forgiven Mom for going to college against his wishes and then working while she was raising Brandon and me. He thinks women were made to stay home and run the house."

"What did he say that caused your dad to tell him off?"

"Granddad said that while Mom was out fulfilling her 'selfish ambition,' she was neglecting her husband and kids. Dad lost it. I remember Brandon and me sitting there paralyzed, afraid to move. I don't remember Dad's exact words, but I remember he slammed his fist on the table and let Granddad know that Mom was a great wife and mother and a talented newspaperwoman. He said things were just fine in our family and that Granddad had better never say another word about it."

"What did Ellen do?"

"She went out to the kitchen with Grandma. I think she was crying. Dad told Brandon and me to go outside and shoot baskets, and I couldn't get out of there fast enough. I don't know what happened after that, but I never heard Granddad bring it up again."

Hailey fiddled with the fringe on the couch pillow. "How did *you* feel about your mother working?"

Owen shrugged. "I never thought about it. Mrs. Bennett was always there when Brandon and I got home from school and during summer vacations. I remember home as a happy place. Mom was always baking something good, and we took turns licking the bowl. Mom and Dad used to play Chinese checkers and Monopoly with us and taught us how to play chess. Sometimes we took turns reading books out loud. At least one of them went to every ball game we had. Some of my best memories are of family vacations—all of us laughing and clowning around in the car. Honestly, I don't remember ever feeling neglected."

Hailey started to say something and then didn't.

"What?"

"Nothing."

"You look upset," Owen said. "Did I say something wrong?"

"I just don't understand why you're so opposed to me going back to work when you just said that it didn't bother you that your mother worked."

"Yeah, but she didn't work full time until we were in school. Daniel's barely a year old. I'd think you'd be glad to have time with him before you get back into the workforce."

"I am...but the thought of spending all day every day with him for the next five years is depressing."

"Then why are we talking about having another child?"

"You're the one talking about it. Not me."

"Honey, it's not fair to Daniel to deny him a brother or sister."

"Both of your parents were only children. Neither complained about it or even thought they'd missed anything."

"Well, I want Daniel to grow up with at least one sibling. Brandon and I had a ball growing up. We were really close."

"Lucky you. My sisters and I fought till we were adults. And now we have families of our own and live a million miles apart. I think the whole sibling thing is overrated."

"We agreed to have at least two children, Hailey."

"I know, but that was before I realized how demanding they are." She reached down and picked up a miniature board book and traced the ABCs with her finger. "I dearly love Daniel. You know I do. I just don't enjoy being on call every second. I need something else to do. I need adult conversation."

"What am I?"

"I'm talking about during the day. It's getting to the point where I can hardly wait for *Oprah* to come on. I have this beautiful little boy—everything I've ever wanted—and I'm desperate to escape from him. What's wrong with me?"

Owen ran his hands through his hair. "Why haven't you talked to me about this before?"

"I've just started realizing it myself. It's not as though I want to abandon my son. I just don't think I make a very good stay-at-home mom."

"For crying out loud, Hailey, you're doing a great job. Daniel's thriving."

"But I'm not. That's what I'm trying to tell you. And at some point, it's going to start affecting him."

Owen got up and sat next to her on the couch, his mind reeling. Finally, he took her hand in his. "I think your taking on an outside job will only add to the pressure."

"I can't keep doing what I'm doing. I'm suffocating." A tear rolled down Hailey's cheek.

"Then why don't we hire someone to help you with Daniel so you can get out and do some things for yourself?"

"Like who?"

"I don't know…a nanny?"

"Do you realize how expensive that could be?"

"We can use my annual bonus."

"That's supposed to go in Daniel's college fund."

"We've got a long time to save for his college. Right now, I'm more concerned about you."

Hailey squeezed his hand. "You'd really be willing to hire a nanny?"

"If we could find one with good references that we all like, yes."

Ellen closed the cover on the novel she was reading and set the book on the nightstand. She turned off the lamp, then pulled the covers up to her chin.

"Good night, honey," Guy said softly.

Ellen turned on her side and faced him. "How come you're still awake?"

"My mind's racing. I'm not prepared to do the opening on Tuesday's court case, and I'm going to be tied up in meetings all day tomorrow."

"I'm sorry. It's because you gave up work time this past week to get our fathers settled."

Guy seemed to be studying her. "I'm concerned about how Lawrence will treat you when I'm not around."

"You can't fight my battles for me. I'll handle Dad."

"Yeah, I can see how well you're *handling* him. He's got your stomach in knots."

"Is it that obvious?"

"It is to me, though you're doing a good job restraining yourself."

"Honestly, he's worse than a two-year-old. Why does he have to make everything so difficult?"

"I doubt if he knows how to break the cycle. Maybe it's up to you."

Ellen felt the muscles in her neck tighten. "To do what— apologize for going to college, for pursuing a career and using my talent—for *neglecting* my family?"

"Of course not. But you're not going to heal if you don't forgive him."

"I've tried a hundred times, but the feelings come flooding back every time he criticizes me." Ellen breathed in and exhaled. "I made such an effort to insure his move here would be as painless as possible. I helped him close on the house, close out his accounts, prepare for the estate sale, pack up his things. Then I pulled a U-Haul trailer all the way to Seaport with him treating me as if I didn't exist."

"Being forced to give up his independence was probably the most traumatic event in his life besides losing your mom."

"That's no excuse for making me feel worthless." Ellen closed her eyes till the emotion passed. "You'd think he could've at least wished me a happy Mother's Day since I spent it helping him get his affairs in order instead of with my kids. But then, we both know what kind of mother he thinks I am."

"Maybe he was just missing your mom and just wanted the day over with."

"I never know what he's thinking. It's so exasperating. I envy the relationship you have with your dad. Roland is such a sweetheart."

"He is. But I have to believe there's more to Lawrence than meets the eye. Your mother always said he had a softer side he kept hidden from everyone else."

"But why from me? I'm his only child." Ellen resented that all the negative feelings were resurfacing. "I used to go crying to Mother, asking why he didn't love me, and she would tell me over and over again that he did. She'd tell me stories about what a doting father he was when I was a little girl. But what I remember are the awful disagreements. All I ever wanted was to hear him say he loved me and that I wasn't a total disappointment to him. Well, forget that."

Guy stroked her cheek with the back of his hand. "Maybe not. It's possible he just doesn't know how to tell you his true feelings. Maybe he needs you to draw him out."

"Guy, the man is losing his memory. Drawing him out would take a miracle."

"So? What've we got to lose by asking for one?"

4

Ellen Jones sat out on the veranda, Monday morning's breeze damp and salty, and listened to the incessant chirping of a mockingbird perched atop the gazebo. Between the branches of a live oak, she could see streaks of flaming pink on dawn's pale blue canvas.

"Honey, I'm leaving now." Guy Jones walked out on the veranda in his tan silk suit and yellow tie.

"You look sharp, Counselor. I hope you don't wilt in this humidity."

"I doubt I'll set foot outside my air-conditioned car between here and Tallahassee. Anything exciting in the newspaper?"

"Not really. But the mayor is sure touting the open house at the People's Clinic Saturday night. Don't forget the Tehranis asked us to ride with them."

"Why don't you treat yourself to something new to wear? Shopping will take your mind off your dad."

"I doubt that. But I would like to get something to set off the pearls the kids got me for Mother's Day."

He smiled. "I knew that."

"But I think I'll spend the morning writing," Ellen said. "I need to get serious about finishing this second novel."

"You've been telling yourself that for months."

"I know. It's hard to write confidently after all the rejections I've gotten on the first one."

"You're going to get published, I just know it. Someday

you'll be holding a copy of *A Shred of Evidence* with your name on the cover."

"I wish I had your optimism."

"I have a good track record of being right on things like this." He bent down and pressed his lips to hers. "I'll call you tonight. I love you."

"I love you, too. So much." Ellen held his hand for a few seconds, all too aware that when he walked out that door she was solely responsible to look out for their fathers until he returned home Wednesday night.

"You okay, honey?"

"Yes, I just miss you when you're gone. Be careful on the highway."

"I will. If you buy a new dress, take a picture of it and e-mail it to me."

Ellen took a sip of coffee and listened to the sounds of the kitchen door opening and closing and Guy's car backing out of the garage.

Would her father and father-in-law be okay by themselves? Maybe she should bake something and drop it by the apartment. Or was that too obvious?

Ellen's heart raced and she suddenly felt like a rabbit in a trap. Would her father resent her checking in on them so soon? Should she call instead? Or was it better just to e-mail them and leave it at that for a day or two?

Lord, don't let me neglect Roland because I'm afraid of how Dad will treat me. I'm not a child anymore. I don't have to think badly of myself just because he does.

Then why do I? Ellen sat rehashing the past until she heard the cuckoo clock strike seven. She got up and climbed the winding stairs to her office in the widow's watch, determined to lose herself in her writing.

❀ ❀ ❀

Owen Jones sat at the breakfast table, eating a bagel and cream cheese while Hailey read through the want ads.

"I'm not comfortable entrusting Daniel to someone we don't know," Hailey said. "I think I'll call a few of our friends and see if any of them has a good recommendation."

"Smart move. I'll also ask around at work." Owen reached over and put another handful of Cheerios on Daniel's highchair tray. "Don't worry, champ. We're not about to leave you with just anybody."

The baby smiled and reached out his sticky hand and grabbed Owen's sleeve.

"Nice move, Daniel. I just got this sport coat back from the cleaners."

Hailey smiled without looking up. "Welcome to my world."

Owen wet his napkin and wiped the smudge until it disappeared, then gulped the last of his coffee and stood. "I need to get going. I've got a meeting at eight. Call me if you get any good leads. I'd like to be around when you do the interview."

"Okay. I think I'll spend the day pursuing this. Maybe Ellen knows of someone."

"That's a thought. Mom knows a lot of people. If nothing else, she could put out a few feelers for us."

Hailey looked up at him, her eyes watery. "I can't believe you're being so sweet about this. I feel like the worst mother in the world."

"Don't." He pressed his lips to hers. "You just need a little help to take the pressure off so you can enjoy being a mom again."

Hailey dabbed her eyes. "I really do think it'll make a difference."

"Of course it will." He reached over and touched Daniel on the nose, evoking a giggle. "What's not to enjoy?"

❀ ❀ ❀

Ellen cut the pan of cooled brownies into squares and put them in a Tupperware container—all but the one she'd taken a big bite out of. If she didn't get these out of the house, she knew she'd end up polishing off the entire batch. She popped the last of the brownie into her mouth and picked up the Tupperware and her purse and went out to the garage.

Why was she feeling intimidated? Taking homemade goodies to her father and Roland was a nice gesture by anybody's standards. How could he fault her for that?

Ellen drove down Seaport Parkway where the branches of the live oaks had formed an awning over the street and provided shade for the stately old homes that lined either side. The spurts of sunlight that shot through the cracks reminded her of her neighborhood in Baxter.

She drove the nine blocks to Ibis Drive and turned right, then continued down the palm-tree-lined street and past the front gate of Colony Reef Retirement Center. She noticed a crowd gathered at the pool and pulled into the empty parking space in front of apartment 201. She sat for a moment. In her rearview mirror, she could see a net had been strung across the pool and a number of seniors were playing volleyball.

She got out of the car, walked to the door marked 201, and rang the bell. Several seconds later, she heard footsteps and then the door opened.

"Why aren't you at work?" Lawrence snapped.

Ellen forced a smile. "You know I don't work anymore." She held out the Tupperware container. "I brought you and Roland some homemade brownies."

Lawrence glanced at the container but didn't take it. "I don't like chocolate."

Ellen felt her neck and face grow hot. *Don't give him the satisfaction of seeing you react to his rudeness.*

Roland's face appeared over Lawrence's shoulder. "Ellen! What a nice surprise. Come in here and let me hug your neck."

Ellen squeezed past her father and embraced her father-in-law. "I baked you some brownies."

"How thoughtful. I hope you can stay a while."

"Sure, for a few minutes. I still have some shopping to do." Ellen sat in one of the chairs facing the couch and pretended not to notice the scowl on her father's face. "Looks like there's a game of volleyball going on at the pool."

Roland nodded. "Yeah, I'd sure like to play, but this bad hip of mine won't hear of it. Guess I'll just have to pick a team and cheer them on. Volleyball is big here."

"Stupid game." Lawrence folded his arms. "I want to go home."

Roland swatted the air. "That's behind us. This is a whole new day, Lawrence. At least we've still got some independence. That's something to be grateful for."

"I don't want to be grateful."

Ellen bit her lip. "So what have you two been doing?"

"Oh, I've been cooking up a storm," Roland said. "I've got some vegetable soup and a chicken-and-rice casserole in the freezer. But tonight we're going to try dinner at the club."

"Sounds like a great idea. What's on the menu?"

Roland smiled. "New England boiled dinner. I can't resist anything made with corned beef and cabbage."

"You like that, don't you, Dad?"

"Won't be as good as your mother's. When is she coming home from Aunt Bessie's so I can stop all this eating-out nonsense?"

Ellen stared at her father searchingly, then glanced over at Roland, who just shrugged.

"Mom isn't at Aunt Bessie's, she's—"

"Dead. You think I don't know that? Why are you bringing up your mother when you know it upsets me?"

Ellen's heart raced. How was she supposed to respond? "Uh, Roland...what else have you been doing?"

"Oh, I measured the kitchen shelves so I can line them with paper. The van takes us to Wal-Mart on Tuesdays, and I'm hoping to get what I need."

"What we *need*," Lawrence said, "is to go home where we can do what we want. This is a bunch of hooey."

"Might as well stop bellyaching, Lawrence. You're not going to stay ahead of Father Time. There's plenty here to keep us busy."

Lawrence pursed his lips. "No yard work. Might as well shoot me."

"Dad, why don't you let me drive you to Bougainvillea Park? The place is just teeming with growing things. I'll bet you'd love it there."

"So you can follow me around like I haven't got good sense?"

"I could read a book. I certainly don't need to hold your hand."

Lawrence stared at her blankly. "Hold my hand for what?"

"If we go to the park."

"What park? If you two are going to keep secrets from me, you can just leave." Lawrence shook his head and stared at his hands.

Ellen locked gazes with Roland and saw in his eyes the same concern she felt. "So how are you getting along with your roommate?"

"We do just fine." Roland lowered his voice. "Every now and then we aren't on the same page, but it's no big deal."

Lawrence looked up. "I suppose you're going to tell Ellen I'm forgetting things?"

"Are you?" she said.

"Am I what?"

Ellen studied her father. "I think it would be a good idea to have a doctor do some tests. There might be medication that can help your memory."

"I'm not going to start popping pills because some highfalutin doctor decides my mind isn't as sharp as it used to be."

"On the other hand, the doctor might say you're just fine, Dad. What have you got to lose?"

Ellen lay in bed staring at the ceiling fan going round and round. She glanced at the clock just as the phone rang, and she reached over and picked up the receiver.

"Hi, Guy."

"Hi, honey. How was your day?"

"Okay. How were your meetings?"

"Productive. We got done early and I actually had a couple hours to work on my opening for tomorrow. So'd you talk to our two charges today?"

"I took some brownies over there. Roland was a sweetheart. Dad was a royal pain." Ellen sighed. "His mind is really going. This was as bad as I've seen him." She relayed to Guy the incidents as she remembered them.

"He didn't seem that bad yesterday," Guy said.

"No, but when I was in Ocala, he said some strange things. I chalked it up to his being a real stinker, but now I'm beginning to wonder how many times he wasn't operating in present tense. He even asked me today why I wasn't working. I thought he was being difficult. Now I think he was dead serious."

"We need to make an appointment and get him evaluated."

"I know. I already broached the subject with him, told him that medication might help. He looked scared, Guy. I actually found myself feeling sorry for him."

"Good. Compassion might go a long way in getting him to cooperate."

"Not with me. You may have to take the lead in this."

"Okay. You know I will. See what you can do about getting him in for an appointment. Anything else going on?"

"Owen and Hailey are looking for a nanny."

"A nanny? Why?"

"Seems Hailey feels she's suffocating being at home with Daniel all day."

Guy snickered. "She's got one little boy. How hard can it be?"

"Not every woman is cut out to be a stay-at-home mom. I think it's a good idea."

"To let some nanny raise our grandson?"

"Settle down, Counselor. Mrs. Bennett did a great job with the boys when I worked. Owen and Hailey are just looking for someone to help keep the house clean and watch Daniel when Hailey needs to get out or has something planned, though it may be difficult to find someone who'll do both. Apparently, professional nannies are trained in child care and don't do housework."

"Is Owen okay with this?" Guy said.

"Actually, it was his idea. I think he'd go for just about anything that would keep Hailey from taking a job right now. This seems like a reasonable compromise."

"And an expense they don't need."

"Owen says they can easily cover it with his annual bonus. He didn't sound worried about it."

There was a long pause.

"Well," Guy said, "he's a smart kid and seems to know what he's doing, but I still have trouble trusting him to use good sense. It hasn't been that many years since his drinking and carousing kept me up at night."

"Oh, he's way past all that. And if Owen can handle being the CFO of Global Communications, we can certainly trust him to figure out how to budget for a nanny."

5

ordy Jameson stood at the entrance to Gordy's Crab
Shack, the midday sun hanging high in the bluebird
sky, and waited to welcome the first of Tuesday's customers. He spotted a woman walking down the pier and realized it
was Ellen Jones and waved.

Ellen smiled and walked up to him and gave him a hug.

"You havin' lunch alone?" Gordy said.

"Yes, I'm looking forward to a working lunch on the back
deck." She patted the leather case at her side. "I brought my laptop.
I'm trying to wind up my second novel. I don't know if I can concentrate, but I'm going to try."

"How about if we seat you at the table in the far corner of the
deck? You can sit out there as long as you like."

"Thanks. That sounds perfect. Goodness, I'm famished. And
I've been craving Pam's cherry pie all morning."

Gordy laughed. "You want a piece before lunch or after—
or both?"

"After is enough of a splurge, thanks."

"Okay, but it's on the house."

Ellen shook her head. "I know better than to argue. One of
these days your generosity is going to hit you in the pocketbook."

"Yeah, that's what Pam and Weezie tell me. But I was doin'
this long before either of them were around. Besides, sales on
whole pies have skyrocketed since those two got their heads

together and had the pastry case put in. Givin' away a few slices isn't hurtin' a thing."

"Weezie seems to enjoy being assistant manager."

"Loves it. Promotin' her was the best move I ever made. The woman's an entrepreneur at heart and a lot more creative than me. Shoot, if Pam and I were ready to retire, we could hand her the keys and walk away without battin' an eye."

"That must be a good feeling," Ellen said.

"Yeah, it is. I hope she's still here when Pam and I are ready to call it quits. But that's a ways down the road."

Gordy glanced over Ellen's shoulder and saw his lunch buddies walking down the pier toward the crab shack.

"Lunch for one?" Gordy heard the waitress say to Ellen.

"Yes, thank you. I'd like to sit out on the deck."

"Shayla, give Mrs. Jones one of the corner tables." Gordy winked at Ellen. "Hope you get somethin' done on your novel."

Eddie Drummond, Captain Jack, and Adam Spalding walked over to Gordy and slapped him on the back.

"You eating with us today?" Eddie said.

"Yeah, save me a place. I wanna make sure Shayla's got the hang of it first."

Adam's eyebrows met in the middle. "Who?"

"Shayla Taylor…Weezie's sister-in-law. I hired her as a temporary while she's waitin' to hear back on a couple of jobs she's applied for. Poor thing lost her husband in Iraq. Too bad she won't be around long. She's real good with customers."

"Never can tell," Eddie said. "If she doesn't get the job she's after, maybe she'll decide to work for you long term."

Gordy shook his head. "Nah, her first love's workin' with kids. Never had any of her own."

"We gonna stand here all day?" Captain said. "If I get any hungrier I'm gonna fight those ornery pelicans for whatever it is they're pickin' at."

"Gross!" Eddie gave Captain a shove. "You're worse than my kids."

"Well, come on then," Gordy said. "Today's special is all the fried clams you can put away."

Ellen savored the last bite of Pam's cherry pie and pushed her plate to the side just as the waitress came by to fill her water glass.

"How was everything?"

"Scrumptious." Ellen glanced at the woman's name tag. "I noticed your last name's Taylor. Are you any relation to Weezie Taylor?"

"Yes, I'm her sister-in-law. Our husbands were brothers."

The word *were* didn't escape Ellen's attention. She didn't see a wedding ring. "I'm Ellen Jones. I eat here frequently, so I'm sure our paths will cross again. Nice to meet you."

"Likewise, ma'am. I may not be here long, though. Gordy was sweet to hire me till I can find a permanent job. I'd really like to work with kids—maybe in a day care or a preschool. It won't pay as much, but I'd love doin' it."

"Have you worked with children before?"

"Oh, yes ma'am. At church mostly. I volunteered my time till Lucas got killed in Iraq, but now I need a paycheck. I don't have the credentials to teach, but I love just helpin' out. Nothin' like all those hugs and kisses to make my day."

"Well, I hope you find what you're looking for, Shayla. It was very nice talking with you."

Ellen opened her laptop and turned it on. She pulled up chapter twenty-seven of her book and began reading just as her cell phone rang. She heaved a sigh of frustration, then picked up her phone and pushed the Talk button. "Hello."

"Ellen, it's Roland. I'm sorry to bother you, but I think we've got a problem."

"What's Dad done?"

"Nothing," Roland Jones said. "I can't find him, is all. He's not in the house. I walked over to the pool and then around the block looking for him, but my bad leg wouldn't go any farther."

"When did you see him last?"

"He grabbed a couple of your brownies and said he was going to his room to watch TV. But when I went to get him for lunch, he wasn't there. I never heard him leave, but I'm sure he's not here. I've looked everywhere."

Ellen breathed in slowly and let it out. *Lord, what do I do?*

"Ellen? You still there?"

"Yes. Stay right where you are, Roland. I'll be there in ten minutes."

"Okay. I'm sure sorry I couldn't find him."

"This isn't your fault. Try not to worry. I'll see you in just a few minutes."

Ellen turned off her laptop and put it in the carrying case. She took out two one-dollar bills and placed them under a Tabasco bottle so the breeze wouldn't whisk them away. She started to leave, then changed her mind and replaced the bills with a five.

She smiled as she passed Shayla and went inside to pay her bill, thinking of all the things she'd like to say to her father when she figured out where he was.

Owen Jones walked in the front door of his house and followed a trail of plastic toys to the kitchen. "Hailey, where are you?"

"In the laundry room."

He dropped the mail and a sack of fish and chips on the countertop, then walked across the hall to the laundry room and saw Daniel sitting on the floor, stacking his plastic rings.

"I thought you were going to lunch with the management team," Hailey said.

Owen reached down and picked up Daniel and held him on his hip, then kissed her on the cheek. "I decided to check in with you instead. Any leads on a nanny?"

Hailey stopped folding clothes and blew a lock of hair out of her face. "No. I had no idea nannies were so specialized. A couple of my friends recommended I contact Nannies For Hire, but when I called, they told me they didn't have any prospects willing to combine childcare and housekeeping duties, that their ladies have been thoroughly trained as childcare professionals and aren't babysitters or domestic help. So much for getting a little help."

"We don't need someone to keep Daniel eight hours a day," Owen said. "No one is willing to split childcare and housecleaning?"

"Not there. I got the impression I was insulting the woman by even suggesting it. I have a feeling it's going to be that way no matter where I inquire."

Owen touched Daniel on the nose and made him laugh. "I thought this was going to be easy."

"Me, too, but we can't justify the expense of a nanny if she won't even help with the housework."

Owen put his arm around her. "You let me worry about that."

"Darling, we have to be realistic. If the person isn't willing to stay busy helping me with other things when I'm spending time with Daniel, what good is she to me? I want someone to share the load, not take my place."

"There has to be someone out there willing to do that."

"How would we find her? I'm really uneasy about putting an ad in the paper."

"Don't get discouraged. Something will fall into place."

"I hope so. Oh, I forgot to tell you—" Hailey looked up— "some guy called this morning—a Tim O'Rourke. Said he would try back later."

"Did he say what he wanted?"

"No. And he wouldn't leave a number."

"Probably selling something. I don't know anyone by that name."

Ellen got a glimpse of her father-in-law in the picture window when she pulled up in front of apartment 201. She got out of the car and hurried to the front door, reaching it just as Roland stepped out on the stoop.

"I'm so sorry," Roland said. "I would've kept looking for Lawrence, but this darned hip of mine isn't worth a plug nickel."

Ellen put her hands on her father-in-law's shoulders. "This is not your fault. Let's take my car, and you can show me where you've already looked. How long do you think he's been gone?"

"Hard to tell when he left, but he went in his room around nine thirty."

Ellen helped Roland into the front seat and then backed her Thunderbird out of the parking space.

"I looked all around the pool, then walked that way." Roland pointed down Ibis Drive.

Ellen drove in the opposite direction, her speed at a crawl, her eyes searching one side of the street, then the other. "Did Dad say anything that would give us a hint where he might've gone?"

"Not really. He doesn't always make sense, and I try not to pay too much attention to his complaining. I thought I had him talked into going over to the pool this morning, but he couldn't find his hat."

"That faded old ball cap he's had forever?"

Roland shrugged. "I don't know. But he was sure upset he couldn't find it."

Ellen stayed on Ibis Drive and drove all the way around the complex and back to the entrance. "Well, if he decided he wanted to buy another hat, he may have walked down to that sporting-goods store he commented on the day we arrived."

Ellen turned right out of the retirement center and drove to the end of street and stopped at a red light, her fingers tapping the steering wheel. "I'm sure Dad is enjoying worrying me to death. But I thought he'd be more considerate of you."

"Oh, Lawrence is just having a hard time. It isn't easy putting your independence on the shelf. Makes you feel like your life doesn't have much meaning anymore."

Ellen was surprised to see Roland's eyes brimming with tears. She reached over and touched his arm. "Please don't feel that way. We all wanted you closer in case you need our help."

Roland half smiled. "You're sweet, Ellen. But let's face it, Lawrence and I are just a couple of has-beens who don't have much to offer anymore."

"Yes, you do! We love you. We enjoy your company and are thrilled that Daniel will get to know his great-grandfathers."

Roland kept his eyes straight ahead. "The light's green."

Ellen heard a horn honk and turned right onto Seaport Parkway and drove two blocks to The Outdoor Store. "I'll check here first." She pulled into a parking space and set the brake. "Watch for Dad, okay? I won't be long."

Ellen got out of the car and pushed open the glass door and quickly walked up and down the aisles without spotting her father. Finally, she went up to a man with a name tag. "Excuse me." Ellen took her wallet out of her purse and held out her father's picture. "Has this man been in here today? His name is Lawrence Madison. He's my father. He may have come in looking for a ball cap or a wide-brimmed hat."

The salesman shook his head. "Sorry. I don't remember him."

"Would you mind checking with the other employees? It's important that I find him. He just moved here and may not be able to find his way home." *Or he's taking his sweet time, hoping to make me sweat.*

"Uh, sure. Wait here. I'll be right back."

Ellen looked through a display filled with billed caps and every imaginable style of outdoor hats for men. Would her dad have paid these kinds of prices? Where else would he have gone on foot? Ellen suddenly felt hot.

"Ma'am?"

Ellen turned and saw a different salesman standing there. "Yes?"

"I think I sold a blue cap to the man in this picture—maybe an hour or two ago. He paid cash so I never got his name."

"Did he seem all right?" Ellen said.

"Yeah, I suppose. He said something about his daughter throwing out his favorite hat."

"Did you see which way he went?"

"Not really. I did notice he put on the cap as he walked out the door."

"Okay, thanks." Ellen hurried toward the exit, her heart racing.

Where else could she look? Should she report him missing? Was it too soon? Maybe it was smarter to go back to the apartment first and see if her father had gone home.

She opened the exit door just as her cell phone rang. She reached in her purse, grabbed the phone, and put it to her ear. "Hello?"

"Did you know your dad is down at Gordy's?" Guy said.

"No! Roland and I have been out looking for him! How do you know he's at Gordy's?"

"Because Gordy just called me at the office after he couldn't reach you at home. He apologized all over himself for calling me in Tallahassee, but said Lawrence seemed disoriented and upset. Apparently, he wandered into the crab shack and asked one of the waitresses if she'd call his daughter. He gave her your name but couldn't tell her your address or phone number. The waitress remembered you being in there earlier and asked Gordy if he knew how to reach you. Thankfully, he did."

"Roland and I have been pulling our hair out." Ellen told Guy everything that had happened after she left the house with the intention of having a quiet working lunch by herself. "I can't imagine why Dad went to Gordy's. I doubt if he's even heard of the place."

"Let's just be glad he did," Guy said. "Why don't you go pick him up and then call me back, and we'll figure out what we need to do."

Owen Jones walked into Global Communications and took the elevator up to the third floor. He nodded at the receptionist and walked into his office. He picked up a stack of phone messages, his eyes stopping on one from Tim O'Rourke. He had called at twelve-thirty and said he'd call back.

Owen walked out of his office and over to his administrative assistant's desk.

"Helen, what can you tell me about this call from Tim O'Rourke?"

"Just that he wanted to speak to you about an important matter."

"Why didn't he leave a number?"

Helen's pale blue eyes grew wider. "I don't know, Mr. Jones. Maybe he's on the road and can't be reached."

"Did you get the impression his call was business related?"

"He didn't say that. I just assumed it was."

"Okay. If he calls back, come find me. He called my house this morning and pulled the same song and dance, and I don't want him bothering Hailey if he's not going to leave a message."

6

Ellen Jones marched into Gordy's Crab Shack just after two and spotted a blue ball cap visible over the back of one of the booths. She walked in that direction and saw her father sitting across from Gordy Jameson, taking a bite of what appeared to be apple pie.

"I'm sorry you had to call Guy in Tallahassee to reach me," Ellen said to Gordy. "I was out looking for Dad."

"No problem." Gordy slid out of the booth. "Lawrence and I have been talkin' baseball." He winked. "The pie's on the house."

"Thanks," Ellen said, "for *everything*."

"Let me know if I can do anything else." Gordy patted Ellen's shoulder and walked toward the kitchen.

Ellen slid in the booth opposite her father, her arms folded on the table. "You promised not to leave the retirement center without someone being with you!"

Lawrence acted as though he didn't hear her.

"Why didn't you come back to the apartment?"

Lawrence shifted his weight and didn't make eye contact.

Ellen softened her tone. "Dad, you don't have to feel ashamed if you got confused. You don't know your way around Seaport."

"I wasn't confused!"

"Then why did you end up here?"

"None of your business."

"Dad, I'm more than annoyed! I was worried sick about you.

51

Was this your way of getting back at me for bringing you here? Is this how it's going to be?"

"Just take me home. I'd rather talk to your mother."

Ellen paused, aware that her father was wringing his hands. Should she correct him? Let it slide? Go along with him? *Lord, help me say the right thing.*

She reached over and touched her father's arm. "Mom was much gentler than I am. I'm sorry I raised my voice. I just care what happens to you, that's all."

Lawrence was silent for several seconds, then looked up. "Why aren't you at work?"

"I'm here to pick you up, remember?"

"Well, it's about time! The bus left me off over an hour ago. That hippie's been talking my ear off ever since."

Ellen started to correct him and then changed her mind. "Sorry I'm late, Dad. I'll take you home now."

Ellen sat in her father and father-in-law's apartment, waiting for the evening news to come on and wondering why she ever thought this arrangement might work.

Roland turned up the volume.

"Good evening. I'm Shannon Pate."

"And I'm Stephen Rounds. Welcome to *Regional News at Six*. Seaport police are looking for a suspect in the stabbing death earlier today of a souvenir-shop owner. Jared Downing is on the scene and has the story. Jared…"

"Stephen, just after noon today, police responded to a 911 call made by an employee of the Sun Haven Souvenir Shop in the six-hundred block of Beach Shore Drive. When they got here, the employee led them out to the alley behind the establishment, where the owner, Jackson Kincaid, lay dead from a single stab wound to the chest.

"According to the employee, Kincaid had gone out back to

dispose of some boxes after checking in new merchandise. When he didn't come back, the employee went looking for him and discovered his body lying next to the Dumpster.

"Police were then called, and a short time later, thirty-six-year-old Kincaid was pronounced dead at the scene. No wallet was found on the victim, and police believe theft was the motive for the killing.

"Hannah Kincaid, the victim's wife, said the couple had moved here last year from Ft. Lauderdale, confident their three young children would thrive in a smaller community. Tonight, those children are fatherless.

"Andrew Connor, the owner of Fish Tales Eatery and Gift Shop two doors down from Sun Haven, gave the police a description of a man he saw sitting on a beer crate behind Flamingo's Bar and Grill around 11:45 this morning. He describes the suspect as a tall, thin, gray-haired Caucasian male wearing khaki shorts, a yellow golf shirt, and a blue baseball cap.

"Anyone having information that might help police locate this man is asked to call the Seaport Police Department…"

Ellen stared at her father, her heart pounding. "Is that where you were…in the alley?"

Lawrence stared at his hands as though he didn't hear a word she said.

"You don't remember? Or you don't want to talk about it?"

"When's your mother coming home? It's time for my dinner. Why isn't she cooking my dinner?"

"Roland is cooking dinner tonight," Ellen said softly. "Look at me, this is important. Do you remember being in an alley today? That witness gave a perfect description of you."

Silence.

"Dad, please. I have to know what happened. A man was murdered."

Lawrence wrung his hands, then looked at her, his eyes brimming with tears. "I want to go home."

Ellen got up and knelt next to the couch, her hand on his. "It's okay, Dad. You're safe with me. Did you see a man stab someone?"

Lawrence pulled his hand away from hers. "He cut me a piece of pie."

"Dad, that was Gordy, the man who stayed with you till I picked you up."

"When are we having dinner? Why are you starving me?"

"Dad, I need you to calm down! This is very important!" Ellen was thinking she was the one who needed to calm down. "If you were in the alley, you had to have seen something. I'm going to call Police Chief Seevers. He's a friend of ours. Maybe something you tell him will help him find the man who did the stabbing."

"I want to go to bed."

"I know this has been exhausting. But I need you to stay awake while I call Will Seevers and see when he can talk to you."

Ellen got up and took her phone out of her purse, then turned on the voice-activation feature and spoke into the receiver. "Police." She looked over at her father, thinking about what he may have seen and wondering if he would be able to recall a single detail of it. She wasn't about to subject him to the usual protocol.

"Seaport Police Department, how may I direct your call?"

"This is Ellen Jones. I need to speak directly with Chief Seevers."

"What is the nature of your call, ma'am?"

"My father may have seen the man who stabbed that souvenir-shop owner today. I'd like him to talk with Chief Seevers."

"Investigator Backus is handling that case and would be glad to speak with you."

"I've dealt with the investigator before. I'd really prefer to speak with Chief Seevers. Would it be possible for you to get a message to him?"

"That would be highly irregular, ma'am."

"I know. So is my situation. My father is elderly and has special needs. I don't mean to be unkind, but the investigator is not terribly gentle or tactful. Chief Seevers and I worked together on the Hamilton kidnapping case, and I'm much more comfortable with him."

"All I can do is pass this information on to Investigator Backus and let him decide. What is your phone number?"

Ellen gave the woman her cell phone number.

"I'll make sure he gets this information right away."

"Thank you." Ellen disconnected the call.

"Why aren't you at work?" Lawrence said.

Ellen sighed and decided not to try to explain it again.

Roland got up, his hands on his lower back, and stretched. "Guess I'll go warm up the soup and put some rolls in the oven."

Ellen wondered what Roland must be thinking. How could she leave him alone with her father after all this?

She glanced at her watch. "Dad, I'll be right back." She walked down the hall to the bathroom and closed the door, then pressed the autodial for Guy's apartment on her cell phone.

"Hello."

"Oh, good, you're there," Ellen said.

"Yeah, I just walked in. What's up?"

"You're not going to believe the newest development." Ellen relayed to him what she had just seen on the evening news, her conversation with her dad, and what she had said in her subsequent call to the police. "Did I do the wrong thing by asking for Will? I don't want to take advantage of our friendship."

"He might be willing to do you a favor and talk to your dad, but don't count on it. That's not really what the city pays him for."

"I know. I may have to relent and let Dad talk to Investigator Backus, but I figured I didn't have anything to lose by asking."

"Honey, I'm sorry you're having to deal with all this by yourself.

I'll try to get home early tomorrow night. You going to be okay?"

"As long as I stay in thinking mode. What should I do about tonight? Dad's much worse than I thought, and I can't saddle Roland with the responsibility of looking out for him."

"I agree. You're going to have to take your dad home with you."

"He'll never go willingly."

"Then call Owen and get him to side with you. You can't leave him there."

"What about Roland? I'm not comfortable leaving him by himself." Ellen sighed and leaned against the sink. "Maybe I'll just stay here tonight until we figure something out."

Beep.

"Guy, that's my call-waiting. I'll call you back after we've talked to the police."

"Okay, honey. Try to stay calm and take it one step at a time. Wish I were there to help."

"That's two of us. Love you."

"Love you, too."

Ellen switched over to the other caller. "Hello."

"Ellen, it's Will Seevers. I understand you wanted to talk to me…"

Police Chief Will Seevers hung up the phone and looked over at Investigator Al Backus. "Will you stop with the martyr routine? You know Ellen and Guy are friends of mine."

"What's the woman's beef anyway?" Backus said.

"Her father needs careful handling, and she didn't think you were the one to do it. You have to admit tact isn't your strong point."

"Hey, I can do whatever it takes to get the job done."

Will smiled. "Yeah, Al. I remember you being tactful—once. You can go with me to question her father if you promise to let me do the talking."

"Okay, I'll keep my mouth shut. So she thinks the old guy saw the assailant?"

"It's possible. Unfortunately, he's showing signs of Alzheimer's. The best she's been able to determine is that he was walking home from The Outdoor Store and got confused and ended up in the alley and then at Gordy's. Her father didn't seem to know where he'd been, but Ellen says the description given on the news of the man in the alley fits him to a T, right down to the blue cap."

Al rolled his eyes. "If the guy's that out of it, why waste time trying to get his statement?"

"He might give us enough to find the perp."

"Yeah, right. My grandfather has Alzheimer's. Trust me, we're never gonna know if what the man says is real or not—if he remembers anything at all."

"Well, before we blow him off—" Will pushed back from his desk and stood— "how 'bout we go hear what he has to say?"

7

Owen Jones put the last of the dinner dishes in the dishwasher and turned the On switch. "Sorry to rush out of here, but Mom would like me to be there when the police take Granddad's statement. We can talk more about the nanny situation when I get home."

"I don't know what else there is to talk about," Hailey Jones said. "The whole thing's turning out to be a fiasco."

Owen put his hands on her shoulders and looked into her eyes. "We're *going* to find someone. Just be patient, okay?"

Hailey nodded. "You'd better get going. Call me after the police leave. I'm dying to know what this is all about."

"Me, too." He pressed his lips to hers. "If that Tim O'Rourke calls again, see if he'll leave a number and find out how late I can call him back."

Owen felt Daniel tugging at his pant leg and reached down and picked him up. "Don't you give Mommy a hard time about going to bed, hear?" He tickled Daniel's tummy then handed him to Hailey. "I can't imagine I'll be late."

Owen went out the side door and walked under the breezeway to the detached garage. He put the top down on his Jaguar, then backed out of the driveway and headed for Seaport, wishing he'd watched the evening news so he'd have a better handle on what was going on. His mother's sentences had all run together, but the gist of her call was that Granddad had gone out by himself and gotten lost and possibly witnessed a stabbing.

Owen wound his car through the residential neighborhood, then turned on to Main Street, stealing glimpses of the gulf beyond a seemingly unending row of restaurants, businesses, and souvenir shops.

Up ahead he saw the Seaport exit and merged into a stream of traffic headed east. When he saw his way clear, he got into the left lane and pressed on the gas until his Jaguar seemed to be sailing, the evening breeze whipping his hair, the sun an orange ball in his rearview mirror.

An invigorating sense of happiness charged through him—that same sort of high he'd sought in his bachelor days, though back then the high had come from partying, drinking, pursuing women, and smoking pot. How quickly he had lost interest in that lifestyle when he fell in love with Hailey. And even more so when he'd gotten right with God. And now that they had Daniel, life just kept getting better and better.

Owen's vibrating cell phone brought him back to the moment. He took it out of his shirt pocket and saw his home number lit up on the screen. He flipped it open and put it to his ear. "That was quick. What's up?"

"Tim O'Rourke called again. I told him you were out and would be glad to call him later, but he wouldn't leave a phone number. He sounded mad—like he didn't believe you weren't home. I asked if he could tell me what his call was regarding, and he hung up on me."

"I'm getting tired of this guy bugging us. Next time he calls, why don't you just hang up on *him*."

"I don't want to antagonize him. Something about him gives me the creeps. I just want you to talk to him so he'll stop calling."

"I'd be glad to if the guy ever bothered to leave a number!"

There was a loud whooshing sound, and Hailey's voice faded in and out. "Listen, honey, you're breaking up. If the guy calls again, give him my cell number."

❀ ❀ ❀

Ellen sat on the couch with her father, frustrated because he couldn't seem to make sense of the details stored in his mind.

"Okay, Mr. Madison," Will Seevers said. "I'd like you to try again to picture the man you saw with a knife."

Lawrence stared at his hands.

"Dad, tell the chief about the man with the knife."

"He cut me a piece of pie."

"The man in the alley?" Will said.

"Had a belly on him. Big fella. He waited at the bus stop. Ellen saw him."

Ellen looked at Will and mouthed the word "Gordy."

"What was the man wearing?"

Lawrence stared at his hands. "Had Old Glory on his shirt."

"A flag T-shirt?"

"Had a gut on him, I'll tell you that."

Will looked over at Ellen. "I assume Gordy was wearing his usual navy polo shirt with the crab shack's logo?"

Ellen nodded.

"Mr. Madison, when you saw the man in the Old Glory shirt, what was he doing?"

"Running over the broken glass," Lawrence said. "Don't you know anything?"

The doorbell rang.

Ellen rose to her feet. "Excuse me. That's probably my son." She went to the front door and saw Owen standing on the stoop. She put her arms around him and held him a few seconds longer than usual. "I'm so glad you're here."

"How's it going?"

"It's not. Dad's confusing what he saw in the alley with what he saw at Gordy's. Come sit with us. I think they're just about to give up."

Ellen introduced Owen to Chief Seevers and Al Backus and then resumed her place next to her father.

"Okay, Mr. Madison," Will said, "I want you to close your eyes for a minute and try to picture the man's face. Can you tell me anything about him—anything at all?"

Lawrence closed his eyes for what seemed an eternity, and then opened them and stared blankly at Will. "Who are *you*?"

"I'm Chief Seevers."

Lawrence held his gaze, a puzzled look on his face. "Sure don't look like any Indian I've ever seen."

"Dad, this is the *police* chief. You were telling him what you saw today."

"It was a fine day. Ellen's mother brought me cold mint tea and served up some of that lemon cake I like so much."

Ellen locked gazes with Will. "I really need to get him to bed."

"Mr. Madison, thank you for talking with us," Will said.

"Do I know you?"

"Uh—well, not exactly. We'll have to get acquainted some-time."

Out of the corner of her eye, Ellen noticed Investigator Backus tapping his fingers on the arm of the chair. What was it about him she disliked so?

"Will, do you think you'll need to question Dad further?" Ellen asked.

"I don't know. It seems obvious he's confusing Gordy with the man he may have seen in the alley. But if Gordy wasn't wear-ing a T-shirt with a flag, it might mean the assailant was. It's not a lot to go on."

Ellen sighed. "I'm sorry. Maybe after he's rested something will come back to him."

Will stood and Backus followed his lead. "I'll be interested to see if we find glass in the alley."

❧ ❧ ❧

Owen hung up the phone with Hailey just as his mother emerged from his granddad's room and came and sat next to him on the couch.

"What a day!" Ellen said. "Dad's finally asleep."

Owen glanced out into the kitchen and saw Papa sitting at the kitchen table, reading the newspaper. "Mom, what are we going to do? We can't leave Granddad here with Papa."

"I know, honey. I'm staying tonight, but tomorrow morning, I'll have to insist that Granddad come home with me until your father and I can come up with a better plan."

"Papa shouldn't be by himself either."

Ellen looked out into the kitchen. "I know. But he should be okay for a couple of days until we can make other arrangements."

"Meaning what—assisted living?"

"I don't know, Owen. I hate this! Why do parents have to get feeble and helpless…? Ellen put her fist to her mouth and seemed to choke back the emotion. "I wish Mother were here."

"Don't cry. Would it help if I took Papa home with me tonight?"

"It's sweet of you to offer, but I can manage. Besides, Hailey doesn't need any added pressure right now. Which reminds me, any leads on a nanny?"

Owen shook his head. "Hailey says they all want to be involved with children full time and don't want to do any house-work at all. We need someone flexible. Hailey's really down about it. She's getting vibes from the agencies that none of their people are willing to juggle childcare and housecleaning. We're willing to pay the same money. I don't know why it's such a big deal."

"Everyone is so specialized anymore," Ellen said. "Are you set on finding someone through an agency?"

"Not really. We just don't know where else to look for some-one capable and trustworthy."

"Maybe I'll ask Weezie Taylor's sister-in-law."

"Are you talking about Weezie down at Gordy's?"

Ellen nodded. "Her sister-in-law Shayla is working there temporarily. She was my waitress today at lunch and told me she's looking for a job at a day care or preschool. Maybe she'd be interested or knows someone who might be happy with the arrangement you're talking about. Surely not everyone who loves working with kids wants to do it eight hours a day."

Owen lifted his eyebrows. "Including Hailey." He sank into the back of the couch. "Mom, how are you going to sleep on this cushy sofa tonight?"

"I'll be fine."

"Why don't you let me stay here with Granddad and Papa? You can go home and sleep in your own bed."

"No, you need to be with Hailey and Daniel, and you've got to go to work tomorrow. The more I think about it, it's probably best if I take both your grandfathers home with me in the morning. We've got plenty of room. Then when your dad gets home tomorrow night, we can figure out what we're going to do."

"You can't possibly be thinking of letting Granddad live with you."

Ellen's eyebrows gathered. "Certainly not permanently. But after the episode today, I'm not sure how much care he actually needs. We may have to keep him with us until we get him evaluated by a doctor."

8

Owen Jones eased his Jaguar into the right lane and exited the highway at Port Smyth. He reached in the glove box for two Excedrin, then popped them into his mouth and washed them down with a gulp of bottled water.

Why did he feel so guilty? Maybe he should have insisted that his mother go home and let him spend the night with his grandfathers. He wondered if his offer to bring Papa home with him had sounded sincere and if he'd successfully masked his relief when his mother turned him down. What right did he have to expect Hailey to take on more responsibility right now?

His cell phone vibrated and he put it to his ear. "Hello."

"Owen Jones?"

"Yes."

"This is Tim O'Rourke. I was beginning to think you were avoiding me."

"Most people are courteous enough to leave a phone number. What is it you want?"

"I have something that belongs to you."

"Really? And what is that?"

"I'd rather show you. Where can we meet?"

"You didn't answer my question, Mr. O'Rourke."

"And you didn't answer mine."

Owen paused, dumbfounded by the audacity of this man. "Who do you think you are? You've harassed my wife, my secretary. You've finally got me on the line, so cut the game playing!"

"Oh, this isn't a game. We've got serious business to discuss. Tell me when and where."

"I've got news for you, *Tim*. There's no way I'm going to meet some guy I don't even know to discuss something he won't reveal over the phone. Call back when you're ready to shoot straight with me. Until then, stop bothering me." Owen disconnected the call, his heart racing faster than the motorcycle that whizzed past him, his mind exploding with words he had vowed never to say after Daniel was born.

His phone vibrated again and he started to answer the call, then decided not to. Owen waited for what seemed an eternity, then checked to see if the caller had left a message. He had. Owen played it back.

"You need to see for yourself what I'm talking about. It would make things a lot easier on both of us if you just told me where to meet you. Needs to be someplace private. And you need to come alone. I'll call back after you've had time to think about it."

Owen tossed the phone on the passenger seat and gripped the steering wheel with both hands. Where did this guy get off telling him what to do? He spotted the Seafood Extravaganza sign up ahead and realized he'd missed his turn.

He switched lanes without thinking and glanced in the rearview mirror just as he heard a long horn blast and saw the front grill of an eighteen-wheeler just a few yards behind him.

Owen swerved back into the left lane and made a sharp U-turn, his tires screeching, and drove in the opposite direction on Main Street, wondering what Tim O'Rourke had in his possession that was so all-fired important he wouldn't talk about it over the phone.

Owen pulled his car into the detached garage and went into the house by the side door. He stopped in the doorway to the kitchen and saw Hailey sitting at the table putting pictures in a photo album. He knocked gently. "I didn't want to startle you. It's nice to see you looking so relaxed."

Hailey looked up and smiled. "I'm trying to get caught up with this photo album and Daniel's baby book." She glanced at the clock. "I can't believe it's been forty minutes since you called. Are you just wiped out?"

Owen walked over to where she was sitting and kissed her. "Not too. Is Daniel down for the night?"

"Yes, and don't you dare wake him up." Hailey's eyes seemed to search his. "You look stressed. Are you having second thoughts about Ellen staying with your grandfathers?"

"No, I'm fuming over the conversation I just had with Tim O'Rourke. What a jerk!"

"I gave him your cell number. So what's the deal?"

Owen lifted his eyebrows. "Says he's got something that belongs to me and wants to meet with me privately." Owen told Hailey everything he could remember about the conversation and then let her listen to the phone message. "I resent this guy trying to manipulate me. Why doesn't he just say what it's about?"

"Are you going to meet with him?"

"No way. He can either give me the courtesy of an explanation…or he can take a hike."

"Aren't you curious about what he has that's yours?"

"Not especially." Owen picked up a photograph of Daniel playing peekaboo with Granddad and Papa. "The more I think about it, it reeks of some elaborate sales ploy."

"Well, *I* sure don't want to talk to him."

"Now that he's got my cell number, I doubt he'll call here again. But if he keeps being a pest, we'll get an unlisted number. Two can play this game."

"So much for the Do Not Call List."

Owen pulled out a chair and sat at the table and put the photo back on the stack. "I forgot to tell you something when I called earlier. Mom mentioned that one of the gals working for Gordy might be willing to split childcare and housekeeping responsibilities or maybe knows someone who would. She's going to check into it for us."

"I didn't think it would be this hard to find someone."

"Just try not to worry about it. It'll fall into place."

Hailey slid the photo into the plastic sleeve, then looked up and caught his gaze. "Why don't we pray about it?"

"I'm sure Mom'll do enough of that for both of us."

"But remember what the pastor said about married couples praying together. I really wish we could start doing that."

"Honey, God already knows what we need whether we say it or not." Owen patted her hand and rose to his feet. "You go ahead and work on the album. I think I'll read the newspaper and try to unwind."

Ellen Jones opened the door to her father's room and peeked inside. He seemed to be sleeping soundly. She pulled the door shut and walked past Roland's room and into the living room. She turned on the TV, eager to watch the eleven o'clock news and dreading an uncomfortable night of tossing and turning on the sofa.

How hard it was to see her father slipping away, knowing she would likely never be able to make peace with him. She had made guarded attempts in the past, but when he came back with his usual caustic remarks, she decided it wasn't worth it.

Ellen thought back on her girlhood days and tried to recall a tender memory of her father—anything that might help salve the pain of his ongoing disapproval. Had he ever affirmed her? She couldn't remember. Ever since she'd been old enough to have a mind of her own, they had never seen eye to eye.

Ellen had always held the hope that someday he would soften and see that she had been a good wife, mother, *and* journalist—and would have made a good daughter if only he would have accepted her for who she was. Ellen batted her eyes to stop the stinging. Why did she miss her mother so much?

The TV anchor's voice brought her back to the present.

"....Police Chief Will Seevers told reporters earlier this evening that police have spoken with a witness who may have seen the assailant in this morning's stabbing, but he would not comment further while the case is still under investigation.

"Andrew Connor, the owner of Fish Tales and a business acquaintance of stabbing victim Jackson Kincaid, has already set up a memorial fund for the Kincaid family and put in five thousand dollars of his own money. WRGL News reporter Jared Downing spoke with Connor earlier this evening and here's what Connor had to say:

"'I can't tell you how heartbreaking Jackson's murder is for those of us who knew him and Hannah and the kids. But a tragedy like this always hurts more than just the victim and his family. I set up the memorial fund not just because Jackson's wife and the kids have financial needs, but because people here need a tangible way to reach out to make this awful situation a little less awful. Here's a chance for the community to pull together to help one of their own. I really hope folks will dig deep into their hearts and pockets and be generous.'

"Contributions can be made to the Jackson Kincaid Memorial Fund at Fish Tales Eatery and Gift Shop located at 106 Beach Shore Drive, or by sending a check to the address shown on the screen..."

Ellen couldn't listen anymore. She wondered how the victim's children were coping with the loss of their father. She thought it sad that in many respects she had also lost her father when she was a child.

Owen turned off the TV and the lights and walked into the nursery and laid his hand gently on Daniel's back.

"I love you, son," he whispered.

He stood for a moment and felt the baby's breathing, then walked out of the nursery and into the master bedroom and climbed into bed, hoping he had wound down enough to fall sleep.

He draped his arm over Hailey and pulled her close, her long, thick hair feeling like a warm blanket next to his skin. He stroked the soft tresses and inhaled the clean, almost flowery scent of her hair.

He closed his eyes and tried not to think about the back-to-back meetings he had in the morning or the budget cuts he'd been forced to make or how to break it to the board of directors that the company was operating at 5 percent over budget. He wondered if Tim O'Rourke knew he was the CFO of Global Communications.

Owen rolled over on his back, his hands clasped behind his head. Why was he still wasting brainpower thinking about *that* creep? What could the guy possibly have of Owen's? And why all the secrecy?

He had replayed the phone message over and over in his mind, and one comment wouldn't leave him alone: *You need to see for yourself what I'm talking about.*

See what? Did the guy have something to blackmail him with? Owen racked his brain, trying to think of something he'd said or done that someone could hold over him. Nothing came to mind.

He exhaled loudly, threw off the covers, and sat up on the side of the bed. Too bad he didn't have Tim O'Rourke's phone number so he could call him back and spoil *his* night's sleep.

Ellen punched the throw pillow and turned on her side, thinking this cushy sofa could double as a torture tool. She heard the kitchen clock ticking and Roland snoring and the sinister yowling of a cat outside. The air conditioner clicked on, and the irritating noises were drowned out by the hum of the motor.

Ellen got up and spread the thermal blanket on the floor and tossed the throw pillow on one end. She got down on the floor and wrapped herself in the blanket, thinking the hard floor couldn't be any more miserable than that marshmallow heap she'd been wrestling with for the past several hours.

She was reminded of the story of "Goldilocks and the Three Bears" she had been reading to Daniel. "Too hard. Too soft," she mumbled. If there were such a thing as "just right," she'd sure like to find it before morning.

Ellen stared into the darkness, her back aching and her eyelids heavy. The air conditioner shut off, and she waited expectantly for the annoying sounds to crawl through the stillness and find her ears.

She started to doze off when a clicking noise caught her attention. What now? She listened intently, then realized someone was jiggling the handle on the front door! The pounding of her heart was audible. Had she locked it? She couldn't remember.

She jumped to her feet and hurried to the door, relieved to find the deadbolt locked. She put her eye to the peephole and saw a shadow. She groped for the porch-light switch but felt only a smooth wall. Should she yell? Make a noise? Call the police? *Lord, I need wisdom!*

Ellen banged on the door with both fists. "Go away! I'm calling the police!"

Instantly, the shadow disappeared.

She moved to the picture window and peeked through a crack in the drapes in time to see a dark figure dissolve into the blackness.

She groped her way to the sofa and collapsed, then drew in a slow, deep breath and exhaled, repeating the process until her pulse slowed. Should she report it to the police? Not tonight. She was too exhausted to go through all that, and the would-be intruder was probably blocks away by now.

Ellen grabbed the throw pillow off the floor and hugged it to her chest. First thing in the morning, she would pack up her father and father-in-law and take them to her house. She could hardly wait for Guy to get home from Tallahassee.

Suddenly the room was flooded with light. Ellen saw her father standing with his hand on the light switch, a familiar scowl on his face.

"Thanks for waking me up!" he snapped. "The least you could do is keep the volume down on the blasted TV! Why don't you go back to your own house? You're more trouble than you're worth."

It was all Ellen could do not to shout at him, to tell him what a cruel, despicable, ungrateful old grouch he was.

Sometimes I hate you, she thought.

She brushed past him and went out to the kitchen, hoping to find solace in what was left of the brownies.

9

The next morning, Ellen Jones sat in the wicker rocker on the veranda of her home, Daniel asleep in her arms, Lawrence and Roland inside watching Andy Griffith reruns. She looked over at Hailey and smiled.

"I'm so glad you came over. I've about had it with crisis management. It's so relaxing just to sit here and rock a baby."

Hailey Jones took a sip of lemonade. "It was nice getting out. You never said—did the police get any other reports of attempted break-ins?"

"Not at the retirement center. But they tried to assure me this kind of thing happens all the time—probably a cat burglar looking for easy access."

Hailey looked out at the gazebo and seemed to be miles away.

"Honey, are you worried about finding a nanny?"

"No one seems interested in the arrangement we want. Owen mentioned you thought Weezie Taylor's sister might consider it or know someone else who would. I didn't want to bother you with it since you've had your hands full."

"If you'll get me the portable phone and the number for Gordy's, I'll call Shayla right now."

Hailey went inside and came back a minute later with the phone in one hand and a piece of paper in the other. "Here you go."

"Thanks." Ellen dialed the number. "It's a little early, but she's probably there. She was the sweetest lady."

"Gordy's Crab Shack," said a familiar male voice.

"Hi, it's Ellen."

"Oh, good," Gordy Jameson said. "I was gonna call you and see how Lawrence is doin'. Will stopped by on his way home last night and told me Lawrence may have seen the guy who stabbed Jackson Kincaid. I *was* surprised to be on the suspect list."

"Sorry," Ellen said. "Dad was obviously confused about where and when he saw a knife."

"Will got a kick out of razzin' me anyhow. So how's Lawrence doin' today?"

"He needs to be looked after. I decided to bring him and my father-in-law to our house, especially after what happened last night." Ellen told Gordy about her near run-in with a burglar. "If it's not one thing, it's another."

"You've got a lot on your plate. Why don't you bring Lawrence down here when you need a break? We seemed to hit it off."

"I couldn't do that to you."

"Why not? We had a good time talkin' baseball."

"Did Dad seem lucid?"

"Off and on. But he sure knows his facts. Reminds me a little of my dad. I wouldn't mind hangin' out with him."

Ellen smiled. "You're sweet to say that. But I'm not about to saddle you with that responsibility."

"Hey, I'm dead serious. Drop him off some morning when you need to go do somethin'. We don't open till eleven. Pam and I'll keep an eye on him."

"I just might take you up on that. Listen, I called about something else. Is Shayla there?"

"Yeah, she's settin' tables."

"Could I talk to her? I promise not to keep her."

"Sure. Hang on."

Ellen stroked Daniel's soft, fine hair, thinking childcare was a piece of cake compared to what she was facing with her father.

"Hello."

"Shayla, it's Ellen Jones. You may remember me. I was in there for lunch yesterday and then came back to pick up my father who'd wandered in."

"Yes, ma'am. How can I help you?"

"You mentioned you're looking for a position in a preschool or day care. I was wondering if you might consider working for my son and daughter-in-law. They need someone who will split childcare and housekeeping duties. The agencies don't seem to have anyone willing to do that."

"Yes, ma'am. Licensed nannies don't much like to do cleanin'."

"My kids have just one little boy—a year old. My daughter-in-law isn't holding an outside job and doesn't really want to hand off Daniel for the entire day."

"Well, that arrangement would suit me just fine."

Ellen looked at Hailey and nodded.

"I'm not hung up about workin' with a lot of kids," Shayla said. "I just like little people and spendin' time with them. And I sure don't mind rollin' up my sleeves and doin' housework. I cleaned houses for years. Thing is, I can't claim the title nanny 'cause I haven't been certified."

Ellen chuckled. "Neither have first-time moms, but they've managed since the beginning of time." Ellen held Hailey's gaze and mouthed the words, *Do you want to talk to her?*

Hailey nodded.

"Shayla, my daughter-in-law is sitting right here. Could you talk to her about this?"

"I'd be happy to."

Ellen handed the phone to Hailey, and Daniel began to stir. He squirmed and stretched, his tiny fists clenched, then opened his eyes wide and smiled at Ellen.

"Hi, cutie." She pressed her lips to the baby's soft cheek. "Let's go get your diaper changed while Mommy talks to the nice lady."

Ellen got up and went inside, all too aware of her father sitting expressionless in front of the TV, his arms folded tightly to his chest. She wondered if anyone would be as enthusiastic about caring for him.

Owen Jones walked out of the boardroom and over to the elevator. He got in and pushed the button for the third floor, then crossed the hall and went into his office and closed the door.

If the board had listened to me six months ago, we would be out of the red by now.

He glanced at his watch, then picked up the phone and dialed home.

"Hello."

"Hi, honey. I just got out of my second meeting. Two down, one to go."

"How were they?"

"So-so. The department heads are well aware they've overspent. But, just once, I wish the chairman of the board would look at me as if I'm an adult male with a brain instead of a kid he should be calling *sonny*. If he'd opened his hairy ears and listened to me in the first place, we wouldn't be in this shape. I've frozen salaries until we get back on budget."

"I'll bet that went over well."

"Tough. They hired me to keep them in line. One of these days they're going to get serious about listening to me." Owen sat back in his chair and rubbed his eyes. "Sorry, I'm probably overreacting. I didn't sleep a wink last night. So did you talk to Mom?"

"Yes, she got Granddad and Papa moved in at her house. I took Daniel over there, and she rocked him till he fell asleep. We had a real nice visit. She also put me in touch with Weezie Taylor's sister."

"Really?" Owen listened while Hailey gave him the details of her conversation with Shayla. "Wow, does that ever sound hopeful. When can we meet her? I've got lots of questions."

"She's done at Gordy's at seven. It'll take her forty-five minutes to get here. I hope you don't mind that I told her to come even though Daniel will be down for the night."

"Not at all. If she seems right, she can meet Daniel later. We would need to have a trial period anyway." Owen glanced at his watch. "Honey, I need to get ready for the next meeting. I'll see you about six, all right?"

"Okay. Love you."

"Love you, too."

Owen hung up the phone, and a second later he heard Helen's voice on the intercom. "Mr. Jones, Tim O'Rourke is holding on line one."

"Okay, Helen. Thanks."

Owen sat staring at the blinking button, thinking he didn't want to seem too anxious to talk. He took a slow, deep breath and let it out, then picked up the receiver. "Hello."

"Have you thought any more about when and where we can meet?"

"What's your angle, O'Rourke? What are you selling?"

"I told you, I have something that's already yours."

"Funny, I'm not missing anything."

"Yeah, you are, but there's nothing funny about it. I'm giving you the chance to name the place and time, but you're going to see me one way or the other."

"And I told you, I'm not agreeing to meet you without knowing why. I'll not be manipulated."

"We'll see about that." *Click.*

Ellen heard the doorbell ring and dried her hands with a kitchen towel, wondering which solicitor she would have to try not to be rude to this time. She hurried to the door, surprised to see Police Chief Will Seevers standing on the porch.

"I just came by to give you a status report on the stabbing case," Will said.

"Please, come in."

Ellen led the chief into the living room, where he stopped and seemed to be admiring the oil painting hanging over the couch.

"Isn't that the old-timer who hangs out on the beach and builds those elaborate sandcastles?" Will said.

"As a matter of fact, it is. Guy and I bought this painting at a gallery in the old art district. Did you know Ned?"

Will smiled. "I used to bump into him all the time...and that beggar of a pelican that followed him around. Haven't seen him in a while."

"He's gone to be with the Lord. I met him on the beach a couple years ago, and we developed a special relationship—a sort of father/daughter thing." Ellen felt a twinge of grief. "Please have a seat. I'm anxious to hear about the case."

Will sat on the couch across from her. "I thought you might be interested to know that the *only* place in the alley we found broken glass was between the crime scene and the back of Flamingo's Bar and Grill next door—where one of the merchants said he saw your father sitting about 11:45 the morning of the stabbing."

"So Dad must've seen the assailant."

"Well, he was sitting in the right place at the right time. It would be impossible not to see a man running down the alley...or even the stabbing if he was looking in that direction. We told the shop owners in the area the suspect may have been wearing a T-shirt with a flag impression and may be sporting a gut that hangs over his belt."

"I just hope Dad wasn't confused about that, too."

"Well, it's all we've got to go on."

Ellen glanced up and saw Lawrence standing in the doorway.

"Why are you talking about me behind my back? Who is *he*?"

"Dad, it's Police Chief Seevers. Remember, you talked to him about the man in the flag T-shirt?"

Will stood and offered his hand to Lawrence. "I want you to know that my department is taking the description you gave us seriously."

Lawrence seemed to be processing the words, but Ellen wasn't sure whether or not he recognized the chief.

She pointed to her watch. "Dad, the Marlins game starts in five minutes. It's on 1640 AM—"

"Think I don't know that? I'm old. I'm not stupid."

Ellen waited until her father went down the hall and into his room, then said to Chief Seevers, "I moved Dad in with me. After all that's happened, I can't be sure he's safe unless he's supervised."

"Probably a good idea. By the way, I read the report you filed about the prowler you ran off."

Ellen nodded. "Unfortunately, I caught only a glimpse of a shadow that I'm not even certain was a man's. I just assumed it was."

"Odds are you're right." The chief stood. "Well, I won't keep you. I just wanted to let you know where we are in our investigation. I'll keep you posted."

Ellen sat out on the veranda, the late afternoon breeze warm and muggy, and anxiously awaited Guy's return from Tallahassee.

Lord, I'll never be able to get along with Dad in the same house. Please show us another way.

She heard the kitchen door open and Guy's voice calling her.

"Ellen, honey, I'm home. Where are you?"

"Out here!" She got up and hurried inside and fell into Guy's open arms. "Am I ever glad to see you."

"It's nice to be missed. How are our dads doing?"

"Oh, same as usual. Mine's moping around, and yours is going out of his way to be a sweetheart. At least we haven't had any incidents since I brought them home—other than I'm feeling chained to the house. I'm not even comfortable going up to the widow's watch to work. I'm afraid Dad will wander off."

"Don't worry. We'll get this resolved as quickly as we can. We just need to get Lawrence evaluated and figure out what level of care he needs."

"But what about Roland? He can't live by himself, and I can't bear to think about putting him in assisted living."

"It isn't really that different from the retirement center. Dad wouldn't have any problem making friends, and we could see him all the time, even bring him here when we want."

Ellen sighed. "I know, but it's psychological. Too much too soon."

"Honey, look at me."

Ellen looked up into Guy's dark eyes and saw only kindness.

"Dad can handle it. What he can't handle is being responsible for Lawrence."

"Poor Roland," Ellen said. "You should have seen the fear in his eyes when we couldn't find Dad. We should never have let them move in together."

"How could we possibly have known Lawrence was this bad?"

Ellen raised her eyebrows. "Well, since I could count on one hand the times I'd seen him since Mother died, we couldn't. But what does that say about what kind of daughter I am?"

"Honey, don't even go there. Your father has rebuffed all your attempts to warm up to him. The lack of relationship isn't your fault."

"Well, it's certainly my *problem*."

A loud crash came from the bathroom, and then muffled cries for help.

Ellen dashed toward the bathroom, Guy on her heels. She was surprised to see her father standing in the hallway, a blank look on his face. She squeezed past him and stood outside the closed bathroom door.

"Roland, are you all right? Roland?" She heard only moaning.

"You go in," Ellen said to Guy. "I don't want to embarrass him."

Guy turned the knob and looked inside. "Oh, Dad, what in the world...Ellen, go call 911! Hurry! There's blood all over the place."

10

Ellen sat in the living room knitting an afghan, her mind racing through every possible injury Roland could have sustained in his bathroom fall. She couldn't remember when she'd seen so much blood. Why hadn't Guy called from the hospital yet?

Ellen picked up the remote and turned down the volume on the TV. "Dad, that thing's making me a nervous wreck."

"Now I can't hear it!" Lawrence snapped.

"Well, I'm sure the *neighbors* can." Ellen paused for a few moments, aware of the heat coloring her face, then got up and handed the remote to her father. "I didn't mean to be ugly. I'm worried about Roland, and I think I'll go in the bedroom and try to relax. Guy should call soon."

"I want to go home."

"Dad, don't be difficult. This isn't easy on me either."

"You only think about yourself!"

Ellen bit her lip. *If I were thinking only of myself, I wouldn't put up with your abuse!*

"Your mother cares about what's best for me. I wish I were with her instead of you."

Well, that's two of us, Ellen thought.

The phone rang and she hurried into the kitchen and picked it up. "Guy?"

"Sorry it took me so long to call. They wouldn't let me use my cell phone inside the hospital, and I didn't want to get too far away from Dad. Bottom line: They stitched up the nasty gash on his head, but he needs a hip replacement."

"Good heavens! Is that really necessary?"

"Dad's arthritis is so bad there's just no cartilage left. The reason he fell is the hip gave out. It happened a few times when he was living alone, but he never told us. And apparently his orthopedic doctor suggested over a year ago he should get it replaced, but Dad was hoping to put it off."

"Don't you think we should get a second opinion?"

"Honey, this *is* a second opinion. You've seen how Dad struggles to walk. Another bad fall and he could really be laid up. If he doesn't have the surgery, he'll have to rely on a walker. You should've seen how he balked at that."

Ellen glanced at the calendar. "When do they want to schedule it?"

"Under normal circumstances, they'd send him home and set it up for sometime within the next few weeks. But the doctor's aware of our circumstances, and since Dad's already in the hospital, he thinks they can work him in sometime tomorrow."

"*Tomorrow*? Are you comfortable with that? Is Roland?"

"He wants it over with and insists there's no reason to postpone the inevitable. And considering what we've got on our plate, I'm not going to argue. It's important to get him back on his feet as soon as possible."

"Don't they need his medical records? And what about all that pre-op testing they do? Is the doctor even reputable? What do you know about him?"

"Ellen, take it easy. The doctor is with Southside Orthopedic Specialists. You can't get any better than that. He'll get Dad's medical records faxed over in the morning. And most of the pre-op can be done tonight. Unless his tests show he's not healthy enough for the surgery, there's no reason to put it off."

"This is so unexpected, my head's spinning! How long will he be in the hospital?"

"Probably three to five days. Then a week or two in the rehab hospital…maybe more, depending on how he does. Of course, he'll need to do rehab at home for weeks after that."

"Poor thing," Ellen said. "How is he?"

"In good spirits, but I think he's a little scared. I'm going to stay till he's asleep and then I'll be home. The doctor thinks it might be afternoon before he can do the surgery, but I want to get back over here early in case they take him sooner."

"Guy, I want to be there when they do the surgery."

"What would you do with Lawrence?"

"I don't know."

"Maybe Hailey and Owen could help out. You probably should call them tonight anyway, just so they know what's going on."

"You're right." Ellen glanced at her watch. "I'd better do that before it gets too late. I love you. Give Roland a hug for me."

"I will. Keep my side of the bed warm."

Ellen hung up the phone and dialed Owen's number.

"Hello."

"Hi, it's Mom. Did you and Hailey have a chance to visit with Shayla?"

"Yeah, she just left. Hailey's going to check out her references, but both of us feel like she's the one. Daniel woke up crying when she was here, and they seemed to connect. She got him back down without a peep. I'm not even sure *we* could've done that."

"I'm so glad. Assuming everything checks out, when do you think she'll start?"

"Tomorrow. Of course, Hailey won't leave Shayla alone with Daniel until we've checked out her references and are comfortable with the arrangement. But unless something unexpected surfaces, I think we've got ourselves a nanny."

"That's wonderful, honey. But doesn't she have to give notice at Gordy's?"

"No, he was giving her hours just to be nice."

Ellen smiled. "Sounds like Gordy. Listen, I have some bad news. Papa fell this evening and is in the hospital. They're going to do a hip replacement sometime tomorrow."

"Oh, no. Where'd he fall?"

"In the guest bathroom. Your dad had just gotten home from Tallahassee, and we heard a loud crash and a cry for help." Ellen told Owen the details, and even as she relived the ordeal, the reality started to sink in. "I'd love to be at the hospital during the surgery, but I can't leave your granddad by himself."

"I'll come stay with him. Oh, wait…I can't. I've got another round of meetings tomorrow. Hailey could probably come over."

"No, don't worry about it. Your dad and I can switch off. We'll manage."

"You sure?"

"Yes. I don't really have to be there. I just wanted to. I'm sure Roland won't be in the mood for company."

Owen hung up the phone and went into the living room where Hailey sat cross-legged on the couch, looking through the list of Shayla Taylor's references.

"I am *so* excited," Hailey said. "I just know she's going to work out. Who was on the phone?"

"Mom. Papa fell in the bathroom and is having his hip replaced tomorrow." Owen flopped on the couch and told Hailey everything his mother had told him. "I think I'll head over there after work tomorrow and stay with Granddad so Mom can go to the hospital."

"She really won't leave him alone—not even for a couple hours? I mean, couldn't he watch TV or something? It's not like he's helpless."

"I know. But she doesn't trust him not to pull another stunt." Owen lifted his eyebrows. "Granddad's stubborn…and liable to do anything just to spite Mom. Like I told you, this has been going on all my life. Granddad's mind may be slipping, but for the most part, his tactics haven't changed."

"Did Ellen say whether or not the police checked out what he told them?"

"Actually, I forgot to ask her. Maybe there'll be something on the news." Owen thought about his conversation with Tim O'Rourke and wondered if Hailey needed to know. He decided she did. "Honey, I didn't have a chance to tell you this before Shayla came over, but O'Rourke called me at work today."

"Why am I not surprised? What did he say?"

"He's insistent that he's got something that's mine, and determined we're going to meet—one way or the other."

"What's that supposed to mean?"

"I don't know, but I didn't like his manipulative tone. I'm not going to talk to him anymore, and I don't want you talking to him either."

"What am I supposed to do if he calls?"

"Just hang up on him."

Ellen sat out on the veranda, a cool, moist breeze blowing off the gulf, self-pity oozing from every fiber of her being. It wasn't supposed to happen this way. She had vowed years ago that if or when the time came for her father to need care, she would hire it out—not take him into her home.

Lord, it's not fair! Dad turned his back on me years ago. I don't want to take care of him! I don't want his bitterness and resentment and hateful disposition in my house.

As hard as she tried, Ellen had never been able to let go of those last bittersweet moments before she left for college…

She stood in the driveway, the old Corvair packed to the hilt with every conceivable possession that could be squeezed into her dorm room, and said goodbye to the ivy-covered brick house she had grown up in. Her father's stern profile was visible through the screened-in porch, but he wouldn't even turn and look at her.

Ellen felt a hand on her shoulder.

"He's a stubborn man," her mother said. "But you mustn't think that his disapproval of your choice to go to college means that he disapproves of *you*."

"I don't think he can separate the two." Ellen wiped a tear off her cheek.

"Your father won't admit it, but he's going to miss you terribly."

"Yes, I can see how torn up he is that his only child is leaving home." Ellen cringed at the sound of her sarcasm and fell into her mother's waiting embrace. "I'm going to miss you so."

"Only till you get out on the highway. Just think about how long you've dreamed of this. I'm already envisioning the day when I can brag about my daughter the journalist."

Ellen smiled in spite of herself. "I've thought about it for so long it doesn't seem like a dream anymore. I know it's going to happen."

Her mother tilted her chin up and looked into her eyes. "Ellen, promise me that you won't let your father's weaknesses become your own. Don't shut him out. Don't let him shut you out."

"What am I supposed to do? I can't force him to accept who I am."

"Then learn to accept who *he* is." The look on her mother's face pierced her heart. "If you could get a glimpse of the man I see, it wouldn't be so hard to love him…"

The blast of a distant tugboat brought Ellen back to the present. *Lord, have I ever really loved my father? Or understood him? I want to honor You in the way I treat him. But it's so hard.*

"Why are you out here?" Lawrence stood in the doorway in his pajamas.

"It's quiet and peaceful."

"I want to go home."

"Dad, I'm sorry we had to sell the house. But it was important that you be closer to us so we can help you."

"Just wait till you're old and can't fight back."

For a split second, Ellen had a sense of what that might be like. "Why don't you come sit with me."

Her father seemed to be looking at something beyond her. "Who goes there?"

Ellen turned quickly and looked into the dark backyard. "There's no one out there, Dad."

He walked to the top of the steps and cupped his hands around his mouth, "Who goes there? Show yourself!"

Ellen exhaled loudly. "There's no one there."

"Shows how much you know about it."

He went down the steps and Ellen followed him, afraid he would stumble in the darkness.

"Look over there, next to the gazebo! See him hunched down?"

Ellen was aware of the neighbors' dogs barking. She felt a shiver crawl up her spine. "Come on, let's go back inside."

Lawrence ignored her and marched toward the gazebo. "Come out, you lily-livered snake!"

Ellen grabbed his arm. "Dad, no."

"There're enemy soldiers moving this way! Provisions are getting low and my men are exhausted! I need to call for reinforcements!"

Ellen tightened her grip and spoke softly. "Okay, let's go back to camp and make that call."

"What?"

"You said you needed to call for reinforcements."

Lawrence yanked his arm free. "Why'd you drag me out here? What's wrong with you?" He scowled at her and shook his finger. "If you don't stop this lying, young lady, I'm going to have to ground you."

Ellen followed her father up the steps and then turned around and looked into the black nothingness. The dogs were still barking.

II

On Thursday morning, Gordy and Pam Jameson raced hand in hand down the pier to Gordy's Crab Shack, a heavy rain drenching them and Pam squealing like a schoolgirl with each puddle she stepped in.

"Hurry and get the door opened!" she hollered, her bangs plastered to her forehead, water beaded up on her face and dripping off her nose and chin.

Gordy put the key in the lock and pushed open the door, then lifted Pam in his arms and stepped across the threshold, his hearty laughter filling the empty restaurant. "You look more like a drowned rat than the girl I married!"

Pam poked his ribs with her elbow. "I told you we should take the car and not our bikes. Yuck! I hate the feel of wet cotton." She shook her short hair and combed her fingers through it.

Gordy took a handkerchief from his pocket and handed it to Pam. "Here, darlin'. Your mascara's runnin' down your face."

"How lovely." Pam patted her face dry. "Looks like you're going to have to find something for Billy to do inside today."

"Yeah, I think you're right."

The front door opened and Weezie Taylor stepped inside and closed her umbrella. "Wooooeeeeee, it's comin' down!" Her ivory smile took over her face and she looked at Pam and then Gordy. "And the two of you are thinkin', 'What's Weezie doin' here this early?'"

"I'm sure you're gonna tell us," Gordy said.

"I've got a dentist appointment this morning and thought I'd check in with you first and make sure you're cool with Shayla quittin' to work for Owen and Hailey."

"Sure, no problem. I told her she could work here till she found what she wanted. We've got a couple of day waitresses beggin' for more hours. It's not posin' a hardship."

"That's what I thought. I just wanted to hear you say it. I can't thank you enough for bein' so good to Shayla. The other reason I came by is to tell you Guy Jones's father fell last night and is having surgery on his hip today."

"Aw, I hate to hear that." Gordy looked at Pam and wrinkled his nose. "The Joneses've sure got their hands full. How'd you find out?"

"Shayla just called me from Owen and Hailey's house. She thought I'd want to know and said to tell you and Pam."

"Yeah, thanks. I'll call the house later and see what I can find out. Okay, ladies, I've got work to do."

Weezie took her thumb and forefinger and held up the sleeve of Gordy's work shirt. "That soggy thing oughta make you feel *crabbier* than the logo." She titled back her head and let out a robust laugh he was sure could be heard across the pier. "Kinda lends a whole new meanin' to the words 'crab shack,' doesn't it?"

Gordy chuckled. "Maybe when the rain lets up, I'll ride my bike down to the souvenir shops and buy a T-shirt."

"Then get me one, too," Pam said. "I'm going to freeze in this air conditioning."

Weezie took hold of Gordy's arm. "Come on, I'll drive you down there and wait while you run inside. Talk nice to me, and I'll loan you this big ol' umbrella."

Owen Jones went in his office and started looking through his stack of phone messages and saw that Tim O'Rourke had called at 9:15. He walked out to his administrative assistant's desk.

"Helen, I asked you not to talk to this guy anymore."

"Yes, sir, I know. I told him that, and he hung up. But I thought you'd want to know he called."

"I really don't. If he calls again, you have my permission to hang up on him."

Helen sat with her hands folded on her desk, a row of wrinkles across her forehead. "I have a really hard time being rude."

"Listen, Helen. O'Rourke's the one who's rude. The man has my cell number, so there's no excuse for him disrupting your workday trying to get to me. Just cut him off."

"Yes, sir." She tapped the face of her watch. "It's ten o'clock."

"Already? I need to get back downstairs. If Hailey calls, tell her I haven't heard anything more about my grandfather, just that his surgery is scheduled for eleven."

Owen went back in his office and picked up his briefcase, then hurried out to the elevator and pushed the button for the ground floor. He took his cell phone out of his pocket and accessed his messages and found only one. He played it back and recognized Tim O'Rourke's voice:

"You're not going to get rid of me by ignoring me."

Owen put his phone back in the pocket of his sport coat and waited till the elevator opened, then walked across the hall to the boardroom, hoping he could put his annoyance on hold and his best foot forward.

Ellen Jones glanced outside at the billowy gray clouds, dreading the thought of spending the entire day cooped up indoors and wondering which tormented her more: the blaring of the TV or her father's sulking? At least he seemed lucid this morning and hadn't been combative. She glanced at her watch. Roland would be going into surgery in thirty minutes.

Her phone rang and she quickly picked it up. "Hello."

"Mrs. Jones?"

"Yes."

"This is Meg in Dr. Roper's office. We've been able to schedule an evaluation for your father on Thursday, June 5, at 9:00 a.m.. I'll go ahead and send the forms to you so you can fill out his medical history and bring it with you to the appointment."

"That's two weeks away," Ellen said. "Is there no way to get him in sooner?"

"I'm afraid not. Dr. Roper is booked solid."

Ellen turned her head and lowered her voice. "But I really can't leave him alone, and we're not set up to care for him at home."

"Yes, ma'am. I hear you. But truthfully, most of our patients are in similar circumstances. I gave Lawrence the first cancellation we had. Otherwise, it would've been four to six weeks before we could see him."

"All right, thanks. We'll see you then."

Ellen hung up the phone and looked at the date and time she had jotted on a Post-it note, convinced she wouldn't survive two more weeks in the house with her father.

The phone rang again.

"Hello."

"Ellen, it's Gordy. I called to check on Guy's dad. I thought maybe you'd be over at the hospital."

"No, I'm home with *my* dad. How'd you find out about Roland?"

"Shayla told Weezie. I understand she started workin' for Owen and Hailey this mornin'."

"Yes, she did. The kids are thrilled."

"Anything Pam and I can do to help you?"

"Not really. The surgery is scheduled for eleven, and I'm just waiting here with Dad. Guy's been at the hospital since early this morning."

"Well, if you decide you wanna head over there, bring

Lawrence down here. Pam and I will keep an eye on him."

"I couldn't do that. You've got a business to run."

"Actually, my paperwork's caught up and I've got plenty of help scheduled in. I could work in a few games of Chinese checkers with Lawrence and then let him have lunch with my buddies and me on the back deck. Think he'd like that?"

"I can't imagine he wouldn't. Gordy, are you sure? I don't want to take advantage of your generosity."

"Hey, have you ever known me to get into anything I didn't wanna get into?"

Ellen smiled and glanced at her watch. "I could bring Dad over in about twenty minutes. Would that work?"

"You bet. Come whenever you want."

Police Chief Will Seevers sat at his desk sipping lukewarm coffee and rereading the preliminary autopsy report on Jackson Kincaid.

Kincaid had died of a single stab wound to the chest made by an eight-inch blade, consistent with that of a hunting knife. The angle of the entry wound suggested the attacker had used the right hand and was approximately the same height as the victim; and the depth of the wound suggested considerable strength was used to thrust the knife. Conclusion: the perp was likely a strong, right-handed male about five-feet-nine-inches tall. No DNA evidence was found on the victim or under his fingernails. The victim's body had no defensive wounds.

Will took off his glasses and rubbed his eyes. Why didn't a healthy young guy like Kincaid put up a fight?

Investigator Al Backus entered the room and flopped in a chair. "This case is already cold."

"It hasn't even been forty-eight hours, Al."

"Yeah, but expecting retailers to remember some paunchy

guy wearing a flag T-shirt is like expecting a school teacher to notice a kid with a runny nose."

Will put his glasses back on. "I get your point. But at least it's *something*. For now, let's run with what Mr. Madison told us. Don't forget Andrew Connor saw him sitting behind Flamingo's just before the stabbing. We know for certain he was there."

There was a long moment of silence.

A grin spread across Al's face. "Wouldn't it blow your mind if the *old man* did it?"

Will wadded up a piece of paper and tossed it at him. "You read the autopsy. Get out of here and find me something that makes sense."

"Okay, but my guess is that some transient stabbed Kincaid for his money and took off. And since our Yankee-Doodle dandy has no doubt ditched his shirt, that leaves me with the impossible job of tracking down a pot gut."

"Look, I know we've got zilch." Will put his feet up on his desk, his hands clasped behind his head. "Knock on doors if you have to, but somebody out there must've seen a man wearing a flag shirt in the area at the time of the murder. I'm not willing to just blow off what Lawrence Madison told us."

Gordy sat in a booth across from Lawrence, his arms folded across his chest, tickled to see the look of victory on Lawrence's face. "That's three games in a row. You cleaned my plow."

A smile stretched Lawrence's cheeks, and it was obvious he didn't realize Gordy had let him win all three games of Chinese checkers.

"Well, I know when I've been whupped." Gordy started picking up marbles and putting them back in the game box. "You hungry? Three of my buddies come here for lunch, and we can eat with them out on the back deck. They're all baseball fans."

Lawrence stood. "Got any fried clams?"

"The best in town."

Gordy put the game in the closet. He led Lawrence down the hall and onto the back deck, and then over to the round umbrella table where Captain Jack, Eddie Drummond, and Adam Spalding were seated.

"There you are," Captain said. "We wondered if you were gonna join us today. Why aren't you wearin' your crab shack shirt?"

"Pam and I got caught in the rain this morning. I went down to one of the shops lookin' for somethin' dry to wear. These flag shirts were on sale for ten bucks apiece."

Adam covered his smile with his hand. "Guess they didn't have an *extra* extra large."

"Hey, wise guy, it wasn't supposed to be a fashion statement."

"So who's your friend?" Adam said.

"Guys, this is Lawrence Madison, Ellen Jones's dad. He just shamed me at Chinese checkers, and I asked him to join us for lunch."

Gordy shooed away some pesky grackles underfoot and seated Lawrence at the table between himself and Adam.

"Lawrence used to own a hardware store." Gordy put his hand on the old man's shoulder. "Eddie there in the coveralls is an auto mechanic at Sears. Captain with the anchor tattoo operated a commercial fishin' fleet till he retired. And super-hunk Adam there on your right is livin' off his inheritance and tryin' to decide what he wants to be when he finally gets off his duff."

Eddie rolled his eyes. "He's a disgrace to us working-class folks. Spends more on entertainment than I do on my mortgage."

"Hey, it's a tough job, but somebody's got to do it," Adam said. "So, Lawrence, think the Marlins are going to do anything this year?"

"Not if they keep playing like a bunch of girls."

Captain guffawed. "I like this guy already."

Gordy sat back and listened to the baseball banter, amazed that Lawrence could spout off facts about Willie Mays, Mickey Mantle, and Hank Aaron, yet seemed confused about how the Marlins had done in the past week.

The waitress came and took their orders and the conversation drifted to other things. Lawrence became quiet and seemed to be studying his fingernails.

"Gordo," Eddie said, "did your buddy the police chief say whether or not they've got any suspects in the Kincaid case?"

"You know I don't discuss what Will talks to me about."

"Well, excuuuuuuse me for asking, but it's a little unsettling to think the guy who did the stabbing could be sitting right here on this deck and we'd never know it."

"He's not here," Lawrence said matter-of-factly.

Eddie leaned forward on his elbows. "How would you know?"

"Leave it alone," Gordy said. "Talk about somethin' else."

"Come on, the man deserves to be heard." Eddie winked at Adam and then locked gazes with Lawrence. "So what'd he look like?"

"Had Old Glory on his shirt." Lawrence pointed to Gordy's T-shirt. "Had a gut on him, too."

Eddie laughed. "So Gordo, where were *you* at the time of the murder?"

"Havin' lunch with you clowns."

Captain grinned, his eyes turning to slits. "Maybe we better call Will and report having seen a suspicious T-shirt."

Gordy chuckled in spite of himself. "Why do I put up with this abuse?"

Eddie turned his prodding eyes on Lawrence. "So did you actually see the guy stab Jackson Kincaid?"

Gordy gave Eddie a swift kick under the table.

"Ouch! That hurt."

"Yeah, it was supposed to, hardhead."

Lawrence scowled at Eddie and seemed to be groping for words. Finally he said, "Listen, young man, I haven't got time to waste on someone who's only interested in a paycheck."

Eddie shot Gordy a what's-he-talking-about look.

"I spent years building the store's reputation," Lawrence said. "There's no excuse for treating a customer that way. You're fired!" He pushed back his chair and started to get up when the waitress came to the table carrying a big tray.

"Okay, guys. Four orders of crab cakes and one fried clams. Who's got the clams?"

Gordy motioned for her to set the plate in front of Lawrence. "There you go, bud. Watch that plate. It's really hot."

"Well, this is quite a treat," Lawrence said. "Roland told me we were having pasta salad."

Eddie lifted his eyebrows. "Who's Roland?" he mouthed.

Gordy held up his palm as if to say don't ask.

12

Ellen Jones pushed open the front door to Gordy's Crab Shack just before three and was hit with the scent of old wood and the awareness that the dining room was quiet and empty of customers. Weezie Taylor was talking to a pair of waitresses and waved from across the room. Ellen spotted her father sitting in a booth by himself, a newspaper open in front of him. She went over and slid in the booth facing him, her arms folded on the table.

"Roland's hip surgery went well. He's going to be fine. Are you ready to go home?"

Lawrence turned the page. "Where's your mother?"

Gordy walked over and stood at the end of the booth. "How's Guy's dad?"

"Doing well, thanks. He'll be in the hospital for three to five days and then in the rehab hospital for a week or so. I'm relieved the worst is over. So what did you guys do?"

"Oh, Lawrence and I played some Chinese checkers and then joined the guys for lunch. We've just been hangin' out since. Pam brought him a slice of her triple-berry pie with a scoop of ice cream, and that went over big. Your timing's just right. I think he's about exhausted that sports page."

"I really appreciate this," Ellen said. "Guy was pleased I was able to wait with him during the surgery."

"I was glad to do it. Lawrence and I had a good time. With all that's goin' on, you and Guy gonna be able to make the big gala at the People's Clinic tomorrow night?"

"Oh, definitely. Owen and Hailey offered to bring Daniel over to the house so the three of them can spend some time with Dad while we're out."

"So they can *babysit* me," Lawrence said. "Won't come right out and say so."

Ellen felt the color flood her face. "We're riding over a little early with the Tehranis. Apparently, Ali lined up a professional photographer to take pictures of all the founders before the doors open at six."

"Yeah, Pam wants me spiffed up for this. Talked me into rentin' a tux."

Ellen smiled. "I've never seen you in a suit—not even at your wedding."

"Well, to my way of thinkin', our gettin' the clinic built and open is a miracle worth suitin' up for."

"I know. It's such a testimony to the power of forgiveness and cooperation. Who says Christians, Jews, and Muslims can't get along?" She slid out of the booth. "Well, Dad, shall we go?"

"Do you have to ramrod everything?"

Ellen bit her lip. *Don't react. Don't give him the satisfaction.* "Why don't you choose what you'd like for dinner? I'll make whatever you want."

"I'm not hungry."

Gordy put his hand on Lawrence's shoulder. "You come back so I can have a rematch on Chinese checkers. I'll even serve up some more of those fried clams."

Lawrence nodded.

"Thanks again," Ellen said. "Give my best to Pam."

"Will do. See you tomorrow night."

Gordy stood at the front counter changing out the register tape when Eddie Drummond came through the front door.

"What're you doin' here in the middle of the afternoon?"

Eddie went over and leaned on the counter. "How about filling me in on what's up with your buddy Lawrence. That whole scene at lunch was weird."

"Yeah, sorry. I should've given you a heads-up first. The poor guy's a little senile. I knew throwin' too many questions at him would confuse him all over again."

"What do you mean *again*? Is he the one who talked to the police?"

"You heard what he said."

"Did he get a good look at the guy—other than his T-shirt?"

"Why are you askin' me?"

"Because Will Seevers is your best friend. Come on, Gordo, I know he tells you stuff."

"And you know I don't repeat it."

Eddie put his hands in the pockets of his coveralls. "Andrew Connor brought his car in to be worked on this afternoon. We got to talking, and he told me the investigator working the case thinks the killer was a transient and is long gone by now. The shop owners are pretty upset. They think the police didn't move fast enough on this one and have given up on finding Jackson's killer."

"Listen to me, Eddie. Will Seevers is too much of a professional to let a killer get away without stayin' hot on his trail. Anyone who thinks otherwise doesn't know him very well. Why are you gettin' involved in this? Why don't you tell Andrew to call Will if he has a beef?"

"Well, don't get mad at me. All I did was tell him what Lawrence said."

"He already knows what Lawrence said. The investigator told the merchants everything the cops know."

"Yeah, well, they think they're getting the runaround."

❧ ❧ ❧

Owen Jones wadded up a Best Burger wrapper and dropped it in the paper bag, then washed down the last bite of a triple cheeseburger deluxe with a gulp of Dr. Pepper.

He backed out of the parking space, pulled onto Beach Shore Drive, and took his cell phone off his belt clip and pressed the autodial.

"Hello."

"Hi, Mom. What's the latest on Papa?"

"He's awake and talking and ate a little bit of his dinner," Ellen said. "Your dad just called from the hospital."

"Well, get ready to head over there. I'm almost to your house."

"You're so sweet to do this."

Owen smiled. "Tell that to Brandon next time he whines about me being your favorite. Does he even know what's going on with Papa and Granddad?"

"Of course he does. Let's don't talk about your brother. Tell me Hailey's assessment of Shayla."

"Loves her. Couldn't say enough nice things about her."

"Did she check out her references?"

"Uh-huh, first thing this morning. Everybody raved about how great she is with kids and how honest and dependable she is. Weezie's endorsement probably cinched it, though I think the way Daniel took to her held as much weight as everything else combined."

"Oh, that's so wonderful, honey. What a load off your shoulders."

"Yeah, it helps a lot. Okay, let me get off the phone and put both hands on the wheel. I'll be there in a couple minutes."

Owen disconnected the call and nearly dropped the phone when it vibrated in his hand. "Hello."

"Have you made up your mind where and when you want

to meet?" O'Rourke's voice was unmistakable.

"I already told you I'm not meeting you. Stop calling." Owen hit the disconnect button.

A few seconds later, the phone vibrated again, but he didn't answer. After a minute, he checked to see if the caller had left a message. He had. Owen played it back.

"I tried to give you the option, but now I'm mad. We're going to play this my way." The line went dead.

Owen dropped his cell phone on the passenger seat and stopped at a red light, his heart pounding and his thoughts racing. He banged the steering wheel with his palms. "I hate being manipulated!"

A gray-haired man in the car next to him rolled up his window.

Owen snatched his phone off the seat and pressed the autodial. "Hello."

"Honey, did Tim O'Rourke call the house?"

"No, why?" Hailey asked.

"He just called my cell. He's mad I won't talk to him. Says we're going to play it *his* way."

"What's that supposed to mean?"

"I don't know, but I'm one step away from getting an unlisted number and having my cell number changed."

"Owen, this is ludicrous. Why don't you just meet him and see what he wants? It can't be any worse than this."

The car behind Owen honked, and he realized the light had turned green. He pressed hard on the accelerator and put a city block between him and the driver behind him. "Honey, you still there?"

"You need to get off the phone and pay attention to the road."

"I know. You really think I should agree to meet him?"

"If you get to decide where, yes. What have you got to lose except these annoying phone calls?"

"I resent him manipulating me."

"I know, but is it any worse than being harassed?"

"I shouldn't have to put up with either! Truthfully, I never considered actually meeting the guy. I'll have to think about it." Owen turned left, his tires screeching, and drove up the hill toward Live Oak Circle. "Honey, I'm at Mom and Dad's street. I'll call you later."

Police Chief Will Seevers got in his squad car and fastened the seatbelt. In his side mirror, he spotted Gordy Jameson on his bicycle pulling up on the driver's side. He rolled down the window.

"Looks like you're gettin' away a little early," Gordy said. "Guess your mouth's waterin' for Margaret's Thursday-night meat loaf."

Will smiled. "Caught in the act. What's up?"

"Eddie Drummond stopped by this afternoon. Told me that Andrew Connor and some other shop owners have the impression the cops've decided Jackson Kincaid was murdered by a transient. That true?"

"We haven't made that determination."

"I didn't think so. But, that's the spin. They also think the police didn't move fast enough on this one and have given up on findin' Jackson's killer."

"Says who? Where do they come up with this stuff?"

"Accordin' to Eddie, the investigator workin' the case."

Will was thinking he needed to have a little powwow with Al Backus. "Listen, bud. We're just beginning to find the pieces to this puzzle. We need every retailer down there to be vigilant in case the guy is working the area. Do they think I want to find another body?"

"I know it's irritatin', but I thought you should know the scuttlebutt so you can put a stop to it. Another thing you need to know is that Lawrence Madison had lunch with the boys and me today. We started out talkin' baseball, but when the subject came around to the Kincaid case, he told the guys just as sure as you please that he saw the killer, and he was wearing a flag shirt like mine." Gordy told Will what had transpired at the lunch table.

"You shouldn't have let him discuss the case."

"I stopped it as soon as I could. Lawrence didn't say anything we hadn't already heard on the news."

Will tapped his fingers on the steering wheel. "What I find interesting is that he didn't confuse you this time with the man in the alley, even though you were wearing a similar shirt."

"Yeah, kinda surprised me. He seemed pretty darned certain about the whole thing before his mind checked out and he tried to fire Eddie."

"Maybe I should try talking to him again. Tell Eddie to keep his nose out of it, and I'll see if I can smooth things over with Andrew and the others. By the way, you and Pam doing anything special for Memorial Day weekend?"

"Nah, it's one of our busiest weekends."

"That restaurant's going to kill you."

Gordy laughed. "At least we'll die happy."

Owen sat out on the veranda of his parent's home, laughing with his grandfather and remembering some highlights of his boyhood.

"Granddad, you were the one who took me and Brandon to our first ball game, remember? We drove to Atlanta over Memorial Day weekend."

Lawrence nodded. "Braves won four to two after that rookie right fielder hit a grand slam in the ninth."

"Yeah, the whole place went nuts. We yelled our heads off. It was so much fun. I still have the ball cap you bought me. But the best part was all the junk food you let us eat. Man, did we ever put it away."

"Your brother upchucked all over the backseat of my new Chevy."

"Gross! I'd forgotten about that."

Lawrence smiled. "One of the best times I ever had with you two."

Owen glanced at his watch, then got up and stretched his back. "I wonder how Papa's doing?"

"Raking in the dough, though he won't admit it."

Owen studied his grandfather's face. "I'm talking about Roland."

"I know. He just won that big lawsuit for Sears and Roebuck. Could probably go the rest of the year without a win and still be sitting pretty."

What do I say now? Owen wondered. *Papa won that case before I was born.*

A twig snapped. Owen turned his head toward the dark backyard. "Did you hear that?"

The neighbors' dogs on either side were suddenly yapping. Owen reached inside the house and flipped the floodlight on, then jogged down the steps, across the yard, and around to the backside of the gazebo. He didn't see anyone. He stood perfectly still for a few moments and let his ears be his eyes. Nothing.

He waited a minute, then bounded up the steps to the veranda, where his granddad still sat in the wicker rocker.

"What're you doing, boy?"

"Oh, nothing. I thought someone was out there."

The French doors opened and Ellen stepped outside, Guy behind her.

"How's Papa?" Owen said.

Guy put his hand on Ellen's shoulder. "Doing remarkably well, all things considered. I, on the other hand, am bushed. Think I'll take a hot shower and crash."

"Yeah, you don't want to be wiped out for the big gala tomorrow night," Owen said. "Hailey and I think it's so cool the clinic's finally going to open. You should be proud of yourselves."

"I'm proud of everyone who pitched in. It took a lot of hands working together to make the clinic a reality. Hard to believe that we're finally turning the keys over to the volunteer medical staff."

Ellen smiled. "You're going to have to find something else to fill the void." She turned to Owen. "So what have you guys been up to this evening?"

"Granddad and I talked about stuff he used to do with Brandon and me when we were little. You know, hikes, camp-outs, baseball games."

"Took you on your first snipe hunt." Lawrence winked.

Owen rolled his eyes and shook his head from side to side. "That's the one memory I'd just as soon chuck."

"For some reason, I don't remember that," Ellen said.

Lawrence shot her a crusty look. "You were probably at work."

Owen saw his mother's smile turn into pursed lips. "Is there a reason the spotlight is on?" she said.

"I thought I heard something. I'll go turn it off."

"I'll get it. Goodnight, everybody." Guy pressed his lips to Ellen's and went inside.

A few seconds later the light went off.

"You said you heard something," Ellen said. "What was it?"

Owen swatted the air. "Oh, nothing. Must've been a cat or something."

13

Ellen woke up early on Friday morning and put on her running clothes, then sat in the chair next to the bed and laced up her Nikes.

Guy fluffed his pillow and turned on his side facing her. "I figured you'd head straight for the beach."

"I can't tell you how much I've missed watching the sunrise. I haven't been jogging since before all my back-and-forths to Ocala to get Dad's affairs in order. I feel trapped. I haven't even seen my friends."

"Don't hurry back. I'll get Lawrence's breakfast."

"Thanks. Maybe he'll eat for you. I think he starves himself just to irritate me."

"He's not going to starve."

"He eats like a bird."

"Didn't you tell me he polished off a plate of fried clams at Gordy's?"

Ellen exhaled. "Yes, but he's not eating balanced meals. When I'm around he just picks at his food, even when I know it's something he likes."

"Maybe you give him too much."

"He always seems to have room for dessert."

Guy smiled. "And you thought the two of you were nothing alike."

Ellen grabbed her pillow and tossed it on his head. "Having a sweet tooth is probably the *only* thing we have in common."

"You both loved your mother."

"And we both miss her so much it hurts. The difference is he takes out his anger on me."

Ellen stretched across the bed and kissed Guy's stubbly cheek. "Thanks for keeping an eye on Dad. I won't be gone that long. Once the sun gets high enough, it's going to be too hot to run."

Ellen went out the front door and down the steps, then started jogging toward the beach, feeling as though she had just sprouted wings. She ran down the hill and across Beach Shore Drive and jogged along the surf toward the horizon, her eyes drinking in the soft pink glow dawn had spread across the expanse.

Ellen inhaled the damp, salty air and began to thank God for who He is and for the many ways He had blessed her. She prayed that Roland would recover completely, that tonight's gala would be a grand celebration, and that Shayla would be a good influence on Daniel. She prayed for Guy and her kids, for the Kincaid family, and for her friends. Finally, she sat in the sand and leaned back on her hands and prayed that God would heal her relationship with her father.

That would be nothing short of a miracle.

She fixed her eyes on the horizon in anticipation of a new day, which spoke to her of God's faithfulness more than just about anything else in nature. As far as she could see, the sky had turned the color of a lava flow and was streaked with golden pink and indigo. Ellen sat spellbound until the sun hung above the horizon and the rich colors on the Artist's palette faded to pastel shades.

She took a slow, deep breath and let it out, tempted to applaud and wishing she were the uninhibited type that could shout His praises. *Lord, Your works amaze me. Surely One capable of all this can help me get along with Dad.*

Ellen rose to her feet and looked out over the blue-gray ripples of the gulf. In the distance, she spotted a freighter and its translucent thread of brownish smoke. A prop plane flew overhead, a red-and-yellow banner trailing behind it, displaying the words "Support the Kincaid Memorial Fund: Shop and Eat at Fish Tales."

She whispered another prayer for the Kincaid family and then started jogging toward home, sending a huddle of unsuspecting sandpipers scurrying in all directions.

Ellen looked down the beach and saw a familiar figure running along the surf toward her.

"Mina!"

Mina Tehrani waved her arms and ran about fifty yards till she reached Ellen. "I have missed you…my friend…I was starting to get worried." Mina leaned down, her hands on her knees, and tried to catch her breath.

"I'm sorry I haven't called," Ellen said. "It's been such a struggle." She told Mina about the situation with her father and father-in-law. "I had thought I'd just wait and fill you in tonight on the way to the gala. I'm sorry you were worried."

"No, I am sorry for your pain. I know the relationship with your father is not a good one. So is he now living with you?"

"Only until we get him evaluated and find out what his needs are. He's miserable living under our roof. Can't say that I'm enjoying it either. Enough of that…Ali must be so excited that the clinic is finally going to open."

"Oh, he is a crazy man." Mina laughed. "He cannot say enough about how people here proved that Muslims, Jews, Christians—everyone—can get along if they work together. He is off work today at noon to prepare what he wants to say at the gala. He knows media will be there."

"Are you scheduled at the hospital today?"

"No, I'm off until Monday. It will be a nice break. Sanaz is coming home for the holiday weekend. She is proud to see her father recognized this way. Guy too. Everyone who worked so hard to make the free clinic possible."

"It's exciting on many levels, not the least of which is that our families have become friends."

Mina put her arms around Ellen. "I thank Allah for you. We will pick you up at five fifteen. Let's hope we have a cool breeze tonight or our husbands will wilt in their tuxedos."

"Are you still going to wear your pale blue formal?"

"Yes, Ali likes it very much."

"Well, I'm wearing the long, black silk dress I showed you, unless my sugar habit has made it a tight fit."

Police Chief Will Seevers popped the last bite of a sausage biscuit into his mouth and took a sip of coffee. There was a knock at the door.

"You wanted to see me?" Al Backus said.

"Shut the door and sit down." Will took off his glasses and set them on his desk.

"You mad about something?"

"You bet I am! Just where do you get off telling the shop owners that we've decided a transient killed Jackson Kincaid and that we don't think we're going to get the guy?"

"I never said that."

Will leaned forward, his elbows on his desk. "Then suppose you tell me what you *did* say."

Al made a tent with his fingers, his foot tapping the floor. "Andrew Connor was pressing me about witnesses and where we were with the case. I might've implied it could've been a transient."

"Could've been?"

"All right. I said I thought it was a transient. It was my personal opinion. I wasn't speaking for the department."

"Wrong! Any time you open your mouth, you're speaking for the department. And now we've got a pack of disgruntled merchants who think we didn't move fast enough to catch Kincaid's killer. How unprofessional can you get, Al? You know better."

"I can't believe Connor went crying to you over it. He agreed with me."

"He shouldn't even know what you're thinking as long as this case is under investigation!"

Al's cheeks looked flushed. "Look, I crossed the line by throwing in my two cents. But it doesn't take a rocket scientist to think the killer was probably a transient who killed Kincaid for whatever was in his wallet. All those guys had to be thinking the same thing."

"Well, if they weren't, they certainly are now!"

"Sorry."

"Sorry isn't good enough, Al. I want you to march right back down there and eyeball each and every one of those merchants and tell them we're working our tails off to find out who killed Jackson Kincaid. We've barely scratched the surface."

"What am I supposed to tell them we're doing? You know as well as I do that we've got nothing solid—just some old man's mixed up story about a guy with a pot gut wearing a flag shirt."

"Gordy told me Lawrence Madison was down there for lunch yesterday and seemed pretty lucid when he was talking to Gordy's buddies about it. I think I'll go over to Ellen's and see if I can get Mr. Madison to remember anything else."

Police Chief Will Seevers parked his squad car in front of a stately, vine-covered house with dormers and a widow's watch and admired the enormous, flamboyant tree in the front yard. He got out and walked up the front steps and rang the doorbell. He heard footsteps and the volume go down on a blaring TV, and then the door opened.

"Hi, Will," Ellen Jones said. "Dad's waiting in the living room. Your timing is good since he seems agreeable at the moment. Are you and Margaret geared up for the gala tonight?"

"Yeah, we're pretty fired up." He smiled. "Plus, I can't wait to see Gordy in a tux. The only time I've seen him spiffed up was at our senior prom. And I'm not going to tell you how many years ago that was."

Will followed Ellen into the living room where Lawrence Madison sat on the couch, his arms folded across his chest.

"Dad, I'm going to turn off the TV so Chief Seevers can talk to you."

"Can't hear the darn thing anyway. Think I'm a lip reader?"

"Will, why don't you sit there on the love seat?" Ellen said. "Would you like something to drink? I've got Diet Coke, lemonade, or bottled water."

"Lemonade sounds great."

"Dad, you want something?"

"I want to go home."

Ellen left the living room without comment.

"Gordy told me you had lunch with the guys down at the crab shack," Will said. "Also says you cleaned his plow at Chinese checkers."

"Who are *you*?"

"I'm the police chief—Will Seevers. I've come to ask you a few questions about the man you saw in the Old Glory T-shirt."

"Had a belly on him, I'll tell you that."

"Did you see his face?"

Lawrence's eyebrows gathered and he just stared.

"The man in the Old Glory T-shirt," Will said. "Did you see his face?"

Ellen came in the room and handed Will a glass of lemonade, then sat on the couch.

"What am I, chopped liver?" Lawrence said.

"Did you want something to drink?"

"Not really. Could've at least asked me."

Ellen sat on the couch, her eyes wide with an I'm-sorry-he's-acting-this-way look.

"Mr. Madison," Will said, "you seem to be the only person

111

who may have seen the man who stabbed and killed a local shop owner. I keep hoping that maybe we can help you remember what the man looked like."

"Where'd it happen?" Lawrence said.

"In an alley not too far from Gordy's Crab Shack, where you had the fried clams."

Lawrence had a blank stare on his face.

"Dad, remember you had gone out to buy a ball cap?" Ellen said. "And tried to find your way back to the apartment but got confused?"

"I did?"

"Mr. Madison, we think you sat down to rest behind one of the shops, and that's where you saw the man in the flag shirt running."

"Had a belly on him."

"That's right," Will said. "Can you remember what his face looked like? Anything at all?"

"*Where* was I?"

"Near the alley, Dad. The man was running down the alley over the broken glass."

Lawrence nodded. "Had Old Glory on his shirt."

"Right. Was he wearing glasses? Did he have a mustache or beard?"

Lawrence didn't respond.

"Could you tell if he was white or black? Can you remember anything at all about him?"

"He had a knife. Cut a piece of pie."

Ellen sighed and looked at Will. "I think he's back at Gordy's. For some reason the two incidents just seem to run together and he doesn't recall anything in between."

"Don't worry about it. This was a long shot anyway."

"I'm sorry," Ellen said.

"Don't be. I appreciate your letting me try. I'll see you and Guy this evening." Will drank down the last of the lemonade and rose to his feet. "Mr. Madison, thanks for talking to me."

Lawrence looked up at Will. "Had a sunburned head. Should've worn a hat."

"The guy was bald? Okay, good. Anything else come to mind?"

Lawrence caught Will's gaze and held it. "How did you get in here?"

"I'm the police chief. Your daughter let me in."

Lawrence turned to Ellen. "Why aren't you at work?"

Ellen sighed, then got up and looked as though she were going to say something to Lawrence but didn't.

Will followed her to the front door and heard the TV go on in the living room.

Ellen exhaled loudly. "You can't be sure of anything Dad says. One minute he's right there with you and the next he's somewhere in the past."

"But what if he's right?" Will's eyes searched hers. "How would you feel about me bringing an artist over here to work with him? Maybe if your father saw some rough sketches he could give us more. But be honest. I don't want to push him too hard."

"Let me see how he is after you leave. If he doesn't seem upset, I don't see any reason why not."

"Good. I'll see you at the gala. We can talk then."

14

E arly Friday evening Owen Jones exited the highway in Hailey's Lexus SUV and merged onto Beach Shore Drive.

"Look, Daniel." Hailey Jones pointed to the billboard advertising Water Wonderland. "We're almost to Grandma and Grandpa's house. There's the big beach ball."

"I'm sure that makes a lot of sense to his one-year-old brain," Owen said.

"You never know. He might remember it the next time."

Owen put on his blinker and changed lanes. "Honey, I hope you don't mind us giving up the chance to go to the gala. I know Mom and Dad appreciated our offer to stay with Granddad."

"Not really. I didn't have anything to wear anyway."

He tried not to smile. "Yeah, I guess you need more than three closets full of clothes to find something that would've worked."

"I'm a size bigger since I had Daniel."

There was a moment of steely silence and Owen knew he'd better say something. "You look the same to me."

"And you're a terrible liar. Let's talk about something else."

Owen turned into the Publix parking lot and pulled into a space close to the door. "You want anything from the deli besides roasted chicken, potato salad, green beans, and rolls?"

"Why don't you get a lemon meringue pie for you guys and a pint of low-fat Dutch chocolate ice cream for me?"

"All right, sounds good." Owen started to open the door and then paused. "I just realized I didn't get a call from Tim O'Rourke today."

"Good. Maybe he gave up."

"We can only hope." Owen got out of the car and looked over at Hailey in the passenger seat. "Maybe I should get Popsicles for Daniel."

"You'd better not unless you plan to hold him over the sink!"

Owen laughed. "I'm just kidding. I'll be right back."

Ellen Jones inched her way down the elaborate buffet that had been set up under a white pavilion on the grounds of the People's Clinic. She arranged her plate with samplings from a lavish array of hot hors d'oeuvres and admired the colorful arrangements of fresh-cut flowers donated by local florists.

"The contributors really went all out," Guy Jones said. "I knew it would be nice, but this is better than nice."

Ali Tehrani walked over to them. "Can you believe the turnout? People are beaming with pride that they had a part in this."

"As well they should," Guy said. "The inside of the clinic looks great. I love the way the signature tiles were used for trim. Do we know how many there are?"

"Two thousand, eight hundred, and thirty-seven—each signed by someone who helped build this facility or donated materials or brought refreshments for the workers. We proved that cooperation works, yes?"

Guy turned and put his hand on Ali's shoulder. "That's an understatement, friend. A community project that got Muslims, Jews, and Christians to work together in peace for eighteen months is more like a miracle. This clinic should be the pilot project for the entire country. If the media doesn't get the word out, shame on them."

Ali smiled. "It is a great victory for all."

Mina walked up and linked arms with Ali. "Even the temperature is agreeable. What a perfect evening."

Ellen glanced over at Gordy and Pam Jameson laughing and talking with the mayor and Dr. and Mrs. Kohler and Professor Stephen Hardy. "It's impressive that everyone here contributed something quite personal to this project. In every sense of the word, it really is the *People's* Clinic".

"Aren't you and Mina going to enjoy some of this food?" Guy said to Ali.

"Yes, later. There are many hands yet to shake."

A man with a camera tapped Ali on the shoulder and said something Guy couldn't hear.

"If you'll excuse me," Ali said, "some media people would like a tour of the facility."

The man with the camera whisked Ali and Mina across the lawn and into the clinic.

"Ali is the man of the hour and he deserves it." Guy added several more delicious-looking hors d'oeuvres to his plate.

"Come on, handsome." Ellen tugged at the sleeve of Guy's tuxedo. "Let's go talk to Gordy and Pam."

Owen and Hailey sat cross-legged on the living room floor at Guy and Ellen's house, helping Daniel build a tower out of colorful plastic blocks.

"Come on, Son," Owen said. "Show your great-granddad how we do this."

Daniel rubbed his eyes then lowered himself to the floor and crawled over to Hailey and laid his head in her lap.

"I'm afraid he's had it," Hailey said. "Let me go back to Ellen and Guy's room and see if I can rock him to sleep. Come on, little man."

"Mom and Dad should be home soon."

"Where'd they go?" Lawrence said.

Owen wondered how many times tonight Granddad had asked that question. "Uh, to the big gala at the free clinic. You want another piece of that lemon meringue pie?"

Lawrence winked. "Now you're talking."

Owen went out to the kitchen and cut a slice of pie for Granddad and one for himself, then grabbed clean forks and paper napkins and returned to the living room. "Here you go."

"Always been my favorite," Lawrence said. "Your grandma's was the best. But when it comes to lemon meringue pie, there's just good and better." Lawrence took a big bite, then stopped chewing and seemed to be staring at something beyond Owen.

"What're you looking at?"

"That Peeping Tom on the back porch!" Lawrence put down his plate, got up, and went to the French doors and flung them open. "Who goes there?"

"Maybe it was just something reflected on the glass."

"Think I don't know a face when I see one?"

Owen turned on the floodlight and stepped out on the veranda, his eyes moving from left to right across the backyard.

"He's out there, boy. I saw him. Probably an enemy scout."

Owen went down the back steps and out into the yard and looked in all the dark corners and behind the gazebo, then came back up on the veranda. "Sorry, Granddad. I didn't see anyone."

Hailey came outside and stood next to Owen. "What're you guys doing?"

"Oh, Granddad thought he saw a Peeping Tom—an enemy scout." Owen put his lips to Hailey's ear. "I looked. There's no one out here."

Hailey gave Owen a gentle jab in the ribs. "Well, *you're* the one who heard something last night."

"Probably a cat."

"Well, do you hear the neighbors' dogs barking? I don't think you should just blow it off."

"What do you want me to do—call the police and tell them the dogs are barking?"

"You think this is funny? For all you know, it could've been that weirdo Tim O'Rourke. Maybe he's following you."

"Don't go getting paranoid on me."

Owen heard footsteps inside the house and then his parents came out on the veranda, their faces beaming.

"What a wonderful evening!" Ellen exclaimed.

"Big turnout?"

Guy nodded. "Huge. At one point the crowd was so tight it was hard to mingle. Ali's speech was the highlight."

"Your father was recognized along with the other founders," Ellen said. "WRGL is going to broadcast the entire event after the eleven o'clock news."

"Did everyone look as gorgeous as the two of you?" Hailey said.

Guy laughed. "Oh, you should've seen Gordy. Pam had him spit-shined, tuxedo and all. I never knew he could look that good."

"What about his hair?" Owen said.

"Had the back of it in a short ponytail. He looked like a husky version of some of the movie stars we've seen at the Oscars."

Ellen smiled. "I doubt if anyone had ever seen him in a suit, much less a tux…So why are you all standing out here with the light on? Where's Daniel?"

"Asleep in the Pack 'n Play," Hailey said. "We're out here because Granddad saw someone peeking in the French doors."

"Only there's no one out here," Owen said.

His mother caught his gaze, and he wondered why she seemed so intense.

Lawrence turned to Ellen, his white eyebrows scrunched together. "Where have *you* been?"

"Guy and I were at the gala for the People's Clinic, remember?"

"You think I can't remember anything?"

"I didn't say that. Were you able to get a good look at whoever was looking in the French doors?"

"Had Old Glory on his shirt! Why are you here? Don't think I'm going to give up my house without a fight!"

Owen's eyes collided with his mother's. "I'll let you guys sort that one out. We need to get Daniel home."

Ellen sat on the couch knitting an afghan, her mind racing and only vaguely aware of the television.

"Ellen, did you hear me?" Guy said.

"Uh, no. I'm sorry. What did you say?"

"I said isn't it great ABC evening news is going to run a short clip on the gala Monday night?"

"Yes, that's wonderful."

"Honey, what's wrong? You've been preoccupied since the kids left."

Ellen set her knitting in her lap. "I'm uneasy about the Peeping Tom. I told you how strange Dad acted on Wednesday night. Then Owen last night and now tonight's incident. It's unsettling, especially after someone tried to break into Dad and Roland's apartment."

"I think you're overreacting. Owen never saw anyone, and your father...well, it's obvious his time clock is way off."

"I know, but I can't shake the feeling. I'm going to go set the security alarm." Ellen started to get up, and Guy took her gently by the arm.

"Honey, for crying out loud, if you're that scared, maybe we should call the police and have them take a look."

"And report what—that our son heard a twig snap and my father thinks enemy soldiers are approaching?" Ellen exhaled. "I honestly didn't think much about the incident with Dad at the time. But replaying it in my mind, I remember the neighbors' dogs were barking."

"Probably at you and Lawrence traipsing all over the back-yard.

"You don't know that."

"Then let's go find out."

Guy got up and flipped on the spotlight, then went out the French doors and down the back steps, Ellen on his heels.

"And just what do you hope to prove?" she asked.

"Notice the dogs are barking?"

"I hear them."

"You see anyone besides us?"

Ellen looked around the backside of the gazebo and let her eyes adjust to the darker places along the fence. Nothing.

"Satisfied?"

"Not entirely. But it seems pointless to call the police. When Will brings the artist over to talk to Dad, I'll mention it to him."

15

ill Seevers walked into the police station and down to his office and set Saturday's newspaper and a cup of Starbucks coffee on his desk. He was aware of footsteps in the hallway and then a knock at the door. He looked up and saw Al Backus standing in the doorway.

"What happened to your three-day weekend?" Al said.

Will flopped into his desk chair and took the lid off his coffee, aware of the humble look on Al's face.

"Relax," Will said. "I'm not here to chew you out. I just need to nail down some thoughts before I try to shift gears and put on my chef's hat for the backyard cookout Margaret's planned. Did you talk to the merchants?"

"Yeah. Everything's cool. I told them we're going to keep plugging away till we get the guy. They seemed satisfied."

"Good. Tell me what information you've given them."

Al sat in the chair, his arms crossed. "The perp was probably a right-handed male, five-feet-nine, paunchy around the middle, sunburned head, possibly wore a flag shirt. Most likely Caucasian—aren't many bald and sunburned Latinos, Asians, or African Americans."

"Didn't jog anyone's memory, eh?"

"Nope. Sounds like dozens of tourists they see every day." He started to say something else and then didn't.

"Spit it out. What're you thinking?"

"Look, Chief, I'm out of ideas. We've got no fingerprints, no DNA, no murder weapon. No *case*."

"We've got a witness."

"Yeah, right," Al said. "We can't be sure of one thing he's told us."

"I'm willing to make some assumptions. The glass was in the alley like Mr. Madison said. And if he was sitting on the beer crate where Andrew Connor said he saw him, then he definitely witnessed something."

Al exhaled loudly. "With all due respect, there's a light on in the attic but nobody's home."

"Don't be so sure."

"Even *if* the old guy's giving us correct information, which I highly doubt, what do you want me to do now—go door-to-door looking for a guy whose head's peeling?"

"I want you to cut the sarcasm and act like a professional!" Will took a slow, deep breath. "Al, listen to me…I know how impatient you get with dead ends, but Kincaid's family deserves to know we did our darnedest to find the killer. As long as we have anything at all to go on, we're going to stay on this one. Got that?"

"All right. I'll spend the weekend poring over case notes and retracing my steps. Maybe something will surface." Al's jaw was clenched and he avoided making eye contact.

"One more thing," Will said. "Don't think for a minute that you're indispensable."

Ellen Jones sat in bed, pillows propped behind her, and smiled as Guy glided into the bedroom, whistling and carrying a breakfast tray.

"Your Saturday treat, madam." He set the tray across her lap, the aroma of warm cinnamon rolls flavoring the air, and handed her Saturday's edition of the *North Coast Messenger*.

Ellen put her nose to the red rose in the bud vase. "I never get tired of this ritual."

He pressed his lips to hers. "And I never get tired of spoiling you." He crawled over her and sat on the other side of the bed.

"What's Dad doing?" Ellen said.

"He's happy as a lark. I gave him the sports page and a couple cinnamon rolls."

"Probably won't eat the rest of the day."

"Let's don't spoil what's left of our morning with negative thoughts. Look at the picture on the front page of the paper."

Ellen opened the newspaper and saw the group picture of the clinic founders, taken before the gala. "You have to feel proud of yourselves. Seeing this goal realized is nothing short of a miracle on several levels."

"Yeah, it was a real faith builder for me. I sure never thought I'd be able to respect a Muslim, much less befriend one. Talk about doing a one-eighty."

Ellen squeezed his hand. "I still pray the Tehranis will be open to the Gospel someday."

"Me too. But hopefully they'll see it in our actions, even if we don't say anything."

Ellen smiled, thinking how much Guy had grown spiritually.

A long time passed in comfortable silence, Ellen reading the newspaper and Guy engrossed in the latest issue of *Time* magazine.

The doorbell rang.

"I'd better get that before Lawrence does." Guy climbed out of bed and left the room. A minute later Ellen heard voices and approaching footsteps, then Hailey walked in the room, Daniel in her arms, Owen and Guy on her heels.

"There's Grandma," Hailey said.

Daniel squealed and wiggled until Hailey set him on his feet.

"Come here, sweetie." Ellen set her breakfast tray on the other side of the bed and took her grandson into her arms and smothered him with kisses. "What brings you kids out before noon on a Saturday?"

"We went by the hospital to see Papa," Owen said. "The physical therapist was working with him, so we didn't stay. We'll swing by later." Owen glanced over at Hailey. "Also, we're bothered by some phone calls we've been getting and wanted to get your opinion."

Owen recounted the calls Tim O'Rourke had made to his home, his office, and his cell phone, as well as O'Rourke's final proclamation that he was mad and Owen was going to play things his way.

"The last time he called was Thursday night," Owen said, "while I was on my way over here. It was that same night that I heard a twig snap in the backyard. I blew it off until last night when Granddad thought he saw someone peeking in the French doors. Now I'm wondering if O'Rourke might be following me."

Ellen's mind raced in reverse. "Something doesn't add up because I had an incident with your granddad on *Wednesday* night." Ellen described Lawrence's strange behavior after he claimed he saw someone lurking in the dark. "When he started talking about enemy soldiers approaching and his needing to get provisions and reinforcements for his men, it never occurred to me that he might actually have seen someone. But why would Tim O'Rourke be sneaking around over here?"

"I can't imagine. Granddad must've been seeing things."

"The neighbors' dogs were barking. And what about Tuesday night at the apartment?"

"This is just too weird," Hailey said. "Don't you think we should report it to the police?"

"Probably, though I'm not sure the police can do anything," Guy said. "This O'Rourke never threatened you, and there's no proof that anyone was out there."

"Maybe not," Ellen said, "but someone tried turning the door handle at Dad and Roland's apartment. That certainly wasn't my imagination. Will wanted to come over today anyway and bring the artist to work with Dad. I think we should call and tell him what's going on."

That afternoon the Joneses sat on the veranda, waiting for Will Seevers and his investigators to finish searching the backyard and the police sketch artist to finish working with Lawrence.

"We're probably all paranoid," Owen said. "If O'Rourke had gone to the trouble of following me here, why didn't he just ring the doorbell and force the confrontation he wants?"

Ellen stood, her hands on her low back, and stretched. "I'm going to check on Dad."

She walked inside where Lawrence sat on the couch with the police artist, who held a sketching pad and pencil and appeared to be drawing a face.

"How's it coming?" Ellen said.

The officer shrugged. "The only facts your father seems remotely sure of are the *Old Glory* shirt, as he puts it, and the man's thick middle. Frankly, I'm inclined to think he's merely remembering what he's been told he said and has lost touch with what he may have actually seen."

Ellen sighed. "I'm sorry. I think all the pressure to remember may have made things worse."

"Well, I think we're about through here."

Lawrence glared at Ellen. "I'm not stupid."

"No one thinks that, Dad."

The French doors opened and Owen stuck his head inside. "Mom, Chief Seevers wants us to come take a look at something."

"Excuse me." Ellen went out on the veranda and filed down the steps behind the rest of her family and followed Will over to the gate.

He pointed to a piece of something tan-colored that appeared to be snagged on the top of a wood slat on the privacy fence. "Do you know of anyone who might've climbed the fence recently?"

Guy looked at Ellen and shook his head. "No."

"Well, looks like someone did. This piece of torn material doesn't look weathered or faded."

Ellen sighed. "So much for keeping the gate locked."

"If your lurker climbed the fence to get in, all he had to do to get out was unlock it. We also found this." Will held up a plastic bag containing a cigarette butt. "Hasn't been out here long, and neither of you smoke. We might be able to get DNA off it, but unless it matches DNA on file, it still won't tell us who left it here."

Owen took Hailey's hand in his. "You think Tim O'Rourke could be a convicted criminal?"

"Let's not speculate," Will said. "Let's see if we can match any of the fingerprints we found here with those we found on the door of the apartment."

Ellen sighed. "Will, you should be home having a holiday weekend with your family. We never expected you to get this personally involved."

"No problem. I was going to bring the artist over here to talk to Mr. Madison anyway. Besides, I never take a whole day off when we're in the middle of a murder investigation." Will took tweezers and removed the swatch of fabric and placed it in a plastic bag. "If it makes you feel better, I'm on my way home. Margaret's got a backyard full of guests coming, and I've been dubbed King of the Grill."

Ellen smiled. "Good. Sounds like a whole lot more fun than this."

"I'll have the lab process this evidence and then get back to you as soon as I know something. In the meantime, I suggest you stay attentive to your surroundings and keep your doors locked—just as a precaution."

16

On Sunday afternoon, Ellen Jones sat at a picnic table in Bougainvillea Park, her eyes closed and a warm breeze tickling her back. She listened to Daniel's squeals of delight echoing from the playground and Guy's playful groaning as he braved a game of Ultimate Frisbee with Owen and a group of young dads. For a moment she was transported back to a Madison family reunion where her own father had eaten up an entire afternoon pitching baseballs to Owen and Brandon. She could still remember the sound of Lawrence's war whoop when Owen's bat sent the ball sailing through the air all the way to the lake.

Ellen opened her eyes and noticed her father sitting at the other end of the picnic table, staring at a ketchup bottle.

"Dad, would you like to take a walk with me?" she said. "That path is lined with bougainvillea bushes and leads down to the pond. It's really beautiful."

She thought her father's eyes looked watery, but he turned away from her and acted as though he were watching two little boys frolicking with a dalmatian puppy.

"Would you like more potato salad? It's Mom's recipe. I know how much you love it."

"Of course you know *everything*!"

Ellen's heart sank. "Dad, I know moving here wasn't easy, but I'm trying to make things pleasant for you."

Lawrence folded his arms across his chest. "Nobody wants me around."

Because you're so disagreeable! "How can you say that? Owen asked you to play catch, but you said you were tired."

"I want to go home!"

"I know you do. I'm sorry." Ellen touched his arm, and he yanked it away from her. "Dad, just because you need a little extra help doesn't mean your life is over."

"Call your mother! Tell her to come get me!"

Ellen hesitated and then pushed out the words, "She's in heaven. She would want us to get along. Why can't you just accept my help?"

"Where'd Roland go?"

"Roland's in the hospital, remember? He had a hip replacement."

There was an awkward moment of silence, and then Lawrence said, "Roland cut me a piece of pie. Had Old Glory on his shirt."

Ellen exhaled a sigh of exasperation and didn't bother to respond.

Hailey came back to the table and put Daniel in Ellen's arms. "He's so sleepy he can hardly keep his head up. See if you can work your magic."

"Come on, sweetie. Grandma will sing to you." Ellen swung her legs over the bench and rose to her feet, Daniel's head resting on her shoulder. She winked at Hailey. "Give me ten minutes."

"Come on, Granddad," Hailey said, holding up a bag of popcorn. "How about walking me down to the pond so we can feed the ducks?"

Lawrence looked up at Hailey, his face suddenly beaming. "Don't mind if I do."

Ellen watched her father and daughter-in-law walk arm in arm across the grass and onto the paved walkway and then out of sight. She blinked the stinging from her eyes and began to sing softly to Daniel.

❦ ❦ ❦

Will Seevers sat at his desk eating a ham and cheese on rye and reading the lab results on evidence that had been collected from the Joneses' backyard.

None of the fingerprints found on the French door or gate latch, except for those of family members, matched the prints from the door handle at the apartment. The fabric taken from the fence was consistent with that used to manufacture Dockers-brand khaki pants. The cigarette butt was Camel brand. DNA from the cigarette was that of a male, but couldn't be matched to anything on file at the National Crime Information Center.

Will set the lab report on his desk, took off his glasses, and rubbed his eyes.

Al Backus walked in and flopped into the chair. "So what'd it tell us?"

"Not nearly enough." Will handed the report to Al. "There's nothing to link what happened at Lawrence Madison's apartment to whatever's been going on at the house."

Al skimmed the report. "Maybe there isn't a connection."

"My gut tells me there is." Will sat back in his chair, his hands behind his head. "I want to look at mug shots of all the Tim O'Rourkes arrested in the state of Florida in the past two years. Too bad the Joneses didn't have a surveillance camera in their backyard."

Later that night, Gordy's Crab Shack was packed with customers, many more still waiting outside to be seated. Gordy Jameson pushed open the door to the kitchen, relieved to see six fruit pies on the cooling rack.

"Darlin', you are the one!" he said to Pam. "Seems everybody who's come in tonight has ordered pie for dessert."

Pam Jameson smiled. "I had to take half the pies out of the

case out front and serve them to tonight's customers. I can't seem to get them out of the oven fast enough."

The doors flung open and Weezie Taylor danced into the kitchen. "Whoooeeee! We are packed out and they're still comin'!" She walked over to Pam and gave her a high five. "Dessert sales are up 150 percent, girlfriend! We're finally sellin' the stuff faster than boss man here is givin' it away!" She let out a hearty laugh that nearly rattled the pans.

Gordy chuckled. "Good. Maybe you two will get off my case. I'll leave you to gloat. I've got customers to greet."

Gordy left the kitchen and saw Will and Margaret Seevers sitting in a booth with their daughter Meagan. He walked over and slid in next to Meagan. "How's my favorite teenybopper?"

Meagan giggled, exposing a band of silver across her teeth. "Fine. I leave tomorrow for my field trip. Thanks for helping me earn my airfare."

"You're welcome. Every kid oughta see Washington, D.C. I hope you have a great time." Gordy looked up at Will. "Anything new on the Kincaid case?"

"Nothing I can talk about," Will said. "We're following some leads."

"Okay, I need to get to work." Gordy slid out of the booth and looked back at Meagan. "Take a ton of pictures. When you get back, Pam and I will have you over so you can tell us all about it. Plus, I want a rematch on dominoes."

"Uncle Gordy, why put yourself through that when you know I'm just gonna clean your plow?'"

"Hey, that's my line." Gordy chuckled. "To be honest, Meg, I'll use any excuse to spend time with you before you get to the age when you find it embarrassin' to be seen with me."

"That'll *never* happen," Meagan said.

Gordy looked knowingly at Will and Margaret, certain that it would. "Okay, I'm outta here. Back to work."

Gordy ambled around the crab shack, greeting customers

and handing out a few coupons for free dessert. He spotted Ellen and Guy Jones and Lawrence Madison sitting at the corner table by the window and walked over to them. "Hey, good to see you. Been enjoyin' the long weekend?"

Ellen nodded. "We had a picnic this afternoon with Owen, Hailey, and Daniel."

"Beautiful day for it." Gordy looked at Guy. "How's your dad doin'?"

"Coming along fine, thanks. We just got back from the hospital. He's being transferred to the rehab hospital tomorrow. Depending on how he does, he'll be there between seven and ten days. They expect him to regain almost full function."

Gordy spotted Andrew Connor standing in line at the take-out window. "That's great to hear. Enjoy your dinner." He laid three coupons on the table and winked at Lawrence. "We've got plenty of that triple-berry pie you liked so much."

Gordy went over to Andrew and shook his hand. "Welcome, friend. How come you're not eatin' at your own place?"

Andrew smiled sheepishly. "Shhh. Don't tell my customers, but I'm not crazy about deli sandwiches and quiche." He patted his generous middle. "Give me fried grouper and french fries any day. So how's business been?"

"Great. This is always a big weekend. How about yours?"

"Way better than anticipated," Andrew said. "I had to pull Cheryl and the boys in to help out. We're much busier than last year."

"The Kincaid's place closin' down might've had somethin' to do with it," Gordy said.

"Heck of a way to get more business, but we can sure use the money."

Gordy raised his eyebrows. "Yeah, college'll drain you. So how'd Rory like his first year at Florida State?"

"Uh, actually, he put college on hold for a while."

"Really? Last time I saw him he seemed gung ho about it."

"Yeah, I know." Andrew lowered his voice. "Rory's got some growing up to do. Cheryl and I want to make sure he's got good sense before we send him off to college, if you know what I mean."

"Yeah, I hear you."

Andrew rolled his eyes. "Be glad you don't have kids. You'll live longer."

"Listen," Gordy said, "I wanna make a donation to the Kincaid Memorial Fund. I'll get with you after the long weekend."

"Thanks. We've raised almost nine thousand dollars so far."

"I heard you put up the first five grand."

Andrew shrugged. "Somebody had to get the ball rolling. Jackson's family deserves it. Have you heard whether or not the cops have any suspects?"

"According to the newspaper, they don't. But I guarantee you Will Seevers won't throw in the towel till he's exhausted every effort."

"Yeah, we're all counting on that."

Gordy shook Andrew's hand and patted him on the shoulder. "Good to see you. Give my best to Cheryl."

"Dad, what are you staring at?" Ellen said.

Lawrence's eyes seemed fixed on something, and she wasn't sure he even heard her question. "Why is *he* here?" Lawrence finally said.

Guy glanced up and then said, "That's Gordy. He's the owner of this place. You had lunch with his friends, remember?"

"Had Old Glory on his shirt. Cut me a piece of pie. Why are we here?"

Ellen locked gazes with Guy, who looked as helpless as she felt.

"Here we go, folks," the waiter said. "Two grilled grouper dinners and a fried clam dinner."

"My dad gets the clams," Ellen said.

The waiter set a plate piled high with golden brown clams in front of Lawrence. "Be careful, sir. That plate is super hot."

He gave Ellen and Guy their meals and removed their salad plates. "Will there be anything else right now?"

Guy shook his head. "Looks like we all got what we ordered."

"Excellent. I'll wait a few minutes, then bring you more jalapeno cheese bread."

Ellen closed her eyes as Guy said the blessing. When she opened them, she noticed Lawrence staring at his plate.

"Mmm…those fried clams look yummy," Ellen said. "Can I have a bite?"

"Eat your own dinner!"

Ellen coughed to cover her smile and saw Will Seevers walking over to the table.

"Glad I ran into you," Will said. "I called your house and your son's house earlier today and got answering machines both places. The lab report came back, and none of the fingerprints at the apartment match what we found at the house—with the exception of family members. We got DNA off the cigarette butt. Unfortunately, it doesn't match anything on file. The swatch of material that was snagged on the fence is consistent with the fabric used to make Dockers."

Guy sat back in his chair. "Well, that narrows it down to several *million* possible suspects."

"We're in the process of reviewing the files on all the Tim O'Rourkes who've been arrested in the state. That might yield something."

"I hope it does," Ellen said. "This is very unsettling."

"In the meantime, remember to use caution. Don't give this lurker a chance to get inside your house."

"You think we should keep the security alarm on?" Ellen said.

"Couldn't hurt. Probably a good idea to leave the front and

back porch lights on after dark. I don't want you to overreact, just think smart. I'll get back to you when I've reviewed the arrest records for the Tim O'Rourkes."

"Okay, Will. Thanks."

Will turned and walked toward Margaret and Meagan, who were standing at the cash register.

Guy took a sip of water, his eyebrows forming a dark, bushy line. "Well, on a positive note, no police chief would allocate this much time and manpower unless he thought the effort was going to lead somewhere."

"Well, let's just hope it leads somewhere before you have to leave for Tallahassee."

17

Ellen Jones stood in the alcove of the widow's watch, a warm mug of coffee in her hands, and watched Tuesday morning's sky turn into a glowing blanket of orangey hot pink.

She heard a knock on the door and, seconds later, felt Guy's arms around her, his chin resting on her shoulder.

"It's really pathetic when you can't feel safe sitting out on your own veranda," he said. "I hate leaving for Tallahassee with this hanging over us."

"I know. I'll keep the security alarm on. I just wish the police would figure out who this Tim O'Rourke character is and what he's doing snooping around here."

"I'm just as concerned about the kids," Guy said. "They don't have a security alarm, and Hailey and Daniel are there all day."

"I feel better knowing Shayla's in the house."

"I really hate leaving like this, but I've got a meeting with the partners at nine and another with a new client at eleven. I need to get on the road."

Ellen pulled Guy's arms around her tighter. *Lord, protect us while we're away from each other.* She rested for a moment in Guy's embrace, then turned around, her arms cradling his neck. "God will take care of us. I'll check in with Hailey often and take Dad with me when I go to the rehab hospital to check on Roland."

"Honey, he was fine when we saw him yesterday. My father

doesn't expect or need you to be there every day. They're working him hard. He's tired."

"I know, but I think he'd enjoy a hug and a smile. I don't have to stay long. I just hope *my* dad is cooperative while you're gone. If he refuses to go anywhere with me, I don't know what I'm going to do. I don't dare leave him here alone."

"Tell me again when we take him for his evaluation?"

"Nine more days, but who's counting? Thursday, June 5 at 9:00 a.m."

"I'm sorry the brunt of this falls on you. I'm going to check my schedule and see about coming home tonight instead of Wednesday and just work from my office here. In the meantime, promise me you'll be careful—and smart."

Ellen smiled. "Once a newspaperwoman, always a newspaper-woman. My instincts are on tilt. I'm not about to let down my guard."

Guy looked over her shoulder, his eyes squinting. "What's that airplane pulling, a banner?"

Ellen turned around and saw the same plane she had seen when she was jogging on the beach. "It's an advertisement to support the Kincaid Memorial Fund by eating at Fish Tales."

"I read in the paper that the guy who owns that place has already collected eighty-seven hundred dollars for the family. Amazing." Guy kissed Ellen on the forehead. "I really have to go. You going to come downstairs where you can keep an eye on Lawrence?"

"I suppose I'd better." Ellen looked around her quaint workplace and felt a twinge of regret. "I've totally lost the momentum on this second novel. I don't know what difference it makes since I can't seem to get a contract on the first one."

Owen Jones added sliced strawberries to his bowl of granola, poured milk over the top, then sat at the kitchen table across from Hailey.

"I'm glad Shayla's here," he said. "There's no way I'm leaving you and Daniel alone."

"I wonder why Tim O'Rourke hasn't called again?" Hailey Jones took a sip of coffee. "It still amazes me that he followed you to your parents' house and hid out in the yard."

"Who knows what makes a weirdo like that tick. I just wish Chief Seevers would figure out who he is and keep him away from us."

"Can the police do that? I mean, technically, they can't even prove he's done anything illegal."

"Maybe his DNA will match what was on the cigarette butt."

"First they have to find him."

"They will."

"But wouldn't they have to have a court order to get his DNA?"

Owen stopped chewing for a moment. "Are you trying to depress me or what?"

"I'm sorry. I'm just trying to be realistic. On TV the police never seem able to do anything until a crime has been committed."

"Much more talk like this and I'll just stay home."

Hailey pushed her long blond hair behind her ear, and Owen was thinking how pretty she looked without makeup.

"Are you planning to go out today?" he said.

"I need to go to the grocery store."

"I don't want you going anywhere by yourself. And I don't want Shayla here alone with Daniel. If you go to the store, take them with you, okay?"

"All right. That's a good idea."

Shayla Taylor waltzed through the doorway, Daniel in her arms. "There they are, sweet baby boy."

Daniel giggled and stretched out his arms, reaching for Owen.

"Come here and give Daddy a kiss good-bye."

Owen took Daniel in his arms and pressed his lips to the boy's warm cheek. "You smell good. What did Miss Shayla rub on your skin?"

"Oh, just a little baby lotion after his bath. I *love* a clean baby. Makes people wanna give them all that kissin' and huggin' they need."

"Daddy's got to go to work now. You be good." He handed Daniel back to Shayla and was pleased the boy didn't resist. "Are you sure you're all right with our situation, Shayla? We really don't know anything about this Tim O'Rourke."

"That's okay, Mr. Jones. The Lord does. And since He's controllin' my life, I got no cause to get worked up over things He already knows about. This job was an answer to prayer, and I'm grateful to be workin' here."

Owen was thinking Shayla either had more faith or was more naïve than anyone he knew. "Well, good. I appreciate your attitude. I feel better knowing you're not uneasy."

"I see no cause for lettin' this O'Rourke fella give us a spirit of fear. Me and Mrs. Jones will use good sense, but I have a feelin' the day is gonna go just fine." She glanced at her watch. "And if you don't mind me sayin' so, sir, you're runnin' late."

Owen smiled without intending to. "You're right." He got up and put his arms around Hailey and held her a little longer than usual. "I'll check in with you. Promise me you'll stay alert and will call me if anything strange happens."

"I promise."

Ellen spread cream cheese and strawberry jam on both slices of a wheat bagel and carried it on a saucer over to the breakfast bar. She started to pour another cup of coffee, but the blaring of the TV in the living room had set her nerves on edge and she didn't want more caffeine.

She took a bite of bagel, her eyes resting on a photograph she had attached to the refrigerator of Julie, Ross, and Sarah Beth Hamilton. Ellen glanced at the clock on the oven. Julie should be home from taking Sarah Beth to preschool. She picked up the phone and dialed.

"Hello."

"Julie, it's Ellen."

"Hi, stranger. Ross and I were just talking about you and Guy last night. We missed seeing you at church Sunday."

"We went to the early service and then met the kids for a picnic."

"So how are things going with your father and father-in-law? Is the apartment working out?"

"So much has happened since I talked to you last, I hardly know where to begin." Ellen told Julie about Lawrence getting confused and ending up in the alley and possibly witnessing Jackson Kincaid's murder. Also about Roland's fall and subsequent surgery. And about Tim O'Rourke and what the police found in the Joneses' backyard.

"For heaven's sake, Ellen, why didn't you call and ask for prayer?"

"That's what I'm doing now."

"I'll get you on the prayer chain as soon as we hang up. So are you and your dad there by yourselves till Guy gets back from Tallahassee?"

"Yes, but I'm keeping the security alarm on." Ellen glanced at the keypad on the wall by the kitchen door and saw the red light was on. "No one's going to get in the house without me knowing it, whether I'm here or out running errands."

"I sure hope the police figure out what's going on soon."

"That's two of us. Guy's hoping to come back tonight and work here at home."

"Are Owen and Hailey worried?"

"They're certainly concerned. But they haven't seen anything strange at their place. The whole thing's bizarre."

"I can't believe how much has happened in the past

couple of weeks," Julie said. "You must be on overload."

"I could use a breather. Let's talk about something else. How much longer is Sarah Beth in preschool?"

"Actually, she's finished till September. Poor baby cried when I didn't take her to school this morning. It's useless trying to explain summer break to a three-and-a-half-year-old. At least VBS starts in two weeks."

"Well, tell Sarah Beth I miss her and want to see her real soon."

"Okay. Listen, you play it safe and keep me in the loop. We'll be holding you up in prayer."

"Thanks, Julie. I know you will."

Ellen hung up the phone and saw Lawrence standing in the doorway.

"Why are *you* here?"

"Dad, I live here, remember? You're staying at my house."

"Why aren't you at work?"

"I don't work for the newspaper anymore."

"Well, don't expect a pat on the back. Never could understand women in the workplace. You belong at home, taking care of your family."

Ellen waited until her anger had passed, thinking how absurd it was to get riled up over the same things over and over again. "Did you finish your breakfast?"

"I ate what you put on my plate."

"I'd like to visit Roland at the rehab hospital and would appreciate it if you'd go with me. I'm sure he'd be glad to see you."

Lawrence looked at her and seemed to be processing her words. "I suppose you'll be sticking *me* in one of those places."

"Roland had a hip replacement, Dad. He's only there till the physical therapists can get him walking again."

Lawrence fiddled with the buttons on his shirt. "Maybe we should take Roland some brownies. He likes brownies."

"All right. That's a good idea. I'll make a fresh batch, and we can take them over to him while they're still warm. Would you like me to make lemon pudding for tonight's dessert?"

Lawrence shook his head. "I won't be staying for dinner. I need to drive back to Ocala before it gets dark."

Ellen didn't say anything and wished her father's evaluation wasn't nine days away.

Owen pulled his Jaguar into the parking lot of Global Communications and then into the space reserved for the CFO. He walked in the side entrance and past the employee break room, then got in the elevator and went up to the third floor. When the door opened, he almost ran headlong into his administrative assistant.

"Oops. Sorry, Helen."

"I was just on my way downstairs to get some things from the supply room," Helen said, her hand on the hold button. "I'll be right back."

"How was your long weekend?"

"Relaxing, thanks. How about yours?"

"*Not* relaxing," Owen said. "I'll tell you about it later. Right now, I'm looking forward to hiding in my office and tackling the stacks of paperwork I couldn't get to last week because of our marathon meetings."

Helen's eyes grew wide. "Uh, you can't. Your brother is waiting for you in your office."

"Brandon's here?"

"They just got in from Raleigh." Helen put her hand over her mouth. "I can't say anything else. Act surprised."

"Well, that won't be hard. I haven't seen him since Hailey and I moved here. He's never even seen Daniel. What do you mean *they*?"

"I've already said too much." Helen looked at Owen with pleading eyes. "Please don't tell him I ruined his surprise. He seemed so tickled about it."

The elevator door closed, and Owen turned around and started walking toward his office, wondering if his brother had brought his girlfriend home to meet the family.

The aroma of freshly brewed coffee became stronger and more inviting as Owen got closer to his office door. He picked up his pace and began to whistle and breezed through the doorway. A second later he stopped cold and didn't have to fake his surprise.

Sitting on the couch was a man Owen guessed to be in his early forties and a little girl with blond curls and huge blue eyes.

"You're not...uh, sorry. I was expecting someone else."

The man grinned derisively. "I told you we were going to play it my way."

Owen's heart sank. The voice was Tim O'Rourke's.

18

Owen Jones closed the door of his office, then spun around, his arms folded tightly across his chest. "Okay, O'Rourke, you've got one minute to tell me what you're doing here or I'm calling security."

"Don't talk down to me, you arrogant—" Tim O'Rourke rose to his feet and looked as if he were going to lunge at Owen but, instead, grabbed the little girl by the hand. "I told you I had something that belonged to you. Her name's Annie."

Tim put his hand on Annie's back and prodded her toward Owen. She stopped about halfway between the two men, clutching tightly to a well-worn teddy bear.

"What do you mean she's mine? I've never seen this child before."

"How about we go back five years and take a little trip down memory lane. Does the name Corinne O'Rourke ring a bell?"

Owen shook his head. "No."

"How about Raleigh, North Carolina, and a fundraiser for Senator Poston? A cab ride to the Spartan Hotel? A freebie with a gorgeous blonde?"

"I've dated a lot of good-looking blondes," Owen said.

"This was no *date*! You spent the night in bed with my wife!"

Owen suddenly felt flushed. "I didn't know. She wasn't wearing a ring."

"Then you *do* remember her!" Tim said.

"I vaguely remember the incident. I don't remember what she looked like."

Tim reached in his pocket and pulled out his wallet and held Corinne's picture in front of Owen's eyes. "Remember now? Or did you even bother looking at her face?"

"Look, I was single and reckless. All I was looking for was a good time, not a relationship—or a commitment."

"Guess that backfired."

Owen glanced at Annie and hated that she was trembling. "I'm sure I wasn't the only man Corinne had been with."

"You were the one who got her pregnant."

"You can't know that."

"Oh, but I can."

Owen threw up his hands. "You think I'm buying this? If you're after money, forget it!"

"I don't want money, you idiot. I want out from under! Annie's not mine, and I don't want to raise her!"

"Well, where does Corinne fit into this? If she's so all-fired sure I'm the father, why doesn't she have the decency to confront me herself?"

Tim's face was expressionless, his gaze fixed on the little girl who stood between them. "Corinne died two weeks ago. You're Annie's only living relative."

Police Chief Will Seevers sat at the table in his office, Investigator Al Backus next to him, reviewing the mug shots on the seven Timothy O'Rourkes arrested in the state in the past two years.

Al raised his eyebrows. "The only baldy here is six-two."

"I'm not surprised," Will said. "My guess is we're not dealing with Tim O'Rourke but a perp who's five-nine with his gut hanging over his belt. And it's not Owen Jones he's after."

"Someone who wants to make sure Lawrence Madison doesn't say too much."

"You got it." Will got up and paced in front of the windows, his hands in his pockets. "I need to go tell Ellen what

I'm thinking. For now, I want one of our police cruisers on the Joneses' street at least once every hour."

Only living relative? Owen struggled to find his voice, his eyes moving from Tim to Annie and back to Tim.

"What'd she die of?" Owen finally managed to say.

"Her Mustang was hit broadside by an eighteen-wheeler. She lived two days in ICU." Tim's eyes looked vacant. "And the doctors discovered she was HIV positive. I'm sure she didn't know."

HIV positive? Owen's mind raced with the implications.

Tim's chin quivered slightly. He went over and sat on one end of the couch, his hands folded between his knees. "I just tested positive. You'd think if she was going to cheat on me, she could've at least protected us both. Well, I'll be darned if I'm raising her kid."

"Look, I'm sorry about the HIV. I really am. But I'm not going to be railroaded." Owen looked over at Annie, who had crawled into a corner and buried her face in the teddy bear. "I want you to take the child and leave, or I'll call security."

"Better have a look at these first." Tim picked up a manila envelope lying on the couch and tossed it to him.

Owen reached inside and pulled out a familiar silk tie and the business card he had used when working for the CPA firm in Raleigh. Also a pink envelope.

"Where'd you get these?"

"Corinne had them tucked away. When she was lying there in the hospital all hooked up, all she could think about was what would happen to Annie if she died. Didn't give a thought to me. I told her I didn't want to raise Annie by myself, that I had always suspected the kid wasn't mine. She finally admitted it. Told me she had worried every day since Annie was born that I would discover the kid's blood type couldn't have come from the two of us. Said Annie's father was a guy named Owen Jones who she'd invited to her hotel room after a fundraiser for Senator Poston."

Owen rolled his eyes. "She happened to remember my name just like that after five years? Give me a break!"

"No, you left that tie and business card in her hotel room, and she took it as an invitation to call you, so she kept them. And when Annie was born nine months later and her blood type wasn't O, she knew you were the only man who could be Annie's biological father. She held on to this stuff in case she ever needed to contact you. Read the letter. Corinne spells out everything."

Owen stared at the pink envelope but couldn't bring himself to open it.

"Corinne told me where to find the manila envelope and told me to read the letter. She begged me not to abandon Annie but to take this stuff to you and see if you'd raise her."

"So that's why you've been trying to get me to meet you."

"Yeah. After Corinne died, I went to your old CPA firm and told the HR person I was an old friend who'd lost touch. She said you'd taken a job here. Wasn't hard to find you."

Owen raked his hands through his hair. "I've got a wife and son. We want another baby. This'll ruin everything."

"I can't help that. The kid's yours. At least Corinne left you something living. All she left me is a death sentence."

Owen quickly dismissed the frightening possibilities. "You think I'm going to let you waltz in here and saddle me with a four-year-old I never even knew existed? There's no proof that any of this is true! For all I know, you're just looking for a patsy."

"Why don't you read the letter?"

"Anyone could've written it!"

"There're things in there only Corinne could know."

"I don't care what it says! I don't believe I'm this girl's father!"

"Then take a paternity test!"

"I refuse to be forced into this. There are plenty of people who want to adopt a child. Let someone else take her! Doesn't she have grandparents? Another family member?"

Tim clenched his jaw. "I told you, you're it. I came a long way to do this favor for Corinne, but I'm not taking Annie home with me!"

"Well, neither am I!" Owen shouted.

The room was suddenly pin-drop still except for the sound of Annie's sniffling. Owen looked over at the little girl huddled in the corner, her pensive blue eyes brimming with tears and looking remarkably like his mother's. His heart sank. He wanted to take back his words and to banish her into non-existence at the same time.

Owen turned to Tim O'Rourke, whose face had turned red and glistened with perspiration.

Tim jumped to his feet and fumbled with his shirttail and, in the next instant, held a handgun, the barrel pressed against his temple. "I can't take any more! I just want the pain to stop!"

Owen held out his hand, his voice calm and steady. "Give me the gun, man. This isn't the answer."

"Stay back!" Tim said, his voice quavering. "I'd be doing us all a favor!"

"Daddy...?"

The helplessness in Annie's voice clawed at Owen's conscience, and he felt as though he were paralyzed, his eyes locked on to Tim's, the banging of his heart seeming to fill the room.

God, don't let him do it!

Ellen took the pan of brownies out of the oven and set it on the cooling rack, aware of Lawrence in the doorway, dressed in a bulky blue sweater.

"Dad, why don't you put on a short-sleeve shirt? It's ninety degrees outside. You're going to suffocate in that sweater."

Lawrence's eyebrows furrowed. "We going somewhere?"

"Over to the rehab hospital to see Roland. We're taking him brownies, remember?"

The look on his face told her he didn't.

"The police chief called a few minutes ago. He wants to come by later this morning and talk to us about the man in the Old Glory shirt."

"Had a middle on him, I'll tell you that."

Ellen smiled. "Would you like to have lunch at Gordy's? We can have fried clams."

"Now you're talking."

Owen watched Annie O'Rourke race over to Tim and wrap her arms around his leg.

"Tim, just stay calm, man." Owen felt as though his heart would pound out of his chest. "We can work something out."

Tim stood in front of the couch, holding the gun to his head. "You don't get it. I don't want to work something out. I want *out*. Corinne's the lucky one. Why should I wait around to die of AIDS?"

"You're upset. You're not thinking clearly."

"You don't have a clue what I'm thinking!" Tim's hand shook as he pushed the barrel of the gun more snugly against his temple. "You've got success. Money. A *real* family. I'll bet you live in the perfect house on the perfect street in the perfect neighborhood. You're the one who deserves to die of AIDS, not me. I never cheated on Corinne."

Owen glanced at Annie, tears trickling down her face, and wondered if she was about to see the only father she'd ever known blow his brains out. "I am *so* sorry for getting involved with Corinne. I had no idea she was married."

"Like it would've mattered! Were you so righteous that you'd have walked away from something that gorgeous if you *had* known?"

"I had no scruples back then. I've changed. Didn't you ever do anything you were ashamed of later?"

"Don't change the subject! I never cheated on Corinne!"

Owen paused for several seconds, trying to think of a way to calm Tim down. "Look, man. I'm sorry for what I did. If I could go back and undo it, I would."

"Not good enough! You're going to take responsibility for it." He lowered the gun and peeled Annie's arms off his leg, then pointed the gun at Owen and ordered him to stand over by the desk.

Tim went over to the door and locked it. "Now open the letter and read it—out loud!"

"Okay, okay. Stay calm. I've got it right here." Owen wiped the perspiration off his upper lip, then opened the pink envelope, unfolded the letter, and started to read:

Dear Tim,

I'm writing this letter because I'm certain you're not the biological father of my daughter, Anna Kathleen O'Rourke, and I think you suspect as much.

Her father is Owen Jones, a young man I met at a fundraiser for Senator Poston nine months before Annie was born. Owen and I had far too much to drink, and I invited him to my room at the Spartan Hotel.

He left this tie and business card in the room when he left, and I saved them, thinking he intended them as an invitation for me to call him. I never did. But when I found out I was pregnant, these items took on new importance and I put them away for safekeeping.

After Annie was born, I made it a point to find out her blood type, which was B—yours and mine is O, so any children of ours would also have O. I'm certain that Owen Jones's blood type is the same as hers.

I don't have the courage to tell you this right now. I'm too afraid of your reaction. But I know if anything ever happens to me, you can't handle raising Annie.

You've never loved her. Perhaps deep down, you've always known she's not yours.

I'm not proud of my infidelities, but I am proud of my beautiful daughter. She is the one worthwhile contribution I've made to this world. If something should happen to me, I beg you to take the items in this envelope, including this letter, and find Owen Jones and tell him that Annie is his daughter. Please don't make her pay for my mistake.

I'm sorry for the pain I've caused.

Corinne

P.S. To Owen Jones: Just so you'll know it's really me, Corinne O'Rourke, writing this, here are some things that stood out to me over the course of that evening: You had dated Senator Poston's daughter when you were in college. You loved the taste of beer and green olives. You had a tiny blue light on your key ring that lit up the entire room when you pressed the button. You had a heart-shaped birthmark on your right shoulder blade. And in your black leather Ralph Lauren wallet, you had a photograph of you and your sister Hailey.

Hailey! Owen put the letter back in the envelope, thinking there was no way he was going to jeopardize his marriage to Hailey by confessing that his one-night stand with this woman happened during the time they were dating. And that there were others.

"Satisfied?" Tim said.

Owen slid the pink envelope into the manila envelope and didn't say anything.

Annie looked up at Tim and started to whine. "I want Mommy. I wanna go home."

Tim grabbed her by the arm and shoved her toward Owen. "You're going home with him!"

Owen took the little girl's hand, then bent down and picked up her shabby teddy bear and led her over to his desk chair and set her in it. He turned and took a slow, deep breath. "How about putting the gun down, Tim?"

"No."

"Come on, man. You've just gone through a horrible ordeal. No one in your shoes would be thinking straight. Let's talk this through."

Tim waved the gun at Owen. "You're not in a position to tell me anything. You're the one who should pay. It's your fault all this happened!"

19

Gordy Jameson stood on the back deck of Gordy's Crab Shack, vaguely aware of Billy Lewis wiping down the plastic chairs and umbrella tables with Clorox water. A damp, balmy breeze blew off the gulf, and off in the distance he saw half a dozen white dots on the horizon, probably fishing charters headed toward blue water or any number of sunken vessels where reef fish were plentiful.

He heard the back door open and then felt warm hands kneading his shoulders.

"Hi, love," Pam Jameson said. "What has you so lost in thought?"

"Oh, just a little fishin' fever. Maybe we should take the boat out one day this week. It'd be good for us to get out on the water after workin' the holiday weekend. I sure don't wanna burn out my *cash cow*." He slipped his arm around her and winked at Billy.

Pam chuckled. "Then I'd better make plenty of pies so Weezie won't run out. She'll have a conniption fit if we don't make our 200 percent increase in dessert sales this month."

The corner of Gordy's mouth twitched. "Really bugs her that I keep givin' it away and sales keep goin' up."

The back door opened again, and Gordy turned and saw Will Seevers standing in the doorway.

"Hey, Will. What brings you in so early?"

"I'd like to have a cup of coffee with my best friend. You got a few minutes?"

"Yeah, sure. Let me come in where it's cool."

Gordy went inside and followed Will over to a booth and sat across from him. "What time does Meagan's plane leave?"

"About one. Margaret and the other mothers put the kids on a bus to Tallahassee at seven this morning. Meagan didn't sleep a wink last night. Think how much fun it would've been if *we'd* have gotten to do something like that at thirteen."

Gordy laughed. "Yeah, I think the most excitin' field trip we took in those days was to the Old Seaport Dairy."

"Here you go," Pam said. She put a mug of steaming coffee in front of Will and then Gordy. "Okay, guys. You've got the place to yourselves. It's back to the ovens for me."

Will glanced up as if to make sure Pam was out of earshot, then ran his finger around the rim of the coffee mug. "What I'm going to tell you stays between us, okay?"

"Yeah, sure. What's on your mind?"

Owen stood motionless, images of Hailey and Daniel racing through his mind as he looked down the barrel of Tim O'Rourke's gun.

"Give me one good reason why I shouldn't kill you," Tim said.

"Because that little girl behind me will never get over it, and she's not the one you want to punish."

"I have to kill all three of us. It's the only way." Tim glanced beyond Owen, his arm tautly outstretched, the barrel of the gun starting to shake. "Someone has to pay."

"You're not a killer, man. You didn't even cheat on Corinne when you knew she'd been unfaithful. You're bigger than this, Tim. Put down the gun." Owen eased forward a few inches.

"Stay back! I mean it! Get over there by Annie!"

Owen slowly backed up, his palms held out in front of him, and stood next to the desk chair where the child sat, silent. He put his hand on the arm of the chair and Annie's little fingers closed tightly around his thumb.

"This is not what I came here to do!" Tim said, his eyes brimming with tears. "Why couldn't you have just agreed to take Annie?"

"Look, if it means that much to you, I'll take her. You can leave. I won't try to stop you."

"Shut your lying mouth!" Tim said. "You think I'm stupid? The minute I leave here, you'll call the police and I'll be locked up for threatening you! It's over."

Helen's voice came over the intercom. "Mr. Jones, you have a call on line one. It's your broker."

"Tell him I'll call him back."

"Do you want me to hold your calls?"

"Uh, yes, thank you."

"Would you like me to bring you coffee and refreshments? One of the salesmen brought in Krispy Kreme doughnuts."

Owen looked questioningly at Tim, who shook his head and mouthed the words, *Get rid of her.*

Owen's mind raced faster than his pulse. If he told Helen to call 911, would it push Tim over the edge? Did he dare chance it? "No thanks, Helen. That'll be all."

Owen was aware of Annie tightening her grip on his thumb. "Tim, this is between you and me. How about letting Annie leave?"

"No, she's not going anywhere."

"Why not? She isn't the one you want to hurt."

"How do you know what I want?" Tim shouted, and then glanced over at the door as if he were double-checking to be sure it was locked. "Maybe I want to take you both down with me. Maybe I'm sick of being used by everyone else. Maybe just once *I'd* like to be in control!"

Owen sensed a frightening urgency in Tim's voice. "Look, man. Killing us and yourself will only put you in charge for a few seconds. You still have to face God. You believe in God, don't you, Tim?"

"What's it to you?"

"I don't think He wants you to do this."

"Then He should've protected me from HIV! What've I got to live for now?"

Owen stared at Tim, unable to think of a single reason and wishing he knew how to talk about spiritual things the way Hailey did.

"Yeah, that's what I thought," Tim said, cocking the gun. "You got anything else to say before—"

"Wait!" Owen's mouth watered as a wave of nausea rushed over him. "Please don't kill me. I've got a little boy who needs me. I'll take care of Annie just like you asked me to. You can walk out that door right now and never look back. Nobody else knows about the gun, and I don't have to tell the police anything that happened in here. It stays between me and you."

"You expect me to believe that?"

"Come on, you came here to leave Annie, and I've agreed to take her. That's what you really wanted. So why not leave the way you planned? I give you my word I won't send anyone after you. I just don't want to die."

"Yeah, well, I didn't either." Tim O'Rourke lowered the gun and took a step toward Owen and Annie, his eyes fixed on the little girl's fingers still clutching Owen's thumb. "I'm sorry Mommy died, Annie." Tim let out a sob and, in the next instant, seemed to inhale it. "Daddy's sick, and I don't want to live any-more. This man is your real daddy. He's going to take care of you."

Tim moved his eyes to Owen, a tear escaping down his cheek. "I've decided to let you live. I want you to suffer for the rest of your life remembering what a mess you made of mine." Tim put the gun barrel in his mouth.

Owen spun around and dropped to his knees in front of the

desk chair and pulled Annie to his chest, the deafening sound of a gunshot paralyzing them for what seemed an eternity.

He was aware of a loud ringing in his ears. People hollering. Fists pounding the door. Someone shouting his name over and over. He held tightly to Annie, urine running down her legs and pooling on the carpet, and realized they were still alive.

Will Seevers took a sip of coffee and looked up at Gordy. "I have reason to believe the guy who killed Jackson Kincaid is still in Seaport."

"What makes you think so?"

Will told Gordy what had been happening at Ellen and Guy's house with Lawrence and Owen thinking someone was in the yard, and about Owen's phone encounters with some guy named Tim O'Rourke. "We tried to make a connection and can't. My guess is whoever's been sneaking around the Joneses' place is looking to keep Lawrence Madison from talking."

"I sure don't like hearin' that."

"I know. I hope I'm wrong, Gordy, but I can't afford not to go with that premise till I know differently. Since you spend time with Mr. Madison, I thought you should be made aware of it. I don't want him talking about the case with your buddies, okay?"

"Yeah, okay, Will. I'll make sure it doesn't happen. Do you think this guy wants to hurt Lawrence?"

"I don't know anything for sure. But if I'm right about it being him, he's already killed once."

Owen sat next to Annie on a couch in the CEO's office, his hands folded between his knees, Annie wrapped in a sheet the paramedics had provided. The Department of Children and Families would be there any minute to take her away.

On the other side of the closed door, authorities scrambled

to get statements from the Global Communications staff, and crime scene investigators had arrived to reconstruct the scene inside Owen's office.

"You're going to be okay, Annie," Owen said gently. "Some nice people are coming to get you. They have a lot of experience with little girls and will take really good care of you."

"I want my mommy," Annie said.

Owen didn't know how to respond and was glad when the door opened and Helen stuck her head in the room.

"How are you doing?" she said.

"I'm numb at the moment. I think we both are."

"Can I get you something to eat or drink, honey?" Helen said to Annie.

"I want my mommy."

Owen caught Helen's gaze and, for a split second, they commiserated.

"I saw Hailey pull up," Helen said. "Do you want me to ask the police to let her in here?"

"Uh, no. Would you ask her to wait in the reception area? I'm going to stay here with Annie until DCF arrives."

"Okay." Helen pulled the door closed.

Owen sat in silence for a few minutes and then said, "Does your teddy bear have a name?"

Annie nodded. "Milton."

"Milton, huh? That's a nice name."

Annie turned and looked up at him, her blue eyes wide and questioning. "Are you my daddy now?"

"Well…that's what your other—I mean, that's what your daddy said, but I don't know if it's true."

"Is he with the angels?" Annie said. "Mommy's with the angels."

"I'm sure he's with your mommy." Owen was thinking he wasn't sure of anything, least of all where Corinne and Tim might be.

Annie took Milton by the paws and bounced him up and down on her knees. "Can I come to *your* house?"

"I don't know anything about taking care of little girls. The nice people at DCF are going to find you a happy place to live."

"I have a swing at my house. And a twicycle. And my doggy's name is Oscar." Annie pushed the curls out of her eyes. "He's a wiener dog."

Owen smiled without meaning to. "You mean a dachshund?"

"Yes, and Mommy bought him a gween bowl with his name on it. Do you got a dog?"

"No, but I have a little boy. His name is Daniel."

"Do you got a little girl?"

Owen sighed, guilt clawing his conscience like fingernails on a chalkboard. "Annie, I need you to listen to me. Some nice people are going to be here soon, and you're going to go with them."

"But I wanna come with you." A tear rolled down her cheek.

Owen reached over and stroked Annie's blond curls, thinking how much her round blue eyes looked like his mother's. "I know you do. But you can't."

"Why?"

"Because there are laws to protect little girls when they can't live with their Mommy and Daddy anymore. These people will keep you safe."

"Oscar keeps me safe. He barks weally, weally loud when the mailman comes."

Owen glanced at his watch and wondered what was taking DCF so long.

"Your name is Owen."

"That's right," he said, surprised she remembered.

"And *Daddy*."

Owen jumped up and looked out the window, his hands deep in his pockets. There was a knock on the door. He turned and saw a woman, whose hair was pulled into a single braid, standing in the doorway with a nylon bag in her hand.

"Mr. Jones, I'm Janet Stanton from DCF. I'm going to be Annie's caseworker."

Owen stood with his arm around Hailey and watched CSIs coming and going from the office where Tim O'Rourke's body still lay. The door to the CEO's office opened, and Janet Stanton emerged with Annie, who had been outfitted in a bright blue dress that made her eyes look like sapphires.

"That's Annie?" Hailey Jones said. "What a beautiful little girl."

"I should say something to her. I'll be right back." Owen went up to Annie and squatted in front of her. "Don't you look pretty?"

"I got a new dwess. This one is dwy."

"I see that. Is Miss Janet taking you to your new home?"

Annie's eyes suddenly brimmed with tears. "I want to come to your house!" She threw her arms around Owen's neck.

He held on to Annie and looked up at Janet as if to say, *What do I do now?*

"I'll be in touch," Janet said. "I have all the appropriate information and phone numbers. Annie, we need to leave now. Can you tell Mr. Jones good-bye?"

Annie shook her head and didn't loosen her grip.

Owen heard her sniffling and caressed her back. "I'll see you again soon. Miss Janet will make sure you have everything you need. Do you think you can be a big girl and trust her? She seems awfully nice."

"Don't leave me," Annie pleaded.

Owen swallowed the emotion and wondered if he was going to get through the farewell without losing it. "I'll tell you what. If Miss Janet says it's okay for me to visit with you, then we'll talk about it in a few days, after you're settled. It's been a sad day. Miss Janet wants to take you some place happy, okay?"

Annie nodded and loosened her grip and then let go. "Okay."

Owen took a handkerchief out of his pocket and wiped the tears off her cheeks. "You and I are buddies, right?"

Annie nodded. "And Milton."

"Yes, and Milton."

Janet reached down and brushed away the hair that was stuck to Annie's damp face. "Do you like grilled cheese sandwiches?"

Annie nodded. "And pickles."

"Me, too. Let's go get a grilled cheese for lunch." Janet glanced at Hailey and then locked gazes with Owen. "It's hard to say what kind of an effect today's experience will have on her. But it's obvious she feels safe with you. Why don't you and your wife talk things over, and I'll be in touch in the next few days."

Owen's eyes followed Annie O'Rourke as she walked away, Janet holding her left hand and Milton dangling from her right.

"What did the caseworker mean when she said you and I should talk things over?" Hailey said. "What things?"

Owen felt as though his mouth were filled with cotton and his heart with lead. He could hardly grasp that in a single instant his life had been changed, his entire history rewritten.

"Owen, are you all right?"

"Huh? Sorry, honey, I'm still out of it. The police are finished with me. Let's go home."

20

Police Chief Will Seevers started to walk out of his office and head for Ellen Jones's house when he heard the receptionist's voice on the intercom. "Chief, you still there?"

"Barely. What is it?"

"Police Chief Davison is on line one. Says it's important."

"Okay, thanks." Will went over and picked up the phone. "Hey, Mack, how are things in Port Smyth?"

"Oh, we're cleaning up a real mess," Mack said. "I understand you're looking for a guy named Tim O'Rourke."

"Yeah, how'd you know that?"

"I spent some time this morning with a young fella named Owen Jones. Says you know him."

"Yeah, I do."

"Well, we got a 911 call from Global Communications a couple hours ago. O'Rourke swallowed his gun in Jones's office."

Will put his hand on the back of his neck. "Good grief."

"Jones told us you'd been investigating a prowler at his folk's house and thought it might be this O'Rourke fella."

"Yeah, but we'd eliminated him as a suspect. Any idea what he was doing in Owen Jones's office?"

"Yeah, Jones told us the whole story."

Will listened as Mack Davison told him everything he knew about O'Rourke's phone calls, how he had gained access to the office, and his claim that Owen Jones was Annie O'Rourke's biological father.

"I'll tell you what," Mack said. "Jones and that little girl are lucky to be breathing right now. Could've gone the other way real easy."

"So O'Rourke claimed the little girl is Owen's?"

"Yeah, he had a manila envelope full of stuff to prove it. I'm sure we'll be turning that over to DCF."

"At least Owen and the little girl weren't hurt."

"Not on the outside anyway. I have a feeling it's going to be a long time before they can put this out of their minds."

Owen got in the passenger side of Hailey's Lexus and sank into the seat, wishing he could disappear.

"Did you think to call your mom and tell her what happened?" Hailey asked.

"No."

"Well, you need to before she hears it on the news." Hailey handed him her cell phone.

"I don't feel like talking to anyone right now."

"All right, I'll call her. What do you want me to say?"

"Just tell her Tim O'Rourke's dead and we don't have to worry about him anymore."

"You know Ellen's not going to be satisfied with that explanation. She'll want details."

Owen sighed. "Honey, tell her whatever you want. Let's just get away from here, okay?" Owen closed his eyes and for a split second was back in his office looking down the barrel of Tim's gun. He opened his eyes and stared out the window.

"Ellen, it's Hailey. Owen's all right, but a horrible thing's happened. Tim O'Rourke showed up at Owen's office and ended up shooting himself…Yes, he's dead…I just picked up Owen and we're on our way home…I don't have all the details right now. The guy had his four-year-old daughter with him, and she's been turned over to the Department of Children and Families...I know, it's heartbreaking...Owen gave his statement to the police, but we haven't had a moment to ourselves to discuss who the guy was or what he wanted...I need to get Owen home. He's pretty shaken..." Hailey tapped Owen on the shoulder and mouthed the words, *Do you want to say something?*

Owen shook his head.

"Ellen, we'll call you later, okay...? I'll tell him. We love you, too."

Hailey clipped her cell phone on the visor. "She said to tell you she loves you. She sounded worried."

"Do you mind if we go some place quiet?" Owen said. "I'm just not ready to go home. I need to get my head on straight."

"All right. Daniel will be fine with Shayla. Why don't we go sit in the park under our sycamore tree? When you're ready to tell me what happened, I'll be there to listen. You don't have to talk till you feel like it."

Feel like it? Owen knew he would never feel like it, but he would have to tell Hailey everything—and soon.

Ellen Jones turned on the TV to the local news station and saw only regular programming. She turned it off and went into the kitchen where Lawrence was drinking a glass of lemonade at the breakfast bar.

"You act like you've got a bee in your bonnet," Lawrence said.

"Hailey just called. Tim O'Rourke went to Owen's office and shot himself. Owen's not hurt, but I don't know what happened."

The doorbell rang and Ellen rushed to the front door, glad to see Will Seevers standing on the porch.

"Sorry I didn't get over here earlier," he said. "Something came up. Is this a good time?"

"Did you know that Tim O'Rourke shot himself?"

"As a matter of fact, I did. That's why I'm late. Chief Davison over in Port Smyth called me and filled me in."

"Well, I wish someone would fill *me* in. Hailey called and gave me a quick overview. Said she was going to take Owen home, that he was pretty shaken."

"All I can really tell you is that O'Rourke went to Owen's office with his four-year-old daughter and waited until Owen arrived. There was some sort of confrontation, and O'Rourke shot himself."

Ellen studied Will's face. "What kind of confrontation?"

"You'd have to ask Owen. Chief Davison just wanted me to know O'Rourke was dead from a self-inflicted gunshot wound and no one is going to be charged with anything."

"How did he know to call you?"

"Owen told him we were looking for O'Rourke and why."

Ellen noticed Will was avoiding looking directly at her. "What aren't you telling me?"

"Like I said, you need to ask Owen. Can I come in and explain why we eliminated Tim O'Rourke as a suspect even before this happened?"

"Yes, of course."

Ellen led Will into the living room, where Lawrence was already seated on the couch.

"Hello, Mr. Madison," Will said. "You're looking chipper today."

"Dad, you remember Chief Seevers? He's here to talk about the man in the Old Glory shirt."

Lawrence's eyebrows gathered. "Do I know you?"

"Yes, we've met."

Ellen sat on the couch next to her father and Will sat on the love seat facing them.

"If Tim O'Rourke isn't the one who's been snooping around here," Ellen said, "then who is?"

Will clasped his hands between his knees. "Unfortunately, I

think it may be the man who stabbed Jackson Kincaid. Mr. Madison is the only one who has given a description of the attacker or claims to have seen him."

"You think Dad's in danger?"

"I don't know. But I can't afford not to think that way. I suggest you keep the security alarm on all the time. I'm having a police cruiser go up and down the block around your home once an hour, 24-7. That should deter whoever's been out there."

"But Dad isn't even sure of what he saw!"

"Kincaid's killer doesn't know that."

Owen sat on a familiar wrought-iron bench in Port Smyth Park, his arm draped around Hailey's shoulders and his eyes looking up at the glints of sunlight coming through the branches of the giant sycamore tree. It was here he had come with Hailey to relish the news that she was pregnant. It was here they had sat, planning out the nursery, and here they had brought their infant son for his first family outing. Would it also be here that life as they had known it would cease to be? Would Hailey stand by him? Leave him? Grow cold to his touch?

Owen heard the four o'clock whistle at the Holstein Bakery plant across the river. He couldn't put off telling Hailey any longer. *God, if You'll help Hailey forgive me, I'll do anything—even start going to Sunday school. But please…don't let me lose her over this.*

"You still awake?" he said.

Hailey squeezed his hand. "I'm here. Are you feeling less stressed?"

"I need to tell you what happened."

Owen focused his eyes on a little girl sitting on a blanket, seemingly having a tea party with a Raggedy Ann doll, a man sitting on a nearby bench, his head buried in the newspaper.

"Tim O'Rourke was the husband of a woman I met at a

fundraiser for Senator Poston. Her name was Corinne. She died in a car accident a couple weeks ago."

"I'm sorry. But what does that have to do with you?"

Owen felt as though his mouth were wired shut. How could he find the right words to lessen the blow?

"Owen?"

"Uh, Tim came here to give me something he says belongs to me."

Hailey's eyebrows furrowed. "Something of Corinne's?"

"Yes. And mine, according to him."

"What?"

Owen took a deep breath and slowly let it out until he had just enough air left to say, "Annie."

Hailey's hand went limp. She sat for maybe a minute and then turned to him. "*You* are Annie's father?"

"I don't know. Tim said I am."

"Just the fact that you don't know says a lot!" Hailey let go of his hand. "The guy was obviously unstable. We can't just take his word for it!"

"I know that. Let me back up and start at the beginning." Owen told Hailey everything that had happened in his office from the time he walked in and found Tim and Annie sitting on his couch until Tim shot himself. "I haven't had time to process the whole thing. But my blood type *is* B. It's possible I'm Annie's father. I guess only a paternity test could prove it one way or the other."

"That means you slept with this Corinne when you were dating me." Hailey started to cry. "How could you?"

"Honey, we weren't dating exclusively then. We weren't committed."

"Obviously!"

"Look, I never hid the fact that I sowed some wild oats when I was single."

"Well, you left out the part about sleeping around when you

weren't spending weekends at my apartment. Or didn't you think that was important?"

Owen put his hand on his neck and rubbed. "Those other women weren't important. *You* were. Once I realized I was falling in love with you, I never even looked at another woman."

"There were others?"

"A few. But not after we decided we were serious."

"And just when was that defining, magical moment?"

"Come on, honey, neither of us was dating the other exclusively. You were dating other men."

"Well, I sure didn't sleep with anyone else!"

Owen put his elbows on his knees and rested his chin on his palms. "I had no morals. I admit it. But I wasn't a Christian yet. I didn't see anything wrong with what I was doing."

"And it never occurred to you to protect yourself from HIV?"

"I usually did. Corinne and I were drunk."

"Did you even think to get tested?"

Owen shook his head.

"I can't believe you played Russian roulette with *my* life! What kind of love is that, Owen? What kind of man does that?"

A curtain of silence fell between them.

Minutes passed, and finally Hailey said, "Well, the first thing you need to do is get tested for HIV." She put her hand over her mouth and choked back the tears. "What if it comes back positive? What if you've infected me? What if Daniel has HIV?"

Any words Owen might have mustered were too heavy to pass from his heart to his mouth. He shuddered with regret and fear.

"What are you going to do about Annie?" Hailey said. "You can't just dump her into the system. This isn't her fault either."

Owen opened his mouth and forced out the words. "I haven't thought it through yet. I probably should do a paternity test. But whether I'm her biological father or not, I feel like I should keep in contact with her for a while. The way she clung to me when Tim…" Owen paused to regain his composure. "It's going to be a long time before she gets over what he did—if she ever does. She feels safe with me. Tim told her I'm her real daddy. All she needs is to feel abandoned a third time."

"I agree," Hailey said.

"You do?"

Hailey wiped the tears off her cheeks. "I'm furious with you for being so irresponsible. But I'm not heartless toward Annie. The poor thing has suffered more than any child should have to."

Owen blinked rapidly, but the tears came anyway. "I'm sorry, honey. I confessed all this when I became a Christian and thought this part of my life was behind me. It never even occurred to me that I'd gotten anyone pregnant, been exposed to HIV, or ruined someone's marriage. I can hardly believe this is happening now, when I've finally got my act together."

"What are you going to tell your folks?"

Owen closed his eyes and leaned his head back. "The truth. But I can't begin to imagine how angry they're going to be. It's not as though they didn't caution me time and time again."

21

Early Tuesday evening, Ellen Jones heard the garage door open and walked out into the kitchen and disarmed the security alarm. A few seconds later, Guy Jones walked in the door and locked gazes with her, then set his brief case and hang-up bag on the breakfast bar and pulled Ellen into his arms.

She closed her eyes and allowed herself to feel swallowed up in a sense of safety. "Did Brent give you a hard time about working at home this week?"

"Not at all," Guy said. "Is Owen here yet? I didn't see his car."

"He's on his way."

"What's the big mystery?"

"I don't know. There was obviously something between him and Tim O'Rourke. He and Hailey have been evasive about it on the phone. And Will certainly didn't want to talk about it."

"Poor kid. Had to be tough being there when the guy shot himself. How are you doing with Will's suspicion about Jackson Kincaid's killer?"

"It seems like a bad dream. I quit the newspaper so we could live in peace, and now we have to deal with some killer who wants to keep Dad from talking. When will it stop?"

Guy held her close and gently stroked her back. "Let's take this a step at a time. Where's Lawrence?"

"He's in the guest room watching TV. I'm not even sure he understands what's going on."

"Did you tell him?"

Ellen nodded. "Yes, but Dad didn't even recognize Will. I'm just sure he's got Alzheimer's. One more thing we don't need."

"I heard a car door," Guy said. He let go of Ellen and walked to the front door. A few seconds later, she heard Owen's voice.

Ellen watched her son's face as he walked toward her, and she thought he seemed dark and troubled. "Hi, honey." She put her arms tightly around him. "Why don't you go sit and I'll get you some lemonade?"

"All right. Thanks."

Ellen went out to the kitchen and put three glasses of lemonade on a tray and took them into the living room. "Here you go. I thought maybe Hailey would come with you."

"Shayla couldn't stay late, and it'd be too hard to have a serious discussion if Daniel was with us."

Owen sat with his hands folded between his knees and seemed to be staring at the floor. "Guess there's no need to beat around the bush about this. Tim O'Rourke *did* come to give me something he claims is mine."

"We surmised that much," Guy said. "What was it?"

Owen wrung his hands and looked up at Guy and then Ellen. "Annie."

The silence was suddenly louder than all the jumbled thoughts screaming in Ellen's head.

"Oh no," she said. "Annie is *yours*?"

Owen shrugged. "I'm not sure. But it's possible." Owen sat with his shoulders slumped and laboriously relayed the entire experience, including his reading the contents of Corinne's letter to Tim. "I can't believe this is happening now. I stopped fooling around once I fell for Hailey."

"Well, you're certainly not going to claim responsibility until we find out if you're the girl's biological father!" Guy said. "You'll need to take a paternity test."

"I know that, Dad. But whether I am or not, my marriage to Hailey is damaged. She knows I was sleeping around when we were dating. She's devastated." Owen looked up at Ellen as if to beg for mercy, his eyes brimming with tears. "You tried to warn me, but I wouldn't listen."

"That's hardly the point," she heard herself say. "What's important now is that you and Hailey work through this. And that we find out if Annie is your daughter—and our grand-daughter."

"Corinne's letter said Annie's blood type is B—same as mine," Owen said.

Guy shook his head. "That doesn't prove you're her father. You can't tell me you're the only one this Corinne was sleeping with."

"Annie looks so much like Mom as a little girl it's eerie." Owen made a tent with his fingers. "I kept trying not to see it, but it's plain as day. Wait'll you see her."

Ellen sat stunned, considering the implications and wondering if she could handle another crisis right now.

Owen drove past a row of crape myrtle trees and turned into the driveway, then pulled his Jaguar into the garage and turned off the motor.

He sat with the back of his head leaned against the leather headrest, trying to remember what he could of the events that led to his one-night stand with Corinne O'Rourke. He remembered spotting her talking to Senator Poston's daughter at the fundraiser, looking ravishing in a long red dress that conformed to her feminine curves and had set his mind reeling with possibilities...

"Well, look who's here," Owen had said to Maureen Poston, trying not to stare at the gorgeous blonde standing with her. "I wondered if you'd be here tonight."

"Owen?" Maureen said. "Oh, my goodness, how long has it been? Four years? Five?"

"Something like that." Owen felt the corners of his mouth

twitch as he entertained a flashback of the steamy weekend they had spent together in Acapulco after their college graduation. "So who's your friend?"

"This is Corinne O'Rourke. She works for Daddy's advertising agency. Corinne, this is Owen Jones. We went to college together."

Owen held out his hand to Corinne, his mind ablaze with lustful thoughts. "Nice to meet you." He forced his eyes from Corinne's cleavage back to Maureen's face. "So what's going on in your life?"

He couldn't recall the conversation that followed, only that he could hardly keep his eyes off the voluptuous woman with the alluring blue eyes who made even an attractive woman like Maureen seem dull in comparison. He vaguely remembered being introduced to Maureen's fiancé and a few minutes later being left alone with Corinne, Maureen looking over her shoulder with a wink and a nod.

He and Corinne started off with martinis and basic chitchat, which led to more martinis and stimulating political conversation. Then more martinis and some suggestive talk that finally exploded into action in Corinne's hotel room—something he had no intention of ever telling Hailey...

Owen sat up straight and hit the steering wheel with his palms. How could he have possibly foreseen this?

He got out of the car and walked from the detached garage into the side door of the house. He poked his head in the kitchen and saw Hailey sitting at the table, her face red and swollen. He went over and sat across from her and took her hands in his, unable to think of anything to say that might comfort her.

"How did your parents take the news?" Hailey said.

"They're extremely disappointed, but at least they didn't say, 'We told you so.' I didn't say anything to them about Corinne having HIV. I didn't see the point in giving them something else to worry about."

Hailey pulled her hands free. "Poor Annie. None of this is her fault. Can you even imagine how scared and lost she must feel?"

Owen could well imagine it and wished Hailey would talk about something else. "I honestly don't know what I'm going to do if I *am* her biological father. The kid doesn't even know me."

"She knows you protected her."

"A heck of an icebreaker." Owen waited for a minute, wishing Hailey would make eye contact and finally said, "Honey, look at me. I can't tell you how sorry I am all this is happening. But I promise I've been faithful to you since the first time I told you I loved you. I confessed all this stuff when I became a Christian. God's forgiven me. I need to know you have, too."

"Forgiven you?" Hailey's eyes welled with tears. "I'm not sure it's even registered yet. This could wreck our marriage, not to mention our health, and all you can think about is being forgiven? Well, don't hold your breath, Owen. It's not my job to salve your guilty conscience! You have no one to blame but yourself."

"I know that. But it's history. This happened five years ago."

Hailey wiped a tear off her cheek. "For you. But for me, it's only been eight hours."

Ellen stood in the alcove of the widow's watch, her head resting against the glass, and watched a ribbon of moonlight shimmering on the gulf waters. How she longed to be outside, running along the surf. Or sitting in her rocker on the veranda. Free from fear. From caregiving. From worry.

She looked down and let her eyes search the thick darkness in the backyard. She didn't see any movement and wondered if the lurker had returned or even knew the police had gathered evidence.

The thought of being cooped up in a locked house had been almost more than she could bear. And now Owen's situation.

Lord, help him to work things out with Hailey. And to make the right decision about Annie.

Annie? Ellen could hardly imagine being a grandmother to this little girl she had yet to meet. She tried to imagine the kind of torment that drove Tim O'Rourke to end his life in such a violent way and wondered if Owen was struggling with guilt.

She heard footsteps coming up the spiral staircase and then sensed someone standing in the doorway behind her.

"Honey, what are you doing up here?" Guy said.

"Looking out. Wishing I were jogging along the surf instead of feeling like a trapped animal."

"So let's go jogging."

Ellen sighed. "Right. And what do we do with Dad?"

"Set the alarm when we leave. He's sound asleep."

"What if he wakes up and can't remember where he is? Besides, we can't leave him alone until Jackson Kincaid's killer is caught."

"That may never happen. Plus, we don't know for sure it was the killer who was in our backyard. For all we know, it may actually have been Tim O'Rourke."

Ellen sighed. "I can't believe Owen didn't ask him."

"That's not the kind of question you ask when a guy's holding a gun on you."

Ellen shuddered. "When I think how close Owen came to..."

Guy came over and put his arms around Ellen and rested his cheek next to hers. "Let's be thankful that he's unharmed."

"I don't think his being held at gunpoint, witnessing a suicide, and finding out he's fathered a child equates to 'unharmed.'"

"You know what I mean."

Ellen nestled against Guy's chest. "I wonder if Annie's his."

"I have my doubts."

"Well, regardless, he and Hailey have a long road ahead of them. I sure hope she's able to forgive him and go on."

"Owen's been a good husband and father. She'll get over it."

"Women don't just 'get over it' the way men do. It'll be hard work trusting him again."

"Ellen, it's been five years."

"That doesn't change the fact that he deceived her, which has planted in her mind the idea that he could deceive her again and she'd never know."

"He's changed."

"You and I believe that. But Hailey has to work through it, and we need to pray she will. If Annie turns out to be Owen's, they've got some serious decisions to make."

Owen lay on the wicker couch on the screened-in porch, his knees bent, his hands behind his head, and looked through the tree branches at the bright moon in the night sky. His eyes were tired, but every time he had closed them, he saw either Tim O'Rourke's gun pointed at him or Annie's round blue eyes pleading with him not to leave her.

Hailey didn't want him in bed with her. It was hard to fault her for being angry. No matter how he had tried to justify his actions, he *had* deceived her and put them both at risk for HIV. She had every right to feel betrayed. All he could hope for now was that he would test negative, and that she'd believe he'd been faithful from the time he had first expressed his love for her.

God, please make Hailey know I'm telling the truth.

Owen's eyelids grew heavy and he let them close. A deafening gunshot resounded in his head, and he clutched the throw pillow to his chest, his heart racing, and opened his eyes. He lay trembling in the dark and wondered if Annie O'Rourke was having nightmares. And if anyone besides Milton would be there to calm her fears.

22

On Wednesday morning Police Chief Will Seevers sat at his computer, finishing a cup of coffee and sausage biscuit while he reviewed the case notes on Jackson Kincaid's murder.

Investigator Al Backus breezed through the doorway and pulled up a chair next to the computer and sat, his arms folded. "We're back to square one."

"At least O'Rourke's out of the picture."

"So we're looking for a right-handed guy who's five-nine and bald with a pot gut—who may not even exist. We're spinning our wheels. I think it's time to throw in the towel and admit we're not going to get this one."

"I'm not willing to give up yet. I want you to—"

A voice came over the intercom. "Chief, Jack Rutgers is on line one."

"Okay, thanks." Will rolled his chair over to the phone. "Yeah, Jack. What's up?"

"We've got another stabbing death."

"Where?"

"Bougainvillea Park. A fifty-two-year-old Hispanic male from Waco, Texas. Two joggers found him lying near a park bench at the top of the hiking trail. Chest wound. Just like Kincaid's."

"Okay, Jack. I'm on my way."

Will hung up the phone and looked over at Al. "We've got

another dead stabbing victim. Maybe this time the perp left us some evidence."

Will grabbed his keys and hurried down the hall and out the side door. He jogged over to his car, waited for Al to get in, then headed down Main Street toward Bougainvillea Park.

Ellen ran in the wet sand along the surf, the wind tussling with her hair, and enjoyed a sense of freedom with every gulp of oxygen she took in. Finally, she dropped down in the dry sand and lay on her back, yielding herself to the arms of the beach.

She looked up at the bluebird sky, not even disappointed that she had missed the sunrise. How grateful she was to be free from the chains of caregiving for an entire hour! By the time she got back, Guy would have gotten Lawrence to eat every bite of his breakfast—something she could rarely get him to do.

Ellen's eyes followed a flock of pelicans soaring overhead, and her thoughts turned to her prayer concerns. She prayed for Owen and Hailey's marriage. And for Annie's well-being. She prayed that Daniel and Shayla would develop a healthy bond and that Roland would make a full recovery from his hip replacement. She asked God to help Guy get his work done in spite of having to be at home with the stress. She prayed that the police would find the man who killed Jackson Kincaid. And that God would change her heart toward her father, though she doubted it was even possible.

Ellen closed her eyes and just praised the Lord for several minutes, letting her thoughts rise to the throne of grace.

The sound of giggling distracted her, and she opened her eyes and saw Gordy and Pam Jameson running along the surf toward her, a black Labrador retriever running several yards in front of them.

She waved her arms. "Hi, you two!"

The couple ran over to Ellen and dropped down in the

sand next to her, the Lab bouncing from Gordy to Pam, licking their faces.

Ellen put up her hands in time to keep a wet tongue from swiping her cheek.

Gordy pulled the dog to him and held it by its collar. "Cool it, Dusky."

"What are you doing on the beach on a Wednesday morning?" Ellen asked.

"We're takin' the day off," Gordy said. "Thought we'd go for a walk, then get in the boat and head out to the deep water and see what we can catch. Pam's packed us a feast for lunch."

"Sounds like fun. I'd love a day like that." Ellen wondered if they had read the morning paper or seen last evening's news.

There was an uncomfortable stretch of silence and then Gordy said, "We read about what happened at Owen's office. We're really sorry. It must've been awful."

"Yes, it was."

Gordy's deep voice was suddenly soft. "I know it's real personal and all, but I want you to know Pam and I are here if you need us."

"Thanks. A few prayers would be appreciated, too."

"You've got that."

"Ellen, do you know where the little girl is?" Pam said.

"DCF has her. Her name's Annie. I can't imagine how she must be feeling." Ellen stopped to gather her composure. "I haven't talked to anyone else about this yet. You can imagine what a shock this is to our family. We have a great deal of sorting out to do."

"Just know we're here," Pam said. "Be sure to tell Owen we're so thankful he and Annie weren't hurt."

"Thanks, I will."

Dusky broke free from Gordy's arms and started running in circles and barking.

"That's our cue, darlin'." Gordy pulled Pam to her feet.

"There's no holdin' him back. Let's go fishin'."

"Have a great time," Ellen said.

Gordy held Pam's hand and took off running after Dusky. "We will. See you soon."

Ellen smiled at the sight of Gordy and Pam so happy. It didn't seem possible that it had been a year and a half since she attended their wedding. Or since Owen and Hailey had announced they were expecting Daniel. How Ellen wished she could turn back the clock so Owen wouldn't have to deal with the consequences of his past choices. She wondered what kind of impact the tension between him and Hailey might have on Daniel.

Will Seevers parked his squad car in the central parking area of Bougainvillea Park and walked with Al Backus up a gentle slope to where the hiking trail began. He saw a police SUV parked in the grass next to a CSI van. Half a dozen onlookers who appeared to be joggers were milling around.

Will walked up to Jack Rutgers, who was standing a few yards from where CSIs were taking pictures and gathering evidence. "Same MO as Kincaid?"

"Appears to be," Jack said. "We found a wallet next to the body. No credit cards or money. Just a driver's license belonging to Miguel Sanchez, age fifty-two. Come take a look." Jack led them over to where the victim lay and pulled back the sheet. "Does he look like a Miguel Sanchez to you?"

"Red hair?" Backus said. "No way is this guy Hispanic."

Will squatted next to the body. "I doubt he's fifty-two either. His beard doesn't have a strand of gray in it."

"Judging by how dirty his clothes are," Jack said, "and the fact that he stinks like he hasn't had a bath in a while, I'm thinking he's either homeless or a gypsy like the ones we ran out of here last summer. Maybe they're back."

Will sighed. "That's *all* we need. How long has he been dead?"

"The CSIs say eight to ten hours. That would put the time of death between 10:00 p.m. and midnight."

Will rose to his feet, his mind racing. "Should be easy enough to find out if Miguel Sanchez has reported his wallet stolen."

Al turned to one of the CSIs. "Did you find any DNA under the victim's fingernails?"

"We have to run tests to know for sure, but we got some fibers. No defensive wounds are present, though. Someone probably surprised him."

Al looked at Will, his eyebrow raised. "Maybe our perp followed this gypsy John Doe, hoping to steal the guy's booty."

"Maybe. I want you to start by finding Miguel Sanchez. And see if you can get an ID on the John Doe. Maybe some of the homeless people who live under the bridge know who he is. Maybe there's a pattern in all this, but something doesn't jibe."

"What do you mean?" Al said.

"In both stabbing cases, the empty wallet was found at the scene. How many thieves kill the victim and then stand there long enough to strip the wallet?"

"They usually run with it and pitch it later. Maybe this perp's extra fast. You have a better explanation?"

"Not yet. But something about this just doesn't feel right."

Owen Jones sat in the kitchen, his elbows on the table, his chin resting on his palms. He stared at the picture on the front page of the *North Coast Messenger* of Annie O'Rourke clutching Milton and climbing into the DCF van. He wondered if she was feeling as sad and empty as he was.

Finally, he forced his eyes lower on the page and began rereading the article.

RALEIGH MAN THREATENS HOSTAGES, KILLS HIMSELF

Port Smyth police responded to a 911 call placed at 9:17 a.m. yesterday from Global Communications, a large computer firm located in the north side business district. The female caller said that a shot had been fired inside the locked office of the company's chief financial officer and that two men and a little girl were inside the office.

Police arrived on the scene minutes later and found the office door open and a white male lying on the floor as a result of what appeared to be a self-inflicted gunshot wound. Timothy O'Rourke, 43, of Raleigh, N.C., was pronounced dead at the scene.

Two other people who had been in the office at the time of the shooting, Owen Jones, 31, of Port Smyth, who is the chief financial officer of Global Communications, and Annie O'Rourke, 4, of Raleigh, were unharmed.

Jones told police that Tim and Annie O'Rourke were waiting in his office when he arrived for work and that Tim O'Rourke alleged that Jones was the girl's biological father.

Port Smyth Police Chief Mack Davison told reporters that Tim O'Rourke and Jones argued for several minutes before O'Rourke pulled a .45-caliber handgun from his waistband and shot himself.

No charges have been filed in the case and the medical examiner has ruled the death a suicide.

Annie O'Rourke has been temporarily placed in the care of the Department of Children and Families pending further investigation.

Jones declined to comment.

Owen folded the newspaper and pushed it aside. He exhaled loudly and wondered if Hailey was speaking to him or if he would have to endure the silent treatment all day.

Hailey came into the kitchen, reached in the pantry, and pulled out a box of granola. "Do you want strawberries or bananas on your cereal?"

"Truthfully, I'm not hungry." He looked up at her. "Did Shayla read the morning paper?"

"She's fully aware of what's going on. Thank heavens she didn't make me feel awkward about it."

"Good." Owen picked up the paper and handed it to Hailey. "You might as well read what's in print."

She shook her head. "I don't need to rehash it."

"I just thought you might like to know what other people are reading since you may get asked questions."

"Well, I'm not answering questions for anyone. You're the one who got us into this mess. *You* answer them."

Owen got up and went over to her, his hands on her shoulders, his eyes gazing into hers. "Honey, I'm the same man today I was the day before yesterday. Don't lose the perspective that this happened five years ago. I was wild back then. I didn't believe in God or moral absolutes."

Hailey's face softened, her eyes brimming with tears. "I'm just so scared that I don't really know you."

Owen pulled her to his chest. "You know me to the core. I've got Jesus in my heart now. Can't you see that?"

"I think I do. I just can't bear the thought of being deceived. Without honesty, what do we have?"

Owen held her close and stroked her hair. "Hailey, I love you. And since the first time I said those words to you I have never even considered being with another woman. Please don't punish me for what God has already forgiven."

"I know you're forgiven, but you might have HIV! What are we supposed to do then?"

❀ ❀ ❀

Owen sat in the den, vaguely aware of Shayla playing peekaboo with Daniel out in the kitchen. He realized it was already lunchtime and that he was starting to feel hungry.

The phone rang and he started to let the machine get it, then decided to answer it. "Hello."

"This is Janet Stanton from DCF. May I speak with Mr. Jones, please?"

"This is Owen. Please, just call me by my first name."

"Thank you. I much prefer first names. I'm calling to see how you're doing."

"It's been a difficult twenty-four hours, but I'm working through it. How's Annie?"

"She's been placed with seasoned foster parents. They're sensitive, loving people who're aware of all Annie's been through and trained in ways to help her. But even they're concerned that she cried all night and won't eat anything or let go of her teddy bear. She keeps asking for you."

"Me? Really?"

"Yes, she refers to you as Owen, her other daddy. She wants to see you."

"Is that allowed?"

"It's highly irregular…but considering the circumstances, it might be good for Annie to see someone who makes her feel safe. I guess it depends on how you feel about seeing *her*."

"I'd like to see her. I've hardly stopped thinking about her. In fact, I've decided to take a paternity test. I owe it to both of us to find out the truth."

"And what if the test establishes that you *are* Annie's biological father? Are you willing to be a part of her life for the rest of her life?"

Owen pushed out the words. "Well, sure. How could I not? It's all just a little overwhelming at the moment."

"Of course, it is. I probably shouldn't have called you so soon."

"No, it's fine. I wanted you to. Then it's okay if I see her?"

There was a long moment of dead air.

"Owen, what if the test reveals you're *not* Annie's biological father? Will you just disappear from her life? I think it's important to come to some sort of understanding about this before we proceed. She already seems to have developed a very real attachment to you."

Owen combed his hand through his hair. "It's hard to explain, but Annie and I have been through something I doubt anyone else can understand. I guess you could say we bonded, I don't know. But I care what happens to Annie and would like to help her through this regardless of which way the paternity test goes."

"That's great to hear. I assume your wife's in agreement?"

"Hailey's extremely compassionate and has already expressed concern for Annie's well-being. But right now, she's more concerned about me taking an HIV test than dealing with the other issues. I'm not even sure who to call about the test."

"If you'd like, I can arrange for you to get tested for HIV when you take the paternity test."

"Thanks. I really need to get it behind me as soon as possible."

"How about this afternoon? I think I can collect on a favor and have a local lab work you in."

"That'd be great."

"You could come here to DCF to visit with Annie. I'll make arrangements for you to go get tested afterwards."

"All right, thanks. Let me talk to Hailey and call you back. Do you want me to bring my wife with me when I see Annie?"

"No, not this soon. Let's see how she does with just you."

23

On Wednesday afternoon, Ellen and Guy Jones walked into the kitchen from the garage, Lawrence on their heels.

"Dad, hand me that take-home box," Ellen said, "and I'll put your fried clams in the fridge and reheat them for you later."

Lawrence handed her the box and sat at the breakfast bar.

"I think Roland was glad to see us," Ellen said. "I hope the blood transfusion gets his hemoglobin back to normal. He looks too weak to do the exercises."

"He's doing fine." Guy filled a glass with water and drank it down. "The doctor said it's not unusual for this to happen after surgery. Okay, I've got to get back to work." He winked at Ellen. "Hold my calls."

She chuckled. "Yes, sir. See you at dinner."

A minute later the doorbell rang and Ellen went to the front door and saw Will Seevers standing on the porch. "This is unexpected."

"Have you been listening to the news?" Will said.

"No, we've been out for a few hours. What's going on?"

"May I come in? I won't keep you long."

Ellen led Will into the living room and sat on the couch across from the love seat where he always sat. "I have a feeling this isn't good news."

"It isn't. We have another stabbing victim."

"Oh no."

Ellen listened as Will told her about the body that was discovered at Bougainvillea Park and the discrepancy between the victim's ethnicity and the ID found nearby.

"Unfortunately, none of the fingerprints found on the wallet were on file at NCIC. And none match what we found here at the house. We'll have to wait on the autopsy and see if the angle of the wound will tell us the perp's height and which hand he used to thrust the knife. But the entry wound looks exactly like Jackson Kincaid's. Probably made with the same knife by the same perp."

Ellen shook her head. "Why would Jackson Kincaid's killer strike again in Seaport where his description has been released to the public? This kind of crime would be easy enough to pull off somewhere else."

Will raised his eyebrows. "He obviously isn't planning on getting caught. He may even be taunting the police."

"Or he knows my dad didn't give an accurate description."

"That's a real possibility. But someone's been hanging around your backyard and Mr. Madison's apartment. My gut feeling is the killer knows Mr. Madison saw him and is afraid he can identify him. Whether or not he'll act on that fear is anybody's guess. But I sure didn't expect him to claim another victim."

Ellen sighed. "I haven't noticed anything unusual since your officers checked out the backyard, but I'm afraid to sit out on the veranda right now. I stay inside with the security alarm on whenever I'm home."

"I wish I knew what we're dealing with, but for now, stay cautious and let's stick with the original assumption. We'll keep the police cruiser coming by on the hour."

Owen pulled his Jaguar into a parking space outside the plain red-brick building that housed the Department of Children and Families. He grabbed the still-warm McDonald's sack off the passenger seat and got out of the car and walked in the front entrance.

"May I help you?" the receptionist said.

"My name is Owen Jones. I'm supposed to meet Janet Stanton here at two-thirty."

"Have a seat. I'll see if she's ready for you."

Owen sat in a gray vinyl chair and opened an old issue of *Newsweek* and thumbed through it without reading a word. He couldn't tell if the hollow feeling in his stomach was hunger or nerves.

A young pregnant woman with twin boys he guessed to be about twelve sat across from him. He couldn't believe how dirty the boys' clothes were and tried not to stare.

"Mr. Jones, would you follow me?"

Owen jumped up and followed the receptionist down the gray hallway and into a cheery yellow room with two couches and bright blue beanbag chairs.

Janet Stanton came out of an adjoining room and closed the door behind her, then extended her hand. "Thanks for coming. Annie seems eager to see you."

Owen held up the sack, the delicious smell of a Happy Meal permeating the room. "I thought she might eat this."

"Good idea," Janet said. "By the way, I was able to schedule the tests so you can get them done today after you leave here."

"Thanks. I hope you put a rush on it like we talked about. I don't mind paying the extra money."

"I did. You should know the results of the HIV test tomorrow and the paternity test before the weekend…Owen, I'm sure you realize how very fragile Annie is right now. She's barely four and, in the past two weeks, has lost everything familiar to her: parents, home, dog, playmates. You seem to be the one person she thinks she can count on to protect her. Let me encourage you to take things slowly. Be as honest and as gentle with her as you know how. Are you ready?"

Owen inhaled slowly and exhaled, then gave a nod, wishing Hailey were with him.

Janet opened the door to a pale-blue room with toy-stuffed shelves along the back wall. Blue and yellow plaid carpet covered the floor, and brightly colored balloons had been painted on two of the four walls.

Annie was seated at a low table in the center of the room, holding Milton under one arm.

She looked up, her eyes smiling. "You came!"

Owen suddenly felt as though he had two sets of arms and didn't know what to do with them. Finally, he managed to hold out the sack. "I hope you like Happy Meals."

"Do you got fwench fwies?" Annie's blond curls framed her huge blue eyes.

"Oh, sure. There's a ton of french fries in here. Is it okay if I sit with you?"

Annie nodded. "Do you got a Coke?"

"No, I brought you milk instead. I thought a big girl like you would rather have something to make your cheeks rosy and those pretty blue eyes sparkle."

"You two go ahead and visit," Janet said. "I'm just going to sit here and do some paperwork."

Owen opened the sack, took the hamburger out of the wrapper, and handed it to Annie, then dumped the fries on the wrapper. He opened the milk and put a straw in the carton and set it on the table.

Annie took a big bite of the hamburger. "This is good. Do you got one for you?"

"Uh, no. Actually, I don't."

Annie held up the hamburger. "You can have a bite of mine."

"Okay." Owen took a bite and was surprised at how good it tasted.

"You better have one of my fwies, too."

Owen stuffed a french fry in his mouth. "Oops, these definitely need ketchup. You like ketchup?"

Annie nodded.

Owen squeezed the ketchup from half a dozen small packets and formed a red mound near the edge of the wrapper. "There. Try some of that."

Annie pulled a french fry through the ketchup and popped it into her mouth. "Mmmm."

Owen glanced over at Janet, thinking he'd already run out of things to say. What was he supposed to talk about with a four-year-old stranger?

"My mommy taked me to McDonald's after my pweschool."

"Did you like school?"

Annie gave an emphatic nod. "But I don't like Bwyan Phelps. He's too loud. And he always wants to play monster. I don't like that. Monsters give me bad dweams."

"I sure don't like bad dreams, but I had bad dreams last night. Did you?"

Annie nodded, then tilted her head back, her mouth open, and stuffed in another french fry.

"The one good thing about bad dreams is they only *seem* real, but whatever you see in the dream can't really hurt you."

Annie seemed to be processing the words. She put her finger in the ketchup and dabbed it on her tongue. "My other daddy doesn't like me anymore. He shot his head so he could be with Mommy." Annie's eyes welled. "I miss my mommy. She got dead in a car cwash."

"I know. I'm very sorry." Owen brushed the curls out of her face. "Annie, you don't have to be afraid because you're safe now."

"No, I'm scared of the *monsters*," she whispered.

"What do the monsters look like?"

Annie put down her hamburger and laid Milton on the table and made a circle with her arms. "They are *this* big! And vewy,

vewy mean! Bwyan told me they take mommies and daddies away and won't let them come back!"

"Do you still see these monsters?"

Annie nodded. "Do you got monsters at your house?"

"Absolutely not. I don't allow monsters in my house. Not in my closet. Not in the dark. Not even in my car. Why, I don't allow monsters in my friends' houses either."

"Does your little boy got monsters?"

"No way. And they won't bother you anymore if I tell them not to. Not even at your foster parents' house. You'll be safe there."

Annie's eyes seemed to search his. "Are you sure?"

"Absolutely." Owen put on a stern face and spoke with authority in his voice. "Okay, monsters, listen to me. You may not come to Annie's room. Or her closet. Or any place where Annie goes, whether it's light or whether it's dark. Never, ever, ever again! Now *go away* and don't come back!" He snapped his fingers, then turned to Annie and sucked in breath. "They ran away."

Annie's eyes were huge. "The monsters wan away?"

"Yes, far far away. And that's the last of them. No more monsters. Not ever." Owen avoided looking at Janet. He knew it was risky telling Annie that, but it had worked when Granddad did it for him.

The corners of Annie's mouth twitched. "Can you make the nightmares go away, too?"

"Not always. But I can help you talk about your scary thoughts so they won't turn into nightmares."

"Did you got scawy thoughts last night?"

"Yes, I did. I kept thinking about how afraid I was when Tim was holding the gun. I know how dangerous guns can be. And I knew we could get hurt. It took me a while not to feel afraid anymore."

"Daddy was being cwazy. He scared me."

"He can't hurt you now, Annie. He's gone."

"Why did he got a gun?"

"Sometimes a person's mind gets sick. You know how awful you feel right before you throw up? Well, Tim's mind was feeling sick like that and it made him act crazy. He would never have scared us like that if his mind was well."

Annie stuffed the last french fry into her mouth. "Maybe he's with the angels and isn't sick anymore."

Owen rested for a few moments in the quiet and thought how odd it was having such an intense conversation with a four-year-old. If Annie turned out to be his daughter, what in the world might they be discussing when she turned sixteen? He was suddenly aware of Annie saying his name.

"Ow-en!" she whined. "Pay attention."

He resisted smiling at how funny it sounded that Annie had called him by his first name. "What is it, honey?"

"Are you my daddy now?"

Owen locked gazes with Janet, the words she'd spoken earlier resounding in his head: *Be as honest and as gentle with her as you know how.*

"I don't know, Annie. There's a test the doctors are going to do that will tell if I'm your real daddy. But you know what matters most of all? That we're going to be friends from now on. I'm not going to leave you. I promise."

Annie took another bite of hamburger and hummed happily while Owen weighed the gravity of his promise, realizing the course of his life had just been forever altered.

24

Late that afternoon, Will Seevers pushed open the door to his office and flipped the light switch, then tossed a Doritos bag in the trash and dialed Al Backus's extension. "Al, you there?"

"Yeah, Chief."

"Would you come to my office? Bring us something cold to drink."

"Orange Crush?"

"Sure. Sounds great."

Will grabbed the file on the John Doe case and went over to the table and sat. He opened it and looked through the photographs of the entry wound on the victim's chest.

"Here you go." Al handed Will a can of Orange Crush, then pulled up a chair and sat at the table. "We showed our John Doe picture to some homeless characters camped under the bridge and a few recognized him as Bob. Nobody knew his last name or where he came from. None of them seemed eager to answer questions. We were lucky to make eye contact."

Will picked up a photograph of the victim. "I suppose it's possible one of his homeless *neighbors* could've killed him for whatever was in that wallet."

"They could be covering for someone who wasn't there."

"Maybe. But this feels more like a repeat performance by Kincaid's killer to me." Will put the photograph back in the folder. "The autopsy might give us something to go on."

"Yeah, let's hope. Did you go by the Joneses and tell them what's going on?"

"I told Ellen. She was quick to question why Kincaid's killer would hit again in Seaport, where his description has been released to the media. Makes me wonder if he's taunting us."

Al lifted his eyebrows. "Well, at least we know he's probably still here. I've got a team rechecking the hotels, motels, and B and Bs all over the region for anyone who fits the description we're going with. But we were so thorough on the first go-around. I'll be surprised if it yields anything."

"Any headway on finding Miguel Sanchez?" Will said.

"Nope. No theft report filed by a Miguel Sanchez anywhere in the state in the past year."

"Till now." Jack Rutgers stood in the doorway. "Mr. Sanchez just reported his wallet missing. He's here for the landscaper's convention and was down at Fish Tales last night buying souvenirs for his kids. He's sure he left the wallet on the counter after making his purchase. He went back when the store opened this morning and talked to Andrew Connor, but no one had turned in a missing wallet, so he came here to file a complaint. I think you'll want to hear what he has to say."

"Okay. Why don't you seat him in the meeting room and give him something to drink. Al and I will be right there."

Jack glanced at his watch. "All right. But he's got to drive to Tallahassee to catch a ten o'clock flight."

Owen Jones sat out on the screened-in porch, drained from the afternoon's activities and lacking the energy to get up and go inside where it was cool. He hadn't realized how scared he was of the HIV threat until he went for the test. And now the waiting was pure torture.

He held up the photograph Janet had taken of Annie and studied it. Before the weekend, he would know whether or not he was this little girl's biological father. He wondered if a negative result would change his feelings. Surely the compassion he felt for her losses and the bond they shared as victims of Tim O'Rourke's terrorizing would hold firm whether or not Annie proved to be his flesh and blood.

But a promise never to leave her? What had he been thinking? There was no guarantee the state would even allow him to see Annie long-term. And what if she had behavioral problems? Or was riddled with psychological problems? Or if *she* tested positive for HIV? Was he prepared to stick by her through all that?

It was clear that Janet was disappointed and concerned that he had overstepped his bounds. Maybe she was right. The sound of the sliding glass door opening distracted him.

"Owen, dinner's almost ready," Hailey said.

"Okay. I'll be there in a minute."

Hailey came out on the porch and sat on the wicker couch next to him. "You're awfully quiet. I guess you're as worried about the HIV test as I am."

"Pretty hard not to be. But I'm trying to get my mind on other things, like my time with Annie and everything you and I talked about when I got home. I'm amazed how much you seem to care about her."

"How could I not care about any child who's been through what she has?"

"Well, whether Annie's mine or not, let's hope I have what it takes to be there for her. I'm shaking in my boots."

"Well, that's two of us." Hailey linked her arm in his. "But we might as well face it head-on—and soon."

Owen brought the photo closer to his eyes. "I have a feeling the paternity test will be positive. I can't believe how much she looks like Mom as a kid. Not just the eyes, but her mouth, her button nose, the blond curls. It's almost creepy." Owen glanced over at Hailey. "You don't seem mad anymore."

"Because I'm busy being terrified by the threat of HIV

hanging over us." Hailey laid her head on his shoulder. "Plus, I did a lot of thinking and praying while you were gone. I wasn't exactly Ms. Morality when I met you. I wasn't sleeping with anyone else, but I wasn't thinking marriage either. I was no more committed in the beginning than you were. Neither of us was lily-white."

"I never touched another woman after I fell in love with you. It's so important to me that you believe that."

Hailey squeezed his hand. "I do. It might take a while for my emotions to catch up. But deep down, I know you're devoted to me."

Owen picked up her hand and kissed it. "Heart and soul."

"Miss Hailey!" Shayla hollered. "There's a buzzer carryin' on somethin' fierce in the kitchen. Is there somethin' I can do?"

Hailey brought her hands to her cheeks, then jumped to her feet. "Oh, no, the dinner rolls! I'm coming!"

Will Seevers and Al Backus sat in the meeting room across the table from Miguel Sanchez.

"Okay, let me see if I'm hearing you," Will said. "You went back to Fish Tales this morning to get your wallet, and Mr. Connor told you it hadn't been turned in?"

Sanchez nodded. "That's right. But he's lying. I'm telling you, he took it. The jerk ripped me off! I distinctly remember setting my wallet on the counter. Nobody else was in the store, and he was getting ready to close up."

"How much money was in the wallet?"

Sanchez shrugged. "I don't know, close to forty bucks. But I had to cancel my credit cards, and now I have to fly home without one red cent and nothing for an emergency." He threw up his hands. "Those stinking souvenirs ended up costing me big time! I'm not lettin' him get away with it!"

"I'm sorry, Mr. Sanchez," Will said. "I know this has been a giant headache. But unfortunately there's no proof that Mr. Connor stole your wallet. It's your word against his. We'll go talk to him, but since you didn't see him pick up the wallet, there's not much we can do. At least whoever has your credit cards can't use them now."

"Yeah, well, I'd be dusting the thing for Connor's fingerprints if I were you."

Will half smiled. "We'll be sure to do that."

Twenty minutes later, Will followed Al into Fish Tales Eatery and Gift Shop and saw three customers in the checkout line and two employees, one behind the register and the other helping a middle-aged lady rummaging through a stack of T-shirts. The air was scented with incense. Pelican wind socks hung from the ceiling, and shelves were packed with every conceivable kind of trinket. A red and white sign dangled above the checkout: "Donations can be made here for the Jackson Kincaid Memorial Fund."

Andrew Connor emerged from the adjacent eatery and walked over to where Will and Al were standing. "I suppose that Sanchez fella gave you the same song and dance about having left his wallet on the counter last night?"

"Yeah, what's the deal?" Al said.

Andrew lifted his eyebrows. "I tried to tell him he didn't leave it here, but he's convinced he did. What can I tell you? The guy's wrong."

"But you did wait on him just before closing?"

Andrew nodded. "Sure did. He bought all kinds of stuff for his kids—rubber alligators, squirt guns, T-shirts, hats. And a wooden pelican for his wife."

"How'd he pay for it?"

"Cash. It came to ninety dollars and change. He gave me a hundred."

"Did you see him put the change in his wallet?" Will said.

"No, I was busy putting his purchase into bags. But nothing was on the counter when he left. I know that for a fact since I was the only one here and I closed up. He must've dropped it outside or misplaced it somewhere else."

"Did you touch his wallet?" Will said.

"I don't think so. Why would I?"

"Does the store have a surveillance camera?"

"No. Why?"

Will glanced around the room. "Is there someplace we could talk where there aren't so many ears?"

Andrew nodded. "Sure. Come back to the stockroom."

Will and Al followed Andrew into a room full of cardboard boxes at the end of the hallway.

Andrew grabbed a folding chair and straddled it, his arms resting on the back, and gestured at a couple of other chairs for Will and Al to sit in. "I don't know what else I can tell you."

Al glanced at Will and then said, "Are you aware Sanchez's wallet was found at a murder scene this morning?"

"Murder scene? No. What murder?"

"We found a John Doe in Bougainvillea Park, stabbed in the chest just like Jackson Kincaid. Looks like our perp is back."

"Man, I hope you get him this time," Andrew said. "So how did Sanchez's wallet end up there?"

Al held Andrew's gaze long enough to make him squirm if he were going to. "We don't know. Neither does he. Do *you?*"

Andrew's eyebrows scrunched and then his eyes grew wide. "Me? How would I know? What are you implying?"

"Take it easy, pal. I'm just trying to get at the truth. Sanchez's wallet goes missing after he says he left it on your counter around 9 p.m. He's the last customer of the night, and you're the only other person in the store. Then between ten and midnight, a John Doe gets stabbed and Sanchez's empty wallet is lying next to the body. Nobody knows how it got there. This doesn't compute, if you get my drift."

"Look, I can't tell you what I don't know," Andrew said. "The guy in the park must've gotten his hands on the wallet and then got rolled for it. But I guarantee you, he didn't get it here."

"What time did you leave the store?" Al said.

"I don't know. Late. I had paperwork to do."

"What time?"

"After midnight. I didn't pay much attention. I'm here late a lot during tourist season. It's hard to keep up."

"Can anyone vouch for you?"

Andrew rubbed his hand across his buzz cut. "No, I told you I was the only one here. I think I left a message for my wife on our answering machine, but I don't remember what time. Look, I'm an upstanding member of the community. I run a good business. What reason could I possibly have for stealing a customer's wallet or stabbing some man in the park? I understand you need to get to the bottom of this, but you're wasting your time with me. I can't tell you anything."

"All right," Al said. "We were obliged to check out Mr. Sanchez's allegation, and we appreciate your talking to us. We'll be in touch if we have more questions…Oh, as long as I'm here, I need to pick up a coffee mug for my dad's birthday. Got anything with a sport's theme?"

"Yeah, sure. Let's go take a look."

Will waited while Andrew picked through the selection and then reached up on the back shelf and retrieved a mug with the Miami Dolphin's logo on it. "I thought I had some of these left."

Al smiled. "Sold."

Andrew carried it over to the register, where the line of customers had disappeared and so had the clerk, and rang up the purchase.

"Care to make a donation to the Kincaid Memorial Fund?"

"Yeah, sure." Al folded a couple one-dollar bills and stuffed them into a clear acrylic box on the counter.

Will glanced at his watch, thinking Margaret would be

wondering why he hadn't called to tell her he'd be late for dinner.

"Here you go." Andrew handed the sack to Al. "I'm sorry I wasn't more help. Believe me, *nobody* wants you to get this guy more than I do."

"Don't worry. We will."

Will walked out of the gift shop, bells jingling on the door, and walked a couple yards down the wooden walkway, then said, "Okay, Al, spit it out. I feel your wheels turning."

"Did you notice that Andrew Connor's about five-nine, has a generous roll around his middle, blond stubble for hair—which *could* look bald in the daylight—and has been out in the sun?"

"He fishes on his day off," Will said. "With a friend of Gordy's...Captain Jack something. You have a bad feeling about him?"

"I don't know. Maybe." Al patted the sack with the mug. "At least we've got Connor's fingerprints. I'm curious to see if they match what was found on the wallet—or at the Joneses'."

25

E llen Jones was at the breakfast bar reading Thursday morning's edition of *North Coast Messenger* when Guy came in and sat on the stool next to her.

"Anything noteworthy about the stabbing in the park?"

"The headlines are just a recap of what we heard on the news. I can hardly wait till the killer is behind bars so we can get back to normal again. Though I doubt anything will be normal as long as Dad's living with us."

"Anything new on the O'Rourke case?"

Ellen took a sip of coffee. "No, but the media's going to drag out the drama as long as possible. I'm sure Owen is sick about having his personal business become public knowledge. I know I am. Julie, Mina, and Blanche called and left messages for me, but I haven't returned them yet. I don't know what to say until the results of the paternity test are back."

Guy took a photograph out of his shirt pocket and handed it to Ellen.

"Where'd you get this?" Ellen said. "I thought I put all my childhood photos in the cedar chest."

"Owen attached it to his e-mail. It's Annie."

Ellen couldn't take her eyes off the little girl in the picture. "Good heavens…she could pass for me at that age."

"I'm concerned about Owen," Guy said. "I don't think his faith is strong enough to handle all of this. He barely has his foot in the kingdom now."

"Just think—this may actually be our granddaughter."

"I wonder if he and Hailey have talked about what they're going to do if this girl turns out to be his daughter. She's going to need more than financial support, and Hailey's already feeling overwhelmed with Daniel. This could put a terrible strain on their marriage."

Ellen smiled, her eyes fixed on the photo. "She looks like an Annie."

"Honey, you *can't* be pleased about this."

"*Pleased* is the wrong word. But there are worse things than Owen finding out he has an adorable little daughter that needs him. Assuming, of course, Annie really is his."

"Yes, but think of what it might do to his relationship with Hailey and Daniel. They might never fully recover."

Ellen brushed his arm with her fingers. "God doesn't allow anything to happen unless He plans to use it. Facing the consequences may be difficult for Owen, but God will use it for good."

"You sure about that?"

Ellen nodded. "Positive. That's His promise in Romans 8:28: 'We know that in all things God works for the good of those who love him, who have been called according to his purpose.' That's includes all believers, even baby Christians like Owen who barely have a foot in the kingdom."

After picking at his lunch and finally dumping it down the garbage disposal, Owen Jones went in and sat next to the phone, thinking this had to be the longest day of his entire life. The phone rang and he grabbed it on the first ring.

"Hello."

"Owen, it's Janet. Great news: Both you and Annie tested negative for HIV. I knew you'd want to know right away."

Owen felt as though her words were bouncing in slow motion from one side of his brain to the other. "What a relief!

I've really been sweating this. You're sure?"

"Absolutely. The lab just called. I didn't realize you had authorized them to give me the results."

"Yeah, since you know the situation, I thought I'd be more comfortable hearing the results from you." Owen hated that his voice was shaking. "Frankly, I wasn't sure what to expect. Any chance the paternity test is back?"

"Did you ask them to call the results of that to me, too?"

"I did. I hope you don't mind."

"No, but I don't have it yet. It'll probably be tomorrow. At least you'll sleep better tonight knowing you and Annie don't have HIV."

"I feel like a mountain's been lifted off my shoulders. Thanks for calling."

Owen hung up the phone, his hands shaking, and realized Hailey was standing in the doorway, her eyes round and questioning.

"My test was negative for HIV. Annie's too…" His words trailed off.

Hailey sat on his lap, her arms around his neck, and began to sob and then sob harder.

"Thank you, Lord," she whispered. "Thank you."

Will went in the side door of the police station and down the hall toward his office, a delicious aroma wafting from the sack he was carrying.

A few seconds later, Al Backus was walking next to him, keeping perfect stride. "Connor's fingerprints don't match anything we've found in either stabbing case. Back to square one."

"Well, he wasn't a serious suspect anyway," Will said, flipping the light switch in his office. "What's the word from the team you've assigned to check motels and B and Bs?"

"Nada."

"Anything from missing persons?"

Al shook his head. "Nothing that fits our John Doe."

Will sat at his desk and took the sausage biscuit and cup of coffee out of the sack. "Sorry to eat in front of you, but I'm starved."

"That's all right. I've got a box of doughnuts in my office." Al flopped into a chair. "I guess we'll just have to wait on the autopsy report to see if we're dealing with the same perp. My gut says we are."

"Mine too. But I've been fooled before."

"Wish I could say, 'Let's stick with the facts,' but we're right back to our very iffy description of the perp."

The corners of Will's mouth twitched. "I don't know. You were ready to pounce on Connor because he fit the description, more or less."

"Well, like you said, it's all we've got. But we both know it's not good enough. If the autopsy doesn't give us something new to go on, we're going to be sitting on two murders with a lot of dead ends."

Will took a sip of coffee. "How many homeless people did you talk to yesterday?"

"Sixteen."

"I want you to go back to the bridge and ask more questions. See if the mood feels the same today. Find out who wasn't there yesterday. Press a little harder. Get up in some faces and get somebody intimidated enough to talk about *Bob*."

"Yeah, right. I'll put a clothespin on my nose."

"Go down to Flamingo's, too, and see if anyone noticed what time Andrew Connor left the store.

Ellen ran up the winding staircase to the widow's watch. "Dad...? Are you up there...? Dad...?"

She reached the top of the stairs and pushed open the door

and saw her father standing in the semicircular alcove, his hands clasped behind him, looking out the windows.

"Why didn't you answer me?" Ellen snapped.

Lawrence Madison didn't flinch. "I don't like being hollered at."

"I've been looking for you for the past ten minutes! I worry when I don't know where you are! The least you could do is tell me when you're coming up here!"

"I need permission for that, too?"

"Dad, this isn't about who's in control. It's about making sure you're all right. I'm responsible to help you. Why won't you just cooperate?"

He folded his arms across his chest and didn't answer.

Ellen breathed in and exhaled loudly enough to make sure he heard her. "Owen and Hailey are coming over to visit with us about what happened in his office. Do you remember a man shot himself in Owen's office?"

"The man in the Old Glory shirt."

"I'd feel better if you were downstairs with us. These winding steps are tricky, and I don't want you to fall."

"Sure would solve your problem."

"Dad, let's not do this. I don't want to fight with you. Why don't you come downstairs and I'll get you a piece of lemon cake. Does that sound good?"

He stood like a statue and ignored what she said.

Ellen turned on her heel and stomped down the stairs, across the living room, and into the kitchen. "He's up in the widow's watch," she said to Guy. "I asked him to come down here. Even tried bribing him with a piece of lemon cake, but he's ignoring me. Would you try?"

"Sure." Guy kissed the top of her head. "Don't despair, honey. Just one more week till we go for his appointment."

The doorbell rang.

"I'll let Owen and Hailey in," Ellen said. "Please just work your charm on Dad."

Ellen went to the front door and opened it. She put her arms around Hailey and then Owen, holding on a few seconds longer than usual. "I'm glad you're here. I've been dying to come to you, but I'm so tied down with Dad. Where's Daniel?"

"With Shayla," Owen said. "That seems to be working out great."

Hailey smiled. "I think they're joined at the hip right now. Daniel follows her everywhere and laughs all the time."

"Come in and cool off," Ellen said. "Would you like a piece of lemon coffee cake? It's still warm."

"Maybe later," Owen said. "Ice-cold lemonade sounds good, though."

"Hailey?"

"Just lemonade, please."

Ellen went out to the kitchen and saw her father standing at the sink.

"Why aren't you at work?" he said.

"I'm off today. I wanted to spend some time with the kids."

"Well, that's a switch."

"You want cake or not?"

"I want to go home."

I wish! Ellen pressed her lips together and bit hard. She poured four glasses of lemonade, put them on a tray, and carried them into the living room.

"Okay, here you go."

"This is one of the things I love about living in Florida," Hailey said. "Picking lemons right off the tree and making fresh lemonade. It just tastes better."

Ellen sat on the couch next to Guy and studied the kids' faces. They didn't seem as stressed as she had envisioned.

"We want to run something by you," Owen said. "We were up half the night thinking about how this thing could go with Annie. I don't know for sure what the paternity test will reveal, but I'll be more surprised if she's not my daughter than if she is. You saw the picture."

Guy nodded. "She's a dead ringer for your mom, all right. But that doesn't prove anything."

Owen took a sip of lemonade. "Hailey and I are considering seeking custody of Annie regardless of which way the test goes."

Guy looked at Ellen and then at Owen. "Why would you do that? If she's not yours, let the system place her with someone who can't have kids. Why put yourselves through that?"

"I said *considering*. We know we're in shock right now. We're just talking options. But realistically, Annie could fit nicely into our family. Hailey isn't crazy about going through another pregnancy, but we both want more kids. Annie's adorable. It wouldn't be that hard to love her."

"Son, you're moving way too fast on this!"

"Dad, calm down. We haven't decided anything, okay? We're just talking."

Ellen's eyes moved to Hailey. "How do you feel about it?"

"I'd like to spend some time with Annie. She needs a mother figure right now, and I love kids her age."

"Four is adorable," Ellen said, "but she's going to grow into an adolescent before you know it. Are you prepared for *that* challenge day in and day out? It's a far cry from just spending time with her."

"I know that." Hailey took Owen's hand. "But we both feel incredibly drawn to Annie. Maybe it's a 'God thing,' I don't know. We'd like to spend some time with her and see how she responds to us."

Owen smiled. "She's so darned cute—a real kick in the pants. She told me she had a dachshund named Oscar when she was living in Raleigh. Maybe we should get a dachshund."

"Listen, you two," Guy said, "this is a *huge* step. I'm not saying it couldn't work, but I think you need to take a big step backwards and think about what it would mean. Hailey, you're having trouble dealing with being a stay-at-home mom with just one child. How would you feel with two?"

"Shayla's made all the difference. The time I have with Daniel is so much better when I'm not confined to the house. I love being a mother. I just needed wings."

"And fortunately, I make enough to afford wings," Owen said. "I doubt we'll ever be without a nanny. Truthfully, I think Janet Stanton would jump at the idea of us wanting to adopt Annie."

Guy's eyebrows furrowed. "Maybe so, but we're not talking about getting a kitten. Once she's yours, she's yours forever. You've never raised a child. You haven't begun to experience the rigors of parenting."

"You're right," Owen said. "But do you really think if we had another baby instead of adopting Annie, we would be better parents?"

At four that afternoon, Will Seevers walked across the pier toward Gordy's Crab Shack, not so sure what to think about Andrew Connor.

Al Backus had gone down to Flamingo's Bar and Grill and talked to the bartender, who remembered the lights were off at Fish Tales at eleven p.m. when he went outside for a smoke. But they were back on at two thirty a.m. when he closed up for the night.

When Backus confronted Connor about it, Connor said whoever told him the store lights were off at eleven was mistaken because he was there working. He said he'd forgotten to turn out the lights when he left around midnight and realized it when he came in the next morning.

Will sighed. A simple enough explanation. So why wasn't he satisfied? He decided this job was making him paranoid.

He walked in the front door of the crab shack and saw Gordy Jameson talking to a waitress. There didn't appear to be any customers in the restaurant.

"Hey, Will," Gordy said. "What're you doin' here on Margaret's meat loaf night?"

"I'm not here to eat. Have you got a minute?"

"Sure. Wanna sit here in a booth or go to my office?"

"I think your office might be best."

Will followed Gordy down the hall and into his office and closed the door behind him. "So did you and Pam catch anything yesterday?"

"Yeah, we got into some permit and grouper on light spinning tackle. Had a blast. We brought home some nice grouper filets. Maybe we'll have you and Margaret over and throw 'em on the grill."

"Sounds great…Listen, I need to ask you some questions. As always, this needs to stay between us."

"Yeah, sure, Will. Shoot."

"I'm sure you heard about the stabbing victim at the park yesterday morning."

"Sure did. Have you ID'd him yet?"

"No, we're working on it. Thing is, we found an empty wallet at the scene—empty, that is, except for a driver's license belonging to a Miguel Sanchez. The victim isn't Hispanic, so we know the wallet was probably stolen."

Will told Gordy about Sanchez coming in to file a complaint against Andrew Connor and about the visit he and Al had had with Conner afterwards. He didn't mention that Al had questioned the bartender at Flamingo's.

"You know Andrew Connor. What kind of guy is he?"

"Seems like a real straight shooter. I've never heard anyone bad-mouth him. I admire what he's doin' for Jackson Kincaid's family. Really took the bull by the horns, you know?"

"Doesn't he fish with your captain friend on his day off?"

"Yeah, why?"

"I need you to find out what he talks about. What he has to say about his business. His family. Friends. Finances. That sort of thing."

"Kinda hard to do that without makin' Captain wonder why I'm so curious all of a sudden."

Will patted him on the shoulder. "You'll think of something. I really need this favor."

"Wanna give me a hint what you're tryin' to find out?"

"I'm just trying to cover all the bases. I owe it to Mr. Sanchez to at least establish whether Connor had a motive for stealing his wallet." *Or killing a guy in cold blood.* "If you don't want to do it, Gordy, just say so. But you're in a better position to get honest information than I am. And I don't see any reason to embarrass Connor or his family or cast a shadow on the Kincaid Memorial Fund by letting the media find out about Sanchez's allegation. So can we handle this discreetly between you and me for now? If Connor looks clean, no one will be the wiser."

"All right, Will. I'll see what I can find out. But I just don't see a successful businessman like Andrew Connor stealin' a customer's wallet."

"I know. But Sanchez was so sure that Connor ripped him off he went to great lengths to file a complaint with the police."

"Could be Mr. Sanchez is a loon."

"Yeah, I know, Gordy. I guess I just want to make sure Andrew Connor *isn't*."

26

Late Friday morning, Ellen Jones pushed open the exit door of the Seaport Rehabilitation Center, a blast of hot, moist air smacking her face. "Whew! It's easy to tell summer's around the corner."

"At least the snowbirds are gone," Guy Jones said.

"Where's Dad?" Ellen cupped her hands around her eyes and looked through the glass. "I thought he was right behind you."

"So did I. I'll go find him." Guy pulled open the door and walked down the hallway toward the elevator.

Ellen went over and sat on the edge of the fountain, the rainbow mist cooling her skin, and relished a few moments to herself. At least Roland was recovering well and seemed stronger after yesterday's blood transfusion.

Earlier in the morning, Guy had met with the administrator of Sea Gate, an assisted-living facility not far from their house. As soon as Roland was released from rehab, Sea Gate would be his new home. How she hated that he'd had so little time to get used to the transition from independent living to assisted care.

Ellen took a slow deep breath and let it out. Maybe by this time next week, she and Guy would have a solid diagnosis for her father's failing memory and could make some arrangements for his care. She could hardly wait to get him out of the house and let someone else have the responsibility.

Honor your father and your mother, so that you may live long in the land the Lord your God is giving you.

The words of the fifth commandment echoed off the walls of her conscience and made her want to shout. What was there to honor about her father? Hadn't he dishonored her time and time again with his crushing criticism and cutting remarks? Had he even once said he loved her—or even liked her? It seemed as though he never ran out of new ways to antagonize her.

"It's his own fault I don't want to be around him," she mumbled, her eyes focused on the pattern of the water shooting up from the base of the fountain.

From somewhere nearby, a child's voice found her ears and turned her thoughts to Owen and Hailey and the impending results of the paternity test. Given the crises already demanding her energy, would she have anything left to help with Annie? And would adding a troubled child to the family have a negative impact on Daniel?

Suddenly, Ellen's heart began to race and then race faster until she felt tingly and light-headed and consumed with fear. *Lord, help us make the right choices. I just want my life back. I'm so overwhelmed.*

The sound of Guy's voice caused her to look over her shoulder.

He was walking toward her, Lawrence by his side. "Okay, we're all set. Honey, you okay? Your face looks flushed."

"I'm just a little overheated." Ellen fought the urge to grab her father and shake him. "Where was he?"

"In the atrium, admiring the foliage."

"I need to go home and water my flowers," Lawrence said.

Ellen felt a twinge of compassion and realized it was pointless to remind him he wasn't going home.

"How about us having an early lunch at Gordy's?" Guy said. "I'll bet they've got some of those fried clams Lawrence loves so much."

"Sounds good to me," Ellen said. "I'm about to climb the walls, waiting for the results of Owen's test."

❧ ❧ ❧

Will Seevers stood at the window in his office, his hands in his pockets, and pondered whether he'd crossed the line by asking Gordy to find out what Andrew Connor talks about when he fishes.

"Okay, come and get it," Al said. "One extra-large sausage-and-pepperoni deluxe—minus the onions."

Will went over to the table and sat. Before he had even gotten a napkin opened in front of him, Al had flipped open the box and put a slice of pizza to his lips.

"This is…h-h-hot…" Al's mouth formed an "O," his hand fanning the contents of his impulsive first bite.

Will put a straw in a cup of Coke and handed it to Al. "Here, wash it down."

Al sucked on the straw for several seconds. "Thanks. That's what I get for thinking with my stomach."

"You okay?"

"I'm sure I've blistered my tongue, but I'll live."

Will picked up a piece of pizza and laid it on the napkin to cool.

"You still bugged about Connor?" Al said.

"I'd feel a whole lot better if his story about when the store lights were on had jibed with the bartender's." Will avoided Al's gaze and decided not to tell him what Gordy was up to.

"You don't believe he was working late?"

"Doesn't matter. If the bartender's right about the lights being out at eleven, then Connor wasn't in the store working during the time of the murder."

"It's his word against the bartender's."

"It also bothers me his wife can't tell us what time he got home."

"His old lady's a deep sleeper and never hears him come in," Al said. "But she confirmed that he routinely gets home late."

"I don't care about his *routine*. I want to know where he was Tuesday night between ten and midnight."

"He left a message on the home answering machine at 11:10, but he used his cell phone, so that won't help us. No one can prove he wasn't working." Al's eyes narrowed. "Look, Connor's been cooperative with us and critical that we haven't found Kincaid's killer. We have nothing that links him to either murder."

"Except Sanchez's wallet."

Al sighed. "Which doesn't prove squat."

"Then get out there and find me something."

Gordy Jameson saw Ellen, Guy, and Lawrence walk in the front door. "Hey, good to see you. Want your usual table?"

Guy nodded. "It feels great in here. The heat's downright oppressive."

"Did you and Pam have fun yesterday?" Ellen said.

"Yeah, we anchored over a wreck and caught a boatload of fish. Had a ball."

Gordy motioned to the waitress. "Seat my friends at that table in the corner. And make sure they get dessert—on the house." He winked at Ellen, a smile tugging at the corners of his mouth.

"You're hopeless," she said.

"Yeah, I know." Gordy glanced at his watch and went through the double doors into the kitchen. "Pam, the guys are here. I'm goin' outside to eat with 'em, okay?"

"Okay, love. Tell Eddie the triple-berry pie is fresh out of the oven."

"I will."

Gordy left the kitchen and went out the back door onto the deck, thinking Guy was right about the heat being oppressive.

"Hey, guys!" Gordy went over to an umbrella table where

Captain Jack, Eddie Drummond, and Adam Spalding were enjoying cold drinks.

"How'd you do fishin'?" Captain asked.

Gordy pulled out a chair and sat. "I kept puttin' crabs on the end of Pam's hook, and she hauled in permit as fast I could take them off and throw 'em back."

"You get anything worth eating?"

"Yeah, grouper. It was great takin' a day off."

"So what's your buddy the police chief think about this killer running loose?" Eddie lifted his eyebrows. "It's been a while since we had two murders this close together."

"Why do you always assume Will tells me stuff the rest of you don't know?" Gordy said.

Adam tilted his glass and crunched an ice cube. "I wonder if they've figured out who the victim was?"

"The cops are clueless," Eddie said. "I listened to the news on the way over here. Sure hope they don't let another one slip through."

"Were you just born negative or do you have to work at it?" Gordy spotted the waitress coming to the table.

"Today's special all around?" she asked.

Everyone nodded.

"Give these guys refills on limeades," Gordy said. "I'd like one, too."

"I'll turn in the order and be back in a jiffy with those drinks."

Gordy sat over lunch for forty-five minutes, laughing and joking and chitchatting with the guys, all the while thinking about how he might approach Captain to get the information Will wanted.

Finally, Eddie glanced at his watch. "I gotta get back to work." He pushed back his chair and stood, then put a dollar under the saltshaker. "Have a great weekend, guys."

Adam got up on his feet. "I need to get on the road. I'm driving to Jacksonville for the weekend. My parents are hosting a big party after my baby sister's debutante ball."

"Better keep Daddy happy," Captain said. "Sure don't want him cuttin' off that big fat allowance he gives you."

Adam laughed. "Eat your heart out. See you Monday."

Captain drank the last of his limeade and started to get up.

"You don't have to run off," Gordy said.

"I thought you had to get back to work."

Gordy shook his head. "Not for a few minutes yet. Tell me what you've been up to."

"Oh, same old," Captain said. "A little poker. A little golf. A lot of fishin'."

"You aren't showin' Andrew Connor all your secret fishin' holes, are you?"

Captain chuckled. "Via GPS. He'd never find them on his own."

"He must be an enjoyable fishin' buddy. You've been takin' him out every week for quite a while."

"Yeah, he's cool. Gets Sundays off and can't wait to get out on the water. It's a lot more relaxin' for me than when I was a fishing guide. Andy doesn't get rattled if we don't catch anything. He's just lookin' to clear his head."

"I hear that," Gordy said. "Seems like a real nice guy. Sure is great what he's doin' for Jackson Kincaid's family."

"Did you know the fund is up to almost ten grand now?"

"That's what I heard. Awful generous of him to put up the first five."

Captain nodded. "Yeah, I thought so. Especially considering his business was in the red. I doubt if many people know what a sacrifice that was. He'd be embarrassed if he knew I told you. Don't say anything."

"So he and Jackson were pretty tight?"

"Not really. Andy was always gripin' about how much business Jackson had stolen from him. But he put all that aside to help the guy's family. You gotta admire that."

"Yeah, awful generous of him to cough up that kind of money." Gordy wondered if he was being too obvious. "It's great to see people rallyin' to support the memorial fund. Maybe that'll help business to pick up."

"It's already up 30 percent. Good timing, too, with both his boys starting college in the fall. That's gonna cost him an arm and a leg."

Gordy nodded. "I'm glad things are turnin' around for him."

Captain nodded. "Yeah, if anyone deserves it, Andy does."

Will Seevers read the preliminary autopsy report on the John Doe stabbed in the park, then laid the report on his desk and sat back in his chair, his hands clasped behind his head.

There was a knock at the door, and he saw Al Backus standing in the doorway.

"Yeah, come in, Al.

"Rutgers said you got the prelim on the John Doe."

"Yep, a carbon copy of Jackson Kincaid's except the angle of the entry wound was slightly different. See for yourself." Will picked up the report and handed it to Al.

"Any DNA?"

"No. All we got are red polyester/cotton fibers found on a jagged fingernail, consistent with the fabric and dye used by a North Carolina textile company called Gen-R-Us. They mass-produce polyester/cotton T-shirts in every conceivable color and size, then ship them to more than a thousand outlets around the world for customized imprinting. Most are slated for novelty and souvenir shops."

Al lifted his eyebrows. "So the shirt could've come from almost anywhere in the world."

"Or right here in Seaport."

Al handed the report back to Will. "Well, now we know

we're probably dealing with the same murder weapon and perp that killed Kincaid. Too bad we didn't get his prints on either wallet."

"Were you able to find out anything from the bridge people that might help us ID their buddy Bob?"

"Nah. I'm convinced they don't know anything. The guy was a loner."

"Any new faces in today's mix?"

Al shook his head.

"Okay. Let's forget about the victim for now and concentrate on the killer. We know the perp is five-nine, give or take, and right-handed. He may also be thick around the middle, bald, recently sunburned—*and* was wearing a red Gen-R-Us T-shirt. Find out which Seaport stores sell that brand and color."

"Might take a while."

"I doubt if they all stock red." Will caught Al's gaze. "You might want to start with Fish Tales."

Late Friday afternoon, Owen hung up the phone and went into the bathroom and locked the door. He put down the lid on the toilet and sat staring at the stripes on the shower curtain, his hands shaking, emotion wedged in his throat.

Janet Stanton's words blared like a siren in his head. *"The test proves with 99.999 percent accuracy that you're Annie's biological father."*

It's not as though he hadn't seen it coming. He'd thought of little else in the past three days. But the truth weighed heavier than he had ever anticipated.

How unfair that Annie had spent the first four years of her life being rejected by a man who resented her very existence. But Owen also knew that had he known of Corinne's pregnancy, he would have encouraged her to end it—and this beautiful little girl would never have been born.

Fear seized him and he felt as though his heart were in a vise. What if he couldn't love Annie the way he did Daniel? What if the guilt he felt now turned to resentment? What if Hailey didn't take to Annie the way she had hoped to? Maybe his parents were right. Maybe they were moving way too fast on this and should take a big step backwards. What choice did he have now that he knew for sure Annie was his? He couldn't just walk away from the responsibility. But suddenly, the idea of raising her felt more compulsory than compassionate.

His mind raced with every conceivable negative scenario they might encounter if they had custody of Annie. A knock on the door startled him, and he wondered how long he had been in the bathroom.

"Owen, are you all right?" Hailey said.

"I'm fine. I'll be out in a minute."

"Was that Janet on the phone?"

Owen put his face in his hands, his heart pounding in the silence that followed. *Go away! I'm not ready to talk about it!*

"Owen...? Say something. Don't just ignore me."

"Look, my stomach's upset. Think you could give me a little privacy?"

"All I—"

Owen flushed the toilet to drown out Hailey's voice, and then flushed again.

27

Late Friday night, Gordy Jameson sat in his recliner, the ceiling fan on high, and thumbed through the latest issue of *Florida Sportsman* while listening to the last few minutes of the eleven o'clock news.

He picked up the remote and turned off the TV, then walked softly down the hallway and peeked into the bedroom. Pam appeared to be asleep, her face visible in the moonlight flooding her pillow.

He quietly closed the door and went out to the kitchen and dialed Will Seevers's phone number.

"Hello."

"Hey, Will, it's me."

"I figured. You're the only one who'd call this late."

"I talked to Captain today."

"That was fast. What'd he have to say?"

Gordy leaned back in the kitchen chair, his weight balancing on the balls of his bare feet. "Pretty much what I figured: He enjoys fishin' with Andrew and has a lot of respect for the guy."

"That's it? No insights into why?"

"Sure. Andrew gave that five thousand to the Kincaid Memorial Fund at a time when his business was in the red. Captain asked me not to say anything. Said Andrew'd be embarrassed if people found out what a sacrifice he'd made. You gotta admire that."

"Captain told you Andrew Connor's business was in the red?"

"*Was*. Sales are up 30 percent now. Maybe the increase is his reward for bein' so generous. He came into my place for take-out on Memorial Day. I remember him sayin' he was much busier than last year."

"Gordy, what the heck would boost sales by 30 percent? That seems huge to me."

"I'm only guessin', but Andrew's probably gettin' a chunk of business that would've gone to Kincaid. Plus, tourism's up. And people comin' into Fish Tales to donate to the memorial fund has increased his foot traffic. That could account for some of it."

"I wonder why his sales were down in the first place?"

"Probably increased competition. But tourism hasn't fully bounced back since 9/11 either."

"What increased competition?"

"All those new shops poppin' up all over the place. The pie's gettin' bigger, but each shop owner's slice seems to get smaller. They're all screamin', especially the ones who've been in business a long time."

"Is it the same in the restaurant business?"

"Not for me, but my place is paid for and my overhead's low. But there are plenty of restaurants strugglin' to make it. Of course, Fish Tales is an eatery *and* gift shop. So Andrew might've gotten a double whammy."

"Did Andrew ever talk to Captain about the competition?"

"Yeah, sometimes Andrew needed to unload before he could shift gears and enjoy the fishin'. He complained about business bein' down since Kincaid opened his souvenir shop two doors down."

"You think there was bad blood between them?"

"I didn't get that impression. Competition is always gonna be there whether we like it or not. The fact that Andrew led the charge on settin' up the memorial fund says a lot about what kind of guy he is."

"Is Andrew a family man?"

"Yeah, he's got two teenage boys that help out at the store. His wife Cheryl does, too. I don't know 'em that well, but they seem like carin' parents and hardworkin' folks."

"Any idea where they live?"

"They've got a house that backs up to one of the canals on the west side. Nothin' extravagant, but real nice. Andrew's hopin' to buy his own fishin' boat after he gets the boys through college." Gordy got up and took a can of Coke out of the refrigerator and popped the top. "What can I tell you? From Captain's perspective, Andrew Connor's one heck of a nice guy. Seems that way to me, too."

There was a long moment of dead air.

Gordy walked over to the table and sat. "What's botherin' you?"

"I'm not sure yet."

"Would you tell me if you were?"

Will chuckled. "You ask too many questions. But thanks for doing this, Gordy. I owe you one."

Ellen stood in the alcove of the widow's watch, her head resting against the window, and looked out over the gulf waters, which shimmered in the moonlight.

Mom, Dad, the paternity test came back. Annie's mine.

"Ellen?"

Guy's voice startled her and she looked over her shoulder. "Don't sneak up on me like that. You nearly gave me a heart attack."

Guy came up behind her and put his arms around her, his chin resting on her shoulder. "Sorry. I can't sleep either."

"Owen sounded so desolate on the phone. I had a feeling yesterday when he seemed so enthusiastic about adopting Annie that it was part of the denial stage."

"Well, there's no denying it now."

"I'm not sure he's even gotten angry yet. I suspect that's the next stage."

"Honey, why do you have to analyze everything?"

Ellen sighed. "I don't want any more surprises…I always dreamed we'd have a granddaughter someday. But not like this."

"Well, let's just hope this mess doesn't wreck what Owen and Hailey have worked so hard to build."

"It's obvious they want to do right by Annie. They just need to let their hearts catch up with their logic."

"Maybe. I'll be interested to find out Hailey's impression of Annie after she actually spends time with her. I'm not convinced she hasn't talked herself into wanting what she thinks Owen wants."

Ellen rested her back against Guy's chest. "She wouldn't be the first wife to do that."

"Or the last. But if this is going to work, she needs to be totally honest with Owen about her feelings."

"I doubt she even knows what her true feelings are."

"That's my point. Before those kids take another step, they need to be on the same page. Otherwise, they're just leaving themselves wide open for bitterness and resentment down the road." Guy tightened his embrace. "I'd like to wring Owen's neck for being so careless."

"It's comforting that DCF won't place Annie with Owen and Hailey unless they're convinced it would be a good thing for the child."

"Well, what about *our* child? Seems to me Annie has more options than Owen and Hailey do."

"Like what?" Ellen said. "Foster care? Is that what you want for Owen's daughter?"

"No, but there are a lot of couples who might jump at the chance to adopt her, especially if she's as cute as Owen says she is."

"Even if that's true, I don't think we should encourage it. Owen is thirty-one years old. He's better off financially than most. He and Hailey could offer Annie a stable, loving home. They're quite capable of stepping up to the plate. Why should someone else be persuaded to take responsibility for a child he fathered?"

"I know you're right, honey, but I'm not there yet. It took Owen a long time to settle down and get both feet planted firmly on the ground. I don't want to see this mistake ruin his life."

Ellen turned around in Guy's arms and looked up into his eyes, her own brimming with tears. "Our son's behavior was the mistake, not Annie. God has allowed her into our lives for a reason. We need to learn to love her, not look for excuses to pass her off."

Owen lay in bed, holding Hailey in his arms, his eyes wandering around the moonlit room, his heart trying to process that Annie O'Rourke was truly his flesh and blood.

"Owen, are you awake?" Hailey said softly.

"Yeah. I can't believe it…Yesterday I was so sure that raising Annie was the right choice, and now I'm freaking out. I'd like to put you and me and Daniel in the car and go somewhere far away. But I could never escape the guilt. It's like those big blue eyes of hers are branded into my soul."

"I couldn't forget her either. But your folks are right—we need to slow down."

Owen pulled Hailey closer to his chest. "I can't believe it's only been four days. Seems like a lifetime."

"I know. But if and when we decide to do the home study, it needs to be because we want to, not because we feel guilty or pressured."

"I studied Daniel earlier tonight, after he fell asleep in my arms. If you can get past his hair being dark and straight, his facial features look much like Annie's."

Hailey nodded. "They certainly wouldn't have any trouble passing for siblings."

Owen tried to imagine the guestroom turned into a little girl's room, and what it might be like to cuddle with Annie and read a bedtime story. Going through the motions would be easy. But what if he never *felt* the part? What if he never developed the caring heart needed to nurture this troubled child?

"Have you thought about what you're going to tell people at work?"

"I doubt I'll say anything to anyone except the board of directors. And Helen. They'll be supportive, I know that."

"Can you handle the stares? That would be the hardest for me."

"Truthfully, honey, compared to the pressure I'm feeling about parenting Annie, and the scare we just had with HIV, any criticism or judgments people might have would seem like a walk in the park."

Will Seevers sat in front of the TV munching a bowl of raisin bran and only half paying attention to the giddy young starlet on *The Late Show with David Letterman*. What was it was about Andrew Connor that left him feeling so undone? After what Captain had told Gordy, it wouldn't surprise him if Connor were nominated for citizen of the year.

Will swallowed the last bite of cereal and then drank down the milk. The fact that he had faith in Gordy's ability to read people just added to his confusion. But how much personal contact had Gordy actually had with Connor? Maybe the two of them had rubbed elbows a few times at chamber of commerce meetings. Possibly eaten at each other's restaurants. Engaged in a little business chitchat. But if Gordy were required to rely only on his firsthand experience with Connor to make an assessment, it didn't seem as though he could vouch for the guy's character.

"What's wrong?" said a sleepy voice.

Suddenly, he realized Margaret was standing in front of his chair, her eyes at half-mast.

"Nothing's wrong. Why would you ask that?"

"I heard you talking to Gordy."

"Gordy's fine, honey. Go back to bed."

"Is everything okay between him and Pam?"

Will set his bowl on the end table. "Yes, they're great."

"Well, he didn't call this late without a reason."

"I'm tapping his brain about something. Just police business."

"Are you coming to bed soon?"

"Won't do any good. I'm wide awake."

Margaret sat in his lap, her arm around his shoulder. "You seem consumed all of a sudden by the second stabbing."

"I've just got a lot of questions racing through my mind. One of the hazards of being a cop." He squeezed her hand. "You know how I process stuff."

She glanced at the empty bowl. "Raisin bran?"

"Yeah."

She leaned over and kissed his cheek. "Okay, I guess I don't need to worry until you start dipping into my stash of chocolate."

Will finished watching a second *Seinfeld* rerun and then turned off the TV just as the mantel clock struck two. He wondered if taking a drive would help him relax so he could sleep. At least he didn't have to work tomorrow.

He taped a note on the bedroom door in case Margaret got up looking for him, then went out the front door and got into his squad car. He backed out of the driveway and headed for the beach, thinking he might stop at Burgers and Shakes and get a chocolate malted. He was suddenly aware of how tight his belt was and decided to exercise a little self-discipline.

He drove past Burgers and Shakes and turned onto Beach Shore Drive, amazed at how much of the beach and the gulf beyond he could see by the light of the moon. His memory of the first time he and Margaret had walked the beach under a full moon brought a smile to his face. He was a senior in high school and she was a junior—and both were in violation of their curfews. Will had gladly accepted being grounded for a week and remembered confiding in Gordy that he planned to marry Margaret someday.

He turned into the tourist district and drove slowly up and down streets that were almost devoid of traffic. A few cars were still parked at the nightclubs, probably those of employees closing up for the night. Will pulled over in front of Flamingo's Bar and Grill and looked next door at Fish Tales, which was dark except for the interior security lights and the neon Closed sign in the front window.

Will backed up one door to Sun Haven Souvenir Shop and noticed a For Sale sign posted on the front glass. He wondered how Mrs. Kincaid was going to support three young children and if Jackson had thought to carry life insurance.

Will pulled away from the curb and drove around to the alley. He stopped in back of Flamingo's Bar and Grill, just a few feet from where Lawrence Madison was believed to have been sitting prior to Jackson Kincaid's murder.

Will looked over at Fish Tales and tried to imagine Andrew Connor looking out the side window. He certainly would've had a good view of the alley from there. But what would cause such a busy man to take notice of a guy sitting on a beer crate, much less describe in detail what he was wearing?

In his side mirror, Will could see the ground next to the dumpster where Jackson Kincaid's body had fallen. If Lawrence Madison had been sitting behind Flamingo's, he had to have seen Kincaid's killer, even if his feeble mind couldn't sort it out.

How feasible was it that Andrew Connor might have been the man Lawrence saw with the knife? Connor had never been arrested. Didn't seem to have any enemies. Gave generously to help the Kincaid family. Had cooperated with police. And openly voiced his disgust that the police hadn't found Kincaid's killer—

not typical behavior for a man with something to hide.

Yet, except for not having a bald head, he fit the description of the perp. And it wasn't that big of a stretch to think his blond buzz cut could be mistaken for a bald head in the midday sun by a lost and scared old man. Thanks to Gordy, it was obvious now that Connor may have had a motive—for killing Kincaid, anyway. Nothing about the missing wallet and the John Doe made sense.

Suddenly Will was blinded by light reflecting in his car mirrors and flooding the alley. His drew his gun, his heart pounding, but in the next instant the face of one of his officers appeared at the driver's side window of Will's car.

"Everything okay, Chief?"

Will put his gun in the holster and rolled down the window. "It was until you pulled up behind me like that."

"Sorry. We were cruising by and saw a vehicle in the alley and thought we'd check it out. Didn't expect it to be you." The officer turned to his partner and hollered, "Everything's fine. Cut the high beams."

"I couldn't sleep," Will said. "Figured as long as I'm awake, I might as well keep my mind working on the Kincaid case. Anything happening tonight?"

"No, sir. It's been pin-drop quiet. We've cruised by the Joneses' place on the hour like you told us. Nothing suspicious outside."

"Good."

"You need help with anything here?"

Will shook his head. "I was just replaying Kincaid's murder in my mind. Same questions. No answers." *Not yet anyway.*

28

On Saturday morning, Ellen Jones lay in bed, vaguely aware of muffled voices in another room and then footsteps in the hallway. And whistling.

"Wake up, sleepy head," Guy said.

Ellen let the aroma of warm cinnamon rolls and Starbucks breakfast blend waft under her nose, then opened her eyes just as Guy's lips warmed her forehead.

"Maybe you'd rather sleep a little longer?" he said.

"And miss being pampered?" She felt the corners of her mouth turn up. "Mmm...that smells *so* good. Is Dad up?"

Guy nodded. "He's already had a bowl of oatmeal and bananas and is watching some fishing program on TV."

Ellen sat up, a pillow behind her back, and waited for Guy to place the breakfast tray across her lap.

"I don't know how you get him to behave so nicely," she said. "I think he lives to torment me." Ellen leaned down and put her nose to the red rose in the bud vase and inhaled. "Oh, my. What a beautiful fragrance."

"Nothing but the best for my sweetheart. Here's your newspaper, madam. And a little cream for your coffee."

Ellen chuckled. "You are so...*awake*. What time is it?"

"9:40."

"The morning's half over! Why did you let me sleep so late?"

"You needed it. Do you even know what time you finally fell asleep?"

Ellen blew on her coffee. "Must've been early this morning. I couldn't get Owen off my mind."

"Me either." Guy went around and got in his side of the bed. "I'd like to be a bug on *his* wall. How do you even begin discussing what to do in a situation like theirs?"

"Seems wise to start by spending time with Annie. Judging from what Owen's told us, she's adorable. I can't imagine Hailey won't be taken with her."

"Sure, till the first temper tantrum. Or the first time Annie hauls off and slugs Daniel. Or digs in her heels and won't do what she's told. It's hard enough to cope with negative behavior in a child you've loved from day one. How do you do it with someone else's child?"

"Annie isn't someone else's child."

"You know what I mean. She's been someone else's for four years."

"Well, Owen and Annie seem to have bonded during the ordeal with Tim O'Rourke. A strong basis for trust has already been established, and they can build on that."

"But Hailey and Annie haven't bonded. What if they don't? That's not something that can be manufactured or forced."

"You think you could reserve your opinion until they've at least *met*?" Ellen put her cup on the saucer, then turned and looked at him. "Guy, it's not like you to be so negative. The kids are going to need our support. We've got to be a united front."

"You're right." Guy ran his finger along the edge of her tray, seemingly lost in thought. Finally he said, "Maybe what I'm really afraid of is that *I* won't click with Annie. I'm crazy about Daniel. But truthfully, I don't know that I can love Annie the same way."

Owen Jones sat at an outside table at the Port Smyth Coffee Company, his eyes focused on a single sailboat gliding across the endless blue-gray ripples of the gulf. He was aware of voices and the throaty chirping of grackles in the palm trees and the aroma of hazelnut coming from the steaming cup of coffee in front of him.

He felt a tap on his shoulder and looked up at a shapely brunette stuffed into short shorts and a tank top.

"Sir, is it okay if I borrow this chair?" she said.

Sir? Owen could almost hear his ego deflate. A few years ago, gals her age were falling all over him. Now he was just another thirty-something. "Uh, sure. Go ahead."

"Thanks." She giggled, then picked up the chair and carried it over to a table packed tightly with young people who appeared to be college age.

Owen listened for a long time to the cacophony of voices and uproarious laughter coming from the group, almost wishing he could go back and live his life over, this time using the wisdom he had stored in his thirty-one-year-old brain.

He remembered feeling invincible at their age, indulging his fleshly desires without a thought to the consequences. He shuddered to think how little consideration he had given to the threat of HIV or getting someone pregnant or the marital status of his partners. Even if he had known Corinne was married, he would never have passed up a chance to sleep with her as long as she was willing.

Tim O'Rourke's last words seemed suspended in his mind. *"I've decided to let you live so you can suffer for the rest of your life remembering what a mess you made of mine."*

A gunshot exploded in Owen's memory and caused him to jump, hot coffee spilling down his hand. He grabbed a couple napkins and laid them over the puddle on the table, feeling as if he were going to lose it.

He got up without making eye contact with anyone and hurried down the wooden stairs to the beach and started running and then running faster until he was a considerable distance away from anyone.

Finally, he dropped down in the sand and lay on his back, his forearm covering his eyes, tears spilling down the sides of his face.

God, I'm sorry. I never meant for anyone to get hurt. How am I ever going to make this right?

Will Seevers sat reading the Saturday sports page after devouring one of Margaret's weekend specialties: a Spanish omelet and crispy hash brown potatoes. He had crawled into bed around five a.m., finally exhausted enough to sleep, and didn't hear a thing until Margaret woke him up at eleven and said Meagan had called from Washington, D.C., and was having the time of her life.

He heard the engine of a low-flying plane and glanced out the window and saw a Cessna pulling a red-and-yellow banner: "Support the Kincaid Memorial Fund: Shop and Eat at Fish Tales."

Will wondered how much that kind of advertising was costing Andrew Connor and which had come first: the 30 percent increase or the advertising ploy? Then again, why should anyone fault Connor for advertising the memorial fund? Every dollar was going to the Kincaid family. If it brought Connor some foot traffic and a bump in sales, so what?

Will folded the sports page and laid it on the end table just as his cell phone rang.

"Will Seevers."

"Chief, it's Al."

"What's up?"

"We've already found seven stores that sell red Gen-R-Us shirts, including Connor's. Seems like a moot point if they're available all over town. You want us to keep working on this?"

"No," Will said. "Where are you?"

"Sitting at a red light at Main and Orange Blossom."

"Why don't you swing by my house? I've got a few things I want to talk over with you."

"Now?"

"Yeah, I think we need to change our strategy."

Twenty minutes later, Will sat at the kitchen table with Al Backus and explained what he had asked Gordy to talk to Captain about, and also what Gordy had reported back.

Al's eyebrows scrunched. "With all due respect, Chief, I can't do my job if you don't keep me in the loop."

"I thought Gordy would stand a better chance than we would of finding out what personal stuff Connor talks about. It was a long shot. I didn't see the point of saying anything unless I found a motive."

"Sure smells like a motive to me."

"Yeah, me too. It was pointless to call you at eleven thirty last night. You're the only one I've talked to about this."

"Does Gordy know you suspect Connor?"

"Not really. Naturally, he's curious as to why I'm asking questions about Connor, but I didn't tell him what's going on. Gordy and I have an understanding."

"Yeah. Yeah, I know. Don't ask, don't tell."

Will smiled. "Something like that. He won't open his mouth to anybody about this."

"Okay, so what now? You said we need a new strategy."

Will folded his hands on the table. "It's time we leaned on Connor about his relationship with Jackson Kincaid."

"If the word gets out we're questioning Connor, it might jeopardize the memorial fund."

"I agree. Let's swing by the store tonight at closing and see what he has to say."

Owen lay on the porch swing, his hands clasped behind his head, and counted the wood slats across the ceiling for the umpteenth time.

The door opened and Hailey poked her head outside. "Owen, Janet's on the phone. You want to take it out here or inside?"

"Out here's fine."

Hailey came out and handed him the phone and sat next to him on the porch swing.

"Hi, Janet."

"Hello, Owen. I'm just checking in to see how you're feeling now that you've had time to let the news sink in."

"I'm a little overwhelmed, but I want to do right by Annie. Where do we go from here?"

"I guess that depends on whether you want to be Annie's father or her daddy. Have you and your wife decided whether you plan to seek custody of her?"

"We're talking about it. You said something about a home study."

"Yes, that's the first step. But getting custody of Annie will take some time."

"How much time?"

"That depends on a number of factors, but best-case scenario three to six months after the home study. Could be up to a year."

"Why so long since we know I'm her biological father?"

"Our job is to place Annie where her needs can best be met."

Owen glanced over at Hailey, his eyebrows raised. "Are you saying there's a chance we wouldn't get custody?"

"It's highly unlikely that would happen to a biological parent who wants the child, especially if you pass the home study. That takes about six weeks to complete."

"What's involved?"

"A social worker would be assigned to conduct the home study, which would involve a background check, an evaluation of your home environment, a good deal of Q and A with you and your wife—and with friends and relatives."

"Is all that necessary?"

"Standard procedure. Surely you can appreciate that we need to be sure she's placed in a safe and loving environment?"

"I had no idea how complicated this could get."

"It sounds more difficult than it is. You just need to take it a step at a time."

Owen sighed. "How's Annie doing?"

"About the same. She's eating better, but she talks about you all the time."

"That's a good sign, isn't it?"

"Yes, but I wish you hadn't told her you weren't going to leave her. It's important for Annie's sake that you don't have contact with her for two or three weeks so she can adjust to foster care and let her emotions calm down."

"You're kidding?"

"Annie needs to be comfortable with her foster family until a final determination is made. Like I said, the process takes time."

"Can we see her first?" Owen squeezed Hailey's hand. "My wife wants to meet her."

"All right. Why don't I call you back on Monday morning and we can set up a time?"

Late Saturday afternoon, Will Seevers sat at the kitchen table with Margaret, looking through a stack of travel brochures on Barbados.

"I don't know, honey. We're talking a lot of money."

"Will, it's our twenty-fifth anniversary." Margaret looked at him with those puppy eyes he found hard to resist. "We've got the money put away."

"Yeah, but that's a big wad for just one trip."

"But we only get one twenty-fifth anniversary. And if we book the trip before July, our lodging is almost half price."

"What's wrong with driving to Santa Fe?" he said.

"We've been there. I'd really love to go some place exotic and different."

Will fought back a smile. She was going to flip when she found out he had already bought the tickets. "Is that Swiss steak I smell?"

"Uh-huh."

"You aren't trying to bribe me, are you?"

Margaret smiled coyly. "Did it work?"

Will's phone vibrated. *Not now. Not when I'm about to tell Margaret the trip's in the bag!* "I need to take this call, honey." He opened his phone and put it to his ear. "Will Seevers."

"Chief, it's Jack Rutgers. Sorry to bust up your Saturday, but we've got another stabbing death."

Will looked at Margaret and rolled his eyes. "Okay, Jack. Fill me in."

"An African-American male approximately sixty years old, found across the street from the receiving dock at the Goodwill store. Single stab wound to the chest. No ID on the body."

"Any witnesses?"

"Not to the stabbing. But a lady pulled into the Goodwill parking lot and saw a man running down the sidewalk and thought nothing of it. Then a half hour later left the store and spotted a body lying next to a hedge."

"Can she describe the guy she saw running?"

"We're working on it."

"Okay, Jack. I'm on my way." Will put his phone back on the belt clip and shook his head.

"What happened?" Margaret said.

"Another stabbing. We've got a witness who may have seen the perp." Will got up, then bent down and kissed her cheek. "We'll talk some more about the trip later. And I'll have some of that Swiss steak when I get back."

Margaret smiled. "Whoever invented the microwave must've been married to a cop."

❀ ❀ ❀

Ellen was listening to *Regional News at Six* while she stacked the dinner dishes in the dishwasher, grateful that her father had opted to listen to tonight's baseball game in his room.

"….Port Smyth citizens wishing to voice their opinions are invited to a citywide meeting at seven p.m. Tuesday at city hall.

"And this just in: WRGL News has received a report of another stabbing in Seaport. News reporter Jared Downing is in Seaport, reporting live. Jared, what can you tell us?"

"Shannon, just over two hours ago, Seaport police responded to a 911 call in the three hundred block of Flamboyant Street. A woman reportedly pulled into the Goodwill parking lot and saw a man running down the sidewalk. When she came out of the store thirty minutes later, she noticed a man lying beside these shrubs you can see behind me. She couldn't tell if the man was drunk or if he needed help, so she ran back inside the Goodwill store and got two employees to walk across the street with her and quickly realized the man had been stabbed and wasn't breathing. She called 911, and paramedics arrived minutes later but were unable to revive him.

"No identification was found on the victim, but an elderly couple who happened onto the scene recognized the victim's red athletic shoes and were able to assist police in locating the victim's wife. The victim has now been identified as Jerome Powers, fifty-eight, a longtime custodian of the Seaport Arms Apartments.

"The woman who made the 911 call told police the man she saw running down the sidewalk was Caucasian and may have been wearing khaki shorts and a green cap.

"Though robbery appears to be the motive in this third stabbing death in eleven days, authorities are tight-lipped as to whether or not they believe it's the work of one killer. The first victim, thirty-six-year-old Jackson Kincaid, was found dead in the alley behind his souvenir shop on May 20; and the second victim, a Caucasian male thirty-five to forty years old, was discovered in Bougainvillea Park last Wednesday morning and has still not been identified.

"Shannon, the residents I talked to this evening are scared. They want this killer off the street. And Police Chief Will Seevers had no comment other than to say his department is conducting a thorough investigation.

"This is Jared Downing reporting live from Seaport. Back to you…"

"Obviously, WRGL News will follow this story closely and bring you updates as soon as we have them. In other news tonight, the Palm City ISD is going forward with plans to—"

"Did you hear there's been another stabbing?" Guy stood in the doorway to the kitchen.

Ellen put the TV on mute. "I did. This is so disheartening. What's going on in this town?"

"I don't know, but I doubt Will is getting much sleep these days."

Ellen sighed. "Maybe not. But he's not the one with an eyewitness living in his house."

29

On Saturday night, Will Seevers stood at the window in his office, observing the media presence outside the police station.

"They're like a pack of wolves, ready to pounce," he said to Al Backus.

Al wadded up a potato chip bag and pitched it into the trash. "Kind of hard to blame them. Three stabbings in eleven days makes *me* nervous. I'd feel better if our witness remembered something besides a white guy wearing khaki shorts and a green cap."

"And I wish someone besides Connor's wife and boys could verify he was working in the store all afternoon."

"The medical examiner said the entry wound was much smaller than the other two. Smells like a copycat to me."

"Or just a different weapon." Will looked at his watch. "You ready to go talk to Connor? Fish Tales closes in twenty-five minutes."

Al rubbed his hands together, a smile on his face. "This should be good. Why don't you go out the side entrance and wait for me? I'll walk over to the parking lot and get my squad car and pretend I'm leaving for the night, then circle back and pick you up. Unless, of course, you're just dying to talk to the media again."

"Not as long as I've got more questions than answers."

Al left the office, the clicking of his heels down the long corridor growing faint.

Will picked up the phone and called Margaret and told her

what he was doing, then walked down to the side entrance. He stuck his head outside and looked around. Not a person or car in sight other than the cleaning service van. He went outside and sat on the steps.

Three minutes later Al pulled up in the squad car and Will got in.

"Did the media fire a bunch of questions at you?" Will said.

"Yeah, but it's you they want to hear from. They're dug in, waiting for you to show your face." Al laughed. "Hope they brought their jammies."

At nine p.m., Will and Al walked up to the front entrance of Fish Tales just as a customer came out and Andrew Connor turned off the Open sign.

Will walked inside. "Looks like our timing was just right."

"For what?" Andrew said. "I answered Investigator Backus's questions earlier this evening."

Will nodded. "We appreciate that, but we've got a few more."

"Can't it wait? I need to get the register closed out. And I haven't had dinner."

"We won't keep you long," Al said. "But we waited till closing so we wouldn't embarrass you. You can either talk to us here or down at the station."

Andrew's eyebrows furrowed. "Embarrass me? What are you talking about?"

Al moved a step closer to Andrew. "Why don't you tell us what kind of relationship you had with Jackson Kincaid?"

"I don't understand what you mean."

"Did you like him? Not like him? *Resent* him?"

"I hardly knew the guy."

"Awful nice of you to put up five grand for a guy you hardly knew."

"Look, I felt sorry for his wife and kids. I'd like to think that if something like that happened to me, someone would help take care of my family."

"Didn't bother you that he came all the way from Fort Lauderdale and opened a nice new souvenir shop—two doors down?"

"Jackson wasn't my only competitor. I learned to sharpen my pencil."

Al pursed his lips. "Funny, I heard your business was in the toilet."

"That's not true. Sales are up 32 percent."

"Before or *after* Kincaid's murder?"

Andrew stared blankly at Al, and then threw up his hands. "For cryin' out loud, I'm trying to help out the guy's family. Why are you coming at me like this?"

"Take it easy, Mr. Connor," Will said. "If you've got nothing to hide, you have nothing to fear from the police."

"Good, because I certainly don't have anything to hide."

Al lifted his eyebrows. "Then suppose you answer my question. Were sales up or down before Jackson's murder?"

"Down. But all the merchants have absorbed some of Jackson's business. It's a heck of a way to increase sales. That's probably why they've all been so generous giving to the memorial fund. It's up to just over eleven thousand dollars."

"And you gave the first five?" Al said. "How'd you swing that if your business was failing?"

"I never said my business was failing. I said sales were down."

Al locked gazes with Andrew. "We could get a warrant to look at your bank accounts and business records."

"Okay, so I had a hard time making ends meet—me and every other retailer vying for the tourist trade."

"Enough to get rid of the competition?" Al looked over at Will, a smirk on his face. "Sounds like motive to me, Chief."

"Come on," Andrew said, "if I'd had anything to do with

Jackson Kincaid's murder, why would I be on your case to find his killer?"

Al lifted his eyebrows. "Because you thought we wouldn't suspect you?"

"Of course I didn't think you would suspect me because I didn't do it! How could you even think such a thing?"

"You had motive. And you fit the description of the assailant."

Andrew looked at Al and then Will. "This is crazy! I was in the store working at the time of the murder. I'm the one who described the guy I saw sitting in the alley."

"That's right," Al said. "And I keep wondering why a busy store manager would stop everything and take note of what the man was wearing."

"I told you...he made me suspicious. I didn't like him loitering in the alley."

"Or maybe you saw him face-to-face when you were running away from Jackson's dead body and told us you saw him from the window?"

"What?"

"How else would he have been able to describe *you*?" Al said.

"That's crazy!"

"Well, those are a few questions behind door number one. Let's take a look behind door number two. There's still the matter of Mr. Sanchez's wallet being left on the counter at your store and showing up next to the second victim."

"I told you, he didn't leave his wallet on the counter."

Al smirked. "Yeah, I know what you said. You also claim you were working till after midnight. But the bartender at Flamingo's says your lights were off at eleven."

"Well, he's mistaken. I was right here, working on reorders."

"I'm curious why you'd call your house and leave a message on your answering machine saying you were working late if your old lady's a sound sleeper and wasn't gonna hear it. Maybe you were setting up an alibi?"

"That's insane. My boys check those messages, too. You're twisting everything."

"Did I mention the autopsy showed that the red fibers under victim number two's fingernails just happened to be from a Gen-R-Us shirt, which you just happen to sell in your store?" Al produced a phony grin. "Feel free to start squirming any time."

"I'm not squirming, I'm getting angry! I have half a mind to call a lawyer."

"Yeah, I suppose it's risky talking to the police if you have something to hide."

Andrew's eyes narrowed. "The public's screaming for justice and you need someone to sacrifice. Well, there's no way you can hang this on me. You have no evidence and no murder weapon linking me to any of these crimes, and you never will because I'm innocent. So unless you plan to charge me with something, I suggest you leave so I can get back to closing out my register."

Ellen sat in the chair in the master bedroom, knitting an afghan and longing to be out on the veranda enjoying the sounds of night and the smell of the damp sea breeze. She heard her father's bedroom door open and the blaring of his TV fill the hallway. She looked up and saw him standing in her doorway, a small black bag in his hand.

"I'm going home," Lawrence Madison said.

Ellen realized he had put on a jacket over his pajamas. "Dad, this is your home for now, remember?"

"You act like I can't remember anything! Why are you always on my case?"

"I don't mean to be. I'm trying to help."

"I don't want your help! I want you to leave me alone! I hate it here! I hate *you*!"

Ellen bit her tongue. *Lord, give me strength.* "Would you like some lemon pudding before you go to bed?"

"Stop trying to control me with food. Dad, eat this. Dad, eat that. Well, you eat it! I'm watching the ball game."

Lawrence disappeared from the doorway, and seconds later his door slammed.

Ellen blinked the stinging from her eyes and knitted faster, her heart pounding, her face hot.

Guy came in and sat on the side of the bed. "Was that Lawrence I heard shouting?"

"Uh-huh. He's just being his usual obnoxious self. He went back to his room, so if we're lucky, maybe he'll crash for the night. Better yet, for a week."

"You've been hiding since dinner."

"Yes, I have."

"Want to talk about it."

"It would take too long."

"I've got all night." His dark eyes seemed to walk right into her heart. "Talk to me."

"It's better if I wait till—"

"Till what, you can clean it up? Convince yourself it's less intense than it is? You're the one who always says it's best to be honest about our feelings."

"All right. I'm feeling angry. No, worse than angry—outraged. I'm tired of the violence. And living in fear. And being forced into hiding." She realized her hands were shaking and lowered her knitting and set it in her lap. "I just want my life back. I miss my friends. I miss writing my novel. Jogging on the beach. Sitting on the veranda without worrying that some stupid killer is lurking in the bushes. And I don't want to be responsible for Dad—not that he appreciates anything I do anyway. I just want him to go away." Ellen started to cry. "How awful is that?"

Guy came over and sat on the arm of the chair and pulled her close, his hand stroking her hair. "Honey, you've got an awful lot on your plate. You didn't mention Owen and Hailey's situation, but I know it's adding to the pressure."

"I suppose. But I could handle it a whole lot better if I

weren't cooped up here all day with Dad. I just dread Monday when you leave for Tallahassee. He's much more agreeable when you're around."

Will pulled his squad car in front of a pale-green-shingled beach house, glad to see the lights still on. He got out of the car and walked to the front door. He knocked gently, and a few seconds later the door opened.

"Good, it's you," Gordy said. "I was about to watch the news, but you can fill me in. Boy, do you look beat."

"You going to let me in?"

"Yeah, sure." Gordy held open the screen door and let Will squeeze past him. "Want somethin' cold to drink?"

"Sounds good. Thanks."

Gordy picked up the ice cream carton and spoon he'd left on the end table and walked out to the kitchen. He opened the refrigerator and grabbed two Cokes and handed one to Will. "Sit down and tell me what's goin' on."

"Is Pam asleep?"

"Yeah, she's out like a light."

Will sat at the table and loosened his collar, then took a big gulp of Coke. "Well, suffice it to say it's been an interesting day. How much do you know?"

"That there was a third stabbin' outside the Goodwill store. A black guy was killed. That's about all."

Gordy listened as Will filled in the blanks, starting from when Jack Rutgers's phone call interrupted his conversation with Margaret to his going to the murder scene with Al Backus.

"What kinda guy kills for pocket money?" Gordy said. "Talk about bloodthirsty."

"Yeah, but I'm not so sure we're talking about the same perp. We'll have to see what the autopsy tells us." Will traced the rim of his can with his index finger and seemed to be thinking.

"Somethin' else is buggin' you," Gordy said. "You didn't

come over here to tell me what I could've heard on the news."

"You're right." Will took another drink of Coke. "This stays between you and me. I'm starting to think Andrew Connor killed Jackson Kincaid and our John Doe."

"You can't be serious."

"How about dead serious?"

"But he's such a nice guy. What motive would he have for killing…?" Gordy's face dropped. "Oh no…After what Andrew told Captain, you're thinkin' he wanted Jackson out of business."

"It's certainly feasible."

"Why would he turn around and set up a memorial fund for Jackson's family?"

Will lifted his eyebrows. "Guilt?"

"But Andrew's the one who's been neggin' you for not findin' Jackson's killer."

"Maybe that was all an act. Look, it's not just the first stabbing that's bothering me. I believe Sanchez's story about the wallet. So how could it show up at the murder scene unless Andrew was there?"

"I don't know, Will. There's gotta be another explanation. What reason would Andrew have for killin' the second victim? Wantin' to put Jackson Kincaid out of business was bad enough, but killin' a stranger?"

"Desperate people do desperate things. If Connor thought he could throw us off his scent by killing a homeless guy nobody would miss, why not?"

"Then who killed the third guy—and why?"

"Good question. But the third victim's wife said he had cashed his paycheck the afternoon before and had several hundred dollars in his wallet. Maybe somebody else knew that."

Will twisted the tab off his empty can and dropped it inside. "I need to ask another favor. If Captain asks you if you said anything to me, I need you to play dumb."

"I don't like usin' my friends this way, Will."

"Yeah, I know. I'm sorry. I wouldn't ask if there was any other way."

30

At six o'clock Monday morning, Ellen Jones opened the French doors and marched out onto the veranda and set her coffee tray on the side table, then nestled in her wicker rocker, feeling as though defiance were oozing from her pores.

A minute later she sensed someone standing in the doorway and her heart sank. Couldn't her father at least sleep long enough to give her a little quiet time?

"Honey, what are you doing out here?" Guy Jones said.

"Oh, good, it's you and not Dad. I'm enjoying the fresh air. I couldn't bear the thought of watching another sunrise with my nose pressed on the glass in the widow's watch."

"I thought we agreed this was not a good idea."

"I changed my mind. If whoever was lurking around out here is bold enough to take me on, more power to him."

Guy sat on the edge of the other rocker, his eyes wide, his hands clasped between his knees. "You can't stay out here. I'm leaving for Tallahassee. I have a nine thirty meeting with a new client."

"Drive carefully, Counselor. I'll talk to you tonight."

"Honey, I'm serious."

"So am I." Ellen folded her arms. "If I stay cooped up indoors, I'll be a basket case before Wednesday night."

"The time always goes fast."

"Sure, when I'm writing or with my friends. Not when I'm

fighting Dad day in and day out."

"After his evaluation on Thursday, we should be able to make some decisions on how to best care for him. You've made it this far. You can handle it for three more days."

There was a moment of silence and then Ellen let out a loud sigh. "You're right."

Guy got up and pulled her to her feet, his arms around her. "I'm mad about you, Madam Novelist. You know that, don't you?"

"Yes, but I'm ashamed to say I've been too busy feeling sorry for myself to pay much attention."

Guy pressed his lips to hers, then tightened his embrace. "When we get a handle on things, what do you say we get in the car and head up to the Smoky Mountains and spend a few days at that neat little resort we found? Maybe drive over to Baxter for a weekend and see some of our old friends?"

Ellen looked up at him and smiled in spite of herself. "If we wait till we get a handle on things, we may have to go in matching wheelchairs."

"Things will calm down soon. Life can't stay this intense forever. We're due for a reprieve." Guy picked up his briefcase and kissed the top of her head. "Come on, let's go inside before you talk yourself into believing the threat's over."

Ellen looked over her shoulder at the backyard. "All right, but I'm really sick of living like this."

Owen Jones sat at the breakfast table perusing Monday's edition of the *North Coast Messenger* while he ate granola and strawberries.

"I'm sorry there was a third stabbing that ate up the front page," Owen said, "but at least there's nothing in here about me and Annie. I'd just as soon keep it that way."

"I'm glad the board told you to take another week off,"

Hailey Jones said. "That'll give us some time to think and plan."

"Did I tell you they're moving me to the office with the transom window?"

"No. I wondered what they'd do about your old office. I doubt anyone wants it now."

"They've already pulled up the carpet and put down tile and made it the file room."

"Pretty fancy file room."

"Well, like you said, no one wants it now. I doubt I'll even poke my head in there."

The doorbell rang and Hailey jumped to her feet. "That's Shayla.

Owen reached over and tickled Daniel's tummy, then put a few Cheerios on his tray. "Here you go, big guy. I'd give you the sugared stuff, but Mommy would have my head on a platter."

Owen heard Shayla's robust laugher, then looked up as she came into the kitchen and strolled over to Daniel's highchair. "There's my baby boy! Miss Shayla's gonna let you play in a warm bath and then we're gonna read the *farm animal* book."

Daniel started to giggle and held up his arms for Shayla to pick him up.

"He actually lets you read to him?" Owen said.

"Oh, my, yes. He takes to those board books like a duck to water. You want me to go do somethin' else and come back for him later?"

"No, he's finished with breakfast," Hailey said. "You can take him."

Shayla removed the high chair tray and lifted Daniel into her arms and walked away, talking to him as if he could understand every word.

Owen chuckled. "I like her. It's obvious Daniel does."

"She's great. I guess we need to ask her how she'd feel about taking on two children."

"I'll pay her more," Owen said. "Whatever's the going rate."

"Knowing Shayla, she wouldn't ask us for it." Hailey glanced at the clock. "Do you think you should call Janet and see what time we can see Annie?"

"Honey, it's eight o'clock. The woman's hardly had time to pour a cup of coffee. I don't want to push. She said she'd call, so let's just sit tight."

"Did your mom sound okay when you talked to her earlier?"

"Yeah, more or less. But I can tell she's fed up with being stuck in the house with Granddad."

"I don't blame her, considering the way he treats her. But I'm beginning to think the police were wrong that someone besides Tim O'Rourke was prowling around over there. They haven't seen anything unusual since the night of the big gala."

Owen lifted his eyebrows. "Then again, they don't sit outside anymore."

"Do you think Tim O'Rourke was ever there?"

"Maybe, though I doubt it. He told Helen he had just driven into town from Raleigh that morning."

"I wish the police would hurry up and catch the killer. I can't imagine Ellen feeling unsafe all the time. Especially with Guy in Tallahassee."

"Yeah, Dad hates leaving them right now. But he can't just stay home till they get this guy. May never happen."

Owen was down on all fours, Shayla holding Daniel on his back, when the phone rang.

A few seconds later, Hailey came into the living room, the cordless phone in her hand. "Owen, it's Janet."

"Okay, big guy, the ride's over. Horsey has to answer the phone." Owen got up and took the phone from Hailey. "Hello."

"Did I call at a bad time?" Janet said.

"No, I was just playing with Daniel. Have you arranged for us to see Annie this afternoon?"

"I thought I'd call first and see what time would work best for you."

"I took the week off, so we can be as flexible as you need us to be. How's Annie doing?"

"She's starting to adjust. Her foster parents agree that she seems to have developed a strong attachment to you. Apparently, your name comes up a lot."

"That's good, right?"

"Yes, if you're serious about wanting to get custody of her."

"We definitely are. We've thought about it over the weekend and want to get started as soon as you can arrange it. Hailey is really anxious to meet Annie."

"Well, if any time is okay with you, why don't you meet me at DCF at two?"

"Could we bring a treat for Annie? Or a stuffed toy or something?"

"Sure, but she'll be very excited just to see you again."

"Yeah, I'm really looking forward to it."

"Owen, there's something you need to understand. We're not going to tell Annie you're her biological father or that you're trying to get custody of her. At least not yet."

"Why?"

"You still need to pass the home study. We're talking six weeks, and if that goes well, another three to six months before a decision is final. That's an eternity to a child. Annie really needs to feel safe and content with her foster parents and not be anxious about the future."

"Okay. So what *do* we tell her?"

Will Seevers sat eating his lunch on a wrought-iron bench in Bougainvillea Park, just a few yards from where the second victim had been stabbed. His gut told him Connor did it, but how could he prove it? No judge was going to issue a search warrant without probable cause. And without the murder weapon or the red shirt, he didn't have a case.

He thought about the John Doe and wondered if he had a loved one somewhere who'd like to know what had happened to him.

Will's mind flashed back a year and a half to the brutal murders of Dary Fassih and Issac Kohler, and how the community had rallied around the boys' grieving parents. Will thought it sad that no relative or friend even knew this man had gone to meet his Maker.

What made a guy enter into the culture of the homeless anyway? Was he hiding from something—or someone? Had he been jilted? Was he mentally ill? Lazy? If he'd been unable to find work, why didn't he just go down to the Salvation Army and let them help him get back on his feet? Or apply for government assistance?

Will wadded up his lunch sack and tossed it in the trash receptacle. He had enough trouble trying to get in the mind of a criminal. Why was he using up energy analyzing the homeless?

His cell phone vibrated. He took it off his belt clip and started walking back to his car. "Will Seevers."

"It's Al. The prelim on the third victim is in. Different knife. Left-handed perp. The ME did find some human hair stuck to the blood, and the DNA doesn't match the victim's. Looks like we got a whole nother ball game."

At five minutes until two, Owen pulled his Jaguar into a parking space in front of the DCF building.

"I've got butterflies in my stomach," Hailey said. "I can hardly believe that in a few months Annie could be ours."

Owen took the keys out of the ignition. "Yeah, I know. I can hardly think about anything else right now." He took Hailey's hand in his and squeezed. "Okay, don't forget the present."

Owen got out of the car and waited for Hailey, then put his arm around her and walked inside the building.

"May I help you?" the receptionist said.

"I'm Owen Jones and this is my wife Hailey. Janet Stanton is expecting us."

"Please have a seat. I'll let her know you're here."

Owen sat in the same gray vinyl chair as last time. Hailey sat in the chair next to him, then reached over and picked up a copy of *Family Circle* and started thumbing through it.

Owen glanced across the room at an unkempt young woman biting her fingernails and ignoring the little boy with a Kool-Aid mustache and runny nose who was whining and trying to climb into her lap. A school-age girl with filthy knees sat in the chair next to them and twisted her matted hair with one hand and sucked her thumb with the other. The white collar of her faded red dress looked as if it were stained with mustard. Owen wondered if kids that dirty ever got cuddled.

A young pregnant woman and an older lady stared at Hailey and Owen as if to ask what *they* could possibly be doing there. Owen was suddenly self-conscious of his no-wrinkle trousers and polo shirt and the pretty yellow sundress and designer sandals Hailey had on.

He realized he was fidgeting and finally picked up a December *Newsweek* and thumbed through it, aware that the pregnant lady was still staring. What was taking Janet so long?

Hailey nudged him with her elbow and held up the magazine. "Look how cute these dresses are. I think I'll get my sewing machine out of the attic. It'd be fun making girl's clothes."

"Yeah, I can see you doing that—maybe even curtains and pillows and all that ruffled stuff little girls like."

Owen glanced up again at the child with the dirty knees and wondered how different she might look if someone like Hailey got ahold of her.

"Mr. and Mrs. Jones, Janet will see you now."

Owen took Hailey's hand and followed the receptionist down the gray hallway to the same cheery yellow room as last time.

Janet Stanton met them at the door and shook their hands. "It's been quite a week, hasn't it?"

Owen nodded. "Yeah, it's hard to believe that this time last week we didn't even know Annie existed."

"She's very excited to see you again—and to meet Hailey." Janet smiled. "*Relax*. This isn't a test. It's just a time to get acquainted. Be yourselves. Just remember to be sensitive to Annie and don't make any promises or discuss that you're seeking custody. Are you ready?"

Owen looked at Hailey and then nodded.

Janet opened the door to the pale blue room with balloons painted on the walls.

Annie looked up, then jumped up from the table and ran over to Owen. "Hi!"

Owen squatted in front of her. "Hi yourself. How about a hug?"

Annie threw her arms around him and whispered. "The monsters are *gone*."

"I told you they wouldn't come back." Owen waited a few seconds, then let go of Annie, his hands on her shoulders. "I want you to meet someone."

"Do you got your wife with you?"

"Yes, and I want you to meet her."

Owen stood and took hold of Hailey's hand. "Annie, this is my wife, Hailey. She likes little girls very much."

"Do you got a little girl?"

Hailey smiled. "I have a little *boy*. His name's Daniel, and he's only one year old. Someday he'll be big like you."

"I'm four years old. I can ride my twicycle on the sidewalk. But I'm not allowed in the stweet."

"Well, Owen and I brought you a big-girl present." Hailey handed Annie a pink gift bag with pink and yellow plaid tissue paper. "Go ahead. Open it."

Annie took the bag and removed the tissue paper piece by piece and handed it to Hailey, then reached inside and pulled out a baby doll. She squealed with delight and looked from Hailey to Owen to Janet. "Can I keep her?"

"Yes, she's a gift. Can you tell Hailey and Owen thank you?"

"Thank you."

"Why don't you show them your drawings," Janet said. "I'm going to sit over here in the rocker and read these reports."

Annie took Hailey's hand and then looked up at Owen. "Could you hold my dolly?"

Owen put the doll under his arm and was surprised when Annie took his hand and led them over to the table.

"You can sit, too," Annie said.

Owen sat on one side of Annie and Hailey sat on the other.

"I dwew a picture of my wiener dog. His name's Oscar. But he's not at my new house. We have a owange cat named Charlie. Only Charlie's a girl cat 'cause she gots kittens."

"Kittens?" Hailey said. "Oh, my goodness, I love kittens. How many?"

"Five. And they are weally, weally little. Charlie cawwies them in her *mouth*. Barbara says it doesn't hurt at all—not one bit." Annie put her hands to her cheeks. "And the kitties dwink milk from their mommy."

"Tell me about Barbara," Hailey said.

"Barbara lives at my new house. Pete, too. He's building a pwayhouse for my dollies. And we're going to the zoo. I'm taking the buggy."

Hailey's eyes grew wide, her face animated. "You have a buggy for your dollies?"

Annie gave a firm nod. "Pete fixed the wheels. They were wusted, but now they are vewy, vewy shiny."

"Now you have another dolly to ride in the buggy," Hailey said.

Owen was surprised by the twinge of jealousy he felt at

Annie's obvious fondness for Barbara and Pete. What if she got attached to her foster parents over the next few months and lost interest in him and Hailey?

Owen sat quietly and enjoyed the exchange between Hailey and Annie, thrilled that they seemed to be hitting it off. He absorbed every detail: the adorable way Annie phrased things; the way Hailey knew how to talk girl talk; the way Annie's facial expressions were surprisingly like Daniel's; how much happier she seemed since the last time he saw her; how much fun she was to talk to…and how eager for affection. He had no trouble imagining Annie as their daughter and Daniel's big sister. So why was he scared to death?

Owen noticed Janet putting her papers in a briefcase. He glanced at his watch, surprised that an hour had passed.

Janet got up and walked over to the table. "What a fun afternoon. Annie, can you tell Owen and Hailey thank you for coming to see you?"

"Thank you."

"They need to go to their home now. And you need to go back to Barbara and Pete's."

Annie pushed out her lower lip. "But I want them to stay."

"I know, sweetie, but they have grown-up things to do. Wasn't it wonderful that they came to spend time with you?"

Annie nodded. "They're my fwiends."

"That's right," Owen said. "I prom—I mean, yes, we're definitely friends."

"Can you come to my new house?"

Owen glanced at Janet and then at Annie. "All the nice people taking care of you will decide that. It might be a little while before we see you again."

"Why?" Annie's eyes brimmed with tears.

"Well, because you need time to be with Barbara and Pete and Charlie and the kittens. You need to play with your dollies and go to the zoo. There're so many fun things to do."

"Do you got fun things to do?"

Owen smiled without meaning to. "Yes, but I like seeing you best of all."

"I enjoyed talking with you, Annie." Hailey brushed the curls out of Annie's eyes. "My Daniel is just a baby and can't talk yet."

"Does he got more kids at his house?"

Hailey shook her head. "No, Daniel doesn't have a sister or a brother."

There was a long pause.

"That's okay." Annie patted Hailey's shoulder as if to comfort her. "I don't got a sister and bwother or a mommy and daddy."

Owen locked gazes with Hailey, thinking it was all he could do not to scoop Annie into his arms and tell her he was her daddy, and Hailey was going to be her mommy, and Daniel her brother.

"Would it be okay if I hug you before we leave?" Hailey said.

Annie nodded. She set the new doll on the table, then turned and put her arms around Hailey's neck. "My mommy said I give good hugs. She's with the angels now 'cause she got dead in a car cwash."

In that instant, every selfish concern Owen had about whether he and Hailey should seek custody of Annie turned into raw determination to get it done.

31

Late Monday afternoon, Gordy Jameson was at his desk reviewing the staff schedule and realized Weezie Taylor was standing in the doorway.

"You need somethin'?" Gordy said.

"Just wonderin' why you're so quiet. Aren't you feelin' well?"

"I'm fine. Just have a lot on my plate. Hope you're set up for a big dinner crowd. I expect that coupon you put in today's paper'll drive 'em in."

Weezie's grin stretched her cheeks. "With any luck at all, we'll have them waitin' outside. That'd be fun for a Monday night. We need the extra business if we're gonna exceed last month's figures."

"You're not content with May's 200 percent increase in dessert sales over last year?"

Weezie let out a robust laugh. "Heck, no. It's June now. We're workin' with a whole new set of figures. But I wanna see all the sales go up, not just dessert."

"That's good." Gordy took off his reading glasses and set his paperwork aside. "I think I'm gonna call it a day."

Weezie's round, dark eyes locked on to his. "Boss, you sure you're all right? You're actin' kinda impersonal and distracted. Not like you."

"I just need a good night's sleep and I'll be as charming as ever." The phone rang and Gordy picked up the receiver. "Yeah?"

"Captain is here to see you," Pam Jameson said. "You want me to send him your way?"

"Sure, darlin', thanks." Gordy hung up the phone and tried not to react. "Okay, Weezie, you can go make us some money. I've got company."

"All right, I'm outta here. You get that good night's sleep, hear?"

She turned and left, and Gordy heard Captain's voice in the hallway.

"Hey, girl, where's the fire?"

Weezie laughed her contagious laugh. "Honey, just hang around for the dinner hour. This place is gonna be *red hot*. Weezie the wise and wonderful is workin' her magic."

"I sure miss seein' you at lunchtime," Captain said. "But the smartest thing Gordy ever did was promote you to assistant manager."

"Well, I sure love my job. You take care, Cap'n."

There was a knock at the door.

"Come in," Gordy said.

Captain came in, shut the door, and sat in the chair, his arms folded. "How come you didn't join us guys for lunch?"

"I'm behind on my paperwork."

"Really? I thought maybe you were avoidin' me."

Gordy manufactured a smile. "Gettin' a little paranoid in your old age, are you?"

"All right, I'll ask you outright: Did you tell Will Seevers anything I said about Andrew Connor?"

Gordy reached into his desk and took out a couple TUMS and popped them into his mouth. "I talk to Will about lots of stuff. I didn't think it was a secret that you and Andrew fish together."

"Did you tell Will that Andrew's business had been in trouble?"

"Why would I do that?"

"I don't know, but someone did. When we were out fishin' yesterday, Andrew told me Seevers and one of his cronies came down to the store after closin' on Saturday night. They grilled him about his sales bein' down after Jackson Kincaid opened his store. Implied maybe Andrew wanted to get rid of the competition. They practically accused him of killing the guy!"

"I'm really sorry to hear it," Gordy said.

"Andrew swears I'm the only one he's discussed his financial troubles with—and you're the only one I said anything to. So, how'd the cops find out?"

"Hey, those guys are pretty resourceful. But why would they think Andrew had anything to do with Jackson's murder?"

"Because they're desperate, that's why. This is a buncha hogwash! Andrew's a great guy who's doin' a lot for the Kincaid family."

"He doesn't have anything to fear if he's innocent."

"What do you mean *if*?"

"For cryin' out loud, Captain, stop hollerin'. I'm not the one accusin' him."

Captain looked into Gordy's eyes. "You swear?"

"Yeah. I think Andrew's a straight shooter. I'd tell anyone that, even Will."

"There's no way Andrew did this, Gordy."

"I sure can't see it. But I'm not a cop. One thing I do know: they can't charge him with somethin' if they don't have any evidence to back it up."

"Well, they're not gonna get evidence because he's innocent. How much weight can they give to the description Lawrence Madison gave them?"

"Hard to say. Far as I know, he's the only one who claimed to have seen the killer."

"Except for that lady who saw the guy running down the sidewalk after the latest stabbing," Captain said.

"Yeah, but the cops don't think…"

"Don't think what?"

"Uh, nothin'," Gordy said. "How should I know what the cops think?"

❀ ❀ ❀

Gordy sat in a chaise lounge on the patio, his hand stroking Dusky's fur, and watched the gulf waves turn to white foam on the sand and then slide back into the sea. The sun was hidden behind a glowing white thunderhead that had amassed on the horizon.

Pam came outside and stood next to his chair, her hand on his shoulder. "The pork chops are almost done."

"Sounds good."

There was a long moment of silence.

Finally, Pam pulled up a chair next to his and sat. "You seem out of sorts today. Did I do something to make you mad?"

"It's not you."

"I heard Will's voice last night. Is anything wrong between you two?"

Gordy shook his head. "No. I'm just in a struggle about somethin'."

"Can I help?"

Gordy raised his eyebrows. "It's police business. I'm not supposed to say anything."

"Whatever you tell me stays between us."

Gordy reached over and took her hand. "I know, darlin', but I don't wanna dump this on you."

"Do you think your dark mood is easier for me to handle?"

"Am I that transparent?"

"You are to me. I think Weezie picked up on it, too."

"Did she say somethin'?"

"Only that she hoped you weren't getting sick." Pam combed her hand through his hair. "I certainly don't expect you to break a confidence. But if you need to run your thoughts by someone, I'm here. And I never tell anyone anything we talk about in private."

Gordy exhaled loudly. "I probably should get it off my chest before it gives me a coronary. Will thinks Andrew Connor had somethin' to do with Jackson Kincaid's death. He asked me to pump Captain and find out what they talk about when they're out fishin'."

"*Andrew Connor?*"

"Yeah, that was my reaction. But Will has reason to suspect him in the second killin', too, so I did what he asked."

Gordy told Pam everything he could remember about his initial conversation with Captain, about Will's reaction to finding out Andrew's business had been in the red, and about today's confrontation with Captain.

"I can't believe Will expected you to play dumb," Pam said. "You wear your emotions on your sleeve."

"I was able to dance around the truth when Captain asked me if I'd talked to Will, but it sure felt like lyin'. Me and the captain go back a long way. I hated usin' him that way."

"I'm shocked about Andrew. The times we've talked to him and Cheryl at chamber of commerce meetings, they seemed like really nice people."

"I thought so. But Will's not inventin' stuff to suspect him for. I guess he's gotta check it out. I just hate bein' caught in the middle."

Ellen Jones sat at the breakfast bar watching her father pick at his dinner.

"Dad, would you like some A1 sauce or ketchup for your chopped sirloin?"

"Since when do you care what I like?" Lawrence Madison said.

"Of course I care what you like. That's why I went to the trouble to make you au gratin potatoes, fresh green beans, and chopped steak. You've hardly touched any of it, and you didn't eat lunch either. You need to eat."

"I'm not eating this garbage! I want to go home! Your mother's got dinner ready."

Ellen softened her voice and put her hand on his forearm. "Mom's in heaven, remember?"

He looked over at her and stared for several seconds, then dropped his fork on his plate. "I'm going home. Where'd you hide my car?"

Lawrence jumped up, and before Ellen realized what was happening, he unlocked the kitchen door and yanked it open, setting off the security alarm. He turned around, his hands over his ears, and ran from the room.

Ellen hurried over to the keypad next to the door and entered in the code to disarm the alarm, relieved when the siren stopped blaring. She waited several seconds, then picked up the phone and dialed.

"Seaport Alarm Company."

"This is Ellen Jones, code 00225. My elderly father accidentally set off the alarm. Everything's fine." *Other than I'm losing my mind!*

"All right, Mrs. Jones, thanks for letting us know."

Ellen hung up the phone and stood with her eyes closed, her heart thumping. She took a slow deep breath and let it out.

Lord, I'll never make it to Thursday. You've got to do something!

Ellen sat at the breakfast bar until she felt civil again, and then went to check on her father. He wasn't in his bedroom. She searched downstairs and then went up the winding stairs to the widow's watch.

"Dad, you can come down now. It was just the security alarm."

Ellen reached the top of the stairs, her eyes moving from left to right across the room. "Dad, are you up here...? Dad...?"

Ellen jogged down the stairs and went in and out of every room in the house, calling for her father.

She went out the French doors and down the back steps and checked behind the gazebo, then went inside and out the front door. She searched the front and side yards and glanced up and down the street, then went back inside and searched the house again.

Finally, Ellen collapsed on the living room couch, her body trembling and her emotions on edge. How far could he have gone?

She grabbed her purse and dug through it until she found a digital photograph Owen had taken of her dad. She went out to the garage, backed out of the driveway, and started driving slowly up and down the streets in her neighborhood.

Owen Jones sat at the kitchen table eating dinner with Hailey and Daniel and tried to imagine what it would be like if Annie were there.

"You want more baked chicken?" Hailey said.

"Yeah, thanks. This is good."

"I'm glad to see you've got your appetite back."

"I'm feeling good about the idea of Annie being ours."

Hailey smiled and handed him the platter of chicken. "Me too. She's precious."

"It'll be a lot more work with two kids. You sure you're up to it?"

"Everything in me says yes." Hailey put another piece of chicken on her plate, then looked at Owen. "I'm eager to do the home study. But it's a huge responsibility, and we should be praying about it."

"I am praying about it."

"I said we. Together."

"Honey, we've already been through this. I'm just not comfortable praying out loud."

"How do you know when you've never done it?"

"I just do."

Hailey sighed. "It's not only about you praying with me. It's about our teaching Daniel and Annie to pray. Are you going to relegate all spiritual responsibility to me?"

"Well, you have more time. And you're the one who's gone to Bible study classes."

"But you're the spiritual head of the family."

"For crying out loud, Hailey, I grew up an atheist. What do I know about teaching kids to pray? I hardly know how to do it for myself."

"Then let's learn together. I want our family to walk with God. I don't want our kids growing up as spiritually desolate as we were."

Owen put down his fork and glanced over at Daniel. "I really do want the kids to grow up with a clear understanding of right and wrong and why Jesus died for them. I want them to have a relationship with God. But can't they learn all that in Sunday school?"

"It's a good start. But unless *we* model a relationship with God so the kids will see what it looks like, I'm not sure Sunday school will be enough."

"I've never even been to Sunday school."

Hailey started to say something and then didn't.

"I suppose you want me to remedy that, too?"

Hailey raised her eyebrows. "I wasn't going to push for it until Daniel turned two. But now that we might get custody of a four-year-old, we can't put it off. I think it's vital that we take responsibility to train our children in Christian values. How can we do that if we haven't been trained?"

"I listen to the pastor's sermons. I know right from wrong."

"Do you know the Ten Commandments?"

"Sure. Well, some of them. Don't kill. Don't steal. Don't commit adultery."

"There're seven more."

Owen sighed. "Okay, I don't then. But I'm not out sinning either."

"Unless, of course, you're breaking the other seven com-

mandments you don't know. Do you know why you were cre-
ated?"

"Uh, not exactly. To go to heaven and be with God, I guess.
What's your point, Hailey?"

"I want us to grow together as Christians. I want us to know
at least the basic answers when our kids ask us questions about
faith and morals. And I want us to feel comfortable talking to
God in front of each other."

"You're back to wanting us to pray together."

"Uh-huh."

"I wouldn't be very good at it."

"By whose standard?" Hailey said. "I'm sure God pays more
attention to what's coming out of our hearts than the *words* we
use to pray."

"But what if I sound stupid?"

Hailey touched his arm. "You're not stupid. Why would you
sound that way? I just want us to talk to God together. Could we
at least try it?"

"You really think it's that important?"

"I do."

The phone rang.

"I'll get it." Owen wiped his mouth with a napkin, then
walked over to the wall phone and picked up the receiver.
"Hello."

"Honey, it's Mom. Granddad is missing. He set off the security alarm by mistake, and while I phoned the alarm company to
report it, he must have left the house."

"Are you sure?" Owen said. "Maybe he's hiding."

"I don't think so. I looked everywhere in the house..." His
mother sounded emotional and she paused for several seconds.
"Dad's only been gone thirty minutes. He couldn't have gone far."

"I'll come over there and help you look."

"No, don't do that. It'll take you forty-five minutes to get here. I called Julie and Ross and Mina and Ali, and they're going to help me look. What I really need you to do is pray."

"Yeah, okay. Did you check Gordy's? Granddad might remember how to get there."

"No, but that's a good idea. Listen, I'm going to go. Pray that he doesn't get hurt and that I find him soon."

"We will, Mom. Keep me posted." Owen hung up the phone and looked over at Hailey. "Granddad's missing."

"I gathered that. What happened?"

Owen went back to the table and told Hailey exactly what his mother had said. "Mom asked us to pray."

Hailey took Daniel's hand and then Owen's. "Why don't we pray as a family?"

Owen wanted to let go but glanced over at his son's smiling face and, instead, reached over and took Daniel's tiny hand in his. "Shall we let Mommy start?"

Hailey closed her eyes and bowed her head. "Father, we come to You because Your Word says we can. We ask for Your protection on Granddad, wherever he is. Help Ellen find him. Please don't let her get too stressed out. Keep her calm. Let her feel Your presence. Show her where to look."

Owen felt Hailey squeeze his hand and assumed that was his cue to say something. "Uh, we also pray that Mom won't blame herself, and that You show her positive ways to deal with Granddad's obstinate behavior. Thank you, God."

There was a long uncomfortable pause. Did she want him to say something else?

"In Jesus' Name we pray. Amen." Hailey let go of his hand. "That wasn't so difficult, was it?"

"Not really. But I didn't say much."

"You said what was on your heart. That's all prayer really is." Hailey sat back in her chair. "Are you sure Ellen doesn't want us to drive over and help her look?"

"Yeah, she called the Hamiltons and the Tehranis to help. Knowing her, she probably has half the church praying, too."

Ellen turned into the Quick Stop parking lot and spotted Julie and Ross Hamilton's Ford minivan and Mina and Ali Tehrani standing next to their red Cadillac. She pulled into a parking space and got out and, an instant later, was smothered in hugs.

"You're all so sweet to help." Ellen reached in the pocket of her sundress and pulled out the photograph of her father. "This is a recent picture. Dad's six-one, slender, gray hair. He has on khaki pants and a green and white plaid shirt. His name is Lawrence Madison."

"Why don't we search in different areas of town?" Ali said. "Mina brought her car, too."

"All right," Ellen said. "I'll look here on the south side and check out the beach and Gordy's and the rehab center and a few other places that might be familiar to him."

"I'll go north," Ali said. "Mina, you go east. Ross and Julie, you head west."

"Wait." Ellen wrote down her cell number and handed it to each of them. "Call me if you find him. I have each of your cell numbers and will relay the word. He may be confused and unco-operative. If he won't come with you, don't let him out of your sight till I get there."

"All right," Ross said, "let's get rolling while we've still got some daylight."

32

On Monday evening, Will Seevers sat on the couch reading the newspaper and listening to a new instrumental CD Margaret had bought. The phone rang and he picked it up.

"Hello."

"Why the heck didn't you tell me you'd gone down to Andrew's store and as much as accused him of killin' Jackson Kincaid!"

"Take it easy, Gordy. It was for your own good. I figured Captain would tell you, and I wanted you to look surprised."

"Well, you got your wish. He came in late this afternoon, loaded for bear, and said you and one of your *cronies* had raked Andrew over the coals and implied that maybe he killed Jackson Kincaid to get rid of the competition. Captain also asked me point-blank if I said anything to you about Andrew's sales bein' down. I sidestepped the truth because you asked me to, but I'm done. Don't ask me to do it again."

"All right, I won't. But what you did was invaluable to our investigation."

"What about what's invaluable to *me*? I'm not riskin' my friendship with Captain over this. You're on your own. I can't believe you really think Andrew killed Jackson Kincaid anyway."

"Doesn't matter what I think. I'm going to have a hard time proving it."

"Yeah, well, maybe he didn't do it." Gordy exhaled into the

receiver. "Did you even ask Mrs. Kincaid whether there was a conflict between her husband and Andrew?"

"Give me a little credit. Of course we did."

"And?"

"Said she wasn't aware of any conflict, that the Connors had always been nice to them. It's obvious she's so grateful for what Andrew's done with the memorial fund she can't see straight."

"Or maybe *you* can't. I don't mean any disrespect, Will—you're a great cop and an even better police chief—but it looks like you're graspin' at straws. I mean, even the victim's wife won't bad-mouth Andrew. If the guy's really capable of murder, wouldn't you think he'd be on somebody's bad list?"

Will felt his cell phone vibrate. "Gordy, I've got to go. I've got another call."

"You sore at me?"

"No. Just frustrated I can't pull the evidence together. Talk to you later, okay? Give Pam my love."

"Yeah, same to Margaret."

Will hung up and opened his cell phone.

"Seevers."

"Chief, it's Jack Rutgers. I'm out cruising and just ran into Ellen Jones. Did you know her father's missing?"

"No, fill me in."

"Not much to tell. He accidentally set off the security alarm at the house and then disappeared. She's out looking for him."

"Is she sure about how he disappeared?"

"Yeah, seems to be. I told her I'd keep my eyes open."

Ellen Jones worked her way through a crowd of customers waiting outside Gordy's and walked in the entrance. She spotted Weezie Taylor and waved, grateful when Weezie smiled and walked toward her.

"Evenin', Ellen. You here for dinner?"

"Actually I'm looking for my dad. Have you seen him?"

"No. Is Lawrence missin' again?"

"He set off the security alarm at the house, and the next thing I knew he was nowhere in sight. The Hamiltons and the Tehranis are out looking for him, too."

"I'm so sorry. Wish there was somethin' I could do."

"There is." Ellen handed Weezie a piece of paper with her cell number on it. "Would you keep an eye out for him, and if he comes in, call me right away?"

"Be glad to. Try not to worry yourself sick. He might be lost, but the Lord's got His eye on him."

"You're right. Thanks, Weezie."

Ellen walked out of Gordy's and across the pier to her car and got inside. The sun had sunk behind a mass of gray clouds and it would be dark soon. She leaned her head back and closed her eyes. *Lord, where is he? Please help me find him.*

Ellen reached for her cell phone and pressed the autodial for Guy's apartment in Tallahassee. It rang once. Twice. Three times. "Come on, Counselor. Pick up."

"This is Guy Jones. Leave a message and I'll call you back." Beep.

Ellen disconnected the phone and started to dial his cell number when a knock on the window startled her. She saw Officer Rutgers's face through the glass and rolled down the window.

"I didn't mean to scare you," he said. "I saw you sitting out here and wondered if you'd had any luck finding your father?"

"No. And frankly, I don't know where else to look."

"Is there any chance he might've gone back to your house?"

"I never even considered that." Ellen's heart sank. "I left in such a hurry I'm sure I didn't lock the doors. If he's there, he might not be safe!"

"Why don't I follow you home and check things out, and we'll go from there."

❦ ❦ ❦

Owen Jones sat on the screened-in porch, the last vestiges of day-light still visible in the western sky. He wondered if Annie would fall asleep hugging her new baby doll.

"There you are." Hailey came out on the porch and closed the sliding glass door, then sat next to him on the couch. "Daniel's finally out."

Owen put his arm around her. "I love you."

"I love you, too. What brought that on?"

"I don't know…It was kind of neat praying together. I didn't think I'd like it, but I did. Made me feel closer to you."

Hailey laid her head on his shoulder. "Maybe we could start by praying before meals and get Daniel used to it, too. Right now, he thinks all the hand holding is a game."

Owen smiled. "Yeah, he thought it was pretty fun…Think we should call Mom and check on Granddad?"

"I'm sure she'll call us as soon as there's something to tell us."

"I wonder what happens if she can't find him? It's almost too dark to search anymore."

Ellen waited in the car while Officer Rutgers searched the house. She opened her cell phone and dialed Guy's apartment again.

"Hello?"

"Thank heavens you're home. I missed you earlier."

"You called? I didn't get a message—"

"I know. I didn't leave one. Listen, you should know what's going on here."

Ellen told him everything that had happened, starting with her father's nasty attitude at dinner and finishing with Officer Rutgers following her home.

"He's checking out the house now," Ellen said. "But the lights were out when we got here. I don't think Dad came back."

"I'm so sorry, honey. What a mess."

"What'll I do if I can't find him...? Guy hold on. The officer is coming out of the house." Ellen put the phone on the seat and got out of the car.

"Your dad isn't here," Rutgers said. "There's no one in the house. I locked the back door, so it's safe to go inside."

Ellen swallowed the emotion. "It's too late to look anymore."

"He may come home on his own. But judging from my past experience with seniors who wander off, I'm guessing someone will realize he's lost and take care of him till they figure out where he belongs. Does he have anything on him that gives your name and address?"

Ellen nodded. "I put one of Guy's business cards in Dad's wallet."

"Okay. I'll keep my eyes open while I'm cruising. Why don't I check back in about an hour and let's see where we are?"

"Thank you. I'd really appreciate that."

Rutgers tipped the brim of his hat. "Yes, ma'am."

Ellen got in the car and picked up the phone. "Did you hear that?"

"Yes," Guy said. "Do you need me to drive down there?"

"Absolutely not. You can't do anything more than I've already done."

Beep.

"Guy, that's my call-waiting."

"Okay, honey. Try to stay calm."

"Let me call you back." Ellen switched to the incoming call. "Hello?"

"Ellen, it's Ross. We found him."

"Thank the Lord! Where?"

"At the Old Seaport Dairy. Julie spotted him sitting outside. We're with him now. He's finishing a cup of lemon custard."

"Should I come get him?"

"No, we're about ready to leave. He's fine."

Well, that's one of us. "I can't thank you enough."

"Glad to help. See you in about ten minutes."

Ellen pulled the car into the garage, pushed the remote, and waited until the door closed behind her. She went into the house and turned on the kitchen light, then walked into the entry hall and turned on the porch light.

She paced in the hallway and dialed Mina and then Ali and told them the good news and thanked them for their help.

A few minutes later, Ross and Julie's minivan pull into the driveway. Ellen pushed open the front door and went outside on the porch, her hands in the pockets of her sundress, and tried to look more relieved than angry.

Lawrence sauntered across the front lawn and up the steps, Julie and Ross on his heels.

"Why do *you* look like such a grump?" Lawrence said as he squeezed past Ellen and went into the house.

Ellen put her arms around Ross and then Julie, determined not to get emotional. "Thanks. I don't know what I would've done without you. So tell me what happened."

"Not a lot to tell," Ross said. "After Julie spotted him, we parked the car and walked up to him and told him we were friends of yours and had come to take him home. He didn't even question it."

Julie raised her eyebrows. "The manager, Joe somebody, came out and talked to us. He said your dad had been sitting outside about an hour and seemed confused, so the waitress brought him some lemon custard and kept an eye on him, hoping someone would come looking for him."

"Did Dad say anything on the way home?"

Ross shook his head. "No, but when we pulled in the driveway he said this wasn't where he lived. I told him it was your house, but he seemed mad, like he thought we'd tricked him."

"He's pretty confused right now," Ellen said. "I can't thank you enough for finding him."

"I'll call the prayer chain and tell them the good news," Julie said. "You get a good night's sleep."

Ellen waved as the Hamiltons' minivan backed out of the driveway; and as soon as they drove off, she leaned against the front door, put her face in her hands, and began to sob.

After she regained her composure, she went inside and found Lawrence sitting on the couch, the TV blaring. Ellen picked up the remote and pressed the mute button. "We need to talk."

Lawrence sat with his arms crossed and acted as if he didn't hear her.

"Why in the world did you leave the house? I was worried sick."

Lawrence glared at her. "I want to go home."

"Dad, how many times do I have to tell you your house has been sold? You can't go back to Ocala! I'm trying to help you! Why can't you just cooperate?"

"I don't need your help."

"*Yes,* you do. You're having trouble remembering things. And I'm responsible to see you don't get hurt."

"You're a terrible daughter! You only care about what makes *you* happy!"

Ellen threw up her hands. "You really think I'd put up with your verbal abuse if I only cared about what makes *me* happy? I promised Mom I would watch out for you! I'm doing this for her whether you appreciate it or not!"

"You hate me! You've always hated me!"

"I don't know what I feel, Dad! It certainly isn't love!" The words escaped Ellen's mouth and seemed to hang in the silence like a flashing billboard.

She felt the heat color her face and tossed the remote to Lawrence and ran from the living room, tears blurring her vision.

33

Ellen Jones stood in the alcove of the widow's watch, her head against the glass, her eyes fixed on the sunrise. In the quiet, she could hear her father's spoon scraping the bowl and hoped he had eaten all of his Cream of Wheat.

He seemed fine this morning, as if the events of the night before had never happened. Sometimes not being able to remember might be a blessing.

"I don't know what I feel, Dad! It certainly isn't love!" Ellen was grateful her mother hadn't heard the ugly, awful truth spill out of her daughter's mouth. She was sorry for saying the words, but who could blame her for feeling that way after a lifetime of not being able to please her father, no matter how hard she tried?

Mother had always told her how much her father had delighted in her when she was little. How he had taken Ellen with him to the hardware store and paraded her around like a prized possession. Why couldn't she remember ever feeling special to him or receiving any heartfelt affection? As far back as she could remember, they'd had opposing perspectives on nearly everything that mattered. And he never seemed to tire of pointing out how she had failed to measure up to his expectations.

Ellen took a Kleenex out of her robe pocket and wiped the tears off her face. *Lord, it scares me how hard my heart is getting. He needs me, and I don't want to be needed. Teach me to love him. Show me how to honor my father.*

❧ ❧ ❧

Will Seevers walked into his office and flipped the light switch. He set a cup of Starbucks coffee on his desk and looked through his phone messages. There was a knock at the door. He glanced up and saw Al Backus standing in the doorway.

"This oughta jump-start your morning," Al said. "Some guy looking at fifteen to twenty for armed robbery cut a deal with the DA in exchange for coughing up the perp in the third stabbing— some guy named Leon Hawkins who's been shooting off his mouth at a nightclub on Fourteenth. A couple detectives from vice went to Hawkins's apartment with a warrant and found a switchblade and a wallet with Jerome Powers's driver's license and credit cards stashed under the mattress. Hawkins denies knowing anything about it but hasn't asked for a lawyer."

"This is almost too good to be true."

"It gets better. He's a southpaw. All we need is his DNA to match the hairs we found on the victim, and we can place him at the scene."

Will sat at his desk. "We really need this one, Al. It could go a long way in regaining public confidence and also give us a little breathing room to figure out how Andrew Connor fits into all this. If Hawkins looks good for this, get him to confess."

Al grinned. "No problem."

"All right. Wrap it up neat and tidy and then let's make sure the media jumps on it."

Gordy Jameson saw Captain Jack walk in the crab shack with Eddie Drummond and Adam Spalding.

"Hey, Gordo," Eddie said. "You eatin' with us today?"

"Yeah, let me tell Pam and I'll be right out. Everybody want the special?"

All heads nodded.

Gordy went through the double doors and over to where Pam was making piecrusts. "I'm gonna eat lunch with the guys. Would you keep an eye on things?"

Pam smiled. "As Weezie would say, 'I gotcha covered.'"

"Don't forget the part about not givin' away the farm." Gordy chuckled and kissed Pam on the cheek. "Come get me if you need me."

He left the kitchen, told the waitress to bring four specials and four limeades, then went out the back door to the deck and joined his friends at the round umbrella table.

"We missed you yesterday," Adam said.

"I was behind on some stuff. Anything I need to know?"

Adam smiled. "Not from yesterday. But get this…Andrew Connor just put up a ten-thousand-dollar reward for anyone who gives police information that leads to Jackson Kincaid's killer."

"Amazing," Gordy said. "How'd you find that out?"

"I was in the dive shop across the street on my way over here and saw a big sign in his window."

"Man, that guy's really puttin' up the bucks," Eddie said. "First the memorial fund and now this. Seems like he's doing more than the cops to solve the case."

Captain nodded. "Andrew's a good guy. I think he'd do just about anything he could to bring the killer to justice and make sure the Kincaid family's taken care of."

"Well, the cops are sure sitting on their duffs." Eddie looked sheepishly at Gordy. "Sorry, but it's the truth. They've got three murders and no suspects. What does that tell you?"

Gordy bit his tongue. *It tells me you don't know what you're talkin' about.*

Ellen set a plate with half of a turkey breast sandwich and four apple slices on the breakfast bar in front of her father just as the phone rang.

"Hello."

"Hi, honey, it's me," Guy Jones said. "How are you doing after last night?"

"So-so."

"I take it Lawrence is within earshot?"

"Uh-huh."

"Forty-eight hours from now Dr. Roper should be able to tell us what to do to help him."

"I can hardly wait. By the way, I just heard on the noonday news that the police arrested a man who confessed to killing the third victim. They didn't give many details but said he wasn't being charged in the first two."

"Maybe he will be later. It'd sure be nice to get the threat to your dad behind us."

Lawrence got up and started walking out of the kitchen.

"Dad, wait," Ellen said. "You need to eat lunch."

"You eat it! I'm going home."

Ellen sighed. "I guess you heard that?" she said to Guy.

"Yes, but try not to worry. I'll be home tomorrow night, and Thursday morning we'll tackle this together."

"He just seems so much more belligerent all of a sudden. I'm afraid I can't handle him. He keeps insisting he wants to go home. No matter what I try to talk to him about, it always seems to come back to that."

"Honey, I know it's overwhelming. Just hang on till I get home tomorrow night."

"And pray they don't cancel his appointment."

"They won't. I'll check in later, okay? I love you."

"Love you, too."

Ellen hung up and went into the living room and saw Lawrence sitting in front of the TV, his arms folded across his chest.

"Dad, would you try eating just the apple slices?"

He glared at her and didn't answer.

Ellen walked back into the kitchen and sat at the breakfast bar. A few seconds later, Lawrence came into the kitchen and opened the door underneath the sink and seemed to be looking for something.

"Dad, what do you need?"

"Where's the watering can? I need to water my plants."

"The plants are silk. I don't have a watering can."

He turned and looked at her, his eyebrows furrowed. "Where are your mother's African violets?"

Ellen didn't answer. Would it even register if she told him they had wilted and been thrown out years ago?

Will Seevers went into Gordy's Crab Shack around one thirty.

Pam Jameson walked out of the kitchen and gave him a double take. "Hi, Will. What brings you in this time of day?"

"Is Gordy around?"

"He's in his office. You can go on back."

"Thanks."

Will walked past the kitchen and down the hallway and stopped in front of Gordy's open door and knocked.

"Come in."

Will stepped inside. "Got a minute?"

"Yeah, sure. Come in and sit."

"Did you hear we made an arrest in the third stabbing?"

"Yeah, but that's all I heard. I don't know any of the details." Gordy put down his pencil and sat back in his chair.

"Some punk looking at time for armed robbery cut a deal with the DA and fingered the perp—a guy named Leon Hawkins. Detectives got a warrant and found the murder weapon and the third victim's wallet under Hawkins's mattress. His DNA matched what we found on the victim, and his prints were on the knife and the wallet. *Plus* he confessed."

"A slam dunk, eh?" Gordy raised his eyebrows. "Did he say why he did it?"

"The victim made the mistake of opening his wallet and revealing a stack of bills when Hawkins was in the Quick Stop on Third. Hawkins followed him out of the store and onto a quiet street, and the rest is history."

"How much was the victim carryin'?"

"About four hundred dollars—last Friday's paycheck."

"What a cryin' shame—a man's life for a lousy four hundred dollars." Gordy shook his head from side to side. "By the way, did you hear that Andrew Connor is offering ten grand to anyone who gives information that leads police to Jackson Kincaid's killer?"

"You're kidding?" Will said. "Where'd you hear that?"

"Adam Spalding was in the dive shop across the street from Fish Tales just before he came in for lunch. Said he saw a big notice in the window. Still think Andrew's guilty?"

Will made a tent with his fingers. "Look, Gordy, it's not as though I'm out to get him without a reason. It's not personal. I told you I'm going to have a hard time proving it."

"Yeah, especially if he didn't do it."

"Fair enough. But I've got a responsibility to find the killer, and I can't let the skepticism of other people influence the case. I have to pursue every angle."

"Yeah. Yeah, I know. So did Meagan get back from D.C. okay?"

Will nodded. "She started talking the instant she stepped off the bus last night and didn't stop until she went to bed. Then started in again this morning." He chuckled. "Thanks for contributing to her travel fund. This is a trip she'll always remember."

"Aw, I was glad to do it. Meagan's like my own kid."

There was a long moment of silence.

"Somethin' else on your mind, Will?"

"I just want to be sure you and I are okay. I don't want this case jeopardizing our friendship either. When I asked you to talk to Captain, I honestly didn't think you were going to find out anything that might establish a motive. But once you did, I couldn't ignore it."

"I know that. I just don't want to play cop anymore."

Ellen disarmed the security alarm, then opened the front door and went down the steps and out to the mailbox. Blanche Davis was walking her white poodle down the street and rushed over to her.

"Oh, hello, dear. It's so good to see you!" Blanche said. "We've all been so worried about you."

"The past few weeks have been difficult, but I think we're starting to see the light at the end of the tunnel. It was awfully nice of you to watch Sarah Beth last night so Julie and Ross could help me look for Dad."

"I don't have to be asked twice to spend time with that little doll. How is your father today?"

Ellen bent down and scratched the poodle's chin. "I don't think he remembers what happened."

"Isn't that sad?"

"Well, at least he's unaware of how sad it is."

"I so miss being able to visit with you," Blanche said. "When you get to the place where you're ready for chitchat, I do hope you'll call. I'll even make that chocolate Bundt cake you like so much.

"I would love that. Guy and I are taking Dad for an evaluation on Thursday. I'm hoping things will start to get better after that."

"Are you planning to have your father live with you permanently?"

Ellen didn't say what she was thinking. "I don't know yet. We need to figure out what's best for all of us."

Blanche put her arms around Ellen and gave her a motherly squeeze. "Well, I'm sure you'll make the right decision."

"Thanks for the vote of confidence."

Blanche looked down at her poodle and gently tugged on the

leash. "Come on, Nicki. We girls need our exercise."

Ellen heard a low-flying plane and glanced up at the familiar yellow and red banner it was pulling. She removed a bundle from the mailbox and walked back in the house and entered the code on the security alarm. She went in the kitchen and sat at the breakfast bar and opened the mail, and finally gave in to the self-pity that had taunted her since last night. Why should she have to sacrifice her happiness to accommodate an abusive father who never loved her and neither wanted nor appreciated her help? How she missed her writing and going to Bible study and those spur-of-the-moment lunches with her friends. But more than anything, she missed her quiet time on the beach and evenings at home with just Guy.

Ellen pushed the mail aside and went over to the counter and set the cookie jar on the breakfast bar. She reached in and got a peanut butter cookie and took a bite, then poured a glass of milk, sat on a stool, and began thumbing through the June issue of *Better Homes and Gardens*.

She became engrossed in an article about how to prepare quick and easy romantic dinners for two. She copied down several recipes and put them in her recipe box, wondering how long it would be before she had an opportunity to try them.

The phone rang and she picked it up. "Hello."

"Hi, honey," Guy said. "I had a few minutes before my three o'clock meeting and thought I'd call and see if things had calmed down."

"For the moment. I've actually been reading a magazine and lost track of time." Ellen put the lid on the cookie jar and wondered how many calories she had just consumed.

"Did your dad ever eat his lunch?"

"No, and I decided not to push it. I went outside to get the mail and talked to Blanche for a minute, then opened the mail and have been reading ever since."

"Well, good. I see the partners headed for the conference

room, so I need to go. I'll call you tonight. I love you."

"I love you, too."

Ellen hung up the phone and put the cookie jar back on the counter. She went in the living room and turned off the TV, then walked down the hall to her father's room, surprised he wasn't in there.

She stood in the hallway and called his name. He didn't answer.

Ellen checked the bathroom and the other rooms in the hallway and then checked the living room, dining room, and kitchen.

She stomped up the winding staircase to the widow's watch. "Dad…? Dad…! The least you could do is answer me!"

Ellen scanned the room, then ran back down the stairs, disarmed the alarm, and went out on the veranda. "Dad…!" she shouted. "Are you out here…?" Ellen threw up her hands. "I can't believe this. I turn my back for two minutes…"

She heard the phone ring and ran back inside. "Hello."

"Mrs. Jones?"

"Yes."

"This is Tracy Palmer, the leasing manager at Colony Reef Retirement Center."

"Oh, hi. I trust you got the message I left you about my father and father-in-law staying with me until we—"

"Yes, but that's not why I'm calling. I called to tell you their apartment is on fire. I thought I should let you know right away before you heard it on the news."

Ellen struggled to find her voice and finally said, "Tracy, tell the firefighters that my father may be in that apartment! Did you hear me…? Tracy?"

"Uh, yes, I heard you." Tracy's voice was shaking. "W-what makes you think he's in there?"

"Because he's missing! And he's confused. And he's been talking incessantly about wanting to go home. Please…tell the firefighters to check his apartment! I'm on my way!"

34

Ellen Jones sped down Seaport Parkway, aware that she was driving well over the speed limit. She glanced up through the windshield to see if she could see smoke, but the sky was hidden by a canopy of leafy branches.

Ellen saw a string of brake lights come on in front of her and slowed the car to a crawl and stuck her head out the window, trying to see what was holding up traffic.

Lord, please don't let anything happen to Dad. How would she live with herself if her negligence had caused something awful to happen to him?

Lawrence's words echoed in her mind: *"You're a terrible daughter! You only care about what makes you happy!"*

"Come on people, move it!" Ellen noticed the atmosphere looked a little bluish and she was sure she smelled smoke.

In her side mirror she saw an ambulance, its lights flashing, weaving around cars in both lanes. Finally, it pulled into the center lane and passed her, the sudden shriek of its siren adding to her edginess.

The traffic started to pick up speed, and Ellen saw that cars were being diverted by the police and not allowed to turn on Ibis Drive. She stopped next to one of the officers and rolled down her window.

"Keep moving, ma'am" the officer said.

"My father may be trapped in that fire. Please, I have to get in there!"

The officer bent down and looked in the window and seemed to be studying her face. Finally, he motioned to another officer. "Let this one through."

Ellen turned right, and above the palm trees, she saw billowy black smoke filling the sky. She pressed on the accelerator and raced toward the entrance of the retirement center. She parked her car at the clubhouse, then jogged down to her father's apartment building, where she saw an ambulance and two fire trucks. Firefighters were holding high-pressure hoses and directing torrents of water into the blazing building.

Ellen stopped behind a crowd of onlookers. From what she could see, the ground-level apartment was an inferno and the entire building appeared to be engulfed.

She quickly scanned the crowd and saw a gray-haired man with his back to her, standing taller than anyone else. "Dad!"

Ellen pushed her way through a wall of bodies and reached out and grabbed his arm just as he turned and looked at her.

"Oh, I'm sorry," Ellen said. "I thought you were my father. I saw your gray hair and—"

"Mrs. Jones!"

Ellen saw Tracy Palmer rushing over to her.

"I saw you pull up," Tracy said. "Did you find your dad?"

"No! Did you tell the firefighters to check his apartment?"

"Yes, right after I talked to you, but I've been consoling the tenant in 212. He fell down the stairs trying to escape and injured his back. We just put him in the ambulance."

Ellen heard shouts and then looked up as the roof collapsed and flames and sparks surged into the air. She hurried over to a man in bunker gear who held a walkie-talkie to his ear and tapped him on the arm.

"Sir? Sir! Did you check that ground level apartment on the left? My father could be trapped in there, and I—"

"We checked the entire building, ma'am. Everybody we could get out is out. I can't send any of my people in there now."

Ellen stared at the inferno, her heart breaking, her conscience taunting her with the careless words she had thrown at her father, *I don't know what I feel, Dad! It certainly isn't love!*

Ellen's eyes clouded over and tears trickled down her cheeks. She was aware of a helicopter flying overhead. And a woman crying hysterically about a missing cat. And the muffled sound of a phone ringing. The third time it rang, she groped her pocket and put her cell phone to her ear. "Hello."

"Ellen, this is Blanche. I tried calling your house, but you didn't answer. I'm afraid Lawrence got out again. Don't worry, dear, he's just fine. He's sitting in my porch swing, enjoying a nice glass of raspberry tea."

Ellen turned her Thunderbird into the driveway of the gray two-story house with white Bahamas shutters, which graced the corner of Live Oak Place. Blanche waved from the screened-in porch. Ellen got out of the car, aware that her clothes reeked of smoke, and walked across the lawn and up the steps, her knees feeling as though they might not make it to the top.

Blanche opened the door and put her arms around Ellen and whispered, "For some reason, he thinks my name is Sybil. Was that your mother's name?"

"No, Sybil was his neighbor in Ocala."

Blanche looked over at Lawrence and smiled. "He's been a perfect gentleman. We've had a nice visit, haven't we, Lawrence?"

Ellen stared at her father, trying to grasp the irony that while she stood outside his burning apartment, envisioning his horrific demise and bemoaning that he had died thinking she didn't love him, he was sitting on Blanche Davis's porch, sipping raspberry tea.

Ellen swallowed the emotion. She could hardly believe he was alive and promised herself never again to say or do anything she would regret after he was gone.

"You don't have to run off," Blanche said. "It's so pleasant out here. Why don't you stay and have some raspberry tea and sugar cookies?"

"Thanks, that would be nice," Ellen heard herself say.

"I'll just be a minute, dear."

Blanche went inside, and Nicki came out on the porch and started yapping and running in circles.

Ellen picked up the poodle and sat in a white wicker chair facing the porch swing where her father sat, rubbing the dog's ears and not really knowing what to say.

Finally Lawrence said, "Why aren't you at work?"

"Oh...I thought it might be nice just to take the day off."

"It's about time. You should plan something fun with the boys. They don't see enough of you."

Ellen blinked the stinging from her eyes. "You know, Dad, that's a really good idea."

Ellen sat in the dark living room, vaguely aware of the rhythmic ticking of the cuckoo clock in the kitchen. She replayed over and over in her mind those horrible moments when she thought her father had perished in the fire.

How easy it had been to blame him for the rift in their relationship. His caustic remarks had wounded her more times than she could count; and his lack of support for her college education and her dream of being a journalist had all but done away with any meaningful interaction.

But there came a crossroads, an opportunity for Ellen to soften and allow herself to feel like his little girl again, but she chose instead to slight him...

Ellen had sat next to Guy in the old Chevy Impala, his arm around her, as they pulled into the driveway of the ivy-covered brick house she grew up in.

Guy turned off the motor. "You're awfully quiet. You worried about their reaction?"

Ellen smiled and ran her thumb across the shiny gold band on her left hand. "Not really. Mom will be happy because we're happy. I'm sure Dad will have something hateful to say, but I don't really care. The last thing we wanted was a church wedding."

"You're an adult. You don't have to answer to him."

"I know, but it gripes me he blames the university for turning me into an atheist…as if I'm not capable of thinking for myself. I don't see that his beliefs have changed his hateful disposition one iota." Ellen leaned her head on Guy's shoulder. "I'm glad we decided to elope. It was a fun adventure we can tell our kids about someday."

"Yeah, it was. I just hope that later on you don't regret not having your father walk you down the aisle."

"Why would I want him to give me away? He never cared about anything that mattered to me."

"Well, I plan on caring about everything that matters to you." Guy picked up her hand and kissed it. "Come on, Mrs. Jones, let's go tell your folks your address has changed."

Ellen and Guy walked up to the front door, arm in arm, then went inside and told her parents that they had run off and gotten married over spring break. Ellen offered a carefully rehearsed explanation of how planning a big wedding during Guy's second year of law school would have been overwhelming. But she sensed both of her parents knew the real reason…

Ellen wiped the tears off her cheeks and blew her nose. How she regretted that decision later and every day since. Not only had she robbed her mother of the joy of sharing her wedding day, but the anger and bitterness between Ellen and her father only escalated.

Several years later, her parents moved from Baxter to Ocala. And when her mother died, it was easy for Ellen to emotionally distance herself from her father. She never wrote, rarely called, and forced herself to make a compulsory trip to his home every other year to salve her guilt.

But how had she let herself become so removed from her father's life that she didn't know until Sybil Armstrong called her that he wasn't capable of taking care of himself anymore?

Ellen dabbed her eyes and plucked another tissue from the box. *Lord, You don't have to tell me twice that I've been given a second chance. Show me how to love my dad.*

35

At 4:15 on Thursday afternoon, Ellen and Guy Jones sat in the waiting room of Dr. Hershel Roper's office at the Alzheimer's Institute of Beacon County while Lawrence was in another part of the building finishing up the testing and evaluation.

"This is taking longer than I thought," Ellen said. "At least we got to go out and have lunch together. That was a rare treat."

Guy looked over the top of the *Fortune* magazine he was reading. "I'm just grateful we can get most of the testing done today. I'm impressed at how well this place is set up for diagnostics."

"After the way Dad's been acting, I fully expect the doctor to tell us he has Alzheimer's. I guess my biggest fear is how we deal with it."

Guy reached over and took her hand. "We'll deal with it together. But I don't want you ever put in the position you were the other day. There's got to be a way to keep him safe and you sane."

Ellen smiled. "Might be too late for me."

The door next to the glass check-in window opened and a nurse appeared, clipboard in hand. "Mr. and Mrs. Jones, Dr. Roper is ready for you now."

Together they went into Dr. Roper's office where Lawrence was already sitting in a blue leather chair.

"Please, just make yourselves comfortable," Dr. Roper said.

Ellen sat on the couch, and Guy sat beside her.

Dr. Roper leaned forward, his hands folded on the desk. "Lawrence has been very cooperative, and we were able to do extensive testing today. I've already given him an overview of the diagnosis, and now I'd like to discuss the details with you.

"As I told you this morning, there is no one test that can single out Alzheimer's disease. But there are a number of tests that help us eliminate other things that could be causing the same symptoms. CT scans and MRIs are very useful in helping to rule out other problems. I'm happy to say that Lawrence's brain shows no sign of stroke, brain tumor, or other disorder.

"We also did a physical exam and tested his blood and urine, and everything looks normal. And his psych exam revealed there's no psychological cause for his changing behavior.

Dr. Roper looked down at the paper in front of him. "However, we also conducted a neuropsychological evaluation, which tested Lawrence's memory, reasoning, hand-eye coordination, and language function. And also a mental status evaluation that assessed his sense of time and place and ability to remember, understand, communicate, and do simple calculations. These were the areas of real concern.

"After a team consultation to review all the test results, we're in agreement that Lawrence falls well into the moderate stage of Alzheimer's disease. As I explained this morning, AD is not a normal part of aging. It's a brain disease that causes increasing loss of memory and other mental abilities."

"What do you mean by moderate?" Ellen said.

"We classify Alzheimer's in seven stages, one being the very earliest stage and seven being the most severe. Moderate Alzheimer's is about stage five. Generally at this point, the patient cannot get by without assistance. He needs help choosing proper attire. There is some disorientation in time. He may be unable to recall important facts of his current life but can still remember major facts about himself, his family, and others.

"Unfortunately, there's no way to be absolutely certain that any living person actually has AD. That can be proven only by doing an autopsy on the brain. But when all the usual tests show no other cause for the changes in memory and behavior, we give a diagnosis of probable Alzheimer's disease."

"Can anything be done to treat it?" Ellen said.

"There's no cure, but there are some drugs we can try that might help slow down the progression. Obviously, it would have been more desirable to have caught it in the early stages. Good nutrition, hygiene, and reassurance can go a long way in preserving his comfort and dignity."

Dr. Roper took off his glasses. "AD is the most common cause of severe memory loss in elderly adults. The disease attacks few people before age sixty, but it becomes increasingly common with age. In the past, elderly adults suffering from severe memory loss were often labeled senile, but they were probably suffering from what we now recognize as AD."

"Does it affect life expectancy?" Guy asked.

"Technically, yes, though Alzheimer's patients are almost always elderly and the disease progresses over a ten-to-twelve-year period. However, in the latter stages, the patient undergoes significant physical, mental, and emotional changes, and most become bedridden and require constant care. In their weakened condition, patients are vulnerable to pneumonia and other infectious diseases. I'll give you a packet of information to take with you that will offer a more thorough explanation."

Ellen glanced over at her father, wondering how much of the diagnosis he understood. "What kind of care does Dad need?"

"A lot of TLC, patience, and understanding. And close supervision. Since Lawrence has already wandered three times in spite of your best efforts, I don't think home care is advisable for him. There are a number of quality AD care facilities here in Seaport. I know of two that are operating in converted houses and focus on a much smaller number of patients. That makes for extremely personalized, top-notch patient care. And the homey atmosphere is nice for the families who visit. I'll be glad to provide you with a list of options when you leave."

Guy squeezed Ellen's hand. "Thanks."

Dr. Roper slipped his glasses on and looked from Lawrence to Guy to Ellen. "I'm sure this seems overwhelming. I can't stress strongly enough how important it is that we look at the person and not just the disease. Some of the physical, mental, and emotional changes Lawrence is experiencing are confusing and frustrating for all of you, but remember he didn't ask for this either."

Ellen walked in the kitchen door and disarmed the security alarm, then put the take-home box of Gordy's fried clams in the refrigerator. She wondered if she had ever sat through a quieter dinner out.

Lawrence came inside and sat at the breakfast bar, and Guy went over to the sink and poured himself a glass of water.

"Dad, I'm going to have a glass of lemonade," Ellen said. "Would you like one?"

"I need to go home."

Ellen sat next to him at the breakfast bar and put her hand on his forearm. "Guy and I are going to do everything we can to help you."

He yanked his arm away from her and folded his arms across his chest.

"Did you understand what Dr. Roper was talking to us about?"

"You think I can't remember anything?"

"Then you understand that you might need a little more help than you're used to. We want to make sure you get it."

Lawrence's eyes brimmed with tears. "Where's your mother? I want your mother."

Ellen fought back the emotion and then said, "Mom can't be here right now. You need to stay here with us for a while."

He looked up at Ellen, his eyebrows furrowed. "Is Aunt Bessie getting better?"

Ellen nodded. "Mom's been a real lifesaver."

"That mother of yours has a heart of gold. I just hope Aunt Bessie appreciates her."

Ellen met Guy's gaze, and she could tell he felt as helpless as she did.

Lawrence slapped his hands on the countertop and then stood. "Well, I'd better go turn on the radio. I don't want to miss the last game of the World Series."

"Who's playing?" Guy said, giving Ellen an I-have-no-idea-where-this-is-going look.

"The Marlins and the Indians. If they win tonight, they'll be the first wild-card team ever to win the series." Lawrence walked out of the kitchen.

Ellen sighed. "How can he talk baseball like that and be so confused about other things."

Guy chuckled. "Honey, the Marlins beat the Cleveland Indians in the World Series in 1997. And the series is always played in October."

"Oh."

The phone rang and Ellen picked it up. "Hello."

"Hi, Mom. Have you got time to finish our conversation about Granddad?"

"Sure, Owen. Let me get a glass of lemonade and go sit on the couch."

Guy motioned for her to go sit and he'd get it for her.

Ellen went into the living room and let her body sink into the couch. "Sorry I had to hang up when I called earlier. Dad seemed agitated when I started talking about his Alzheimer's, and I thought I'd wait and give you the details without him listening."

"Before you get into that, did the fire marshal ever determine what started the fire in the apartment building?"

"Yes, some electrical wiring in the wall of your grandfathers' apartment shorted out. All their personal belongings are covered by insurance, but most of what they had were keepsakes. Except for Granddad's bedroom furniture, everything of monetary value was rental property."

"I'm just glad they weren't there."

"Me too, honey."

"Okay, what did Dr. Roper tell you?"

Ellen told Owen every detail she could remember about Alzheimer's disease, including how the current stage of the disease was affecting her father and what they should expect as the disease progressed.

"Does Granddad have the resources to pay for that kind of care?"

"For a while. He's got all the money from the sale of the house, plus his Social Security. He's been living off that and some bonds he bought after he sold the hardware store. If that runs out, your father and I may have to cash in some of our investments. But that wouldn't happen for a long time."

"What about Papa? He moves into assisted living this weekend. Can he afford it?"

Ellen glanced up at Guy and smiled. "Fortunately, yes. Roland was a successful attorney and a shrewd investor. I doubt he'll run out of money if he lives to be a hundred."

"Have you seen him lately?"

"We stopped by the rehab center after lunch. He's getting around beautifully with his walker and seems eager to get out of there and into assisted living. I think he'll make the adjustment just fine. We decided not to mention the fire or Granddad's diagnosis until he gets settled."

"Hailey and I will be glad to bring Daniel over to the house and entertain Granddad so you can get Papa moved."

"Thanks, that would help a lot. It won't take us long since

all we have of his are the clothes I brought home."

"I hope he doesn't get depressed when he finds out about the fire. I guess all his pictures of Grandma got destroyed."

"Yes, but I have some good ones. In fact, I may put one in a frame and take it with me when we drive him to the new place. Honey, how are you and Hailey doing? Any idea when you'll begin the home study?"

"Nothing's been scheduled. Janet Stanton's pulling a few strings to get the process moving faster."

Ellen sensed a little anxiety in his voice. "Are you still feeling good about it?"

"Oh, yeah, really good. Hailey, too. I'm just not sleeping worth a hoot. I can't seem to shake that whole scene with Tim O'Rourke."

"Have you thought about talking to a counselor?"

"Janet told me Annie's seeing a child psychologist. She gave me the name of someone she could get me in to see. Hailey thinks I should make an appointment."

Ellen doodled crosses on the back of an envelope. "It can't hurt."

"Yeah, I suppose. If nothing else, maybe a shrink could give me something to help me sleep."

"It would be better if someone could help you sort out why you're not sleeping. I sense there's more on your mind than just the suicide and finding out you're Annie's father."

"You mean dealing with Hailey's reaction to my getting Corinne pregnant? She's been more forgiving that I ever thought she'd be."

"I'm glad for that. But it's not as though you've really had time to assimilate the fact that your lives are never going to be the same. That certainly doesn't have to be a negative, but you're going to have to step into bigger shoes than you've ever worn before."

Owen sighed into the receiver. "I can deal with that. But

what if I never can feel the same about Annie as I do Daniel? There's no guarantee that'll happen."

"Would it surprise you to know I wondered the same thing when I got pregnant with Brandon?"

"Really?"

"Absolutely. But I had plenty of love for both of you. You will, too. Any idea when you'll be allowed to see her again? Or when we will?"

"Uh, well, it's all kind of up in the air. Lots of red tape. But I promise you're going to gobble her up."

"I'm sure I will. We may have to work on your father."

Owen laughed. "Mark my words: She'll have him wrapped around her little finger in no time."

36

J ust after lunch the next day, Will Seevers turned onto Live Oak Circle and parked his squad car in front of the Joneses' vine-covered house. He got out of the car and stood for a moment, enjoying the ambience of the stately old homes and huge live oaks that graced the neighborhood, then walked up on the porch and rang the bell. A half minute later, Ellen Jones answered the door.

"Come in where it's cool," she said. "I appreciate your stopping by."

Will followed Ellen into the living room and sat on the couch. "What's this about?"

"I thought you should know we had Dad evaluated and he's been officially diagnosed with Alzheimer's. I don't know what that does to his statements about the man with the knife, but I thought you should know."

Will raised his eyebrows. "I'm really sorry. I guess this is no big surprise to you, but I'm sure it's difficult."

"You have no idea." Ellen told Will about her father's latest wandering incident.

"That was *his* apartment building that burned?" Will said. "I guess I didn't make the connection."

"Poor thing was over at my neighbor's having raspberry tea." Ellen looked down at her hands. "The doctor thinks he needs more care than we can give him. We're looking into our options…which brings me to my question: How do we protect him once he's not living here?"

"Interesting you should ask that. Al and I have been thinking it's not necessary anymore."

"Really?"

"You haven't noticed anyone snooping around in almost two weeks, and we have a suspect that knows we're on to him. He's not going to take any chances, especially with us keeping close tabs on him."

Will popped the last bite of a Snickers into his mouth and looked out the window at City Hall and the husky old live oak trees that shaded the grounds.

The Kincaid Memorial Fund had jumped to over sixteen thousand dollars. And Andrew Connor's reward offer for anyone who fingered the killer had gone over big around town. Last night Jared Downing from WRGL News had done a live interview down at Fish Tales with Connor…

"Mr. Connor, your generosity speaks volumes about your concern for Jackson Kincaid's family. Some are calling you a hero. How do you respond to that?"

"Hey, I saw a need and just wanted to help. That's all."

"What made you decide to put up ten thousand dollars in reward money for information leading to Kincaid's killer?"

"The police have nothing. I thought this might help breathe new life into the investigation. Jackson's family deserves justice…"

"You look ticked." Al Backus flopped into the chair next to Will's desk. "Let me guess: You're thinking about Andrew Connor."

"I'm going to get him, Al. I don't know how yet, but he's not going to get away with Kincaid's murder and come off looking like a hero. Not on my watch."

"Then I hope you've got another idea because I'm fresh out. We don't have enough for a warrant. Even if we did, Connor seems too smart not to have covered his tracks. The murder weapon and the red shirt are probably buried somewhere—or washed out to sea."

"He made a mistake somewhere. They all do. We'll just have to wait him out."

Late that afternoon, Ellen pulled her car into the garage and turned off the motor, then went into the kitchen and saw her father sitting at the breakfast bar, eating apple slices.

Lawrence scowled at her. "Why aren't you at work?"

"Uh, I'm done for the day," Ellen said.

"Then why'd you bring work home?"

Ellen tightened her grip on the stack of brochures in her left hand. "This isn't work. It's just…something I promised someone I would read."

"When is your mother coming home?"

"Hi, honey." Guy walked into the kitchen and pressed his lips to hers. "I got Lawrence a snack and have been looking over some contracts for a client. Did you make the rounds we talked about?"

"Yes." Ellen handed him the stack of brochures and glanced over at Lawrence. "Dad, *The Andy Griffith Show* is on in two minutes."

"Why aren't you at work?"

"Did I tell you we're having roast beef for dinner? And green beans cooked the way Mother made them?"

"Come on, Lawrence," Guy said. "I'll set up a TV tray so you can have your snack and watch your program."

Ellen sat at the breakfast bar and laid out the brochures she had picked up at various Alzheimer's care facilities. She heard Guy getting Lawrence set up in the living room, then heard his footsteps behind her.

"That was a whirlwind trip," Guy said. "You must have half a dozen brochures here. Choosing the right place may be harder than we thought."

"Not necessarily. I'm partial to this one. I'd like you to go with me and take a look."

Ellen handed him the Harmony House brochure with a picture of a white mansion and tree-covered grounds on the front. She began to reread the information while he perused it.

"This is a great-looking place."

"I'm sure that's why it was at the top of Dr. Roper's list. I was really impressed. It doesn't have that nursing-home feel to it at all. Has the flavor of home. The living room even smelled of potpourri. It's a little more expensive, but it shows."

Guy looked at the rate sheet enclosed and looked over at her, his eyebrows raised. "A *little* more expensive?"

"Okay, considerably more. But Dad's got substantial savings. I know the disease can span ten to twelve years, but he's eighty-seven, and we don't know how long he's had Alzheimer's, probably a long time. If I had been the kind of daughter who bothered to stay in close touch, I'd have a better handle on all of this."

Guy tilted her chin and looked into her eyes. "Ellen, you know I want what's best for Lawrence, but is this guilt talking? Because I don't think he's going to appreciate the difference in the ambience. The quality of care is what matters most."

"Of course it does. And just look at the ratio of caregivers to patients. This place has the highest rating. Really topnotch." Suddenly Ellen's eyes brimmed with tears and overflowed down her cheeks. "Okay...I feel guilty for avoiding him all those years. I have to live with that—and the fact that he's never liked anything about me and we can scarcely stand to be in the same room together. But it's not too late to do the right thing. Since Dr. Roper doesn't think we should be the caregivers for Dad, the least we can do is provide the most homey and loving environment for him."

Guy held her gaze for what seemed an inordinate amount of time, then kissed her forehead. "Let's go take a look at it tomorrow before we move my dad to Sea Gate."

"Owen and Hailey are bringing Daniel over about nine. They said to take as long as we need."

37

On Saturday evening, Ellen Jones stood at the front door and waved goodbye to Owen, Hailey, and Daniel as their SUV backed out of the driveway, then she went back into the living room where Lawrence stared blankly at the blaring TV. Sometimes his nasty disposition seemed easier to handle than his lack of presence.

She went through the French doors and out onto the veranda, then took refuge in her wicker rocker and tried to let her heart catch up with the events of the day as she listened to the calming sounds of night.

Guy came outside, handed her a glass of lemonade, and sat in the other rocker, neither of them saying anything for some time.

"It's been quite a day," Guy finally said.

Ellen sighed. "It killed me to move your dad into Sea Gate this afternoon. He came here thinking he was going to live with Dad, and it feels as though we've betrayed him."

"Honey, he's *fine*. I think the hospital stay and extended rehab prepared him for it. He'll make friends quickly and get involved in some of the activities there. He loves chess and board games and cards. He'll be busier than he's been in years, and we're just a mile away. I have a really good feeling about it. Thanks for thinking of taking the picture of Mom to the new place. That helped."

"I dearly love Roland. I'd give anything to have that kind of relationship with my father. I'm dreading tomorrow."

"When do you think we should tell him?"

"I don' t know. It seems cruel to pack his things and just take him over there. But if we tell him tonight, I doubt he'll remember tomorrow what we're doing." Ellen wiped a tear off her cheek. "It's a blessing Mom didn't have to make this decision."

"Well, rest assured Lawrence will be better off at Harmony House, and he won't be tormenting you day in and day out. The quality of both your lives will be much improved."

"There's just something so sad about your parents becoming helpless…like children. I don't want to live long enough to be a burden to the boys."

Guy smiled. "I don't know. It would serve Owen right for all he's put us through…Just kidding!"

"Compared to what he's put himself and Hailey through, our part is nothing. It's a tremendous adjustment, learning how to love and care for a tiny stranger, and I'm sure Annie won't be adorable twenty-four hours a day. Hailey may accept our son's past indiscretion with Corinne, but putting all that behind her and taking on the role of Annie's mother will be an enormous challenge. Plus, Owen has scarcely begun to deal with the guilt of Tim O'Rourke's suicide."

Guy shook his head. "He's not responsible for that man's choice."

"Of course not. But Owen has to own up to the fact that he slept with another man's wife and got her pregnant—which ultimately destroyed a marriage and set the stage for Tim O'Rourke's emotional instability."

"We told Owen his fast lifestyle was going to catch up with him. At least I'm finally convinced he really wants Annie."

Ellen looked up at a smattering of stars visible between the tree branches. "So am I. This could just as easily have been a compounded disaster. It's just a shame that little girl had to spend four years with a man who verbally abused her. Heaven only knows how many emotional scars she has."

"Seems Owen's foolish mistake is just going to keep on costing him. If only he'd known, I'm sure he would've chosen differently."

"Wouldn't we all? I never meant for my anger at Dad to turn my love into indifference. One bad experience seemed to lead to another. And before I knew it, I cared more about being right than doing right. I can't believe how far I let it go."

Guy got up and pulled Ellen to her feet, his arms around her. "It's water under the bridge, honey. What's important now is that you make peace, if not with your dad, with yourself and the Lord.

The next day after church, Ellen fixed Lawrence a grilled cheese sandwich, and while he was eating, she went in his room and packed his clothes.

"How are you doing?"

Ellen looked up and saw Guy's reflection in the dresser mirror. "Okay, I guess. Is Dad finished with lunch?"

"Almost. I called the administrator at Harmony House. They're expecting us within the hour. They've got his room ready."

"Why do I have butterflies?" Ellen said. "I know this is the right thing to do."

"Because it's the beginning of the end. I felt like that yesterday when we moved my dad to Sea Gate. Like you said, it's hard to see a parent frail and helpless like a child. But it's the cycle of life."

"Roland could've lived here with us."

"He didn't want to, and I don't blame him. Besides, there's so much to keep him busy at Sea Gate, he's going to love it."

Ellen blinked quickly to clear her eyes. She wondered if her own father was capable of loving anything or anyone.

"If you're through packing Lawrence's things, why don't I take them out to the car and meet you in the living room?" Guy kissed her cheek. "It's going to be okay. I promise." He picked up the suitcase and a few hanging things and walked out of the guest room.

Ellen sat on the side of the bed, her heart pounding. *Lord, please give me gentle words to tell Dad what we're going to do. Help him not to be afraid. Don't let him feel abandoned.*

Ellen took a slow, deep breath, then got up and walked out to the living room where her father sat, the crusts of a grilled cheese sandwich piled on the TV tray. She picked up the scraps and took the plate out to the kitchen just as Guy came in from the garage.

"Okay, we're all set," he said. "Let's go talk to him."

Ellen followed Guy into the living room and started to sit on the couch, but instead knelt beside her father's chair, her hands folded on the arm.

"Why aren't you at work?" Lawrence said.

"Guy and I have something important to talk to you about."

Lawrence folded his arms tightly across his chest. "I'm not selling the house."

"Do you remember going to see Dr. Roper?"

Lawrence's eyebrows furrowed. "Had Old Glory on his shirt."

"Dr. Roper, Dad. You sat in the comfortable blue leather chair, and we all talked about how you're having trouble remembering things? Dr. Roper wants to help you. So instead of living here with Guy and me, you're going to live at a different house."

Lawrence stared at her blankly.

"It's called Harmony House. The people there are very kind."

"I want to go home."

"That's going to be your new home."

"Where's your mother? I want to see your mother."

Ellen steadied her voice. "Take a drive with us and let us show you the beautiful flowers and plants and the waterfall in the atrium."

❀ ❀ ❀

An hour later, Ellen sat on the side of the bed in Lawrence's room at Harmony House, admiring the textured stripes on the light blue wallpaper above the cherry wainscot.

"This bed feels great, Dad. Nice and firm. Just the way you like it. I think you're going to like it here."

"You don't know everything!" Lawrence snapped.

"But I know how much you love flowers and plants, and they said you could have your own flower garden out back. Won't that be great?"

"Stop talking to me like I'm a kid. You think I don't know what's happening here?"

Ellen got up and walked over to the love seat and sat next to her father. She tried taking his hand, but he yanked it away. "Dad, Guy and I looked all over town to find the best place for you. Dr. Roper thinks you need to be where he can help you. We can't keep you safe enough."

"I want to go home!"

"I know you do. But you can't. This is your home now."

"How're we doing?" A pretty woman about forty walked into the room. "I'm Rachel Britton, Lawrence's nurse."

Ellen and Guy introduced themselves and shook Rachel's hand.

"Have you folks been through the orientation?" Rachel asked.

Ellen nodded. "Very impressive."

"I assure you, we will do everything possible to make Lawrence feel at home and help him adjust to his new surroundings. The premises are secured so there's no chance he's going to wander. We have security cameras throughout the house and grounds, so we'll be able to monitor him at all times. You don't need to worry about a thing."

"So what happens now?" Guy said.

Rachel looked at her clipboard. "After we do the usual check-in medical evaluation and tests, we'll get him started on the meds the doctor talked to you about. We'll show him the recreation room, then take him down to the dining room, where our dietician will work with him and find out what his food preferences are. Of course, the information you've already provided us will help immensely in that regard. The food here is nutritious and our chef customizes meal portions to suit each resident's taste."

"Will you give him nutritional supplements?" Ellen said.

Rachel nodded. "We offer special highly nutritious milk-shakes at all hours. Residents can choose fresh fruit shakes or vanilla, chocolate, or butterscotch."

"Maybe *I* should move in," Ellen said.

Guy smiled and shook his head.

"If there are no other questions, I'll let you folks finish visiting," Rachel said. "I'll come get Lawrence and get started in, say, twenty minutes?"

Ellen nodded. "Thank you." She watched Rachel leave the room and wondered how much her father understood of what was going on.

She glanced over at Guy and then at Lawrence. "Dad, we have to leave now. The people here will take good care of you, but Guy and I won't be far away. We'll come visit."

Lawrence's gaze met hers. "Since when?"

Ellen got in the elevator and went down to the ground level, vaguely aware of Guy holding her hand. When the elevator door opened, she walked briskly across the elegant foyer and out onto the front porch, her vision clouded, her conscience accusing her of taking the easy way out.

Ellen stopped and gripped the porch railing with both hands and blinked till her eyes cleared enough for her to walk down the steps and out to the car. She pulled open the passenger door and got inside just as a dam of emotion broke and spilled down her face.

She heard the other door slam and felt Guy take her hand.

"We're doing the right thing," he said.

Are we? Or is it just easier? "If Dad didn't hate me before, he certainly does now."

"Honey, that's nonsense. I'm not sure he even realizes what's happening—at least not consciously."

"I hope Mother doesn't know what I just did."

"What *we* just did. And it's the most compassionate thing we could do. Lawrence isn't safe with us. We can't watch him twenty-four hours a day."

Ellen took a tissue and wiped her cheeks, then blew her nose. "What's so pitiful is that I wouldn't want to, even if it *were* best for him. I've never had that kind of father/daughter relationship, and I never will."

"That doesn't change the fact that he's better off here, where he'll get the care he needs. Maybe as his memory fails, he'll forget there was ever a rift between you."

"I wish I had worked harder to make things right between us before he got this bad."

"Ellen, it's not as though you never tried to get along with him. Your dad has resisted you at every turn."

"Yes, but even after I became a Christian, I continued to justify my resentment. If I had chosen to forgive him and let God work, maybe we could've built something between us."

"You can't go back, honey," Guy said. "You can only take it from here."

Ellen fixed her eyes on a magnolia tree in the side yard next to the flower garden. "It's too late. Half the time he doesn't even know what I'm talking about. All my life I've longed to hear him say he loves me. And I know that can never happen now."

38

Two weeks later, on Father's Day, Ellen, Guy, and Roland Jones sat around the elegantly set dining room table, enjoying the meal Ellen had prepared.

Roland sat back in his chair and patted his middle. "That pork tenderloin was delicious, Ellen. Everything was. I can't thank you enough."

"Oh, it was my pleasure," Ellen said. "We're just so happy you're here with us this Father's Day."

"It bothers me Lawrence couldn't be here, too."

"We stopped by there on the way to church," Ellen said. "He's going downhill really fast. I think even the doctor is surprised. They took him off the meds because they made him sick and he couldn't eat. He's losing weight."

Roland shook his head. "What a shame."

"So Dad," Guy said, "how does it feel to be the chess king of Sea Gate?"

"Well, there're a couple of old duffers who give me a run for my money. We've had a few laughs. I'm just so grateful I can keep my mind active."

Ellen glanced at her watch. "I wonder what's keeping the kids. Owen said they'd be here at three and have dessert with us."

"Honey, it's only ten after. Hailey probably planned something for Owen for Father's Day. It's not as though your pecan pies are going to spoil." Guy winked at her.

"I know. But I haven't seen Daniel in over two weeks. I need a grandma fix."

"Just think," Guy said, "this time next year, Owen will be the father of two."

Roland raised his eyebrows. "How long's the process take?"

"I heard a car door," Ellen said.

A minute later Hailey walked in the house, holding Daniel on her hip and two gift bags in the other hand.

"It's so good to see you." Ellen put her arms around Hailey and pulled Daniel's little hand to her lips and smothered it in kisses. "Grandma's missed you."

She started to reach for Daniel and then froze, her eyes fixed on the little blue-eyed blond girl wearing a pink and white smocked dress and holding tightly to Owen's hand.

Ellen put her hands to her mouth. "Oh, my goodness. Is this…?"

Owen's face beamed, his voice soft. "Annie, this is your grandma."

"Hi, Gwandma," said the sweetest voice Ellen had ever heard. "Do you got cookies at your house?"

Ellen glanced at Owen and then smiled at Annie. "I'll bet I do," she said, finally finding her voice. "I'm so glad to finally meet you. What a wonderful surprise!"

"It gets better," Owen said, his grin the size of the Grand Canyon. "She's all ours."

Ellen sat in the living room, trying to let her emotions catch up to the realization that Owen and Hailey had custody of Annie— and that she and Guy had a granddaughter.

"Son, how did you pull this off so quickly?" Guy said.

"It was totally unexpected. Annie's caseworker, Janet Stanton, came to the house a couple weeks ago and said it was obvious to her that Annie had bonded with me from day one, and that her attachment had only gotten stronger after spending time with Hailey. And since the paternity test proved she's my daughter, Janet asked us how we felt about her going before the judge and asking that the home study be waived and we be given custody. We were totally excited. And the judge went for it."

"Just like that?" Ellen glanced over at Annie sitting on the floor with Daniel, helping him stack red, blue, and yellow plastic blocks.

"Well," Hailey said, "I'm sure it didn't hurt that Annie's foster parents agreed with Janet's assessment, and that we wanted Annie and wouldn't have trouble providing for her. But as it turns out, Owen could've legally gotten custody the minute the paternity test proved he was her father. But since he and Annie were still recovering from the shock of the suicide, Janet didn't want to move too quickly."

"Are you sure you aren't moving too quickly?" Guy said.

Owen put his arm around Hailey and looked into her eyes. "Absolutely sure. We brought Annie home Friday afternoon, and already we can't imagine life without her. What a Father's Day gift. We're going to get started on Hailey adopting Annie as soon as we can."

"You going to keep her name the same?" Ellen said.

"Yeah, we like Anna Kathleen. Obviously, she'll be a Jones."

"She seems relaxed with both of you," Guy said. "It's uncanny how much she looks like your mother."

"Yeah, I told you. By the way, we thought we might stop by and see Granddad. What do you think?"

Ellen sighed. "He's not doing all that well, honey. This is such exciting news, but it'll probably fall flat with him. Why don't you hold off for a little while?"

"I feel bad we haven't driven over to see him. Things have been crazy for us, as you might imagine. Sorry we've been avoiding you, but we didn't want to spoil the surprise. The look on your faces was worth it."

"I'm thrilled for all of you," Ellen said. "And thankful you didn't have to go through the home study and months of waiting. What a precious little girl."

Annie gave Daniel a squeaky toy, then got up and came over to Hailey. "Mama, don't forget the supwise."

"Sweetie, all the daddies have already opened their gifts."

"No, the *other* supwise."

Owen chuckled. "I almost forgot. We left something important on the porch, didn't we, Annie?" Owen took her hand and went out the front door.

A minute later, Annie came inside carrying a dachshund in her arms. "We gots a new puppy, and he is weally, weally fun! We bringed him to my new house, but he got in twouble because he went pee-pee on Daniel's shoe." Annie wagged her finger. "Bad puppy. He got a time out, but he just cwied and cwied, so Mama let him come out of the cage."

"What's your puppy's name?" Guy said.

Annie shrugged. "Daddy says we hafta think about it. Puppy needs a very special name. My other doggy's name is Oscar, so we can't call him that. Here, Gwandpa, he wants *you* to hold him." Annie ambled over to Guy and transferred the squirming tube of rusty-brown energy into his arms and all over the front of his white polo shirt. "Be careful he doesn't scwatch you. His paws are vewy, vewy sharp."

Ellen watched with amusement as the puppy jumped up repeatedly and licked Guy's face, Annie clapping her hands and giggling with delight.

Guy's words came rushing back to her.

"Maybe what I'm really afraid of is that I won't click with Annie. I'm crazy about Daniel. But truthfully, I don't know that I can love Annie the same way."

Ellen laughed without meaning to. *Bet me, Counselor.*

39

Gordy Jameson finished reading the big Fourth of July edition of the *North Coast Messenger* and looked again at a small article on the front page, just below the fold. He wondered if Will Seevers's hackles were up.

FISH TALES COMMITS 20 PERCENT
OF WEEKEND SALES TO
KINCAID MEMORIAL FUND

Andrew Connor, owner and manager of Fish Tales Eatery and Gift Shop, 612 Beach Shore Drive, has designated 20 percent of his holiday-weekend sales to the Jackson Kincaid Memorial Fund. Connor made the announcement just prior to the weekend, when donations to the fund topped twenty thousand dollars.

Connor, who also contributed the first $5,000 to the fund, has been diligent in his resolve to help raise money for the widow and children of Jackson Kincaid, a fellow merchant found stabbed to death behind Sun Haven Souvenir Shop on May 20.

Connor said that Saturday and Sunday's turnout was heartwarming and he expected sales today to exceed both previous days put together.

"This is what community is all about," Connor said. "We *are* our brother's keeper. Everyone can help."

Connor has extended today's store hours to midnight to give people plenty of time to come in after the
fireworks display and make either a purchase or a
donation. Special T-shirts commemorating the event
will be available for ten dollars apiece while they last.

Gordy folded the newspaper, aware that Pam was standing
in the doorway. "What's up, darlin'?"

"Will and Margaret are here and would like us to have lunch
with them. We've got plenty of help, and Weezie *the wise and
wonderful* is working the crowd."

Gordy chuckled. "She's staying on top of her goal for July. I
forgot what colossal increase she's after. Might as well go have
lunch and let her do her thing. The woman's in her element."

Gordy followed Pam out to the booth where Will and
Margaret were seated side-by-side and slid into the other side facing them. "Have you ordered yet?"

"Still looking," Margaret said. "Anything really scrumptious I
should know about?"

"Yeah, the spicy grilled shrimp'll knock your socks off. And
you're not payin' today, it's on me. Happy Fourth."

"Well, that's too good to pass up."

"You guys have plans for the rest of the day?" Will said.

"We'll slip outta here later and catch the fireworks." Gordy
held up his index finger and hailed the waitress.

She took their orders and brought each of them a limeade.

"I suppose you heard about Andrew Connor's latest ploy,"
Will said.

"I wouldn't exactly call givin' money to a victim's widow
and kids a ploy." Gordy took the lime slice off the rim of his
glass and dropped it in his drink. "The guy's generous. I admire
what he's doin'."

"And I don't trust him any further than I could pick him up
and throw him."

"Can't you put police business on hold for one day?" Margaret said.

"Sorry." Will smiled sheepishly. "Old habits die hard."

"So tell us about Meagan's trip to D.C."

Gordy got absorbed in the details of Meagan's trip, and then the four of them batted around personal news and laughed and joked together. He glanced at his watch and realized it was already two o'clock.

"This was like old times," he said. "We've gotta do this more often. You need to go out in the boat with us. Pam and I found this neat little island where we've been hangin' out and doin' some snorkeling."

"Sounds like just what we need," Margaret said. "I have to get this man of mine away from town so he'll stop obsessing about unsolved cases."

"I'm not obsessing," Will said. "I just get antsy when I know 'who done it' and can't prove it."

Gordy slid out of the booth, thinking he wasn't touching that one. "My turn to work the crowd."

"Thanks for lunch," Margaret said. "I'm going to buy one of Pam's triple-berry pies and serve it tonight with vanilla ice cream. The couple next door is coming over to watch the fireworks."

By late afternoon, the crowd finally thinned out, and Gordy went into the kitchen looking for Pam.

"Darlin', I'm gonna ride my bike down to Fish Tales and buy a couple of those special T-shirts Andrew's sellin'."

"We already gave five hundred dollars. Why are you buying T-shirts?"

"So we can wear them to the fireworks display. I'd like people to know we support the memorial fund. Might help encourage donations."

"Okay, you know where I'll be." Pam smiled, a dusting of flour on her chin.

Gordy went out the front door and across the pier and over to the bike stand. He unlocked the padlock on his bicycle and headed toward the souvenir shops.

He pulled up in front of Fish Tales and noticed the WRGL-TV van parked out front and balloons tied to the railing on the wooden walkway. He chained his bicycle and went inside and spotted the sign advertising the T-shirts he had read about in the newspaper.

Gordy stood close to the table and waited until the family in front of him took what they wanted and walked over to the register. He moved up to the table and the messy stacks of white T-shirts and held one up. In the center was a large red circle with the words "Jackson Kincaid Memorial Fund" printed around the circumference. Inside the circle were the words, "I Gave. Keep It Going."

He went through the stack and picked up a large for Pam and one for Weezie and a 2X for himself, then took them to the register, glad that only one customer was ahead of him.

Gordy let his eyes flit around the store, curious about the wholesale cost of this much inventory. He was suddenly aware that a white-haired woman in front of him sounded angry.

"I *know* you have a thirty-day return policy," the woman snapped, "but I bought this weeks ago for my grandson's birthday, which was yesterday. I didn't open the box when you sold it to me. This one's been used. I want a new one."

Gordy noticed the cashier was Rory Connor, who looked much more like a grown man since he had last seen him—and remarkably like Andrew.

"I'm sorry, ma'am, but there's no way we sold you used merchandise," Rory said.

"Then explain *that*," she said.

Rory's eyebrows came together. "Maybe it's rust or something. Did you—"

"Is there a problem here?" Andrew Connor came over and stood next to the lady.

"She wants to return this hunting knife," Rory said. "She *says* we sold her a used one, but—"

"We'll be glad to exchange it for a different one," Andrew said, his face flooded with red. "I'll take it from here, son. Go get another knife out of the case. I'm really sorry, ma'am. It's guaranteed not to rust, and we'll sure stand behind that guarantee."

"Call it rust if it makes you feel better," the woman mumbled, "but this knife has been used."

Gordy noticed Andrew's hand was shaking.

Rory brought another knife and Andrew inspected it, then showed it to the customer. "This one is perfect. See…?"

"Fine, I'll take it," the lady said. "But you ought to be professional enough to admit your mistake. You're not dealing with a fool."

Andrew put the replacement knife in the box and put the box back in the woman's sack. "There you go. I'm very sorry for the trouble."

"Me too." The lady turned and shuffled toward the front door.

Gordy stepped up to the counter and laid the three T-shirts on it. "Hey, Andrew. Thought I'd pick up a few T-shirts to support the memorial fund."

Andrew slid the returned knife under the counter. "I'm sorry, what…?

"I think what you're doin' with the T-shirts is a keen idea. I wanna support it."

"Thanks." Andrew rang up the T-shirts. "That's forty dollars even. I'm covering the sales tax on these."

"Uh, did I accidentally bring four shirts? I thought I had three."

"You did. My mistake." Andrew voided the transaction and started over. "Okay, that'll be thirty dollars."

Gordy handed him two twenties. "How many have you sold?"

"I'm not sure yet. I ordered a thousand."

"We're all proud of what you're doin'."

Andrew glanced over at Rory and nodded toward the back room. "Thanks, Gordy. I appreciate your support."

"Glad to help…"

Andrew stared at him for several seconds and finally said, "Was there something else?"

"I gave you two twenties."

Andrew shook his head from side to side. "Of course you did. I don't know what's wrong with me today." Andrew handed Gordy a ten. "There you go. Thanks again."

Gordy picked up the sack and walked out of Fish Tales, bells jingling on the door. He looked in the front window and saw Andrew grab Rory by the back of his shirt and prod him into the back room.

What was that all about? Gordy went down the steps to where he'd chained his bicycle and noticed the white-haired lady who had exchanged the knife struggling to get her car door open. "Here, let me help with that."

"Thank you, young man. My hands don't work like they used to."

Gordy smiled. When was the last time someone called him young? "I'm glad you got your grandson's knife exchanged okay. The owner's a real nice guy."

"He may be, but I'll tell you one thing…that hunting knife *had* been used. There was dried blood crusted where the handle meets the blade. Do they think I was born yesterday?"

"Aw, I know the owner pretty well. I'm sure he wouldn't sell you used merchandise."

"Really?" The lady arched her eyebrows. "Well, let me show you something else." She slid in behind the wheel and reached inside the console and pulled out a small piece of white packing. "This was in the box with the knife. Does that spot look like rust to you?"

Gordy held the packing and examined a red spot. "Looks like blood."

The woman seemed annoyed. "I took that out of the box because I didn't want to embarrass them any more than I had to. I figured it must've been some kind of mistake. I never expected them to act as though I was the one trying to pull something!"

"You won't be needing this packing now, will you?" Gordy said.

"No, I certainly won't. I appreciate your help, young man. Good day."

Gordy shut the car door and looked up at Fish Tales, a sick feeling in his stomach, his mind racing with possibilities he didn't even want to think about.

He looked down at the drop of red on the packing in his hand, wondering what in the world he had just walked into.

40

Gordy Jameson stood in front of Fish Tales Eatery and Gift Shop, feeling as though his shoes were nailed to the wooden walkway. He folded the stained packing and put it in his pants pocket and tried to decide what he should do. The last place he wanted to be was in Andrew Connor's personal business. But how could he just walk away and do nothing?

He opened the door to Fish Tales and went back inside. He didn't see Andrew or Rory, so he walked over and stood outside the closed door that led to the back room and pretended to be looking through a display of beach sandals.

He heard Andrew and Rory's muffled voices and strained to hear. He couldn't make out what they were saying, but they sounded angry.

Gordy glanced around the store and noticed no customers were waiting at the checkout, and Cheryl Connor had her back to the register and was talking to a WRGL-TV camera. He inched slowly toward the checkout and slipped behind the counter and squatted, then picked up the knife the woman had returned, thinking he should put it in his bag and take it to Will.

"What are you doing back there?" Andrew Connor's voice was loud and unmistakable.

Gordy turned around and flashed the friendliest smile he could muster. "Oh, *there* you are. I wanted to take a look at the knife the lady returned. I think it'd be perfect to use on my fishin' boat."

"Well, let me get you a new one. I'm sure you heard me tell her that one's defective."

"I was hopin' you'd sell it to me at a discount."

"Sorry. I never sell anything that doesn't live up to the warranty claim."

"Yeah, but it doesn't matter for what I need it for."

"It matters to me." Andrew held out his palm. "Give it to me. I'll sell you a new one at cost. Professional courtesy. One businessman to another."

"That's not necessary. This one'll work just fine on the boat. Really."

Andrew's face glistened with perspiration. "It's not for sale."

Gordy looked at Andrew and then at Rory, who had walked up next to him. "It would sure save you from havin' to return it."

"No problem. We do returns all the time." Andrew shot a glance at several customers who were staring. "Gordy, why are you pushing this? I'm offering you a great deal."

Gordy's heart pounded, sweat rolling down his back. "Andrew, I think we both know you're not plannin' to return this one."

"What are you talking about?"

Gordy lowered his voice to a whisper. "Do you wanna call Will Seevers, or should I?"

Rory started to take a step forward and Andrew put out his arm and stopped him. "For what?"

"Look, guys, I hate this. But I can't ignore what I saw and heard when that lady returned this knife. If you've got nothin' to hide, why won't you sell it to me?"

"I told you why. You need to leave." Andrew looked at something beyond Gordy. "Would you please turn off that camera? I don't want this on the news. It's just a misunderstanding." Andrew looked again at Gordy. "I want you out of here."

"Okay. But I'm takin' the knife with me."

In the next instant, Rory lunged at Gordy and knocked the

knife out of his hand, then picked it up and backed up next to his father. "Now leave or we're throwing you out."

Gordy held out his hands in a defensive posture. "Take it easy. Nobody needs to get hurt here."

"Sorry, folks," Andrew said, a phony smile plastered on his face. "Just a little misunderstanding. Everything's fine. This man was just leaving."

Gordy heard the bells jingle on the front door and saw Rory's eyes dart back and forth, seemingly wild with panic. He spun around and tripped over his own feet as he raced toward the back room.

Gordy turned and saw Officer Jack Rutgers and another officer standing by the front door.

"Jack, don't let that kid go out the back!" Gordy shouted. "He may have the knife that killed Jackson Kincaid!"

Gordy was aware of one of the officers running past him, but his gaze was fixed on Andrew Connor, who stood frozen, his eyes vacant, his shoulders slumped.

"I just wanted to protect him," he mumbled. "All I was trying to do is protect my son."

Gordy sat in Will Seevers's office, an empty can of Orange Crush in his hands, the ceiling fan drying his perspiration, and wondered what might have happened had Jack Rutgers and the other officer not been nearby when one of Andrew's customers dialed 911.

Will walked in the office and flopped into the chair next to Gordy. "Way to go, pal! They both confessed."

"Why don't I feel better?"

"It's hard to find out someone isn't who you thought he was." Will patted Gordy's knee. "I can't believe this. What are the odds of the whole thing being captured on tape? If Connor hadn't made such a royal production of giving twenty percent of his sales to the memorial fund, that team from WRGL News wouldn't even have been down there."

"Yeah, well, I don't need to see it on camera. I'll never forget the look on Andrew's face. The guy was devastated about his son."

"Before you grieve for dear ol' dad, you want to hear what happened?"

"Give me the short version. I'm sure I'll hear it over and over for a long time."

"Okay...Jackson Kincaid moved to town and opened his store two doors down from Andrew Connor. Kincaid thrived and Connor dived. Tension mounted, and Andrew and his wife started having marital problems. Serious stuff. There was screaming and yelling at home. Doors slamming. Fists flying. Creditors calling. Cheryl threatened to leave. Andrew swore she'd never see the boys again if she did. It was ugly."

"And the neighbors never reported it?" Gordy asked.

"I don't think anyone knew. Cheryl started drinking again after five years on the wagon. Rory tried to cope by taking drugs, then started venting his frustration by knocking his younger brother around. Andrew was beside himself but couldn't afford family counseling and didn't want to press charges against his own son. Rory's anger just kept escalating and his fuse got shorter and shorter. The kid made no bones about blaming Jackson Kincaid for wrecking their family. But no one expected this."

Gordy shook his head from side to side. "How'd he kill him?"

"The morning of May 20, there was a big blowup at home, and Rory came to work mad—and high. He spotted Kincaid out at the Dumpster and says something drove him to take a knife out of the display case, go out to the alley, and stab him. Afterwards, he stripped Kincaid's wallet and made it look like theft."

"Talk about cold."

"Drugs will do that to you. Rory ran down the alley and in

the back door of Fish Tales and bumped into his father. He confessed what he'd done, and Andrew told him to wash the blood off his hands. Wanted to know if anybody saw him."

Gordy raised his eyebrows. "Lawrence Madison?"

"Bingo. Rory wasn't sure how much Lawrence saw, but Andrew looked out the window and got his description and turned it in to us, trying to make like Lawrence could be the assailant."

"That's really low."

"It gets worse," Will said. "When the investigation started getting too close to Rory, Andrew panicked. He took a knife exactly like the one Rory used and stabbed the homeless guy in the park and planted Sanchez's wallet next to his body."

"*Andrew* did that?"

"Thought if it looked like we were dealing with a pro, it might throw us off Rory's trail. He'd have done just about anything to cover up the boy's guilt and keep him out of jail."

"Can't imagine bein' *that* desperate."

"We've got both murder weapons. Andrew buried his in his grandmother's orange grove. We've already recovered it right where he said it would be."

Gordy rubbed the stubble on his chin. "So how the heck did the other knife end up getting sold?"

"Rory wanted to be seen on the sales floor immediately after the stabbing. He haphazardly rinsed off the knife and put it back in the box, thinking he'd get rid of it later. But when he went back, it was gone. Somehow it got put back in inventory and sold. We'll have to wait for the DNA test to confirm it, but I'm sure the dried blood is Kincaid's. That spot on the packing should be his, too."

"I'm surprised they confessed. You don't have their DNA on anything."

"They don't know that." Will leaned forward, his hands between his knees. "Frankly, they seemed relieved. I think the guilt was eating them up. Wanna bet that's why Andrew set up the memorial fund for the Kincaids?"

Gordy sighed. "He sure fooled me. So who was snooping around at Ellen and Guy's?"

"Rory. Early on, he was hoping to get to Lawrence and scare him into keeping his mouth shut. But once he heard about the old guy's state of mind, he decided it wasn't necessary. But he wasn't the man Ellen scared off at Lawrence's apartment. That was probably a cat burglar."

"Was Rory wearing a flag shirt when he killed Jackson?"

Will nodded. "Andrew made him take it off and threw the thing in the trash. I'm sure it's in the landfill by now. The red T-shirt Andrew wore when he stabbed the John Doe got laundered and put in his drawer at home."

Gordy felt as though a boulder had rolled onto his stomach. "How does somethin' like this happen, Will? Andrew Connor always seemed like a nice guy to me. Rory was an Eagle Scout, for cryin' out loud."

"Anger is no respecter of persons. The worst thing anyone can do is store it up. One way or another, it always explodes, either in tragedy or illness. I see it every day. Alcohol and drugs only compound the problem."

"Feels like I'm invading their privacy, knowin' all this stuff."

"Well, I'll tell you one thing…it was risky going back in the store and confronting Andrew. Took a big man to do that."

Gordy patted his belly. "That's me, all right."

"You know what I mean."

"Yeah, but I really don't know how you do this for a livin'."

"It's rewarding when we get the bad guys."

Gordy swallowed hard. "I still have trouble thinkin' of Andrew and Rory as bad guys."

"They each killed a man, Gordy. I let God judge what's on the inside, but it's my job to lock them up."

"Yeah, I know. Somebody's gotta keep the Jackson Kincaid

Memorial Fund goin', too. Maybe that's somethin' Pam and I could do."

"Speaking of Pam, you need to go home and put your arms around her. I sent Margaret over there a couple hours ago to stay with her."

Gordy sat in a chaise lounge on the patio, unmoved by the incessant booming or the kaleidoscope of exploding color that lit up the night sky. He smiled at the *oohs* and *aahs* coming from the beach, but was content to be out of the crowd and at home with Pam.

"I'm so glad you're all right," she said, squeezing his hand. "I can't stop thinking about what could've happened."

"Andrew and Rory didn't want to hurt me, darlin'. Will said they seemed relieved to finally get caught."

"Do you think Cheryl knew what they'd done?"

"Said she didn't. Her eyes looked as dead as a POW's when I saw her. I doubt she'll ever get over it. The younger brother either."

Pam shook her head. "What a shame they have to suffer for Andrew and Rory's mistakes. The Kincaids, too. It's just awful."

"What do you think about us keepin' the momentum goin' on the Memorial Fund? Now that the Connors won't be doin' it, somebody should. The goal was fifty thousand. With this bizarre twist, contributions might soar. It'd be great bein' a part of somethin' positive in all this."

"Yes, it would. I'm all for it."

"Good. I'll see what would be involved in our takin' over."

Gordy was lost in thought for a few moments, then chuckled without meaning to.

"What's so funny?" Pam said.

"Oh, I'm just wonderin' what kind of marketing scheme Weezie'll cook up once she finds out all that foot traffic will be headin' our way."

41

The next afternoon, Ellen Jones walked in the front door of Harmony House and saw her father sitting by himself in the parlor, seemingly staring at nothing. She went over and sat next to him on the couch.

"Hi, Dad."

"Why aren't you at work?"

"I came to tell you the big news. Gordy caught the man in the Old Glory shirt." Ellen patted his hand and he yanked it away. "Chief Seevers put him in jail. Everyone's talking about it."

Lawrence folded his arms across his chest and didn't respond.

"Can you believe how beastly hot it is? We could really use a good rain. It would be good for your flowers, too. I just snuck a peek at them. They're really coming along nicely."

"I want to go home."

"Owen and Hailey said to say hi. They have a little girl now."

Lawrence turned and glared at her. "Don't you ever stop talking?"

"Hello, Ellen." Rachel Britton came over and stood in front of the couch. "Could I talk to you in my office?"

Ellen turned to Lawrence. "I'll be right back." *As if it matters to you.*

She followed Rachel into her office and sat in the chair next to her desk. "Dad's his usual charming self."

"Lawrence isn't responding well to anything we're doing,

but I want to assure you, we're giving him the best possible care. I'm sorry he seems so unhappy. We spend more time with him than any of our other patients. The disease affects each one so differently."

Ellen nodded. "My father was difficult on a good day when he didn't have Alzheimer's. I'm not surprised that he's not doing well. But I'm so sorry for you, for us...and especially for him." Ellen sighed. "I wish I understood what he's thinking and what would make him feel better."

"I suppose until we find a way to reverse this disease, we'll never know what any of them are thinking. I just wanted to reassure you and to find out how you and your family are handling Lawrence's situation. We do have a support group, if that interests you."

"My husband and I attended a few meetings in the beginning. I think we're handling Dad's situation as well as can be expected."

"Good. Well, that's really all I had to say. Thanks for coming in my office. I don't like talking in front of my patients."

Ellen got up and started to leave, then turned around. "Rachel, do you think it would be upsetting to Dad for us to bring his great-granddaughter to see him? She's four."

"I'm sure it's fine as long as she understands that he may not act like other people she's used to."

"Annie's never met my dad, so she doesn't really have any expectations. I don't know whether the little-girl chatter will bother him or not. I guess we can always cut the visit short if it does."

Ellen left Rachel's office and went out to the parlor and sat on the couch next to Lawrence.

"I told you I'd be right back," Ellen said.

Lawrence ignored her.

"Roland is doing better now. He's getting around without his walker."

"I want to go home."

"You have a lovely home. Just look around. You've got the prettiest flowers of anyone living here."

Lawrence jumped up from the couch and walked toward the elevator.

"Where are you going?"

"I need the watering can. I promised to take care of your mother's African violets."

Ellen blinked to clear her eyes. "Okay, Dad. Let's go find it."

Ellen sat out on the veranda for five minutes before the heat and humidity drove her back inside. *Wouldn't you know it? I'm finally free to go out there and now it's too darned hot.*

The doorbell rang, and Ellen got up and looked out the peephole. Blanche Davis stood on the porch without her white poodle—a sure sign she hoped to be invited in.

"Hi, Blanche."

"Did I come at a bad time, dear?"

"No, come in where it's cool. Would you like some lemonade?"

"That sounds wonderful."

Ellen led Blanche out to the kitchen and poured two glasses of lemonade and sat at the breakfast bar.

"How's that adorable little granddaughter of yours?"

Ellen smiled. "Thriving. She's the perfect addition to Owen and Hailey's family. It's amazing to watch them interact. Annie and Daniel are crazy about each other."

"That's so good to hear. And how is Lawrence?"

Ellen felt her dark mood returning. "The same. I know the Alzheimer's can make him indifferent, but I sense he's depressed, too. I don't know what to do about it. He's right where he needs to be."

"I know he is. I'm so sorry he seems unhappy."

"It's nothing new. It just bothers me more because he's helpless."

Blanche took a sip of lemonade. "You never said why the two of you aren't close."

Ellen was quiet for a moment, then she said, "From the time I was old enough to think for myself, if I said something was black, Dad said it was white. Used to drive my poor mother crazy. But when I finally got old enough to defend my position, Dad got more controlling, which made me angry and bitter. Of course, that fueled some bad choices on my part, which caused more anger and bitterness between us. I guess it's been a vicious cycle all my life."

"Can't you just apologize and move on?"

"I wish. It's more complicated than that."

Blanche's sincerity was magnified in her thick lenses. "Ellen, my father died without me ever telling him I loved him. I've always regretted that."

"I don't remember ever saying those words to my dad either. Oh, I signed all my cards 'Love, Ellen,' but I've never actually told him that."

"*Do* you love him?"

Ellen ran her index finger around the rim of her glass. "I didn't used to think so. But the more he slips away from me, the more…I don't know. I guess the more I need to believe we had *something* worth remembering…" Ellen's words failed.

Blanche reached over and patted her hand. "Don't worry, dear. You still have time."

Ellen lay on the couch, watching the ceiling fan go round and round. She finally had the house all to herself, yet couldn't concentrate on anything. She hadn't added a single word to her second novel. Hadn't called Julie or Mina or even Hailey. Hadn't even put her dinner dishes in the dishwasher. It was as though she were grieving.

She'd been miserable ever since her conversation with

Blanche. Her mother's words replayed over and over in her mind.

"Ellen, promise me you won't let your father's weaknesses become your own. Don't shut him out. Don't let him shut you out."

"What am I supposed to do? I can't force him to accept who I am."

"Then learn to accept who he is. If you could get a glimpse of the man I see, it wouldn't be so hard to love him."

Ellen was aware of the phone ringing. She went out to the kitchen and picked up the receiver on the wall phone. "Hello."

"Hi, it's Hailey. I'm taking Daniel to a birthday party in the morning and wondered if you might like to have Annie to yourself for a few hours. Shayla has a doctor's appointment and I gave her the day off."

"I'd love it. You want me to come get her?"

"Could we meet halfway—at the Waffle Hut at the Port Winnie exit?"

"Sure, what time?"

"Nine?"

"That would work fine."

"After the party, I'll drive over to your place so you can spend a few minutes with Daniel."

"Well, don't hurry," Ellen said. "Let Daniel take his nap first. I've got errands to run, and this might be a good time to take Annie to meet Granddad. I'll take her to lunch someplace fun and then bring her back here and make good on my promise to give her a pedicure and paint her nails. I'm sure she hasn't forgotten."

Hailey laughed. "Are you kidding?"

"Okay, honey. I'll meet you in the Waffle Hut parking lot at nine in the morning.

42

Ellen Jones walked up the steps and onto the big front porch at Harmony House, her hand holding tightly to her granddaughter's. She stopped outside the front door and looked down at Annie and the baby doll tucked under her arm.

"Remember what we talked about?"

Annie Jones gave an emphatic nod. "Gwanddad might say funny things. But his mind is just pwaying twicks on him 'cause he gots a boo-boo in his bwain."

"That's right."

"Does he live in this giant house by hisself?"

"No, you'll see lots of great-grandmas and great-grandpas and people who are visiting them."

"Does he got a dog or a kitty?"

"No, but you can tell him all about yours."

Ellen looked through the beveled glass and saw people in the parlor. She pushed open the door and recognized several patients sitting with visitors.

Annie looked up at the chandelier, her blue eyes wide and round. "This is a vewy pwetty pwace! Does it got stairs like at your house?"

"It has an elevator. Granddad lives on the second floor."

Ellen walked Annie across the parlor and into the cherry-paneled elevator and pushed the button for level two.

Annie giggled as the elevator went up quickly and stopped. "My tummy fell down."

The elevator door opened, and Ellen turned right and walked down to Lawrence's room and stopped in the doorway. He was sitting in a glider chair.

"Hi, Dad. I have a surprise for you." Ellen walked into the room, holding Annie's hand. "This is—"

"Ellie!" Lawrence's face lit up and it was as though life came back into his eyes. "You little dickens. Where have you been?" He reached out his arms to Annie. "Come over here and let me get a good look at you."

Annie glanced questioningly at Ellen, and then went over and stood in front of Lawrence. "I'm *Annie*. This is my fwiend Dolly. She likes you."

"Well, I'd better have a look-see," Lawrence said.

Annie held up the doll with both hands. "She only gots one shoe. I think the other one falled off in the car. She won't cwy if you hold her."

Lawrence took the doll from Annie and cradled it in one arm. "Hello, Tiny Tears. I'm glad to see you're over your cold."

Tiny Tears? Ellen remembered playing with a Tiny Tears doll in the back room of her father's hardware store.

"No, her name is *Dolly*," Annie said. "Mama and Daddy bought her for me when I was weally little. But I'm bigger now. And I live at my new house. Daniel is my baby bwother, and I have a puppy named Snickers. He gets in lots of twouble."

Lawrence handed the doll back to Annie. "Did you get in trouble today?"

Annie shook her head. "I didn't got any time-outs."

"Then you know what *we* get to do."

Annie smiled, her cheeks dimpled. "What?"

"Why, we get to go to Aunt Bessie's and pick blueberries. Then your mother will make her special cobbler and put a big scoop of vanilla ice cream on it and let it melt, just the way you like it."

"Mmm...I love ice cweam," Annie said. She looked over at

Ellen, her hands cupped around her mouth, and whispered, "We're pwetending."

Ellen nodded but was thinking this was all too real.

"Does Aunt Bessie got lots of bwueberries?"

"Are you kidding? She's got a bushel…and a peck…and a hug around the *neck*." Lawrence grabbed Annie and pressed his lips to her neck and blew until she squealed with delight.

"Do it again!" Annie pleaded. "It feels tickly."

"I think Dolly needs a nap," Ellen whispered. "We need to get very quiet."

Annie handed the doll up to Lawrence. "You can wock her to sweep."

"Come on up here." Lawrence lifted Annie into his lap. "You hold Tiny Tears, and I'll do the rocking."

Annie laid her head back on Lawrence's chest, the baby doll clutched to her own, and seemed completely relaxed as the glider moved slowly back and forth and Lawrence hummed "Rock-a-Bye, Baby" slightly off key.

Ellen sat on the side of the bed, absorbed in the moment.

"I want to get down now," Annie finally said.

Lawrence put his hands around Annie's waist and gently set her on her feet. "Don't run off, princess. We didn't say the magic words."

Annie turned around and looked up at him, the corners of her mouth twitching. "What words are they?"

"I say, 'I love you, sweet Ellie,' and then you say…"

I love you too, Daddy. Ellen's eyes clouded over, her heart stirred by the memory that had been lost for decades. She fought to regain her composure and glanced over at her father, thinking the conversation was getting too confusing for Annie.

"But we're just pwetending," Annie said to Lawrence. "You're not my daddy."

Ellen went over and slipped her hand into Annie's. "That was such a fun game, sweetie. Granddad seemed to enjoy it very much."

"Why aren't you at work?" Lawrence snapped.

"I thought you might enjoy having a young visitor. Looks like I was right."

"I want to go home."

"Why don't we go down to the rec room and watch Jeopardy?"

Lawrence folded his arms across his chest, his mouth a straight line of defiance.

"Don't be gwouchy or you gotta have a time-out," Annie whispered. "Come on. I'm a vewy, vewy good helper, and I will take you to the elebator."

Lawrence didn't say anything, but let Annie take his hand and lead him down the hallway.

Ellen followed but lagged behind, blinking to keep the tears from clouding her vision and wondering if she could hold it together until she could be alone.

43

Ellen Jones lay on the couch and listened to the sound of the pendulum on the cuckoo clock in the kitchen. She had managed to hold in her emotions until Hailey picked up Annie. But the minute she had waved good-bye and shut the front door, she began to weep. That was hours ago. It seemed as though the river of tears would never dry up.

Ellen sat up on the couch and blew her nose. This was getting her nowhere. She got up and went up the winding staircase to the widow's watch and turned on the light. She sat at her desk and turned on the laptop, then brought up an empty page and started to type:

Dear Dad,

You will never see these words, but I desperately need to write them. I have spent most of my life convinced that you never loved me. Even though Mother told me differently and tried over and over to help me see the man she knew you to be, I chose to cling to my stubborn pride and anger and bitterness. I resented you so much for not wanting me to have any dreams other than your dream for me: to be a wife and mother.

I'm ashamed to admit that I chose to elope with Guy so you couldn't "give me away." I didn't want a church wedding either. I had rejected any thought that you could actually be right, that there might be a God who cared about what I did with my life. But the deepest reason for not wanting you involved was I wanted to punish you for not supporting my going to college and becoming a journalist. I wanted to deny you the thing every father wants most: respect. I wanted to embarrass you in front of your friends. And I wanted to show you I didn't need you. Unfortunately, I succeeded. And every day since I have pushed you further and further away.

Your incessant criticism of me for trying to balance career and family was the deepest wound I've ever felt, probably because Guy and the boys meant everything to me and I never felt as though I had neglected them for a moment. But I wonder now how much of your ongoing criticism was a reaction to my attitude—my callous rejection of *you*?

Though we could never see eye to eye on career and family, how foolish it was to let it divide us. I allowed my anger at you to blot out everything good about you. In my mind, you were the epitome of everything I detested. And yet Mother saw something she so wanted me to see: a tender, caring side that I had convinced myself long ago did not exist in you.

I got a glimpse of it when you thought Annie was your "sweet Ellie." Your gentleness and love toward her nearly broke my heart. How did you and I go from *that* tender relationship to bringing out the very worst in each other? As long as I can remember, I've hated who I am when I'm with you. I always blamed you for our failed relationship. But now I see that my response to you was just as destructive as your critical spirit.

Dad, I'm sorry. I'm so sorry. Please forgive me for letting my stubborn pride prevent what could have been. The more you have slipped away from me, the more deeply I've needed to believe we had something worth remembering. I'm so grateful for the gift God gave me through Annie: a precious glimpse into the past I had long forgotten. I *remember* sitting in your lap. I *remember* our magic words. That's what I want to hold on to. The love is still there, even if it's taken much too long to draw it out.

I don't know how much longer you'll be on this earth. The Alzheimer's is taking its toll. But one thing I promise: I will be there for you, even when you don't know me anymore. I won't walk away like I did all those years ago. I'll honor and respect you and do all I can to help preserve your dignity. I only wish I had done it sooner.

I love you, too, Daddy.
Ellie

The keyboard became a blur. Ellen fumbled to turn off her laptop and sat for a moment, feeling both lost and found. Who but the Creator could have planned such a perfect and timely relief mission for four generations strapped with the consequences of foolish choices? Only the Lord God, in His mercy, could have used the most unlikely of voices to redeem it all for His glory.

Ellen wiped the tears off her face and turned off the light. She walked across the creaky floor and stood in the alcove, gazing up at myriad stars in the heavens and wondering if her mother knew.

44

On the first Saturday in November, Ellen Jones invited Owen, Hailey, and the grandkids to join her and Guy for a family picnic at Bougainvillea Park. A balmy breeze had replaced the hot, thick air of summer, and cloud puffs dotted the azure sky.

The family sat at a picnic table on a grassy slope overlooking the duck pond, enjoying Ellen's fried chicken, potato salad, baked beans, and biscuits.

"I'd almost forgotten how much I love your cooking." Guy winked. "We need to have these get-togethers more often."

"I want the recipe for your potato salad," Hailey said. "Mine never turns out this good."

Ellen smiled. "It was my mother's. I'll write it down for you."

Owen looked out across the park and seemed to be miles away.

"Okay, I need to burn off some of these calories." Guy stood and stretched his back. "Who wants to go to the playground?"

"Me! Me!" Annie said. "Can we bwing Daniel? He likes to swing."

"I'll go with you," Hailey said. "These two are a handful." She got up, Daniel on her hip, and whispered something to Owen, then kissed his cheek.

Half a minute later, Ellen sat at the picnic table alone with Owen. She gathered the dirty paper plates and put them in a lawn bag. "You've been quiet today."

Owen traced the gingham checks on the tablecloth with a plastic knife. "Can I ask you a personal question?"

"Sure."

"Did your making peace with yourself about Granddad take away the pain?"

"Not entirely. Nothing will ever change the fact that I missed out on a relationship with my father most of my life and that a big part of it was my own fault. But at least I know God's forgiven me. Admitting the truth and letting go of the guilt was a huge relief."

Owen exhaled. "I guess I'm still waiting for that huge relief."

"In what way?"

"I know God's forgiven me for sleeping around. But I still struggle with the fact that my getting Corinne pregnant ruined her marriage. Maybe if they'd been happier, Tim wouldn't have killed himself."

"You can't know that. There were a number of other factors, not the least of which was HIV."

"Yeah, but I'll always wonder. I dread the day when I have to tell Annie the whole story."

"Well, that's a long way down the road. You have plenty of time to build a strong relationship with her."

"Her psychologist says she's adjusting well. Both of us still have nightmares sometimes, but they're not happening as often."

Ellen reached over and patted Owen's hand. "By the time Annie's old enough to understand everything that's happened, she'll be a happy and secure young woman."

"Let's hope you're right." Owen took a sip of Coke. "It kills me that she was verbally abused during those first years of her life. It wouldn't have happened if I'd been there for her."

"Well, you can't blame yourself for the way Tim treated Annie. I have to believe all the love and affirmation you give her will eventually override the destructive things he said to her."

"I just wish I could shake this awful guilt."

"You will, Owen. But I suspect there will always be a degree of *regret*. I certainly have it. And maybe that's a good thing. Having to live with consequences is certainly an incentive not to repeat the mistakes."

"I just want Annie to have a normal, happy childhood. I had no idea I could love her this much."

Ellen smiled. "*He* knew. The Lord's handprints are all over this situation on several levels."

"Yeah, I still can't believe the breakthrough with you and Granddad. He lights up every time he sees Annie and still calls her Ellie…Is that ever painful to you since he still treats you so mean?"

"Sometimes. But it's also healing. I remember wishing my parents had taken home movies when I was a child so I could get a glimpse of the doting father my mother described. But movies would never have revealed Dad's feelings the way these flashbacks with Annie have."

Owen seemed to be watching a ladybug crawling on his thumb. "Well, one thing's for sure—the whole experience has forced me to stretch. For a long time, I was content to play church, but now I'm going to Bible study, praying with Hailey and the kids, and reading Annie Bible stories that I'm hearing for the first time."

A few moments of comfortable silence settled between them. Finally Owen said, "Something interesting happened after I left Corinne's hotel room. I didn't remember it until the other day, and now I can't stop thinking about it."

"Tell me."

"The cab driver who took me back to my car said I ought to stop trying to sleep with every blonde in Raleigh and marry one who'd make me happy. Of course, I insisted I *was* happy and gave him my usual spiel about guilt being a by-product of Christianity and nothing more than religious lingo. I don't remember the exact conversation, but when I got out of the cab, the guy gave me the strangest look, like he knew something but wasn't going to tell me. He said he was going to pray for Jesus to change my heart and bring the right *lady* into my life. I thought he was a fanatic." The corners of Owen's mouth twitched. "Now I think he must've prayed double hard because it seems as though God's brought me *two*."

"It does indeed." Ellen patted Owen's hand, aware of happy voices and laughter, then turned and saw the rest of her family walking across the grass.

Annie skipped over to Ellen, waving a half-wilted purple flower in her hand. "This is for you, Gwandma. Mama said I wasn't supposed to pick it so I twied to make it stick in the dirt again, but it falled over."

Ellen pressed her lips to Annie's tiny hand. "Thank you, sweetie. Did you have fun on the big red slide?"

"Yes, and I cwimbed this high!" Annie held up her arms and stood on tiptoes.

"Oh my goodness, that's *very* high."

Annie went around to the other end of the picnic table and looked up at Owen, her eyes the color of the afternoon sky, blond ringlets framing her face. "Daddy, we better go thwow the ducks some popcorn. They are getting vewy, vewy hungwy."

Owen brushed the hair out of her eyes. "Think so, huh?"

Annie gave a firm nod.

"Okay, then. Let's do it."

Annie jumped up and down and clapped her hands. "Bwing Daniel. But you hafta hold him so the ducks can't bite his finger."

Owen swung his legs over the bench and rose to his feet. He winked at Ellen, then reached out to Hailey and took Daniel into his arms.

"Okay, big guy, let's escort your sister to the duck pond."

Annie stood on tiptoes and stretched across the table until she had a large paper bag in her hands. "I will cawwy the popcorn so the cwows won't get it."

Ellen watched Owen amble down the gentle slope toward

the water, Daniel on his hip and Annie romping alongside chattering happily and swinging the paper bag.

"You've got that goofy grandma grin on your face," Guy said. "What are you thinking?"

Ellen laughed, then reached over and took his hand. "Just that whoever said the best gifts come in small packages knew exactly what he was talking about."

Afterword

"For God will bring every deed into judgment,
including every hidden thing, whether it is good or evil."

ECCLESIASTES 12:14

Dear friends,
How blessed we are to live under the New Covenant where God's mercy and grace abound! As believers, we need never worry that our sin, no matter how grave, is out of the range of God's forgiveness.

But we must never forget that even though Jesus' death on the cross wipes away the eternal consequences of our sin, in no way does it negate the *natural* consequences. Sin is always destructive on some level. When we repent of a sin and accept God's forgiveness, we can let go of the guilt, but the regret and consequences may follow us to the grave.

Owen saw nothing wrong with his licentious lifestyle before he became a Christian, and it wasn't until years after he accepted Christ that he encountered the hard truth of Galatians 6:7: "Do not be deceived: God cannot be mocked. A man reaps what he sows." And reap he did!

Ellen, on the other hand, was well aware that distancing herself from her elderly father and refusing to forgive him was wrong, yet she chose to cling to her stubborn pride and ultimately forfeited the opportunity for God to heal the father/daughter relationship she so desperately needed.

Certainly God can redeem for His glory the pain caused by

natural consequences, as He did in this story. And though He does not desire that we carry the guilt and shame of sins we've confessed, it is not uncommon for feelings of sorrow and regret to linger long after the sin has been forgiven. These contrite feelings can be a powerful deterrent to keep us from repeating the mistake. But how much better to avoid the sorrow by not making the mistake in the first place.

Sin is *never* harmless. It may seem so at first, but it produces only bad fruit. Since Galatians 6:7 promises that we *will* reap what we sow, let us be careful to plant wisely today and tend our hearts carefully so that tomorrow's harvest will not suffer a blight of devastating consequences.

Don't miss the dramatic conclusion to the Seaport Suspense series in book four, *Not By Chance*. Mystery and suspense abound, and it promises to be another page-turner. Stay tuned!

I love hearing from my readers. You can write to me through my publisher at http://fiction.mpbooks.com or directly through my website at www.kathyherman.com. I read and respond to every e-mail and greatly value your input.

In Him,

Kathy Herman

Discussion Guide

1. Explain what you think Ecclesiastes 12:14 means: "For God will bring every deed into judgment, including every hidden thing, whether it is good or evil." Does God judge a believer's sin differently than an unbeliever's? Is sin judged differently under the New Covenant than under the old? Is there a difference between conviction and judgment?

2. Explain what you think Galatians 6:7 means: "Do not be deceived: God cannot be mocked. A man reaps what he sows." How was this evident in Owen Jones's situation? In Ellen's? In Andrew Connor's? Has it been evident in any situation in your life? Are consequences limited to believers in Christ?

3. Do you agree that natural consequences are the result of sin and something the believer will have to work through? Do you think God gets involved in the process? If so, to what extent? Are consequences a punishment for sin or merely a result? Explain your answer.

4. Have you had to work through the pain of natural consequences? Did it cause you to question whether or not God had forgiven you? Did you think the consequences were a punishment from God for your mistake? Do you think God's forgiveness is

diminished when we are left to deal with the consequences? Do you have past sins you wish you could go back and undo?

5. Think for a moment about what is written in Romans 8:28: "And we know that in all things God works for the good of those who love him, who have been called according to his purpose." Could you see this principle working in Owen's life? In Ellen's? Can you think of situations in your own life when the principle of Romans 8:28 has been evident?

6. What is the difference between guilt and regret? Should a believer feel either emotion once he or she has been forgiven? If we didn't find our sin disturbing, would we be more likely to repeat the offense? Do you agree with Ellen's thinking that she would always have a degree of *regret*, and that having to live with the consequences was an incentive not to repeat the mistake? Why or why not?

7. Do you think God holds us more accountable for our sin when it hurts others? Once a sin is forgiven, are we still responsible for any pain it may have caused? If so, what do you think God wants us to do about it?

8. When we grieve over our sin, does that necessarily mean we're wallowing in guilt? Can grief be more productive than guilt? Do you think having grief for our sin is what the Bible means by "a broken and contrite heart"? (Psalm 51:17). Explain your answer.

9. Have you experienced a broken and contrite heart as a result of the Holy Spirit's conviction? Have you experienced brokenness as a result of being criticized by another believer? If you've experienced both, how did the two compare? Do you think

there's a difference between experiencing godly sorrow (contrition) for sin and experiencing guilt? What kind of fruit does guilt produce? What kind of fruit do you think godly sorrow produces? Which of the two seems more positive?

10. Should Christians be as forgiving as the One who saved us? Should we judge others when we see them struggling with natural consequences that are different from our own? Is it possible for a person to change completely and still suffer the consequences of choices made years ago? Have you ever felt judged by someone who knew you were dealing with the consequences of past sin? How did it make you feel? Have you ever judged someone else in the same way?

11. Explain what you understand Philippians 1:6 to mean: "Being confident of this, that he who began a good work in you will carry it on to completion until the day of Christ Jesus." Is every believer in Christ a work in progress? If so, how should we treat repentant brothers and sisters who are reaping the consequences of sinful choices?

12. Which character in this story could you most relate to and why? If you could meet one of the characters, which would it be? What life message did you take away from this book?

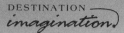